Every family has a few old friends. But those of the sorcerous Crafter family are more interesting than most! Meet . . .

THE CRAFTERS

CHRISTOPHER STASHEFF reminds us why it's important to keep in touch with older relatives.

ESTHER FRIESNER proves that good manners do count.

JODY LYNN NYE illustrates how a school for young ladies can also teach much more practical subjects.

WENDY WHEELER shows that summoning an elemental is not all that elementary.

RU EMERSON reveals why oil and water don't mix!

*This enchanting new shared-world anthology series also includes stories by BARBARA DELAPLACE * BRIAN M. THOMSEN * MORRIS G. MCGEE * ROBERT SHECKLEY * JUDITH R. CONLY * MORGAN LLYWELYN.*

THE CRAFTERS Series
Edited by Christopher Stasheff and Bill Fawcett

THE CRAFTERS
BLESSINGS AND CURSES

THE CRAFTERS

BLESSINGS AND CURSES

BOOK TWO

Edited by CHRISTOPHER STASHEFF
and BILL FAWCETT

ACE BOOKS, NEW YORK

This book is an Ace original edition,
and has never been previously published.

BLESSINGS AND CURSES

An Ace Book / published by arrangement with
Bill Fawcett & Associates

PRINTING HISTORY
Ace edition / August 1992

ISBN: 0-441-12131-4

To our parents,
whom you might say
made all this possible:
Edward and Evelyn Stasheff,
Jeanne and Bill Fawcett

CONTENTS

Prologue	Bill Fawcett	ix
Belonging	Barbara Delaplace	1
Franklin's Salamander	Wendy Wheeler	12
"... A Fortune in Ireland"	Morris G. McGee	32
Her American Cousin	Esther Friesner	57
Whose Ghost There?	Christopher Stasheff	100
Ironsides and Cottonseed Oil	Ru Emerson	153
Miss Crafter's School for Girls	Jody Lynn Nye	191
The Dream Country	Robert Sheckley	225
Oppression	Judith R. Conly	256
Remember the Almost	Morgan Llywelyn	257
A Cursed Booty	Brian M. Thomsen	269

PROLOGUE

The saga of the Crafter Family began in the hills outside Boston at about the same time as the elders in Salem were conducting their much publicized witch trials. In Ireland, Scotland, and Wales they talk of those families whose members "have the weird." The most magically talented son of one of these families found the puritanical fanaticism and suspicion unbearable and emigrated to the American colonies. On an isolated mountain nearly a day's ride from Boston he established a lonely homestead. Amer Crafter was an unusual man for his era, or perhaps any era, in that he accepted the Talent he had inherited and studied it using the tenets of the new "natural philosophy." But the colony was growing and soon Amer had neighbors again.

Where Amer saw a gift, others saw their power as a curse and turned it to darker uses. One of those whom Amer saved from a black coven became his wife. This highly talented couple had six children, all equally gifted. Their children also inherited a wide range of magical talents, often to their own discomfort and danger. When we dream of having the ability to use magic it is easy to concentrate on the novelty of the power and overlook the fact that we would still be a part of our society. Even in the Age of Reason there were many bigots who condemned even the most beneficial use of magic as the Devil's work. As some do even today, normally on cable TV.

The history of the Crafter Family is tied to the growth of the new land they settled in, and the old land a few returned to. These are but a few chapters in that history.

Lower Canada
Anno Domini 1784

By the time the fourth generation of Crafter descendants were born with their own Talents, many had found ways to live comfortably within the early American society. Those few who didn't often simply took to the endless and barely habited forests. The frontier, as always, gave them a place to flee an otherwise intolerable situation. It was both a productive and easy means of escape. The cost of this easy escape was often paid by those left behind.

BELONGING
by Barbara Delaplace

Ungifted. Misfit. Half-breed. She'd lived with those words as a girl.

Tory. Loyalist. Traitor. She lived with those words as a woman.

I wonder if I'll ever feel I belong? Rachel pushed the damp hair off her forehead, then continued to stir the clothes in the near-boiling soapy water of the laundry tub. (There was something about doing the washing that made her reflective.) Growing up in the settlement after the breakup of her family, there always seemed to be someone ready to point out that she didn't fit in, and she'd learned to put on the impassive face of her Iroquois mother whenever it happened. She pushed away the quick stab of sorrow that thoughts of her mother always brought. After so many years, the pain of her death still hadn't faded away. She stirred harder, her tension easing with the physical effort.

Perhaps the pain would have eased if Father had accepted

her death as well. But Nimrod Crafter, ever-rebellious and seldom at peace, had not. And rather than give his daughter into the care of his own parents, who would have welcomed her, he'd left Rachel, a tearful eleven-year-old dressed in deer-skins, with the schoolteacher of the small community near the family's isolated cabin. Then he'd withdrawn to the sanctuary of his beloved forests and Rachel had not seen him again. She'd grown into a woman accustomed to hearing taunts of "Half-breed!" from the cruel and the ignorant, accustomed to walking alone.

Until Michael Wilding came into her life. Tall and broad-shouldered, with a black beard that made his teeth gleam all the whiter when he smiled, he had been drawn to her from the first moment, as she had to him. Their love had only warmed and strengthened through the years since then.

I suppose Father's still with Thayendanegea, she mused. Which meant he'd probably be in Lower Canada, for the great Mohawk leader the settlers called Joseph Brant had gone north after the war, along with two thousand of his people. Loyalists were not welcome in the new republic.

Well, her father wasn't the only Tory in the Crafter fami-ly—and she and Michael had suffered for their loyalty to the Crown. They had been called names, ostracized, and worse. Her husband had once come home from a village meeting bruised and bloody simply for saying that while he hadn't liked the policies of the British government any more than the next man, he didn't agree that revolt against the Empire was the answer. So the small Wilding family had also come to Lower Canada, to the fertile land of the Niagara peninsula. There, the rich soil and abundant land had promised peace and a new beginning.

She inspected the clothing in the tub critically and decided it had boiled long enough. Cold water to cool it all down, that was next.

"Leah! Come with Mommy and we'll go to the stream!"

Rachel's eyes lit up as a dark-haired, merry-eyed whirlwind came rushing to her, spring flowers crushed in one muddy fist. She opened her arms wide to catch the little girl. "Hello, darling! Did you miss me? I missed you."

Leah rewarded her with a grubby kiss on the cheek. "See, Mommy?" she asked, as Rachel swung her up in her arms.

"Yes, precious, they're beautiful flowers. We'll put them in some water. And then your father will be so happy that his little girl picked the flowers for the dinner table tonight! Now, let's get your brother and we'll go to the stream. Will you carry the bucket for Mum?"

"I'll carry the bucket!" Five-year-old Leah loved to help. Rachel put her down and the little girl ran to get the pail.

Baby Noah was gurgling and watching the world with a wide-eyed gaze, snug in his cradleboard. Rachel slid her arms through the straps and eased it to a comfortable position on her back, then stood up. She was about to call Leah again—

—when a strange wave of disorientation swept over her. She was in some other place. Yet she still stood in the clearing in front of the cabin. There was the laundry tub with the embers of the fire still glowing under it. There was the kitchen garden. She tried to step forward, to turn to see Leah, but found she couldn't move—some awful force held her motionless. Only her eyes could move, and they fell on Noah lying in his cradle in front of her: her baby, flushed with fever and twisting restlessly in his blankets. He was desperately ill, and she didn't know how to heal him. She tried to reach out to him, to gather him in her arms, tried to say his name, but the force wouldn't let her. She could only look, fear racing through her. She raised her eyes further and saw Leah lying on her little bed, as flushed and restless as Noah. Her panic grew and she struggled desperately to go to her children. And now she saw Michael lying beyond the children. Sweat shone on his face and he mumbled deliriously. They needed her, she had to go to them. She was gripped with terror. They were her beloveds, more important than anything in the world to her. She had to find the cure . . . .

"I have the bucket, Mommy. Can we go?" Leah stood before her, unaware of the turmoil within her mother. Rachel blinked. Suddenly everything shifted back to normal. She could hear Noah babbling in the cradleboard, could feel him wriggling as he always did. The awful fear drained out of her. *What had happened?* "Mommy?" Leah asked, with a five-year-old's persistence.

It must have been a dizzy spell. She shrugged off further speculation. "Away we go, precious."

The stream was only a short distance from the rough cabin she and Michael had hastily built when they first arrived. There would be a finished house one day, but clearing land, planting crops, and hunting (to say nothing of a lack of neighbours), put that project into the future. And the cabin was weathertight and warm, if small.

At the stream's edge, Rachel took the bucket from Leah and filled it. Her daughter splashed in the water, and she was about to warn Leah not to get her dress soaked, when she felt a sudden chill, like a cold breeze blowing along her nape. She looked across the stream. It seemed to be coming from a dark hollow, a cave formed by the overhanging bank. *It must be my imagination,* she thought.

But the chill grew stronger.

There's nothing there, she told herself more firmly. She straightened, filled pail in one hand, and reached with her other hand to Leah. "Let's go back, precious." The child took her hand, and they went up the trail. Rachel ignored the impulse to look back over her shoulder. Something was *not* peering at them from the hollow!

At the cabin, she took the cradleboard off her back and leaned it against the tree near the laundry tub so Noah could see her. (And so she could see Noah, although she wouldn't admit that to herself.) Leah ran off to pick some more flowers. Rachel poured cold water from the pail until the water in the tub was cool enough to touch, then positioned the washboard and began scrubbing the clothes.

It's just that I don't feel at home here yet, that's all. That's what made me nervous at the stream.

She remembered her uncle Deganawidah, named for the prophet of old, and wise in the ways of men and spirits. He was a wanderer, seldom in one place for very long. "Don't you miss your home, Uncle?" she had asked one time.

He had smiled at her, for he was very fond of Rachel, and called her his pet name. "Little Bird, you carry your home inside you. Once you know who you are and how you stand in relation to the land and the spirits, you're always at home no matter where you are. Do you understand?"

"No, Uncle," she had answered.

"Ah, well, you are very young. But you remember my words. One day you will understand them." And he had hugged her. She could still recall the softness of the wolfskin and the smoky scent of the tanned deerskins he wore.

I guess I still don't know who I am, Uncle. She always seemed a misfit, even within her own family. She knew that she lacked the special talents her parents possessed, her father's gift of knowing thought without speech, her mother's gift of foreseeing events to come. *Ungifted*, she'd overheard her father say one night when she was supposed to be asleep in the loft above her parents' heads.

"She may not have come into her gift yet, Nimrod," her mother's gentle voice replied.

"I could hear thoughts at her age," he said. "And you, Mary"—for her mother had taken a second, New England name when she'd married a New England man—"when could you sense things before they happened?"

"I was very young, too. But many of my clan are gifted in the ways of the spirit."

"So she inherits from both of us. *Something* should have shown up by now."

"You judge her too quickly, my husband. Rachel will know her gift when the time comes."

There had been one time when she thought her mother's prediction had come to pass . . . .

Her uncle was visiting them again. One day he had gone down to the edge of the lake near their lodge to meditate, something he often did. Normally Rachel left him to the solitude he desired at such a time, but this day she had felt lonely and wanted to be near him. So she approached as softly as she could, trying not to disturb his thoughts.

And she had succeeded, for he didn't notice her. His eyes were closed; his face might have been carved from bronze; his seated figure was motionless on the bearskin he always carried with him. Only the long fur of his wolfskin ruffled in the breeze, the head dangling over his shoulder.

But there was a whisper from her clothing when she sat down in front of him, and his eyes snapped open. And for a moment—for a moment she thought the eye sockets of the wolf's head glowed with life, as if a living animal were curled around his shoulders. And the bearskin . . . the empty paws seemed to fill, the shoulders humped, the head lifted and turned to her, dark eyes watchful. For a moment, she saw the guardian spirits that travelled with her uncle.

Deganawidah seemed to know what she saw, for he told her, "You have eyes that see into the spirit world, Little Bird. *Orenda*, the spirit force in all things, flows strongly in you. And one day, you'll be able to call on it."

"Soon, Uncle?"

He smiled at her. "I don't think soon, Little Bird. It's a gift you must grow into." Her face fell, for she so wanted to prove her father's judgment wrong. "But the time will come when you will need it, and be able to use it." She looked unconvinced, and he laughed. "Here, then, Little Bird—I'll give you something to remind you of my promise." And he had taken a thong from around his neck, one that held a small leather case. "There's a bear claw inside this, for our family is of the Bear Clan. You wear it now for me, and remember my words. One day you'll be able to use the spirit power within you."

But it had never happened again, and now she was a woman with children of her own. She suspected the time would never come. But she still wore the necklace he'd given her, the only memento she had of that life with her family. Rachel sighed, then realized with surprise that while her mind had travelled to the past to hear the voices of her family, her hands had scrubbed all the clothes. She called to Leah to come help her, and the two of them rinsed the garments in a tub of clean water, after which Rachel hung them on the clothesline stretched between two trees.

It was nearly time for supper. She picked up Noah and went into the cabin with Leah. The stew she'd earlier set over the fire to simmer was sending forth savory odors, and she had biscuits left from that morning. New potatoes and early peas, picked that afternoon, would complete the meal. "Here, Leah, you can shell the peas for me." So mother and daughter worked together.

She was just finished nursing Noah, or rather, trying to—he was fussing and had little appetite—when Michael strode into the cabin with a double armful of wood and a flashing smile for his family. The wood went tumbling into the woodbox by the fireplace, and he gathered Rachel into his arms.

"Hello, my heart," he said, and kissed her. She could feel the current of his love flowing through her as she returned his kiss, and she leaned into his strength for a long moment. Time apart from each other made time together the sweeter. Then he released her, and she went back to the stove as he turned his attention to Leah. Michael reached down and picked up his daughter. "How's my princess?" he asked, kissing her cheek.

"I helped Mommy. I carried the bucket, and I washed clothes, and I shelled peas."

"All that! You worked hard today, princess."

"And I picked you some flowers, see?" She pointed to the table, where the flowers now stood arranged in a spare mug.

"They're beautiful! Thank you, princess."

"Supper's ready!" said Rachel, and they sat down with her at the table. They joined hands, and Michael began the blessing.

"We give thanks, O Father . . ."

It was a few hours later when Michael checked on Noah, now in his cradle for the night, and spoke to Rachel.

"Rachel, his skin feels much too warm. And he's flushed." A chill went through her and she quickly joined him. Michael was right. Noah was sleeping quietly enough, but she could feel heat radiating from the little body.

"I'll brew some willow bark tea and see if he'll drink it," Rachel said. "That might help."

"A good idea. It's probably minor. I'm sure he'll be fine in the morning."

But she was filled with a sense of foreboding.

Noah drowsily drank a little of the tea, then drifted into sleep. His parents kept a concerned vigil over him, but there was no improvement. Instead the fever seemed to rise, and they took turns gently wiping his forehead with a cool wet cloth and giving him sips of water. Finally Michael said, "My heart, it doesn't need both of us to watch, and you look tired. Go to bed; I'll wake you if there's any change." Rachel was reluctant, but the day's events had taken their toll and she was indeed tired.

"Well, all right. Good night, love."

She kissed him and went into their bedroom, where she

quickly undressed and put on her nightgown. And it seemed
only a few moments after she had laid her head on the pillow
when Michael gently touched her, waking her from a troubled
rest. His face, revealed by the candlelight, was grave, and she
immediately asked what was wrong.

"It's Leah. She's got the fever, too."

Rachel felt ice clamp around her heart. "Let me come and
see her."

"I brought her bed out of the birthing room and put her by
the baby."

Leah was flushed and there was a faint sheen of perspiration
on her skin. "I'll make some more tea," Rachel said, though
somehow she knew it was fruitless. "And since you've been
up all night, I think you should have some rest. It's my turn
to watch them."

Michael yawned in reply. "I'll get some more water first,
then I'll go to bed." He opened the cabin door, letting in the
fresh air and growing light of dawn. "It looks like another
beautiful day." He picked up the bucket and strode away.
Rachel remembered the chill on the nape of her neck, the
feeling of being watched, and fought off a sense of unease
as she watched him go down the trail. When he reappeared
a few minutes later, she breathed a sigh of relief.

"There, that should keep you supplied."

"Thank you, Michael. Now you sleep well." They kissed
and he went to bed.

The willow bark tea didn't help Leah. Slowly her fever
grew, as had Noah's. Rachel bathed them each with cool
water, hoping to lower their temperatures, but it had no more
effect than the tea. She resolutely ignored the fear growing
inside her, the feeling that she was a helpless onlooker in a
preordained scene, a scene she had witnessed by the laundry tub.

She succeeded in keeping the fear at bay until the middle
of the day, when Michael awoke and called weakly to her. She
went into the bedroom, and saw the fever in his face, too. Then
the fear began gnawing at her heart.

"I seem to have caught it now. How are the children?"

She tenderly wiped his face with the wet cloth she carried.
"No better, I'm afraid. Do you feel like drinking some cold
willow bark tea?" She smiled sadly.

"It doesn't seem to have done much good, does it?"

Nonetheless, he dutifully sipped at the tea, then leaned back on the pillow, eyes closed, as if the effort of sitting upright had cost him dearly. Rachel's throat tightened and panic threatened to take over. Then her hand went to the leather case hanging from the thong around her neck and her fingers felt the shape of the claw inside. *I'm of the Bear Clan,* she said to herself, *and my mother came from a great lineage. I'm a Crafter and my father is a fierce fighter. I* won't *give in!*

The hours dragged on, and Rachel kept watch over her family. Noah whimpered and twisted in his cradle. Leah shifted and murmured in delirium. Michael wandered through the paths of fevered dreams, muttering half-audible words. All she could do was offer them water to drink, and try to cool them with sponge baths.

As darkness fell, she realized she'd have to go fetch water, and the thought of the hollow under the bank made her shiver. But she lit the pierced metal lantern, stepped outside, and picked up the pail by the door. Resolutely she walked down the trail, guided by the wavering beams of light from the lantern. Her apprehension increased as she heard the burbling of the brook grow louder. But she made herself keep walking.

She reached the stream bank, and forced her hand to hold the lantern high, forced herself to look across the dark water to the cave under the bank. *You see? There's nothing there.* A glimmer showed in the darkness but she told herself it was probably the gleam of light on a wet rock, nothing else.

But the glimmer seemed to grow, to resolve into two separate gleams. Like eyes, she couldn't help thinking. *Enough! Fill the bucket and go. You have a sick family waiting for you.*

She lowered the lantern and set it on the bank, then stooped to fill the bucket. The gurgle of water as it swirled into the pail seemed unnaturally loud to her. She straightened, lifting the now-heavy bucket, and reached for the lantern with her free hand. Then, like a child picking at a wound, she couldn't stop herself from glancing across to the hollow again—and stark terror shot through her.

There, floating above the dark water, moving towards her, was a dreadful, inhuman scarlet face. It had no body. Long white hair streamed down either side of its horribly twisted features. Flat eyes like beaten copper gleamed madly in the lantern's yellow light. It made no sound as it crossed the water.

Once more Rachel was held motionless as panic grew within her. She knew what she was looking at. Crooked Mouth, her mother had called it, one of the false-face spirits that roamed the forests, spreading sickness and disease. They had terrible strength, and only one powerful in *orenda* could defeat them. And the thing, bobbing horribly in some invisible wind, drew ever closer.

Even in her fear, she found that she could think. Each of her family had fallen ill after coming to the stream, yet she had not. Somehow she had to drive it from her family. Her family was all she had in this new land. Her family was more precious to her than anything else. She had to fight for them, fight to save them. Her hand reached up and clutched the bear claw in its pouch.

I will fight you! she shouted silently at Crooked Mouth.

Its mouth contorted in a fearful, triumphant grin as it floated up to her.

She gathered herself within, reached out for some measure of strength, the strength she could feel all about her, waiting to be gathered. She took a deep breath—

—and a roar echoed through the night air. Rushing up the stream, as though the water were as solid as a forest path, came a huge silvery bear, glowing like the moon. Far behind it gamboled two pale cubs who tumbled over one another in the starlight. The bear snarled at Crooked Mouth and swung a great clawed paw at the scarlet head, hurling it against a tree trunk. The head seemed to burst into a thousand blood-red splinters, which vanished.

And the dread in Rachel's heart, the dread for her family, vanished too. She watched as the bear turned back to its cubs, nosing them gently. She reached out a hand, and the bear raised its head and looked into her eyes for a long moment—

—when a wave of disorientation swept over her. She was in some other place. Yet she still stood by the stream bank. Only now it was bright daylight, and before her Michael and a slightly older Leah splashed in the stream. Noah, a sturdy toddler, sat in the shallow water near the bank, laughing as

he kicked his feet and sparkling drops of water showered around him.

The bear and her cubs had vanished. Rachel was standing in the dark, the lantern tipped on its side, the filled bucket heavy in her hand. She picked up the lantern and looked across to the hollow.

It was just a hollow made by the overhanging bank.

She smiled, and went up the trail to her home.

Philadelphia
Anno Domini 1787

It is not surprising that along with their Talent, some of the Crafter Family inherited Amer's analytical mind. Their own unique abilities also gave them a far different approach to the unknown than was common even in the inconoclastic new United States. This could be an exciting thing in an age where science, as we know it, was being born. A penchant for the new physical philosophies was particularly true of those fourth- and fifth- generation Crafters who remained in the Boston area, which even then was a major center of learning for all of America.

FRANKLIN'S SALAMANDER

by **Wendy Wheeler**

Andrew Crafter Smithson sat in the neatly appointed office of his small house in the prestigious Germantown neighborhood of Boston. His twenty-two-year-old heart sank again as he reread the last few lines of the letter in his hand. The words were written in an old-man's spidery script:

" . . . and so, tho' flattered I am that my early work with that marvelous discovery Electricity has touch'd your Curiosity, and tho' I send heartiest good wishes for your own studies in that Estimable Area, my advanced age together with the New Duties vot'd upon me as the President of Pennsylvania and as Delegate to the Constitutional Congress preclude me from enjoying such

Further and Intimate Discussions of the Science as I
would so greatly enjoy.

Your Humble Servant,
Benjamin Franklin, Esq."

Andrew had read Franklin's *Experiments and Observations
on Electricity* three times. Now he felt like some importuning
young puppy. But he'd so keenly hoped for this interview with
the man. Yes, Franklin was an old man. Yes, those experiments
had been done thirty-five years ago, but the man had been
audacious. Flying a kite in a thunderstorm to catch electricity
in a jar, indeed! In his *Experiments*, Franklin had touched again
and again on issues and theories that both Andrew and his
fellow scientist and correspondent in Italy, Count Alessandro
Volta, now pursued in their attempts to manufacture and store
electricity. Volta had also tried to get an audience with Franklin, while that great man was so long in France. But Franklin
had rebuffed Volta in the same genial and terse manner.

Andrew laid Franklin's letter down and went to stand by the
window, the better to catch a refreshing breeze now that the
heat of summer was fast approaching. He put a hand on the cool
glass of his Leyden jar. It brought back the memory of when
he'd so excitedly demonstrated some of his experiments for
his family—for Grandpa Jim and the Crafter cousins. Andrew
had filled the jar with water and used his Hauksbee machine
to charge the water with electricity. Then, taking a metal T
made for the purpose, he'd touched one end of the T to
the rod on the top of the Leyden jar and the other end of
the T to the metal jacket that wrapped the jar. For a brief
moment, a flicker of yellow light had snapped across the
connection.

Andrew had stepped back, expecting cheers, praise, or at the
least, surprise from his audience. All he'd received were a few
raised eyebrows, some shrugs and some smirks. Then Grandpa
Jim said, "Filling a jar with light doesn't take much Talent,
son." And there it was again. All the Crafters had Talent.
They could scry, they could dowse, they could transmute
metals. Everyone, that is, except for Andrew. But he didn't
need magic, didn't even believe in it. He had his science: his
trade as an astrologer, his electrical experiments. And someday
that pity he saw in the eyes of his family would turn to respect.
That was the real purpose of his work with Volta.

But nowadays, his experiments had reached an impasse. Volta's experiments also. Andrew was certain Franklin would say something, insinuate something, that would make everything fall together. If only he could speak to him just for a few moments.

The Congress Franklin mentioned was to start in Philadelphia this June, only two weeks away. Though he didn't consider himself a political man, Andrew knew what the meeting was for; the newspapers and essays were abuzz with it. The Articles of Confederation, the best the colonists could do as a manifesto for central government during the hectic first days of the Revolution, were to be overhauled. America would have its own Constitution.

Andrew checked his calendar and did a quick survey of his own astrological chart. He could always rearrange his work; the businessmen and farmers who called on him for astrological consultations would be patient if he was gone for a short while. And the auspices were good for a business endeavor. He himself could be in Philadelphia in two weeks, he realized. He might meet Franklin on the street—or maybe in a tavern. Since Franklin's return from France, rumors of his predilection for carousing and for women of low estate had abounded. The word was that he was still a spry old man. Hopefully his mind was also still keen.

Standing in the muggy Philadelphia air had all but turned Andrew's dark woolen attire into a sodden, wrinkled mess. But he had to put forth the appearance of an established man of letters. He ran a hand across his light brown hair which he'd so carefully powdered that morning. It wasn't mussed. The handkerchief at his throat was still in its snug knot, so perhaps the June weather hadn't ruined him.

He'd counted almost a hundred other people standing on the street in front of the Philadelphia State House waiting for a glimpse of the powerful men who would sit in this Congress. Since the war had ended four years before, patriotic fervor was the rage, even to lionizing the leaders of the Revolution. Andrew was more curious than fervent.

He looked around at the periwigs, bonnets and parasols, and wondered again if these people, like him, had work they'd abandoned for capricious reasons. Did they all have an independent income? Andrew did; he received a stipend from his deceased mother's estate.

Andrew had been only five when his mother, Rebecca, died. His father, a respected printer and bookbinder, had invited a longtime friend of the family to live with them. Felicity King had moved into the Boston house with her own two daughters. Gunning King, her husband, lived there too, on the few odd weeks a year he wasn't at sea. Felicity had raised Andrew and his brother and sister as though they were her own children, never seeming to notice any difference between the pale milk of their skin and the rich brown of her own.

Felicity had been almost as bad as Grandpa Jim about the sanctity of the Crafter blood, too. Andrew didn't give any credence to the idea that there was some mystical Talent he should have just because of who his great-grandparents were. It was embarrassing. It was the reason Andrew had chosen such a scientific profession as astrology. The stars spun in the heavens playing their part in the destiny of men. You could read it in a book, plot it out with your pen. It was real.

The first official meeting of the Congress wasn't for another few days, but the delegates were to pay a visit to the State House this morning to sign the registry. A liveried carriage drew up, and out stepped, not a foot, but a stick of some sort. Andrew looked again and saw it was the peg-leg of a scowling older man with flyaway hair and a beaky nose.

"Gouverneur Morris?" he heard. So, this was the urbane and droll Philadelphia lawyer he'd read about. The crowd began to clap, and Andrew joined in. Immediately another carriage drew up; its door opened quickly and a tall man in dark blue with a rigid soldier's posture stepped out and hastened over to Morris. The taller man grinned, making his somewhat stern face seem almost boyish. He shook Morris' hand and then nodded to the crowd.

The crowd began to cheer, first raggedly, then in unison: "Wash-ing-ton, Wash-ing-ton!"

Andrew caught his breath. This was him! This was the man who led the Continental Army and so valiantly won the Battle at Valley Forge! Why, he *did* look powerful and, though it was now a term rarely used by the Americans, regal. "Huzzah!" cried Andrew.

"Pardon me," said a small man at his elbow. Andrew was a few inches short of six feet, but this fellow barely broke five. His sparse hair was caught back in a dark ribbon, and his suit was the same light grey as his eyes. He moved and looked like a rabbit.

"Did you want to see the Colonel?" said Andrew, turning aside.

"Oh, I'll greet George soon enough," said the man, and began ascending the steps to the front door of the State House. Aware that this was a delegate, but not sure which one, Andrew stepped back, almost tripping an older man who walked with a cane as though favoring a gouty foot.

"Pardon," said Andrew, one hand on the man's elbow to steady him. He suddenly realized the crowd had formed a circle around the two of them. Someone began to clap politely. Andrew looked at the man, at the bald head and trailing grey hair, at the odd spectacles perched on his nose, at the brown worsted coat. "Mr. Franklin?" he cried. "Mr. Franklin, it's Andrew Smithson, sir. I came all the way—"

Ben Franklin didn't even seem to hear Andrew. The eyes beneath his shaggy brows had a glint Andrew associated with younger men. Andrew followed his gaze and saw a buxom middle-aged woman, rouged and powdered, smirking back. Franklin gave a gallant waggle of his cane and stepped smartly forward.

"Mr. Franklin?" Andrew tried again, and moved to intercept him. Instead, he collided with a tall young woman wearing mustard yellow. Though slim, she seemed unusually solid, for Andrew and she both nearly lost their footing.

"You made me lose Mr. Madison!" she cried, her dark eyes flashing fury at him. Then her expression changed, as Andrew could feel his doing also. "Andrew?" she said incredulously. "What are *you* doing here?"

"Calliope?" Andrew heard his voice squeak. "Why aren't you in Virginia?"

Calliope King, Felicity's daughter, Andrew's sister by upbringing if not by blood, just rubbed her elbow and grinned at him.

"You have a job here?" Andrew said, looking up at the building before them. The Green Dragon Inn was down a quiet lane. It stood three stories tall, with a coach house and barn, all built of the same grey slate shingles. He knew

Calliope had never been a tavern wench before—her mother forbade it. "How did you acquire it?"

"I convinced the publican. Henry Gant. A very nice man, and this is a very respectable tavern." Calliope tossed her head. Andrew was her elder by less than a year. As children, she'd formed the irritating habit of regularly topping him in height. Now that they were grown, she was shorter than he by only a few inches. Her tallness and her noble air were said to be inherited from her great-grandfather, the first freedman holder of the King name. He was supposed to have been a prince or a priest, a man of rank. Her narrow nose and high cheekbones were from her mother's side, which had some mixture of Indian and white blood. Andrew often thought Calliope looked more like an Italian woman than a Negress. He'd even convinced her to learn a smattering of Italian because of it.

"You can convince anyone of anything," said Andrew. It was true. Calliope could stretch that long neck of hers and speak so commandingly that no one could deny her. Andrew, unfortunately, had a high raspy voice and diffident manner. He found it difficult to get attention. Like today. "What did you mean, I made you lose Mr. Madison?"

Calliope removed her bonnet and hung it on a peg inside the front door of the tavern. Andrew saw she had braided her gleaming black hair in a new style. It made her look almost womanly. He hadn't seen her for three years, he realized now. "Madison is the reason I'm in Philadelphia," she said. "I followed him here when I heard he'd be the Virginia delegate to the Constitutional Congress. And I took this position because this tavern is the meeting place for many of the patriots. All the Masonic groups hold their meetings here—right in that back room. It's a perfect opportunity. I've got my plan all worked out."

"What plan?" said Andrew. She always did the same thing to him, assumed he could read her heart without her having to say. And, truthfully, many times he could. But it had been three years. "What are you talking about?"

"I must beg his leniency for Billy." Calliope bit her lip and her eyes softened. "I met him in Virginia. Oh, Billy's such a wonderful man. Honorable, proud, witty. He'll be a freedman someday, I just know he will. He was Madison's valet, but escaped to the British when they were offering the black men freedom. Now he's been caught again. Madison could free him, and he would, if only he understood what a proud man Billy is."

Through an unexpected lump in his throat, Andrew asked, "Is this important to you? Personally?"

"Oh, yes," said Calliope. She tied a clean white apron around her waist. "May I get you a mug of something? My gift."

"Please," said Andrew. He followed her into the great room. The tables were still half-full of people breakfasting. It seemed a clean, scrubbed place. Andrew would come here for his meals, he decided. "I'm in Philadelphia for a reason, too, Calliope. You misdirected me also this morning."

She handed him a chilled pewter mug. "What could it be? Mother says you never leave your house and your precious electrical machines. It is a real surprise to find you outside of Boston." She bent and brushed his cheek. "Still can't grow a beard, I see."

He jerked his face away. "I'm here on a scientific mission. My friend Count Volta is expecting me to get an audience with Franklin to discuss some of his electrical theories. And I leave my house all the time—I see your mother once a week at least. And she never said *anything* about you leaving your cousin's house for Philadelphia."

Calliope sat down and sighed. "She doesn't know. I traveled here with a nice family who hired me to watch their babies. As soon as I'm successful, I'll go back." She stroked Andrew's arm imploringly. "Please. It's probably best that Mother not be told. We could help each other, you and I."

"Oh," said Andrew, looking at her roguish dark eyes and glossy hair with new appreciation. "I imagine you could get closer to Franklin than I. He has been known to flirt."

"So have I."

"And I could offer astrological consultations to any of the delegates who want to check the auspices. If Mr. Madison is a Virginia farmer—?"

"He is."

"Then we may find him altogether disposed to meet with me. With us. Farmers plant their fields and breed their livestock according to the stars."

"So you'll help me with Billy and I'll help you with your electricity. We always dealt so well together, brother."

"Sister," said Andrew, and finally gave her a welcoming kiss. She returned it heartily, which made his heart heavier. All he kept thinking was, she has a sweetheart. His name is Billy.

Andrew was at the tavern the next day taking a supper of squab and boiled vegetables when Franklin came in. He almost choked on a cold potato, then waggled his fork at Calliope to attract her attention. She had proved to be very popular at the tavern; one young rooster after another set his cap for her.

Now Calliope saw Andrew's signal. The look she gave the older man standing at the doorway, leaning upon his cane, was a considering one. Then she left the bumpkin she'd been talking to to greet Franklin. Andrew saw her say something that made Franklin smile. Then he bent close and said something in return that caused Calliope to throw back her head and shake with laughter. As they moved to the back room reserved for special customers, Andrew saw Franklin make a great show of being infirm so that Calliope, who was as tall as he, tucked his arm in hers and all but supported him.

As they passed closer to Andrew, he noticed bits of thread and lint all across the brown worsted of Franklin's suit. His grey hair seemed unduly flyaway for such humid Philadelphia weather.

Calliope came back into the great room and sat at Andrew's table. He tried to wave her away. "No, don't let him see us together. He may remember me and suspect something."

Calliope just put her head to the side. "You flatter yourself, Andrew. His eye is all for the ladies. He's such an old man—you never mentioned that. And still so spry. I think he likes me, too."

"Good," said Andrew, then had a pang of conscience. "You must not allow him any liberties, Calliope. We only want a meeting with him. Take care."

She looked at him with uncomprehending eyes. "Take care of what?"

"That he doesn't—Well, some men—Oh, go tend your customers." She shook her head, but went. Andrew was greatly encouraged. And it was only fair he make some effort on Calliope's behalf. This very eve he would write a letter to Madison offering his services.

Calliope returned from the back room several times that night. Each time she had something new to tell Andrew. Franklin was conferring with some of the other patriots. Franklin had complimented her eyes. Franklin had presented her with a shilling when she brought him his dinner.

Finally she emerged, pewter pitcher in her hand, triumphant smile on her face. "I got you your interview!" she told Andrew.

"Really? You told him about me and he's willing to meet with me?"

"Not quite." Calliope brushed a crumb from the table. "I thought I would explain things once I was in his house."

"You got an invitation for us to go to Franklin's house?" Oh, she was an excellent girl!

"Just me this first time, but I know I can convince him to see you also once I'm there." Her smile was sly. "I can convince anyone of anything."

Andrew was uneasy. "Exactly what did Franklin invite you to do?"

"To visit him. Tonight. He even told me to come to a special door so we wouldn't disturb anyone else." She began rubbing her hip absentmindedly. "Surely he'll be easy to persuade; he seems quite enthusiastic about my company."

Andrew watched her. "Did he touch you?"

Calliope shrugged. "I think, maybe, he might have pinched me—"

"That does it," said Andrew. "You're not going alone to his house. I'll be there with you."

They were still arguing as they stood at the side gate of the house on Providence Street. Calliope had charged Andrew again and again to tell her why he'd insisted on coming along. Embarrassed to explain such things as lecherous old men to such an innocent, Andrew had not let her from his sight, striding beside her as she made her way to the address Franklin had given her. They'd had to loiter on the street until the night watchman passed with his lantern and billy club before darting up to the tall iron gate.

"All right now, Andrew, just wait for me here." Calliope straightened her bonnet.

Andrew shook his head and folded his arms. "No. I'm coming inside."

Calliope threw out her arms. "For heaven's sake, why? It's me he made the appointment with."

"It's not safe for you alone." That was as much as Andrew would admit.

"He's not a brigand, not a robber. I have no purse for him to take even if he was. Just wait here. Oh, it is open." She'd pushed the gate and discovered it wasn't locked. She sighed loudly as Andrew followed her inside.

The garden inside was well-established, even a little overgrown. Calliope looked around a moment, then stomped over to a small green door on the side of the white clapboard house. She put a tentative hand on the doorknob, finding it, too, was unlocked. Andrew stood right at her elbow as she went in.

"Now where?" he whispered, then he saw the narrow set of stairs leading up.

It was too dark to see, but he could hear the scowl in Calliope's voice. "Up these stairs to a sitting room, he told me. I don't know what he'll do when he sees you came too."

"Be more optimistic, can't you?" whispered Andrew.

Light came from the edges of a doorjamb at the top of the dark stairway. Calliope, on the top step, pushed the door open. Andrew watched her expression change from a scowl to a smile. She gave a curtsey, and a male voice inside the room called, "Delightful to see you, my dear. Please, come in."

Calliope turned; from the look she gave Andrew, he knew she was planning to shut and bar the door. He grabbed the door edge and pushed himself through to prevent her.

"Who's this?" said the male voice.

Andrew turned and saw a small room with a rope bed in one corner. Benjamin Franklin, wearing a dark green robe and slippers, sat in an upholstered chair, his cane across his knees. The satin folds of the robe clung to his skinny shanks and arms. His hair seemed to be standing out from his head. He ducked his chin to glower over the tops of his glasses at

Andrew. Andrew thought he saw a glow around Franklin, a faint one.

"Mr. Franklin, I asked Calliope to help me meet you. It wasn't her fault, sir. I only wanted to importune you in person for an audience."

"Who are you?" said Franklin through gritted teeth.

"Andrew Smithson, sir. I've written you about some electrical experiments—"

"And I wrote you I had no time for such concerns anymore. My interest tonight lies with this young lady. I'll ask you to grant us some privacy." When Franklin reached a hand to the table beside him, a spark of light jumped from his forefinger to the table's edge. Franklin jerked back his hand in irritation. "I have some matters to take up with young Calliope here. Please go."

"No, sir. Not without Calliope." Andrew put an arm around her shoulders.

Calliope snorted and shrugged him off. "Let me stay and talk with Mr. Franklin, Andrew. 'Twill do more good if one stays than if both of us go."

Andrew muttered in her ear, "He doesn't want to talk to you, Calliope." Aloud he said, "You've misjudged her, Mr. Franklin. She's an innocent. You're much too popular a man to chase such girls as her."

"Ah, now I see your game!" cried Franklin. "It's money you want. Some intrigue, some blackmail. Well, let's see who the law believes, the patriot or the young cur and his wench." Franklin stood and went to the open window. Another spark popped as he put his hands on the windowsill, but he grimaced and ignored it. His head out the window, he hollered in a voice amazingly loud for one so old, "Constable! Night watchman! I've intruders in my house! Ben Franklin calling for aid. Hoy! Hoy!"

"Ah, no." cried Andrew. Calliope was gaping, for once silent. "Please sir, don't! We'll go! We'll go!"

The street began to stir. Andrew could see lights as men with lanterns came running. He heard distant whistles; then a bell began to clang. They'd be arrested, jailed, and all because of his obsession with science.

Just then a second Ben Franklin, also dressed in robe and slippers, stepping with a cane, came into the room. This Franklin was glowing like phosphor; his face, his hair, his raiment were all a shining pale yellow. Flickers of electricity danced around him in a corona. He took the chair the first Ben Franklin had vacated.

"Evening," he said to Andrew.

"There's a *what* in my chair?" said Franklin, the first one.

"Another you," said Andrew timidly. "Can't you see it?"

Calliope was goggling at Andrew; obviously she couldn't see it either.

Andrew pointed. In a firmer voice, he said, "There is a man who looks just like you sitting in your chair. Only he is glowing bright with flickers of electricity about him."

"I'm not Franklin," said the figure in the chair. "I've just begun to look like him after all these years. Tell him I'm the elemental he caught when he flew that damned kite in the lightning storm."

"He says he's not you," relayed Andrew. "You caught him in a lightning storm years ago. He's an elemental." He remembered something Franklin had proposed in his papers. "Didn't you say electricity was probably an element, like fire, only unrecognized until now? And just as some say fire has its creatures, its salamanders, so may electricity have its creatures also."

"I don't believe you," said Franklin.

From a door downstairs came a heavy knocking.

"He can't hear me, can't see me," said the salamander, adjusting its robe. "What a frustration it's been all these years. He trapped me and didn't even know it. All I could do was torment him by increasing the charge flowing through his body. It's why he needs all those women."

"He—he says he torments you by charging your body with electricity," said Andrew. He needed to convince Franklin before the constabulary came in. "That's why you need women like you do."

Franklin's jaw dropped. He eyed the chair as though now he could see the being there. Then he put his head back out the window. "Thank you, Constable!" he called. "I've mishandled a family prank, I think. I'm fine. Please excuse me. Yes. Yes. Thank you all. Thank you."

Franklin pulled his head in. His hair was still wild and crackling with electricity. He smoothed it down with one hand. "An elemental, eh? My own salamander. Well, well. You don't know what a plague this has been to me. Thirty-five years. It starts each time as a tingle, then my clothes begin to cling and crackle. Finally I can touch nothing, approach nothing, neither food nor friend nor furniture—nor even the floor—without the most painful shocks." He shot a look at Calliope, but addressed Andrew. "Yes, I will admit more than an ordinary number of intrigues and affairs. But, by damn, it was the only way to obtain relief. That intimate sharing was the one way to mitigate the symptoms."

"He deserved it," said the elemental. "Enticing me into that jar, keeping me from home and kin. All I want is to be released."

"All he wants is to be released," said Andrew. "He'd probably never devil you again if you'd release him, Mr. Franklin."

"Andrew!" cried Calliope, finally finding her tongue. "You know what this is? This is like that story of your great-grandmother talking with that earth elemental—when she found the Chaos for Amer. It's your Talent, Andrew. You've finally found it!"

"Oh," said Andrew, his hand to his mouth. This was what Talent felt like? It was so natural.

"Release the thing?" said Franklin. "How?" He made as if to sit on the upholstered chair, then thought better of it and sat on the bed instead.

"He needn't be so coy," said the elemental. "He sits on me and walks through me all the time. And to release me, all he needs to do is the opposite of that damned procedure that trapped me in the first place."

"He wants you to fly another kite, sir," said Andrew. "Only this time send the key aloft."

"But when will we ever have another lightning storm?" said Franklin. "It's been damnably still weather—"

"Tomorrow night. There will be a storm tomorrow night." The elemental stood and walked to the door. "Trust me. I know these things." Light flashed from the spectacles on its glowing nose. "Resolve to perform what you ought; perform without fail what you resolve." On that platitude, it turned on its heel and left.

"You can expect a storm tomorrow night," said Andrew.

"And we'll be glad to help, Mr. Franklin," said Calliope, "for we have need of your aid also."

"Yes, yes, the discussions of electricity," said Franklin. He was gingerly touching the bedpost to see if he still made sparks.

"Those, yes, for Andrew," said Calliope. "For me, an introduction to James Madison."

"Jim?" Franklin looked up. "He and I take breakfast tomorrow morning. What say I bring him to your victualizing house?"

Andrew was still looking down the hall. "The interview I'd really like," he murmured, "is with *him*."

Madison was the rabbity man in grey Andrew had met that first day at the State House. The small man pushed aside his egg pasty and breakfast cider when Andrew and Calliope came into his private room at the Dragon. "Ben has told me about you two," he said quietly. "He has vast reasons for gratitude, he says, and as his good friend, then so must I. What is it I can do for you?"

Franklin rose, his own plate in hand. "I must tell you both how wonderfully I slept last night, anticipating the surcease tonight's work will bring. Thank you, thank you. Well, eat not to fullness, drink not to elevation, a wise man said. I'll leave you to your private audience with Jim."

Madison was massaging the bridge of his nose with one small hand. "You seem tired, sir," said Andrew. "Will you play a large role in today's Congress?"

"A large but quiet one." Madison's voice was high and light. "I've prepared an extensive proposal which my good friend Hamilton will explain to the Congress, his voice and manner being more suitable for public speaking than mine. It will be, I'm afraid, a challenging summer."

"Maybe more so for you," said Calliope, "for I hear you are a considered and just man, both in your governing and in your personal affairs."

"Doubtless my Dolley would disagree with you somewhat, but thank you just the same. And I'm sure you would like to call upon those very qualities in me now, would you not?" When he smiled, Madison looked almost charming.

"Oh yes, sir. Please, sir. It's about a most honorable man, a man who only wished for the freedom to marry his true love and establish a family that he would support by his own honest work. The simple dream of many a man." Calliope sat beside Madison, her dark eyes moist. Andrew thought how beautiful she was, how much love she had for this lucky Billy. "Mr. Madison, many of us sacrificed for the Revolution. But we won our freedom. And this man has been jailed merely for coveting that liberty for which we all paid the price of so much blood. That liberty we have proclaimed so often to be the right and worthy pursuit of every human being."

"Miss Calliope," said Madison. "How appropriate the name. I declare, you would challenge my old friend Hamilton for persuasiveness. I must reward such ardency, if I can. But what man is this whom I can so affect?"

Calliope laid her hand lightly on his sleeve. "Your valet, Billy."

"Ah." Madison sat straighter. "I see. You're an Abolitionist then, Miss Calliope? That's what inspires your words so."

"I'm a Negress, Mr. Madison." Calliope stretched her own neck to its most regal. "That's what inspires my words so."

Madison blinked several times. Then he took Calliope's hand into his own. "I had no notion. It's as I've grown to understand. There is no difference among men, among races." He looked at her pale gold skin a moment. "Say we make special arrangements for Billy. His case is not popular with my neighbors in Virginny. So say we send him someplace more accommodating. Philadelphia perhaps. Perhaps to work in a victualizing house, much like this one. For a good master, much like Mr. Gant. And say we draw him the contract of an indentured servant, so that at the end of seven years, his freedom is his own and he can live and work—and marry— as he likes."

"Oh, sir." Calliope brought Madison's hand to her lips and kissed it. Andrew saw him flush all the way up his high forehead. "It's just. It's merciful. Can you send a letter on it today, since the Congress has just started?"

Madison threw back his head and roared. "Priceless woman! I observe those tears are sincere, yet still you keep me timely. Of course I will send my letter today."

"I brought paper and pen for my own work," volunteered Andrew. "But you can use some now if you wish."

Madison thanked him, and bent his head over the paper. When he'd finished his letter, which he folded and promised to hand to the secretary of the Congress for posting, he looked at Andrew. "You've been a quiet young man. What is this work you speak of?"

"Astrology, sir—"

"Oh," Madison was enlightened. "You're Smithson, the astrologer who wrote me the letter."

"Andrew!" said Calliope. "How considerate of you."

"Thank you, sister," said Andrew. "And I still make the offer, Mr. Madison. To cast a chart for the Constitutional Congress."

"Yes, please." Madison's grey eyes warmed. "My plantation has prospered, Mr. Smithson, not nominally because of sage advice from several astrologers. June, 1787. We're talking of a Cancer nativity for the Congress, are we not? Hmmm, a mutable sign."

"There are actually twelve celestial houses to consider, Mr. Madison," said Andrew. He had his tables out and was noting any crucial aspects in opposition. "And each house has its say in the horoscope. None rules the other."

Madison nodded. "Like the thirteen states, each with their own constitutions."

"Well, yes," said Andrew. "I'm not a political man, but that would seem reasonable. And though Cancer would be the sun sign, we really see a checking and balancing influence among the Sun sign, the rising sign, and the house in which the Moon falls. Three influences augmenting and mitigating each other."

"Checking and balancing—I like that. My Virginia Plan, I can let you know, says something similar. I propose three separate branches of Federal Government, each one checking and balancing the other . . .Yes, yes, I will lay this out for Hamilton this morning. Oh, excellent. What a help you've been, Mr. Smithson!" Madison jumped up from the table. "A busy day for us all, eh? Miss Calliope, an honor. Mr. Smithson, good luck."

He scampered from the room, leaving Andrew looking dejectedly at his notes. "I was going to tell him he has wonderful auspices in the third house. The house of cooperation among peers."

Calliope kissed Andrew's cheek. "Maybe he'll discover it for himself."

The clouds overhead covered the moon, leaving a darkness so intense the lantern light seemed ripped away by the wind.

Andrew, Calliope, Franklin, and Franklin's secretary, Peter Martin, stood on a hillside outside the city. Also present, though only Andrew could see him, was Franklin's elemental.

Franklin was divesting himself of his clothes, hanging each article over the proffered arm of his secretary. He saw Andrew staring at him. "Men take more pains to mask than mend," he said, merrily tugging off one stocking.

The elemental Franklin was still fully dressed. It shook its head. "Joyful will I be to escape these homilies," it said. "In my original state, I had no need of words or clothes or houses or books. Indeed, you may have been hard pressed then to speak with me, my speech was so strange and random."

Now Franklin was tugging down his breeches.

"Calliope, are you going to stand there gawking?" called Andrew. "Cover your eyes, girl, or your mother will hear of this."

Calliope, holding a parchment kite with a long muslin tail, gave him an impudent grin, then turned her back to Franklin.

The old man began to caper in the moonlight, skinny shanks flashing, pot belly jiggling. "This was how I did the first experiment, children. That didn't show up in my writings, though, did it, Andrew? Heh heh heh."

"I'm glad we can speak," said Andrew to the elemental. They had been conversing for the past hour, at Franklin's house, in the carriage, now on the hill. The others had at first been disconcerted and confused, but soon grew used to Andrew's one-sided conversations. The elemental didn't know science, but it did know its own nature. "Opposites on either side of the kite string, you said?" Andrew asked. "You mean, like a magnet with its two opposite forces?"

"That is it exactly," said the elemental. "I move most at ease along paths set for me with just that positivity and negativity."

"I feel rain," cried Calliope, holding her face to the sky. "We'd better send this kite up now."

A flash lit the dark clouds; then a boom of thunder sounded. The elemental seemed to be less distinct, almost gaseous, though it shone as brightly as ever. It lifted its arms to the sky. "I feel them!" it cried. "My kind await me."

"Send up the kite," said Andrew. They'd already fastened an iron key to it. Now Franklin's secretary took the ball of string from Calliope and began backing away, unrolling it as he went.

"Oh, this airbath is delightful," called Franklin, still capering. "Did you ever hear of the Hellfire Club? Regular airbaths we had, men and women together, no shame at all. Lovely, lovely. Only the British could be so cultured and free at the same time."

"Run with it," called Calliope to the secretary. Andrew saw her shoot a sidelong look at Franklin, then grimace and look away.

A spatter of rain began just as Peter Martin tugged the kite from Calliope's hands. The kite soared out of the lantern light and disappeared.

"Is it up? Is it up?" called Franklin delightedly.

"Yes, sir, I feel it tugging," said Peter Martin. "Will you take the string?"

"Thank you for interceding," said the elemental. "Though in my original state, I would not have known gratitude either. Perhaps this miserable old lecher taught me some worthwhile things after all."

Another flash lit the sky. The thunder roll was almost immediate.

"You're welcome," said Andrew. "And I'm grateful to you, for your helpful discourse and for showing me my Talent." He couldn't wait to take his tale to Grandpa Jim and the Crafter cousins. Such a successful combination of science and magic was rare even in their family history.

"The storm should be closer," called Franklin. The silhouette of his kite could be seen only at each lightning flicker.

"It is close. They're just waiting for me," said the elemental. "That silly old coot. I'll almost miss him. Tell him that for me."

"Mr. Franklin," called Andrew as the elemental walked toward the naked man now starting to shiver in the rain and wind. "He wants you to know he'll miss you."

Franklin turned to face him, face bemused in the lantern light. "Miss me? He will?"

"But not much," said the elemental. It took one more step forward, and now it and Franklin stood in the same place, almost in the same body. The clouds seemed to split open, a fork of lightning as crooked as the Devil's tongue raced across the sky directly toward the tiny dark diamond of the kite.

The results were almost instantaneous: the kite exploded, a ball of light flashed skyward from where Franklin stood, and a boom of thunder flattened all four people to the ground.

Andrew sat up in the now-pouring rain. His chest felt bruised and his ears rang. It took a moment to orient himself. Then he saw that Calliope lay nearby. He crawled to her. Her eyes were closed, but she was breathing. Andrew gasped her name and gathered her to him. He rocked her and rocked her for what seemed forever. Then he felt her stir and heard her say,

"Did you see that lightning!"

"Yes, sweetheart, I saw it. Are you all right? Can you stand?"

"Of course I can." Calliope's tone was indignant. But when she stood, she wobbled and had to hold onto Andrew for balance.

"Mr. Franklin, Mr. Franklin." Peter Martin knelt beside the old man. He'd covered Franklin with his own jacket. "Can you hear me, sir? Wake up. Wake up."

Andrew and Calliope staggered over. "Is he injured?" said Andrew. There were no burns or marks on Franklin's body.

"I feel fine," said Franklin, opening his eyes then. He looked around at them and smiled. "What a capital adventure!"

In the light of the lantern, his face looked calmer, wiser. And what was more, the look he gave Calliope was grandfatherly, Andrew realized. That gleam was finally gone from his eye.

The crowd of young men around Calliope at the Green Dragon Inn the next day was as thick as ever. *They must know she'll be leaving to meet her sweetheart in Virginia*, thought Andrew. The realization that he might burst into tears at her departure both frightened and amazed him. She was his little sister, he kept telling himself. *Put these feelings away*, he told himself.

She came over to Andrew sitting by himself with a chilled mug of cider. "It took two baths to wash the mud and twigs from my hair," she said. "Remember when we used to do Indian dances in the rain?"

"Yes." She was wearing dark crimson and looked very beautiful. He didn't want to prolong the inevitable. "You'll be leaving right away with your message for Billy?"

"No, not right away." Her eyes slid away from his. "I may stay here awhile longer. Or maybe travel back to Boston with you to see my family."

"But what about Billy?"

Calliope gave him a confused look. "I wrote Janine the good news. She should be the one to tell him anyway; they're planning to marry."

Andrew gaped. "Janine, your cousin?"

"Yes."

"Your Virginia cousin?"

"Yes. Andrew, what are you going on about? Is it that you don't want me to travel with you back to Boston?"

"Of course I want you—" Emboldened, he took a breath and babbled. "I want you to go with me to Europe, Calliope, to Italy, to meet my friend Count Volta. I'm certain we'll make headway with our experiments now with what I've learned. Will you come?"

To his amazement, Calliope put her hands to her face and burst into tears. When he put a comforting arm around her, she jerked away. "No! How could you treat me this way? White men often take black mistresses, but I expected better of you. I don't think I can bear it."

He took her by both shoulders. "Calliope. Calliope King, look at me. Did you think that's what I was offering? No, I love you truly and want to marry you. Your mother always taught us all men and women were the same. Well, she wasn't quite correct. There is no other woman like you. And you're the only kind of woman I'd want to marry."

When she brought her hands down, Calliope's thick eyelashes were wet with tears. He wanted to kiss them away, and promised himself to follow through with that later.

"To Italy, you said?" smiled Calliope. "I have your answer, then, *signore. Si, bellisimo, molte molte bene.*"

Ireland
Anno Domini 1781

While some of the Crafter family moved west with the American frontier, others chose to stay in the Boston area. Before the War for Independence one of the most successful of these had been Eben Crafter. Using his native wit and family skills, Eben founded what soon became one of the most successful trading companies in the city. When the war came he was elected Captain of the Boston Militia. When the British occupied the city, Eben's business and home were confiscated the same week as the Declaration of Independence was signed.

Rather than being discouraged by the loss of most of his wealth, Eben took heart in the cause of the new nation. He rose quickly in the ranks of the Continental Army and was mentioned twice by Washington in his dispatches to the Congress. As a reward for his services, Eben was promoted to the rank of major and given the position of second in command of the single-most vital fortress in all the states, West Point. This new appointment was doubly exciting to Major Crafter, as he would be serving directly under one of the most professional and courageous of all the Continental officers.

But things did not go as expected, and within a few months Eben found himself in far different circumstances.

"...A FORTUNE IN IRELAND"
by Morris G. McGee

Eben Crafter laughed aloud. "I've come to Ireland to make my fortune," he whispered to himself, "a traitor to the Continental Army in America and a reluctant servant to His Majesty, King George III." He shivered as the cold rain ran down the back of his neck. He whistled "Yankee Doodle" to himself and tried to put his thoughts about himself in some order that made sense.

It was spring in County Tyrone in the northern part of Ireland, April 1781, on the long and wide main street of Cookstown. The first time he'd seen it, a few weeks before, he asked the Crown Surveyor, "Why so wide a main street and why so long?" The surveyor shrugged and said, "When they planned the town in the last century they thought a great city would grow here; the only things that grew were weeds in the street."

The surveyor had laid out "the meets and bounds" of Eben's estate that lay to the north and west of Cookstown, the estate he had won from the heir of one of the richest landlords in all of Ireland . . . . "Do you play whist, Mr. Crafter, or do you still wish to be called Captain Crafter?" sneered one of the lieutenants aboard ship.

Twenty-one-year-old Royal Navy Lieutenant Lord Larne was the eldest son of the Earl of Tyrone. Lord Larne was Third Lieutenant aboard H.M.S. *Trojan,* a man of wealth, small capacity for strong drink, and an inflated idea of his ability at cards. Larne had a great hooked nose that made Crafter think of a hungry hawk; that and his deeply pocked face made him almost as ugly as the mean spirit within him.

Crafter played with quiet skill, winning £500 in silver during the first week out of New York. During the second week Lord Larne suggested the simple game of *Vingt-et-un,* or Twenty-one, that two could play. Crafter agreed, for part of the Talent—his ability to transmute ordinary metal to silver—also enabled him to see through playing cards. He was the only one in his family who could.

At the end of the third week Lord Larne deeded 10,000 acres of land around Cookstown, County Tyrone, Ireland, to Eben Crafter formerly of Malden, in what had been the Royal Colony of Massachusetts, in lieu of £7,000 in losses at cards.

Eben did not sorrow for Lord Larne, for he was a fool and, after all, he would be Earl of Tyrone when his time came.

He did sorrow for his lost honor and his lost country . . . that late September day when the Commanding Officer of the

Fortress of West Point on the Hudson River, Major General Benedict Arnold ordered, "Come with me, bring the plans of the Fort."

Crafter followed the General in his blue-and-buff dress uniform. Arnold was the man he most admired in the whole Continental Army, Arnold the hero at Ticonderoga, hero at Montreal, hero at Valcour Island in Lake Champlain, and Arnold of Saratoga fame. He had served with Arnold since before Saratoga.

He thought he knew everything about the stolid businessman from Connecticut, and he was sure there was no greater leader in the Continental Army. Crafter followed Arnold without question down the steep steps to the jetty on the river, joined him in the small boat that pulled out into the river. He soon found himself under the guns of the Sloop of War H.M.S. *Vulture* which was anchored a few miles below the great chain—1,097 feet of links of bar iron, 12″ x 18″ links secured to log pontoons that floated just under the surface of the river—the chain that protected West Point and all north of the Fortress.

Only then did Crafter know that Arnold was changing sides. "Well, lad, what of you? I am sending a letter to General Washington today explaining why I had to do as I did. I can send you back with the letter suggesting that you knew nothing of my plans—you did not, for I told no one—poor Major André was captured and from that moment, I was a dead man! I will add a *nota bene*: 'In justice to my officers, Colonel Varick, Major Franks, and Captain Crafter, I am honor-bound to declare that they, as well as Joshua Smith, Esq. (who I know is suspected) are totally ignorant of any transaction of mine that they had reason to believe injurious to the public.' "

Crafter wondered what it would be like to live in America suspected of treason to the end of his days. Life in his America was over; England it was, for better or worse. "I'll follow you, sir," said Eben Crafter.

From Bristol, where H.M.S. *Trojan* landed, Crafter took a coach to London. There he was presented at court as " . . . a loyal son of the Crown, who was once misled but has now returned to the fold." He was amazed that he was awarded £500 by the hand of the Prince of Wales. "You are a good lad," the Prince said. "The people at the War Office tell me that the plans of the American fortress are quite valuable."

The Prince was fat, stupid, smelled of too much perfume, and had a decided lisp. Eben Crafter wondered what would become of England when "Prinny" became King.

Now, in the spring rain he contemplated his fortune: 10,000 acres of land, a run-down manor house, an ancient hill fort with earthen walls, and, just west of Cookstown, a beetling mill—a water-powered mill that processed linen.

The water-powered mill propelled sturdy wooden hammers, or "beetles," over raw wet linen to give it smoothness and sheen. The mill was the only part of the property in good order and repair. The "Manor House" had been built in the 1730's and had never been maintained or repaired.

As the rain ceased for a while Crafter saw Thomas D'Arcy, his young solicitor, crossing the street toward him. "What is it that brings you out on a damp day like this?" he asked.

D'Arcy pulled his cloak closer to his thin body. "There's someone looking for you, Justice of the Peace Benjamin Blackman."

"Who is he?" Crafter wanted to know.

"A lackey of the Earl of Tyrone and an officer of the Crown Courts," said D'Arcy. "He is not a man to cross."

"I have never met him, so not to worry, friend solicitor."

D'Arcy pointed across the street. "He's coming—that's his aide, Captain Smithers, with him—and there, as usual, is his poor wife about ten steps behind."

Crafter watched as the gigantic figure in a rusty black great-coat crossed toward them. He was trailed by a short grey-haired man wearing a red-coat uniform with Scots-type trews instead of the usual knee breeches. But it was the big man who demanded attention. His large body was topped by a small, reddish bald head thrust forward with a cruel, down-turned beaklike nose. He resembled the savage turkey vultures of the Berkshires in Eben's native Massachusetts. He had always been repelled by the carrion-eating scavengers, and he felt the same revulsion for the rapidly approaching figure.

"Crafter, is it not?" the big man croaked in a raspy voice. "I have been looking for you! I am Justice Blackman."

"Indeed," said Crafter. "Why?"

"My friend, Lord Larne, wrote me that you cheated him of his lands near Cookstown."

"He is a fool and he lies," Crafter said in a soft voice.

"MY FRIEND IS A LIAR?" Blackman roared. "YOU WILL RETRACT THAT STATEMENT OR FACE ME IN A DUEL!" His face became redder.

"A fool and a liar," repeated Crafter.

Blackman turned to D'Arcy. "Will you act for this . . . *gentleman*?" he asked, sneering the word. "Captain Smithers will act for me. He will be in the Crown Inn half an hour from now." He moved swiftly away across the street.

Captain Smithers bowed to D'Arcy and followed. Slowly Blackman's wife moved after them; as she passed she whispered quietly, "He wants you dead. Lead will not kill him— *silver* will."

D'Arcy shook his head. "He meant to provoke a duel."

"So it seems," said Crafter. "Go meet with the Captain."

"Four o'clock this afternoon; that's only five hours from now," said a very worried D'Arcy when he returned to his chambers where Eben Crafter waited.

"Do you have a pistol, Mr. D'Arcy?"

"Yes, I carry it on all my journeys to Dublin; the roads are not always safe."

"May I have it? I would also like an hour alone here before we meet Mr. Blackman."

"Here is the pistol; my chambers are yours," said the young solicitor as he left Crafter alone.

Eben took the small bag of lead bullets, selected one, concentrated, then poured the gunpowder into the barrel, inserted the silver bullet, and tamped in the wadding over it.

At four, in a field two miles south of town they waited. Captain Smithers gave the instructions; D'Arcy called out, "Take ten steps, turn, wait for my order to fire. One, Two, Three, Four, Five, Six, Seven, Eight, Nine, Ten, TURN." At once, Blackman fired but missed. "Foully done!" shouted D'Arcy.

Crafter slowly aimed his pistol, waited, then fired. Blackman was hit. He burst at once into roaring red flames. In less than a minute there was nothing left but a smoking small pile of ash that stank of sulphur.

"*Mr. D'Arcy, Mr. Crafter, did you see what I saw?*" Captain

Smithers screamed in horror. "Oh, no, I saw nothing, I was not here, was not here. Justice Blackman was summoned to, to . . . Dublin Castle and so I will swear . . . and you, gentlemen? . . . and you?"

D'Arcy said, "I will speak for Mr. Crafter and myself: We saw nothing . . . we were not even here, you agree?"

As they rode back to town, D'Arcy said, "You are the most interesting client I have ever had. Will there be more surprises?"

"Perhaps," said Eben Crafter. "Perhaps."

"The roof is slate, Squire," said Joe Burke, the property's caretaker, "but it needs new slates on the ridge line and along the eaves. The original slates came from Wales, and they are expensive. We might get some cheaper from an old house that burned last year down in Ballygally. They saved most of the slates after the fire."

Crafter grinned at Burke. "I'm not a squire."

"Yes, you are, sir," Burke whispered. "I can see that. Now, young Lord Larne was no squire—he could never be a squire for all his titles and high and mighty ways and all his money."

"What makes a squire, Burke?" Crafter wanted to know.

"That's easy, sir, he has to care about the land and his buildings, and he has to care for the folk who live on his lands."

Crafter thought a bit. "I see. Well, I shall try."

So Eben Crafter, late of America, found himself a landlord with a caretaker whose wife, Bridgit, cooked in the Irish fashion—in the worst sort of way: boiling the living daylights out of everything. Crafter also had over a hundred tenant-farm families, a mill that processed linen from his lands and from surrounding holdings, and a house very much in need of repair. He needed money to rebuild barns, money to pay farm workers, money to pay house servants. He needed the Talent.

Early one afternoon in late April he locked himself in his bedroom with orders that he was not to be disturbed until noon the next day. He took with him twenty bronze plates, each weighing some twenty-five pounds. He also had ten silver coins from Spain and a handful of English silver shillings.

He concentrated on the silver coins until he had their form and weight fixed firmly and clearly in his mind. Then he put his hands to the bronze plates. A pale blue light seemed to pour from his fingertips; then each bronze became a pile of silver coins. It took hours. As always, he was physically and emotionally drained. He slept until ten in the morning of the next day.

"Burke, saddle my horse," Crafter said as he came out into a rare sunny morning. "I'm going to Cookstown for workers to fix the house and barns." He added, "You come, too, for you speak the Gaelic and we'll need common laborers. We'll also need help from the tenants."

As they rode into the great empty street of the town, they met a couple riding out—a tall man with a bald, skull-like head riding a black stallion, and a girl, a beautiful girl, riding a roan horse that was the tallest horse Crafter had ever seen, eighteen hands, at least. The girl had long red hair that flowed out behind her. Her skin was milk-white, and the figure Eben could make out beneath her flowing green cloak was breathtaking. As they passed he saw her eyes—green with flecks of gold. She smiled at him.

"Have you ever seen such a beautiful girl?" he said to Burke.

Burke looked puzzled. "We just passed old Sean O'Dowd— he was leading a roan horse—there was no one with him."

Crafter twisted in his saddle, and Burke was right! There was one rider on a black horse leading a big roan horse, and there was nobody on the roan.

"Who is O'Dowd?" he asked.

"Why, he lives on your property about two miles from here on the edge of the Tullyhoge Fort that was built before Blessed Saint Patrick made Christians of us all."

"I must needs meet this O'Dowd after we find our workmen," Crafter said, half to himself.

After hiring men who could work with brick and stone and hiring men who could dig ditches and plant trees, and giving Burke orders, Crafter set off at a quick trot toward the ancient hill fort.

He followed the narrow track Burke had pointed out and saw hoof prints in the soft mud. He came to a small thatched cottage that lay close under the green slope of the fort. He called, "O'Dowd, come out, please."

O'Dowd came out the front door, bending his head so he

could fit under the door frame. He was over six feet tall, wiry, and not as old-looking as his bald head suggested. "Yes, Squire," said O'Dowd. "You want me?"

"You know me?" asked Crafter.

"All know you, the American who took Lord Larne's lands and holdings. What may I do for you, Squire?"

"I would like to meet your daughter."

"I have no daughter!" O'Dowd said sullenly.

"You have; I saw her riding with you. She has red hair, a green cloak, and she rides a great roan horse."

O'Dowd answered, "You couldn't have seen her unless . . ."

"Unless he has the gift or the Talent of our people," said the beauty as she stepped through the door.

Crafter looked at her in wonder. She was even lovelier than when he first saw her. "Eben Crafter, your servant, Mistress."

She curtseyed. "Maeve O'Dowd, Squire Crafter," she said, then grinned. "And I'd like to have you as my servant."

"Daughter, mind your manners," growled O'Dowd. He turned to Crafter. "Please come within my house. What is mine is yours," he said, following the ancient Irish formula of welcome.

Inside, there was a warm turf fire and two tall wax candles. The furniture was simple, but well-made and sturdy. "Sit, Squire, if you please," said O'Dowd. "Would you be havin' a wee drop to clear the dust of the road from your throat?"

"An excellent idea," said Crafter, watching the girl, who suddenly disappeared before his eyes. "Oho, what have we here?" The girl reappeared in the middle of the room with an earthen flask and three glasses.

Before Eben Crafter could say a word, there was a glass in his hand. "*Slainte!*" said O'Dowd and his daughter in unison and drank. Crafter drank, too. The fiery liquor warmed his throat—no, seared his throat—and his eyes watered.

"Good Lord, what was that?" Crafter coughed.

"The water of life," said Maeve.

"Whiskey, *Usquebaugh* in the Irish Gaelic and in the Scots Gaelic, too," said O'Dowd. "It is very like the spirits of Scotland: whisky. Irish priests taught the process to the Scots centuries ago."

"I've had the spirits from Scotland, but this tastes stronger," said Crafter. "Much stronger."

"You should try poteen that your tenants make," Maeve said, laughing. "It would melt your teeth."

"Enough," O'Dowd said quietly. "Come within. We know of what you did to Justice Blackman. We felt his evil vanish."

They led Crafter through a door, and he was inside a huge hall, under the hill fort, a room that was at least thirty feet square with a roof twenty feet high. The hall was lighted by a hundred or more tall candles. The walls were hung with tapestries, ancient axes, swords, and shields of bronze and gold.

"Who are you? What are you?" asked Crafter.

"We are *cluricaunes*," said O'Dowd, "part of the Shee— the people who lived here before the Celts ever came to this island."

Maeve continued. "We have some magic powers, but we keep them hidden. We came from the South, near Cork. We left there, for some thought my father a warlock."

"You have power, too," said O'Dowd. "What is the source: good or evil?"

"My powers come from my great-grandparents, Amer and Samona Crafter. He was an alchemist who turned to the study of natural science. He learned to transmute base metals into silver—he hoped for gold, silver was the best he could do. Samona was a witch who gave up her powers, but some of those powers seem to have been passed on to her offspring. I, too, can transmute metals to silver, see through paper—even playing cards. I know if anyone tells the truth, and I'm immune to all spells."

Maeve moved very close to him as he spoke, "You know if one speaks the truth? You will marry me in the month of May, this year."

Crafter looked at her. Her father started to say something, but Crafter said, "Yes!"

So it was on the first Saturday of May in 1781 that Eben Crafter and Maeve O'Dowd were to be wed.

As he dressed that morning in his fawn-colored knee breeches, his fine linen shirt with the white silk neck cloth under his gold-figured Chinese-silk waistcoat, his best white silk stockings, his black shoes with the polished silver buckles, and his new plum-colored broadcloth coat with silver buttons, he gazed into the mirror.

The face that stared back at Crafter was thin, the cheekbones high, the eyes deep-set and blue, the nose a bit too long, the chin firm, and there were dimples in his cheeks when he smiled. He watched as Burke tied the black ribbon to hold his long brown hair in a neat club down his back.

"You look grand, sir," said Burke.

"Thank you. Are we ready, Burke?"

"Yes, sir, I have the carriage and the two white horses ready in front."

"Let's go," said Crafter.

"Do you, Eben Crafter, take this woman to be your lawful wedded wife? To have and to hold from this day forward for richer or poorer, in sickness and in health until death do you part?" asked the round little minister of the Church of Ireland in his surprising bass voice.

"I do," said Eben, looking at Maeve. No longer needing to hide, the Irish beauty was visible to them all.

"Do you, Maeve O'Dowd, take this man to be your lawful wedded husband? To love, honor, and obey in sickness and health until death do you part?"

"I do," said Maeve in a low voice. She turned to Eben and smiled. She looked like a red-haired angel dressed in white.

"Then, by the powers vested in me by the Holy Church, I pronounce you husband and wife," intoned the minister.

With her right hand Maeve lifted her veil away from her face. Eben kissed her gently. "More later," he whispered.

They turned to leave the church and saw that only a half dozen were in the pews.

"No guests, my dear," Crafter said.

"They may be at the house," suggested Maeve.

When they came out into the sunlight, the few offered good wishes. Eben's solicitor, Thomas D'Arcy, handed Maeve into the carriage.

Back home, Eben carried Maeve over the threshold. "Welcome to your home, my dear, and may all your years here be blessed."

She looked at the shabby entryway and then saw Mrs. Burke in her one clean dress. "Bless this house and all who dwell therein."

"Amen!" said Mrs. Burke.

"Mrs. Burke, this is your new mistress, Mrs. Crafter. My dear, this is Mrs. Burke, Bridgit, who cooks and cleans."

Mrs. Burke bobbed a curtsey. "I be cookin' and tryin' ta keep things in good order."

Maeve said curtly, "I can see that this place needs a good cleaning."

Mrs. Burke muttered half under her breath, "*Puga ma hone!*"

"*Puga ma hone*, is it? 'Kiss my ass'? Well, listen to this . . ." Maeve said in a quiet voice, then continued with a streak of Gaelic that became louder and louder. She finished in English: "Do you understand?"

Mrs. Burke wilted and blushed under the torrent of words. Her head bowed, she said meekly, "I'm sorry, my lady. I thought you were one of those Englished kind of ladies who didn't understand nothin'! Forgive me bad manners, and I'll never make a mistake like that again if you'll keep me on."

Maeve looked stern. "I know you won't, for from now on it will be the lady of the house who will be in charge, not some man who knows nothing of a proper home."

Then turning to Eben, Maeve said, "I'll look at the house with you tomorrow. Now we are to have guests. We must be ready."

No guests came except Sean O'Dowd and the solicitor, Thomas D'Arcy. O'Dowd carried two heavy saddlebags and dropped them on the floor. "Mr. D'Arcy, Esquire, I shall need you in your legal capacity," O'Dowd said in formal tones. "You'll help me count out the dowry."

"We never talked dowry, Mr. O'Dowd," Eben said.

"Did you think a daughter of mine would wed without a proper dowry?"

With that, he poured the contents of the bags to the floor. "There should be £4,000, in gold. Count it please, Mr. Solicitor."

D'Arcy counted twice. "I find there are fifty guineas more than the four thousand pounds," he said.

"Let it be, the girl is worth much more!"

"Sir, I agree! I never expected such a noble gift beyond

your wonderful daughter." Eben shook O'Dowd's hand and embraced the older man.

"Now, our guests? I invited all the landowners hereabouts."

"I saw none on the way here," said O'Dowd.

"I wonder why none are here?" Eben asked.

"You wed a 'native,' you know," Maeve said.

Crafter cursed long and loud in anger, then said, "There are two oxen roasting, there is whiskey, wine, and all sorts of sweets—we should invite our tenants. Burke, take my horse and invite every soul from the estate."

"Aye, sir, that I'll do."

Within the hour the floor of the barn was swept; people were eating, drinking, and dancing to the music of the bagpipes, fiddles, and drums. Hands were clapping when little Joe Burke took Maeve into the center and started to do the step-dance. Maeve watched for a moment, then matched step for step. Mrs. Burke grabbed Eben and he, too, danced after a fashion. After several hours all the men picked up the bride, tossed her in the air, and caught her neatly in a chair. They did the same with Crafter. They paraded them out of the barn and around the house three times; they deposited them at the door of the house. "Be havin' a good night's sleep," they shouted with much laughter. "Good night."

Maeve and Eben were alone in the house. He took her by the hand, kissed her, and led her upstairs to their bedroom, which was lit with four tall candles. Maeve turned her back and started to undress; Eben did likewise. She turned to him; he looked with wonder. "You are beautiful," he whispered, "and you *are* a redhead!"

"Oh, you!" she said, waved her hands, and the candles were extinguished. She was in his arms.

"Get up, you slug-a-bed," said Maeve. "We have a home to put in order." She was already dressed, in everyday clothes, so Eben did what any sane husband would do, he got up.

Breakfast was different: the porridge wasn't lumpy, the tea was hot, and there were toasted squares of buttered bread.

The day was full of wonders. Maeve had a dozen of the tenant women and girls helping to dust, clean, and polish all corners of the house; even the window panes gleamed as they had not in ages. At the end of the day, Maeve led

Eben on a tour of inspection. "We're going to need furniture," she said.

"We will have it made in Dublin, when we go there," Eben agreed.

"When?" Maeve wanted to know.

"Tomorrow, if you wish."

"I *wish!*" Maeve said, grinning. "I've never been to Dublin Town."

On an overcast Monday they caught the Dublin mail coach. "I have nothing to wear in the city," Maeve said.

"Not to worry, we'll have everything made for you in Dublin."

The coach shook and rattled on the rutted road south out of Cookstown, through the dreary, colorless town of Dunngannon some dozen miles on. From Dunngannon it was almost twenty hard, bumpy miles to Armagh.

During the ride Maeve chattered happily about the wedding, about the things needed for the house, and she held on to Eben when the coach rocked.

Eben kept the heavy leather bag between his feet. "This is our fortune in silver and gold," he told his young wife. "We must put a good portion in the bank in Dublin." He gave a small purse to Maeve with one hundred guineas. "You should have money of your own," he said. "After all," he added, with a grin, "you are the wife of a rich landlord."

Maeve took one of the gold guineas from the purse, twirled it in the air, and caught *two* guineas.

"Magic?" asked Eben.

"No, my Talent—making gold coins increase in number as many times as I wish."

Eben thought for a moment. "The rich landlord has a richer wife," he observed.

In Armagh, they stopped for the night at The Mitre Inn. "Well-named," said Maeve. "Both the Catholic and the Protestant archbishops have their seats in Armagh."

Before they supped, they looked at the hilly town. Afterwards, they rested in the only good room at the Inn.

The next morning, Eben engaged a well-sprung carriage to take them on to Dublin. Their driver shouted as they clattered over the bridge at Newry, "That's the Town Hall on the bridge. Odd place for it, haint it?"

They moved south fast into the Boyne Valley toward Drogheda. "This is where King James and King Bill fought the Battle of the Boyne," yelled the driver over the clatter of the coach.

In Drogheda, Maeve said quietly, "This is the town where Cromwell killed almost everyone over a hundred years ago."

"The Irish don't forgive and forget, do they?" Eben asked.

"No," said Maeve. "It's forgive and remember!"

As they headed out of town, Eben saw shattered walls that reminded him of ugly, broken teeth.

They drove along the coast to the pretty village of Balbriggan and down through the village of Swords. "A few more miles and we'll see the River Liffy and Dublin," the driver called. He stopped at the top of a small hill to give them a view of Dublin. The sun came out, and a rainbow appeared to paint the steeples and rooftops in radiant color.

"Beautiful," whispered Maeve. "I've never seen a big city before."

In Dublin, they took rooms at The Royal Inn, a block away from Trinity College and only a short walk from Dublin Castle. After they were comfortable, Eben asked the innkeeper to send for a dressmaker and tailor. He used the names suggested by D'Arcy.

In short order the room was busy with dressmakers and tailors, showing samples of cloth, measuring, and giving detailed information: " . . . Lady A always has her gowns sewn by my shop . . . Lord B has all his clothing made by my tailors rather than in London . . ."

The choosing took hours, the measuring hours more, and there were complaints when Maeve ordered that at least one outfit be ready for the levee at Dublin Castle on Friday. The suggestion of a bonus stilled the complaints.

The next day the innkeeper found a lady's hairdresser. In a few short hours Maeve's beautiful red hair was arranged in the latest fashion.

On Friday they took a carriage to the castle, where D'Arcy had arranged that they be presented to the Lord Lieutenant's court. Actually there was only a deputy for Lord Portland. The new Lord Lieutenant was expected some time in early

1782. The castle appeared run-down, but the great hall was well-lit and crowded. All eyes turned when Maeve entered on Eben's arm.

"May I present Henry Grattan, barrister, advocate for Irish legislative independence, John Fitzgibbon, M.P. for Dublin University, Lord Shannon—one of the leaders of the kingdom, Edmund Burke—a friend of you Americans . . ." In a few hours they met almost all of importance in Ireland.

"This young man is Theobald Wolfe Tone, a student at Trinity College." The young man bowed to Eben and kissed Maeve's hand. When he left, Maeve shivered. "There is death following that poor young man," she said.

That night all the young officers and dandies wanted to dance with the beautiful Mistress Crafter. When Eben finally reclaimed her, he whispered in her ear, "I am envied by every man here, and rightly so. You are the most beautiful woman in the room."

On the trip back to Cookstown Maeve said, "You must learn the Irish—the Gaelic—I will teach you." The words sounded strange to Eben at first but he told his teacher, "I learned Latin and Greek at Harvard College so I will learn the Irish."

Maeve mixed her language lessons with stories of the ancient kings and heroes. " . . . King Conoor was King of Ulster, he was at war with Queen Maeve and her husband, King Aillill of Croohan. Conoor's men were all stricken with a weakness and the whole kingdom was protected by one young warrior, Coo-hullin." Maeve recited parts of the ancient poem, *The Cattle Raid of Coolee*. She told of the Knights of the Red Branch, the story of the beauty, Dierdre, her elopement with a handsome young man, the anger of King Conoor, and his cruel revenge. She repeated songs and stories about Finn MacCool and his warrior band, the Fianna.

When Eben asked, Maeve told stories about the Faerie Folk, about the Shee, "It's spelled S-i-d-h-e, but in the usual perverse Irish way it is pronounced *Shee*. I don't know why." She told of her own ancient people. "We were few in this island when the Gaels, the Celts, landed. We survived by blending in, at times by being invisible. It was only that which saved us. About thirty years ago a foul churchman near Cork City accused my parents of witchcraft. It was then that they came north to Ulster and Tyrone. My father found the hill fort and became a tenant of the Earl of Tyrone."

At home, there was unpacking, planning for furnishing and excitement in July, when the wagons delivered the tables and chairs, and all the rest of their purchases. One great case confused Maeve. "What is that?" she asked.

"A surprise," said Eben.

When it was opened, Maeve cried out, "A piano!" It was placed in the south-facing room that Maeve selected as the parlor where guests were to be entertained. "There," she said after it was placed and replaced a dozen times. "It looks right there."

Guests arrived, people they had met in Dublin. Mr. Richard Sheridan M.P., on his way to Enniskillen, stopped to see the "lovely Mistress Crafter" and her husband.

"After we met you at Dublin Castle," said Maeve, "we saw your play, *The School for Scandal*, at the Dublin Theatre. It was very wonderful. I even saw some of the ladies I met in Dublin who seemed very like your characters."

"I hope they did not recognize themselves," he said, and laughed.

Maeve seemed to have the gift of making guests feel at ease. When Harry Henry Grattan visited, he spent hours talking about a true parliament for Ireland. It became common for important Irish leaders to stop at the Crafters' home whenever they were in the area. Eben assured Maeve that she was the reason.

They worked to improve their farm methods, they added to the cattle herd, they bought a fine Arabian stallion to improve their horses, and Eben studied the published works of the Dukes of Norfolk on ways to improve the land.

"We need a better water supply; the springs to the west of the house are not enough for all our livestock," Eben said early in the fall.

"Why not put a well halfway up the hill?" asked Maeve.

"On the hill?" asked Eben.

"Of course," Maeve answered, "I can see water less than twenty feet down. You'll have to dig a series of ponds down lower on the hill, the upper fenced for us, the next for the horses, and at least one or two more for the cattle."

"You can see water below ground? Another Talent?"

Eben had his tenants dig four pools. Then, on the hillside he supervised the digging of, first, a pit eight feet deep; then a long iron bar was pounded deep into the ground with heavy mauls. When they reached a dozen feet, they extracted the bar; water followed. It flowed downhill to the new pools. In less than a week the pools were filled with pure clean water. Eben piped water from the top pool into the kitchen area. "Running water, better than Buckingham Palace!" he exulted.

Late in November one of their guests told of General Cornwallis' surrender to the Americans at Yorktown in October. Maeve asked, "Any regrets?"

Eben said, "No, for I'd not have found you. I am glad that the Colonies have a chance to be free."

In April, 1782 Maeve quietly announced, "We are going to have a son. He should be born by November."

"A son, you are sure?"

"Yes, I'm sure," said Maeve. "Another gift."

In August there was news that the restrictive Poyning's Law was repealed by the English Parliament, giving Ireland some freedom in legal matters. "That law was passed in 1494," Eben remarked. "No wonder the Irish politicians were restive." A short time later, a relief act was passed that gave Roman Catholics in Ireland some rights to education. "Unless people have the same rights as in England there will surely be an American-type revolt."

On November 30, 1782, a son was born to Eben and Maeve Crafter. "We'll call him Sean," Eben said, "after your father, Sean, and my father, John; after all, Sean is the Irish for John. He will be Sean Andrew, for today is the feast day of Saint Andrew."

Maeve smiled. "Himself will be pleased with a grandson to spoil." She was right, for Sean O'Dowd came with an ivory teething ring for the first day, and was properly proud when baby Sean grabbed his finger in his little hands and wouldn't let go.

"Strong he is, like all the O'Dowds," crowed old Sean.

The tenants, too, admired the new baby. The women brought little gifts they had knitted. Bridgit Burke sewed a linen gown and embroidered roses on it in fine red silk thread. Joe Burke carved a jointed wooden puppet with cords that moved its head, arms, and legs. It became young Sean's favorite toy; he'd chuckle when it was moved over his cradle in an Irish jig.

In early spring Henry Grattan arrived bearing gifts for the Crafter heir. "You know, Crafter, you should be active in politics. We are going to have a real Parliament soon in Ireland if only we can be patient enough with the donkeys in Westminster. Oh, by the bye, our English agents are to meet in Paris with the Americans to draft a treaty of peace."

Eben thought of his America, a free nation, and he was glad.

Grattan was followed by a string of Irish gentry who liked Crafter and his pretty young wife.

Every year they spent at least a month in Dublin for theatre, for dances, for shopping, and Maeve said, "gossip." They missed May of 1785, for on the 3rd their daughter was born. "A red-haired queen, she is," said Crafter. "And a beauty like her mother. Shall we name her after the beauty in your story, Dierdre?"

"I'd like that, yes," said Maeve. At the christening she was named Dierdre Charlotte Crafter.

If her grandfather had spoiled young Sean, he outdid himself with Dierdre, saying, "After all, a man has a right to favor a granddaughter a bit if he wants." By the time she was two she was riding in front of him on his horse; by five he had given her a pony of her own.

Eben was more evenhanded. "You spoil them both," Maeve complained, "but it doesn't seem to hurt." Maeve, of course, was as guilty as her father and Eben.

The Crafters worked hard to enhance their estate—putting up glass walls for a south-facing conservatory, improving their lands with lime and fertilizers, rotating crops on their own lands and tenant lands, and most important in Eben's mind: planting trees as windbreaks and holders of the soil.

The work was noticed by neighbors; indeed, Eben was asked to address the new Royal Irish Society in 1790.

When he returned home from Dublin, he told Maeve, "I see trouble. It's in the air as it was in Boston when I was young. I met young Wolfe Tone; he and others are organizing to make a free country, like America or revolutionary France." Months later, Crafter's worries proved well-founded. Tone wrote a tract, "Argument on Behalf of the Catholics in Ireland." This was followed by the founding of the United Irishmen, first

in Belfast, then Dublin. Many of the leaders hoped to bring
Crafter into the movement. He refused with, "One revolution
is enough!"

Many things changed in Ireland. By April 1792 Catholics
were allowed to practice law, in 1793 parliamentary franchise
along with civil and military rights. By 1794 Catholics were
allowed to attend Trinity College.

In 1795 there was greater turmoil: The United Irishmen
had been suppressed in Dublin; Earl Fitzwilliam became Lord
Lieutenant in January and was dismissed in February.

In May, the Belfast United Irishmen invited Eben to an
underground meeting; he again declined.

In June, Wolfe Tone stopped in Cookstown to talk to the
Crafters and say farewell. "I will sail first to America, then go
to France for help. The French Republic is our final hope."

Maeve implored, "Leave Ireland if you must, but, never
return."

"I must, Mistress, for I want to see Ireland free." Tone left
and was later reported with a French fleet that entered Bantry
Bay in the far Southwest to foment rebellion in December.
They were driven off with small losses.

In 1798, young Sean Crafter started the spring term at Trinity College. He had been taught Latin and Greek by his father,
and tutored by graduates who were sent out of Dublin by
worried parents who wished to keep their sons out of trouble—
trouble that seemed all pervasive. Sean was taught Gaelic by
his mother, grandfather, and all the tenants on Crafter lands.

Eben worried in late March when Dublin United Irish leaders were arrested and martial law imposed. He sent an urgent
message to his son to stay away from all politics.

Word came to Cookstown that there was open rebellion in
May in Lienster and the capture of County Wexford by the
Rebels. They were cruelly put down by General Gerard Lake,
the leaders courtmartialed and hanged.

In August the French landed a force in Killala Bay west
of Sligo; with Irish allies they defeated government forces at
Castlebar on the road to Galway. The Rebels fought " . . . for
France, for Ireland, and for the Blessed Virgin."

The Rebels were decimated at Ballinamuck in County Long-
ford by militias from Down, Armagh, and Kerry. The troops
were led by the new Viceroy, Lord Charles Cornwallis, with

General Lake as second-in-command. He accepted the surrender of the French and waited for the next foray.

It came in November when a French naval force was trapped in Lough Swilly, the great Sea Lough that pushed deep into Northern Donegal. With the French was Wolfe Tone. Tone wanted to be treated as a soldier. When that was refused, he committed suicide rather than be hanged. Maeve said sadly, "I saw death on that poor young man. May the Lord have mercy on his soul."

In early March 1799 Joe Burke, Paddy Ryan, and a dozen other tenants came to Crafter, hats in hand. "They're gonna courtmartial at least twenty young lads from your estate, Squire, including my son, Fergus, and Paddy's youngest, Liam. Can you help, Squire? They's to hang if nothing be done."

Eben rode at once to Dublin and the Vice-Regal Court. He sought audience with the Marquess Cornwallis. When Crafter was admitted, he saw a tired old man with a pot belly that seemed to go with his old-fashioned uniform and the heavy, out-of-date, horsehair wig, powdered as if it were decades earlier, and slightly askew.

"I know of you, you were with Arnold after that affair about West Point. I often wondered what happened to you. I saw Arnold a number of times in London . . . a bitter, bitter man. Now, Crafter, what may I do for you? Everyone who comes wants something. Crafter . . . Crafter, do you have a son at Trinity College?"

"Yes, my lord, his name is Sean," said Crafter, wondering what trouble Sean was in that Cornwallis would know of him.

"My daughter Anna, er ahem, my natural daughter . . . I have acknowledged her. Well, she has found your son to be a most delightful young man, and I admit he is a charming rascal. Neither is seventeen yet, but he has asked for her hand."

"My lord?" said Eben, a bit confused.

"There can't be a large dowry, for I still have daughters to marry off; I have also promised to dower my brother William's youngest. You know of him, of course. The Admiral leads the Channel Fleet blockading the French."

"I don't know, my lord. My son is too young to marry. It would make sense when he finishes his degree at Trinity."

Cornwallis smiled. "Agreed. Besides, the government tells

me that if I hold things together for a few years, there will be a property grant and a money grant, too. Yes, yes, that would be better. I could have Anna settled by the time I leave Ireland."

They shook hands; then Eben said, "My lord, I've come on a mission of mercy to plead for some of the young tenants from my estate. They joined the French, but they were young and foolish."

"Really, Crafter, you should know better, you were a soldier; you know rebellion must be put down firmly," said the Viceroy.

"Aye, sir, the leaders, yes, but the poor boys were led like sheep." Crafter spoke with feeling.

"You know," said the Viceroy, "General Lake was advised by London to come down hard on the Ulster Rebels, ' . . . use your discretion freely and inform the magistrates to forget delicacy.'" He continued, seriously. "He burned houses if United Irish membership were suspected. Lake thought Catholic priests a deviant minority. The United Irish oath did ask that they 'be true to the Catholic religion and assist the French if they land,' did you know that?"

"You are speaking of leaders in Dublin and in Belfast and other major centers; I'm talking of young and unsuspecting lads—easily led."

"Perhaps mercy could temper justice. Do you have their names and where they are being held?"

"Yes, my lord, here are the names. Most are being held here in Dublin; only two are in prison in Armagh."

"Major Swainton, come here, please," Cornwallis said in a louder voice. A tall officer entered and stood at attention.

"Draft an order of release for this group of prisoners, to be held accountable by Mr. Eben Crafter of . . . of . . . where do you live, Crafter?"

"Cookstown, County Tyrone, my lord."

"Of Cookstown, County Tyrone, so be it. Good luck, Crafter. Keep those people of yours out of any more trouble. As for that wedding in the next few years, I will visit you in July of this year. I'll bring the girl so you can look her over—she's a pretty thing and headstrong like me," he said with a smile.

The homecoming was both subdued and joyful. Crafter explained to the young men that he stood personal surety for each of them: if they were to be in trouble again, they would be hanged and he would be imprisoned. "We understand, Squire, and we are all owin' our lives to you, thanks be to God," said young Liam, Paddy Ryan's son.

At home Maeve asked, "We can afford them passage to Canada or even to America, can't we?"

Eben agreed, and in a month all were safely on their way to a New World.

On December 10, 1800, by Special License, in the chapel at Dublin Castle the wedding of Sean Crafter, B.A. and Anna Cornwallis, Spinster, was celebrated. The groom was flustered as are all grooms; the bride was beautiful as are all brides; and the parents proud as are all parents. The reception in Dublin Castle was the highlight of the social season and was, in part, a farewell for the Viceroy, who planned to return to India in 1801.

Eben and Maeve stayed in Dublin a few days, then returned home to Cookstown.

The day before Christmas, Eben rode to visit his father-in-law for a pre-Christmas drink.

"You'll like this batch," O'Dowd said. "I distilled it ten years ago and put it aside in an old oak wine cask from Portugal; it has smoothed as it aged. It's the best I've ever made."

After two large whiskeys each, O'Dowd said, "Go outside into the sun, I want to show you something most wonderful."

A few minutes later he came out bearing a great two-handed sword with a gold hilt richly worked in the ancient Irish way. The blade was flecked with rust but still very sharp. "The sword of Brian Boru, the last Ard Righ, the last High King of All Ireland. He defeated the Norsemen outside Dublin at Clontarf in 1014. Alas, he died after the battle. That led to anarchy: the O'Brians of Munster fought the O'Neils of Ulster; they both fought the O'Connors of Connaught. What followed was hate that allowed the English to divide and conquer. Damn them!" O'Dowd said bitterly.

"Sad it was, but the sword is a thing of beauty," Eben said. "I have never seen such work."

"It is for you and my grandson," said the old man. "I want this treasure to stay in Ireland; see here on the hilt in the Irish

'I belong to Brian, King of Munster' as clear as when the swordsmith finished his work."

Eben swung the sword with both hands. "It would take a strong man to use this in battle."

Just then a rider galloped toward them, a portly man on a black horse, dressed in naval uniform. "Crafter," he shouted, "I have been looking for you!" The man had a great beaklike hook of a nose—it was Lord Larne, the former owner of the land on which they stood.

"Lord Larne, I have not seen you in years. What do you want?"

"My lands that you have stolen from me by magic. I met some of your Loyalist relatives from New York who now live in London. They say that you control magic!"

"Lord Larne, you were a terrible card player and that is all," said Eben quietly.

"I am no longer Larne, I am the Earl of Tyrone, Rear Admiral of the Red in his Majesty's Navy. I am the most important member of the nobility in this half of Ireland. I intend justice and revenge," he said, dismounting and drawing his sword.

"Stop, stop this, sir," said O'Dowd, who moved to intercept the attack. The sword flashed in the winter sunlight and bit deep into the old man's chest. He fell with a moan.

Crafter brought the two-handed sword up, at the ready to attack. At that moment Maeve appeared behind Eben. She shouted, "He was at our house, he has powers, satanic powers like his friend Justice Blackman. Silver, silver is the answer!"

"So, that was Blackman's fate? Well, you have no silver there. You are a dead man and so is your wife, one of the poxey natives, I see. By all the powers of Satan, I order you to stand powerless."

Eben turned his sword so that the hilt formed a cross as he backed slowly away. "Silence by all the powers of good in this world," he intoned.

The big man shuddered but continued to advance.

Eben swung the sword so that his hands were on the blade. He concentrated all his powers on the blade. Blue light seemed to flow from his fingers; the blade was bathed in a blue aura. It was done: SILVER! With a scream of rage, Eben slashed at the neck of his enemy. The sword cut deep, and, with a cry of anguish, Larne's head bowed forward and he was dead.

Maeve bent over her father, who whispered, "I will die, will die very soon: the wound is mortal, I know. Eben must carry me into the Great Hall inside the hill fort. Take him, too, and his horse. Nothing must be left outside."

Eben did as he was told. He gently carried the old man inside, placed him in his favorite chair, and kissed him on his forehead.

Then he dragged the dead body inside and left it on the hearth. The horse balked but finally was led inside. Eben tied him to a heavy table leg.

"Now, daughter, you know what you must do," O'Dowd said in a weak voice. His head fell to the side; he was dead. Maeve wept as she kissed her father farewell. Eben carried in the sword of Brian Boru and placed it in O'Dowd's dead hands. "He should bear this sword for all time," he said.

Maeve kissed her father again, then led her husband back into the little cottage, and closed the door. As she intoned a series of Gaelic words and touched the door with her hands, the door faded into the whitewashed wall and disappeared. They were alone in the cottage. "It will stay thus for two hundred years," she said with tears in her eyes. "For now, you are safe, we are safe."

Back at home Maeve spoke of Larne's—Tyrone's—threats. "I was frightened for you," she told Eben.

"All is over now," said Eben. "Nothing more can happen."

"Yes, it can," his wife answered. "A letter came from London for you."

The letter was from Mrs. Arnold.

"My Dear Mr. Crafter,
I received your very kind letter on the death of my dear husband, General Arnold. He thought very highly of you, and I, too, remember you as a kind young man.

When General Arnold died on June 14th, we were all devastated. He was, however, in constant pain from that wound in the leg he suffered at Saratoga.

His funeral was attended by many notables of the Kingdom. The Prince of Wales sent his personal condolences.

The General thought highly of you and in his will has left you the sum of 100 guineas ' . . . for a good and

brave young officer,' he wrote. It will be forwarded to
you by his bank.

I want you to know that the General spoke of you
often in the kindest terms.

> Your Friend in Sorrow,
> Peggy Shippen Arnold
> (Mrs. Benedict Arnold)
> Number Ten, Portman Square,
> London"

"Perhaps all is over," said Eben. "Lord Cornwallis is sure
that Ireland is cursed for at least a hundred years. He is sure
that Catholics will battle Protestants and Protestants battle
Catholics, forever."

Maeve said, "We'll live for a better Ireland for our children
and our children's children."

Eben held Maeve close as the day drew to an end.

England
Anno Domini 1804

While life on the American frontier was dangerous, the civilized society of England could be no less hazardous. London society was rich, full and enticing to young Delilah Crafter when she was sent from Boston to live with her aunt in London and gain some "polish." Beyond the hazards of living in the land against whose army her family had fought, there were also darker dangers. While easily capable of protecting herself and her honor under normal circumstances, the excitement of London society could be overwhelming. Even more ominously, none of social or magical skills could save her from losing her heart to the right man.

HER AMERICAN COUSIN

by Esther Friesner

Huntingdonshire
Near London
April 1804

My dearest Caroline,

I trust that you and your dear parents have enjoyed an uneventful journey to Bath and that the waters will help your papa's gout. But oh! Had I but some magical power at my command capable of simultaneously relieving that good man's afflictions and whisking you back to my side this instant, I vow I should employ it at once, though the use of sorcery is reputed to cost the user thereof her very soul.

For it has happened. Disaster. I am undone.

It came to pass almost to the letter as you predicted when last we were together. Do you recall it? We had wheedled a modest tea from Cook and conveyed it to the river bank, there to feast with equal relish upon sweetmeats and the exquisite poetry of Lord Byron. I can still see your sweet face, smiling around a mouthful of jam tart, as you said to me: *Mark my words, Delilah, once your father moves that woman into your house, she will set about finding the swiftest way to move you out of it.* (You also dropped a goodly portion of tart onto my copy of *Childe Harold's Pilgrimage.* You *will* recall to purchase me that promised replacement at Bath, will you not, darling?)

O evil prophecy! O more than Sybilline foresight! O Caroline, how badly I now require the comfort of a friend! I face the abyss, the nadir of all Fortune, torments unspeakable from which every gently bred lady must pray most earnestly for deliverance or death.

She wants me to marry.

Yes, yes, I know what you will tell me. To marry, it is written, is better than to burn. Yet I swear to you, I do not feel at all subject to spontaneous combustion. Marriage is not for me. I have seen the beast at too close quarters to desire intimate acquaintance with the nuptial state. I do not, of course, refer to the marriages of our own blessed parents—Papa's *first* marriage, I mean. Exceptions prove the rule.

Have you forgotten the many visits you and I paid to the homes of our schoolfriends? In every case, the wife was a shabby, mousey, lacklustre sort of creature. Though she decked herself with a rajah's ransom in jewels and wore gowns that were the last word in *la mode*, the poor jenny wren had about as much spirit as a damp tea towel. The husband, on the other hand, was ever and anon brimming with spirit—and small wonder! He breathed brandy in much the same way as a fish breathes water. At least the fumes of the bottle somewhat mitigated the exhalations of the stable and the kennel which were his especial *parfum*. When he did not sweat, he swore; when he did not swear, he swaggered; and when he did none of the preceding, he collapsed in a chair beside the fire and snored. A pretty picture!

So no, thank you, I do not choose to wed.

Let your imagination frame my reaction, then, when Step-mamma summoned me into the front parlor not two hours ago and said, "Delilah, a gentleman from London will be calling upon us tomorrow. His name is Mr. Horatio Culpepper, of the Derbyshire Culpeppers. His people are distant connections of my family, so I can readily vouch for the young man's credentials. I would take it as an especial favor were you to look upon him kindly."

I could feel the blood mantling my cheeks. There was such awful *meaning* behind her words. Still, innocence is always a lady's first, best shield, as we have learned beyond doubt or debate from our readings, my devoted Caroline. I stood tall—too tall, alack! You know how I gangle and tower—and replied, "What would you have me do for the gentleman, Stepmamma?"

A fleeting look of distaste crossed her mouth. So it always does whenever I refer to her by that title. She has asked me a score of times to call her Lydia if I cannot bring myself to call her Mamma, but I can do neither one nor the other. Lydia Jane Naseby would be a friend's name, and she is no friend of mine, yet to call her Mamma—!

Call her what I might, she would have her way. "When Mr. Culpepper arrives, it would be courtesy were you prepared to entertain him a little by performing upon the spinet. Oh, and I shall ask you to pour at tea, if you do not find that too taxing." She extended her right hand so that I might see the thickness of white gauze bandaging it, and tossed those golden ringlets of hers which are my bitterest envy. "Some of us are not intended by Providence to bake," she said lightly. Her musical laughter followed me from the room.

Need I elaborate? Your sensitive soul, dear Caroline, is twin to mine. You can tell as well as I what she intends! To parade my spinet-playing would be bad enough, but to couple it with a display of how well I preside over the tea things—well! Mr. Culpepper and I had best hie us to St. Uffa's straightaway and save the niceties. He must be wealthy. Stepmamma would find that a prime feather to tuck into her bonnet were she able to rid herself of me and at the same time secure a profitable alliance for the family.

Being privy to the low state of my mind, you may doubtless know whence I write you this. As always, when feeling poor in spirit, I have retreated to Mamma's old attic chamber.

I do not know what possessed my dear departed mamma to spend so many hours closeted away in this miserable hole. Certainly it suits my melancholic humor and is a paramount retreat for the brooding spirit, but she seemed to like it. The walls are bastioned with bookcases, nearly all of which are crammed with a host of musty tomes. Those wanting books are instead supplied with ranks of oddly shaped wooden boxes and equally malformed glassware. These containers attract almost as much dust without as they hold within. The one time I did meddle with Mamma's things, I could not stop sneezing for days thereafter.

One of the books lies open before me on the very table I use to write you this. Thus it has lain since Mamma left it so. Her quill remains beside a crystal inkwell whose contents have evaporated to black residue. The open page reveals lines and lines of Mamma's clear, fine hand. I will not trouble you with the text as it is an impenetrable admixture of Latin, Greek, and some few phrases in plain English which still manage to baffle me by their obscure referents. I vow, the only portion of the volume that makes any sense to me is the initial inscription:

> *Honoria Marie Crafter*
> *Her Book*
> *Presented to Her Upon the Occasion*
> *Of Her Sixteenth Birthday*
> *And in Recognition of Her Most Impressive*
> *Knowledge and Talent*
> *By Her Beloved Uncle Juvenal Sylvan*

"Knowledge and Talent!" Ah, that was Mamma, to the life. It is difficult to picture her of an age with myself, and in possession of so doting an uncle, or to imagine how bitter his disappointment would be to learn that her only child has little knowledge and less talent, apart from the feminine arts. Papa never did see the point in giving a Classical education to a female, and poor Mamma did not live long enough—I was but six years old when she died—to persuade him otherwise.

When I lay my hand upon the open book and trace the alien Greek characters with my fingertips, I can almost believe her nigh. My whole heart desires her presence, her counsel, and her comfort. It pains me deeply to realize that this kind Uncle Juvenal must have known her better than ever I did or may.

Ah, me! Of what use these musings? My profuse apologies for so burdening you, dear friend, with the freight of an overladen heart. May the Season at Bath pass quickly, that you may return all the sooner to

> Your Misfortunate Friend,
> Delilah

*   *   *

April 1804

Dear, distant Caroline,

My head whirls. My heart pounds with wild dismay. All my meed is woe and desolation, and my soul is as a barren, windswept crag where prowls the ravening wolf and circles the cold-eyed bird of prey.

Yet first, lest I forget, commend me to your parents and pray convey my sincere wishes that you are all having a pleasant time at Bath.

O Caroline, whatever shall become of me? He has arrived, the loathsome Culpepper! And not alone. The wretch has had the temerity to bring, unannounced and uninvited, a friend of his from London. This "gentleman"—and you shall see I use the term guardedly—is an American. There! I have said the word. How well you know that my own dear mamma's forebears emigrated from the uncultured shores of that rampant wilderness in the days immediately following the Colonies' revolt. They had sense.

One of the few extant memories of Mamma vouchsafed me is how she would recount the tale of her grandpapa's extended rants against the treacherous Yankees. He was a choleric man, to judge by the portrait she hung in the attic chamber. A beady, burning eye regards the world askance from beneath the tightly curled and trimly powdered wig. Not even the mice have dared take liberties with that canvas, and my own infirmity of purpose is confirmed by the fact that I allow it to hang there still. Touch it? I? I daresay not!

I believe I must have burst into infant tears of fright when first I saw it, for I distinctly recall Mamma saying to me: "Hush, my darling Delilah. That is only my grandpapa Thomas Crafter. Death has come for him already—O pity kindly Death, to have to deal with such a man! I know he looks harsh and forbidding, child. That is because he was. Still, he was one of the most Talented souls our family ever produced, and fond enough of me to say that I appeared to have inherited his Talent."

In memory, I hear my baby lips lisp, "Talent for what, Mamma?"

I must have asked that question, for I likewise recall her laughing reply: "Oh, there will be plenty of time later on for me to tell—nay, show—nay, better still, teach you, Delilah love. Here. You would best be getting on with this for a start." She took a slim book from one of the shelves and placed it in my chubby hands. It was bound in blue buckram and had a snippet of white ribbon marking a place. I opened it, expecting simple words and pretty pictures, such as were my delight. Figure instead my childish anger to discover that there were no pictures at all, and the text was unreadable, the very characters thereof foreign. O outrage! I knew my letters well, and was infuriated to think that here were a whole new set to be conned. I threw down the blue book and said so, vehemently.

Mamma laughed at my tantrum, I am certain. "What, poppet, do not fret. Of course you do not understand the letters. It is all Greek to you." (Here I *know* she laughed; to this day, on hearing a particularly wicked bit of wordplay, Papa shakes his head and remarks, "How your dear mamma would have loved that one!")

Picking up the discarded book, she set me upon her lap and opened it to the beginning, where she showed me the initial text was written in English after all. "This book has been in my family for generations," she told me. "My grandpapa Thomas had it from his father, and he from his father before him. My own papa and my brother Jason had no head for Greek—in our family, Uncle Juvenal always says, one either enjoys familiarity with the Classics or does not—so Grandpapa gave it to me. See, dearest? Here is where we shall begin your education, at the beginning of the book where the lessons are so simple you might even teach yourself, as I did. But you shall not need to do so."

"Teach me now, Mamma!" I begged. My eagerness pleased her, and she bent her head over the pages so that I could smell the haunting scent of the orange-flower water she adored. But before she might begin my lesson, the bell of St. Uffa's tolled the hour for tea. Mamma shut the book and told me to hurry downstairs, lest Cook be cross. "We shall have time for Greek, and Latin, too," she promised. "Time for that and more. There is so much knowledge I want to share with you, Delilah!" She framed my face with her soft, white hands and added, "So sweet, so pretty, and so—yes, by the sharpness of your wit you could not help but have the Talent. Oh, I can hardly wait to see how much of it you do have! But wait we must, at least until tea is done. Never mind. There will be time. Plenty of time, my dearest one."

But there was not time. That very evening, as Mamma and Papa were taking their habitual promenade, my poor mamma caught sight of her friend, Penelope Hawkins, across the street. Miss Hawkins had been gravely ill, and Mamma was so pleased to see her up and about that she disengaged herself from Papa's arm and impetuously dashed into the road to greet her. Alas, she did not see the phaeton bearing down upon her, nor did the crespuscular light permit the driver to see her and rein up his steeds until too late.

I was at the parlor window when Papa brought her poor, broken body into the house. Never will I forget the sight of her bloodstained dress, the material the very color of the little blue book we had shared scarcely two hours ago. Papa walked like a man gone blind. He laid her body down upon the parlor couch despite Nurse's shrill exhortations to remember that "the child" was present. When she saw he would not heed her, she flapped around the parlor, searching for me. I shrank into the folds of the draperies, willing myself invisible. I knew that something was dreadfully wrong, yet, for my life, I did not want to be taken from the room. Papa then burst into wild lamentation—so wild that Nurse, fearing he might do himself a mischief, summoned the footman. Between the two of them, they forcibly conveyed him upstairs. I later heard the front door slam as the footman ran out just ahead of Nurse's shouted orders to fetch Papa a physician.

I was conveniently forgotten. The room was awfully still. I stole from my hiding place to stand beside Mamma's body.

I stared at her face, but it was so pale and bruised and torn that I could not bear the sight for long. I averted my gaze to the open window. Outside, I could see our street transformed into a turmoil of people. A swooning Miss Hawkins was being conveyed back into her own home by her bachelor brother. Your own dear mother, my Caroline, was there as well, her face a twisted mask of grief and shock. The driver of the phaeton huddled on the seat, his face in his hands. Some of the crowd shook their fists at him while the few rational souls present who recognized the bitter workings of chance and fate attempted to hold them back. One among them was speaking earnestly to the distraught driver—words of comfort, I suppose.

"It will not work," said a voice behind me. "The guilt will prove too much for him. By week's end, he will be dead by his own hand. Hanged, I believe."

I turned and saw that I was no longer alone beside the couch. A tall gentleman dressed all in black knelt before me like a suitor. I have no idea of how he managed to enter undetected. I attribute it to a momentary lapse of attention on my part.

"So you are Delilah," he said. Strange, I can recall every detail of his dress—quite the epitome of fashion, he was—but his face remains virtually a blank in memory. It was white, I do believe, and angular to the point of fleshlessness, were that possible in a living man. His eyes were so huge and black as to seem all pupil, or all void, although I know that too to be an impossibility. His forehead was so high that I can not recollect where his hair began, or even if he had any at all. How odd.

It is equally odd that I did not bolt from the room then and there. I always was shy of strangers—Mamma chided me for it many a time—yet I did not seem to fear this one. He regarded me long and hard. "Ah, yes," he said at length. "Amer's very chin, and Samona's midnight hair. You'll be stubborn, or a beauty. Or both, may the powers help us all! Especially if you take after your ancestors in more than appearance." Here he shuddered, and a curious clattering sound rang through the parlor.

"Who are you?" I asked. Rather, I demanded. Never before or since was I so bold.

"A friend," he said, and turned his famished face towards Mamma. How hollow and miserable his voice! "A kindly friend, some call me."

There was something in the way he stared at my poor mamma's body that made me, young as I was, understand that here was another being who shared in equal measure with Papa and me the devastating sorrow of Mamma's passing. In kinship and simple compassion, then, I took his hand in mine. It was exactly like grasping a bundle of dry sticks.

He looked up. "Do you seek to comfort me, child?"

I swallowed my own tears and nodded. "You were her friend," I managed to say.

"So I was, so I was." He shook his head slowly and got to his feet, towering above me. "As good a friend as I have been to many of your family, my dear; to Amer and Samona, in their time, and to Ahijah and Arabella and Margarethe and the rest in theirs, and to Baldwin and Thomas—"

Of all the names the gentleman rattled off, I recognized that one. "Thomas? You were a friend to my mamma's grandfather?" He nodded, an affirmative gesture which did not have precisely the effect he might have foreseen, for on the instant I flew at him in a passion, small hands and feet flailing, and belabored him without let or mercy.

"Liar!" I shouted. My abrupt bereavement demanded outlet, and took it in pointless wrath. "Liar, liar, liar! How could you know my mamma's grandfather? He was *old*, and you—and you—"

The stranger grasped my wrists and effortlessly kept me at arm's length while he gathered his assaulted wits. "And *I*, miss, am older than that," he told me.

I kicked him in the legs, every blow making a sound like drumming my heels against a chair-rail. "You can't be that old!" I bawled, lunging and squirming in his grip. "No one can be that old! Great-grandpapa Thomas is *dead*, and—and Ahijah was the name of my great-granpapa's father, so you couldn't know him and *he's* dead, and—and—"

Suddenly the gentleman in black swept me from my feet and held me tight against him. "Only one death matters so very much to you now, doesn't it, my little one?" he asked softly. His voice was tender, yet it cut me to the heart and I began to cry. "There, child," he said, running those spindly, brittle fingers through my tangled hair. "When you are older, you will understand. For now let it suffice to know that I will be your friend, too."

I was snivelling terribly, I fear, for the stranger gave me his pocket kerchief and bade me blow my nose. I did so, but when I would return him his own he directed me, "Keep it. If you are a true sprig of old Thomas' tree, you'll be glad to own such a useful souvenir some day."

I gazed in wonderment at the kerchief, which he bestowed with as much ceremony as though it were a bolt of best Cathay silk. In truth it was plain black cotton, the hem poorly stitched and the corner embroidered with a tipsy "*D*". All six-year-olds are natural skeptics with the manners of untrained foxhounds. Small marvel that I dried my tears and asserted, "This isn't useful; it's dirty." I blew my nose into the black folds again to ratify my statement.

The stranger lifted one thin, white finger. "I said *if*," he replied. "And I am famous for seldom speaking in the conditional tense, believe me." With that, he vanished. Oh, I do not—I *can* not mean he played the ghost. Most likely he excused himself in the ordinary way and departed by the front door. The footman returned just then with Dr. Greeley in tow, and Nurse flew down the stairs to greet them. She caught sight of me in the parlor and whisked me up to the nursery forthwith. The strange gentleman probably made his exit in the teeth of all that confusion.

That is the only logical explanation, is it not?

None of which, I know, enlightens you any further in regard to the hideous fate which has befallen me, *à la mode de Culpepper*. Pray forgive my digressions, precious friend. In your absence, these letters are the only solace I may find beneath this roof. I must not abuse your patience. *Eh bien, continuons!*

My extended divergence from the topic to hand is, I see, assignable to my earlier mention of Great-grandpapa and his aversion to Americans. (Mamma once told me the old fellow claimed he could smell them out in a crowd!) This, in turn, brings me back to Mr. Horatio Culpepper's American companion, Pericles Factor. O, do not the very syllables of that name jar upon the ear, sweet Caroline? No less did the man himself jar upon my sight.

I was in our smallest garden when they arrived, the one which in happier times was Mamma's private herbary. It has mostly run wild since her death, yet Papa is indifferent to all of Cook's suggestions that he tear down the brick walls separating it from the kitchen garden, to enlarge the latter. Some pretty yellow flowers of cinquefoil held my attention— I thought I recognized them from a sketch in Mamma's notebook, although her comments thereunder were all written in Greek. Some quality of the plant must have fascinated her, for the alien characters were heavily underlined and decorated with a plethora of exclamation marks uncommon to the tongue of Homer.

"Well, if that ain't the purtiest thing!" a deep voice boomed, and a huge paw swept in under my nose to uproot the dainty flowers root and all. Oh yes, Caroline, I have transcribed the "gentleman's" speech exactly as I heard it. Yet my meagre powers of description fall short of conveying the full impact of his raw, uncultured voice and its monstrous accent.

The Americans may have defeated our bold English troops a time or two, but they are condemned to be ever vanquished by our sweet English language.

My unwelcome caller bowed low, doffing his hat with so extravagant a flourish that the brim dug a channel in the garden dust. "You must be Miss Delilah," he said, white teeth flashing from a face sunbrowned as a bargeman's. "Pericles Factor, at your service."

I confess, Caroline, his person was not without those superficial charms of tint and form that less perceptive women are pleased to settle for as attractive. Thank Heaven you and I know better! What boots it that a man like Mr. Factor be molded on the heroic scale, with broad shoulders, trim hips, clusters of jet-black curls such as are the crowning glory of Lord Byron himself, eyes the disturbing violet of iris flowers, and a demeanor merry as a Vauxhall Gardens revel? *We* seek the poet's soul, you and I, in the men upon whom we ultimately mean to bestow our favors.

Which we do not mean to bestow at all, of course.

"Here, ma'am," the creature went on, thrusting the ravished cinquefoil blossoms into my face. "Sweets for the sweet."

"That is, I think, 'Sweets *to* the sweet'," came a voice with all the gumption of a gutted mouse. From out of Pericles' muscular shadow there slunk a person shaped like a cabbage. He bowed to me as well as his complete lack of a waist allowed. Sunlight glistened from his nearly hairless pate. "Horatio Culpepper, mum," he said stiffly. "Connection of your mother's. My friend, Mr. Pericles Factor. Said we might find you out here. Your mother, I mean. From America. Mr. Factor, that is. Said you would see to us, talk to Cook about tea. Having a bit of a lie-down. Terrible headache. Your mother has."

I glowered at him most terribly and said, "You must mean Stepmamma, sir. My mother is *dead*."

The effect of my words was what one might achieve by pouring a bucket of iced water over an owl. Mr. Culpepper suffered some form of inward collapse and muttered obscure apologies. Mr. Factor, however, remained unploughed.

"These are gonna wilt bad if you don't do something about 'em quick. Tell you what, ma'am: You can put 'em in water inside first, before you get us our tea," he said, pressing his still-ignored floral tribute firmly into my hand and using the same action to give me a gentle but determined tug in the direction of our house.

O Caroline, what could I do and still remain a lady? I complied, silently cursing Stepmamma at every pace.

And so they have had their tea and are presently in the rooms assigned them, overseeing the unpacking of their things. I may have poured tea and passed the cakes, but I did *not* play the spinet for either of them. Nor shall I. The oafish Factor looks as if he would prefer a rustic reel to a Mozart sonata, at any rate, and as for my appointed swain, one hesitates to play Bach for the delectation of an animate plum pudding.

Should you wonder how I have managed to elude my unwished-for duties as hostess, I know you will have nothing but praise for my resourcefulness, dear friend:

I am studying Greek.

Yes, that is to be my shelter and my salvation, let Stepmamma pout how she will. The idea sprang full-blown to mind as I sat above the tea things, watching Mr. Factor pour his beverage into the saucer and blow upon the steaming brew before slurping it down. Mr. Culpepper consumed his drink with rather more aplomb, reserving his own excesses of bad manners for the devouring of every tea cake in sight, save those Mr. Factor managed to scoop up.

I could not bear to observe these concerted swillings. Rising from my place as soon as manners might allow, I heard myself announce, "Your pardon, gentlemen, but it is the hour for my Greek lesson."

"Greek?" quoth the uncouth Factor. "I hear tell you English gals like to muck around with odd stuff, but why'd you want to trouble your pretty head with Greek?"

Mr. Culpepper, on the other hand, appeared strangely elated by the news. "Now, Pericles," he said, beaming. "I think it just wonderful that Miss Delilah takes an interest in the Classics." Astonishing to report, he was not at all tongue-tied when addressing his friend, yet let his conversation turn to me and: "Latin, too? Fine tongue. Greek, that is. Studied it some myself. Latin, I mean. Pericles, here, he's got 'em both. Said so, anyhow. Didn't you, Peri? Latin and Greek, Harvard, Yale, somewhere, once? That old book of your family's—?"

Pericles guffawed and dealt the hapless Culpepper a strong buffet on the back. "Aw, now, H'raysh"—thus does the Yankee tongue mangle the sweet syllables of Mr. Horatio Culpepper's Christian name!—"you know I never did have me any sort of a head for furrin languages."

Here he gave Mr. Culpepper a swat so fierce that I marvelled at what passes for male camaraderie. The poor, plump little man lurched forward, his hands skidding among the tea things and quite upsetting the cream. As I rang for Maisie to clear away the resulting mess, I heard Mr. Culpepper say in that peculiar, staccato manner of his that yes, yes, he must be mistaken, quite wrong, surely thinking of another friend, the Classics were not Mr. Factor's meat at all, and so on.

Perhaps my imagination runs too rampant, darling Caroline, but I have reviewed my memories of teatime and the conviction remains: He was afraid. Mr. Horatio Culpepper was purely terrified of his supposedly dear friend, Mr. Pericles Factor.

Whatever can it mean? Sitting here, poring over the first introductory lessons of Mamma's old Greek text, I freely admit that I do not know.

But I do intend to find out.

Think, then, often of

> Your Bemused Yet Determined Friend,
> Delilah

* * *

May 1804

O Dearest Caroline, whatever shall I do?

Forgive the haste with which I write and all accompanying failures of proper Form and Art. My brain reels. Well has my Papa lectured that learning is a dangerous superfluity in woman. Would that I had never opened that accursed volume! One woe doth tread upon another's hem. I am undone!

And I will thank you, in the name of our sweet friendship, to limit your reply to what small guidance you might offer me in my peril. I really do *not* need to hear about the "utterly charming young gentleman from Huntingdonshire with the imploring brown eyes" who has so clearly turned your head from things that *really* matter. How can you stoop to vulgar Bath flirtations at a time like this?

Better if you had followed my example and lavished your time upon books rather than jumped-up Huntingdonshire pups, be their brown eyes ever so wheedling. For I confess, much pain and difficulty though Mamma's texts have brought me of late, I find the pursuit of the knowledge they contain to be strangely compelling. The Greek I mastered with unwonted ease, the initial difficulties of the first few chapters once surmounted. It was as if I had been born to mastery of the tongue, somehow. Mamma spoke of certain members of our family having a certain Talent. *Could this be mine?* I wondered.

It must be that Talent of one sort of another has some bearing upon my facility for the Attic language, since I admit my studies were neither focused nor single-minded. I was too intrigued by the odd relationship I earlier observed between Messrs. Culpepper and Factor. You will recall—if your pet suitor has not quite driven all recollection of me from mind— that I mentioned the fear I sensed emanating from poor little Mr. Culpepper when he gainsaid the American lout. Minded to discover more, I did not hide myself away in Mamma's old room half so much as I originally planned. My Greek studies should have suffered thereby; they did not. In the course of a scant week I find myself possessed of both a workable knowledge of Greek, a smattering of Latin (I have found another elementary text among the volumes of Mamma's library), and the sure and certain conviction that Mr. Culpepper is in mortal danger at the muscular hands of his so-called "friend" Mr. Pericles Factor.

Yes, it is so. I know it for a fact. Criticize me if you must for what I shall now tell you:

It was only last night my theories achieved confirmation. My daily observations of our two guests hinted ever so subtly at an occult relationship between the twain which was not conducive to Mr. Culpepper's health or peace of mind. Daily over the tea things I watched him growing paler and weaker. He no longer gobbled up every tea cake in sight. He reached such a pass that he neglected to partake of even bread-and-butter. In vain did Stepmamma urge him to second helpings over supper. His jowls lost their rosy hue as we watched. His breeches' buttons no longer placed us all under strain.

Mr. Factor, on the other hand, blossomed. His hale complexion achieved the rosiness of rare roast beef, his well set-up form acquired the muscular perfection of an Apollo, his already attractive features reached the epitome of masculine beauty, leaving even dear Lord Byron's storied face in the dust.

By these tokens, dear Caroline, do not think I have been at all affected by the gentleman's charms of person. I am not one to be swayed by trivialities. A pair of entreating eyes holds for me but the opportunity for scientific observation, the better to document the odd phenomenon whereby formerly sensible girls have their brains set all of a tizzy by what are, upon further study, merely two eyes like many others.

Figure in your mind, can you spare the thought, the concern now growing in my heart for poor Mr. Culpepper. The sensation of dread I felt emanating from him whenever we were in Mr. Factor's presence was not to be ignored. It clung like a miasma of some foul and weed-choked tarn to our every moment. The raven of Despair swung low above us, croaking unintelligible syllables of hideous yet occult meaning. Indeed, the whole situation became quite Gothic and literary in its overwhelming immanence.

I could bear it no more. Unprepossessing as Mr. Culpepper's physical attributes might be, I could not in good conscience stand by unmoved while the poor man withered before my eyes. Some chord of human sympathy there is which can not be ignored. I determined to speak with Mr. Culpepper alone and get to the bottom of matters.

The chance to do so presented itself with strange dispatch. I know this for vain fancy, Caroline, but I could swear that Mr. Culpepper somehow *knew* that I wished solitary converse with him, and procured the occasion. But of course that is folderol. It is my habit each evening to thrash out those problems besetting me by addressing my mirror-image while brushing my hair for bed. I am always entirely alone at these moments, and speak in a whisper. How could he have overheard? Coincidence is odd, is it not?

All that aside, I found him walking by himself in Mamma's ruined herb garden in the rain. My surprise was great. I myself was there only because my Greek and Latin has by this time grown wieldy enough to permit the decipherment of much of Mamma's old notebook. It is quite fascinating reading, really. There are directions contained therein for the compounding of curious draughts and philtres whose effect upon the human heart—But that is immaterial. Suffice it you to know that Mamma's instructions were specific as to the hour and meteorological conditions that must attend the garnering of the ingredients. (Did you know, dear Caroline, that tansy leaves gleaned before teatime in a drizzle are requisite for a most subtle potion guaranteed to attract admirers of the opposite sex, whereas those plucked near noon in sunshine are only good for distilling a sovereign sunburn remedy?)

"Oh, Mr. Culpepper!" I cried. "Do come indoors. You will catch your death."

"My death?" The little man leaned against the crumbling brick wall of the garden and sighed as though his heart would break. "That will come soon enough." His recent lack of appetite had whittled his previously rotund form admirably and given him the illusion of height. If I did not know better, I would have sworn he had grown four inches. Too, perhaps through the blurring effect of the falling rain, his hair seemed to be more golden, the features of his face less pudding-y and more hawklike, his eyes an astonishing, nigh feline green. Then I blinked, and the chimera was gone. He was weeping.

I could not bear it, Caroline. Boldly I took his arm and guided him into the house. I could hear raucous snoring coming from the front room. Mr. Factor was taking his ease. Papa and Stepmamma's voices came from a side room, and the servants were going about their tasks here, there, and everywhere. To speak with Mr. Culpepper undetected and apart was impossible, unless I conveyed him to the sleeping chambers upstairs. I need not tell you that *this* was not an option by any means whatsoever!

That is why I silently urged him to hasten up the stairs to the attic and shut fast the door to my sweet mamma's study behind us.

Ah, Caroline, could you have but seen the look of rapture that then crossed his features! He lingered but an instant upon the threshold of the room and breathed deep of the particular exhalation of old books. "It is true, then," he murmured, eyes aglitter.

"What is true, sir?" I inquired. My question seemed to wake him from some happy reverie. He was his old, nervous self once more.

"Why—why, what I thought," he replied. "About you. Studying Greek, Latin. Love of learning. Very rare quality, that. In a woman. No offense. Valuable. No mere pastime, is it? The books." He waddled over to the table where Mamma's notebook lay open beside a newly purchased one of my own. (Into your bosom alone will I confide that my readings of Mamma's scientific observations have inspired me to independent explorations in realms botanical.) "This yours?" he asked, reaching for Mamma's tome.

I know not what possessed me to fling myself between him and the table. No more can I account for the impulse compelling me to catch up the notebook and press it to my breast. I have always been a private person. Perhaps I did not wish to share any relic of my poor, dear mamma's with one who remains essentially a stranger to me.

Scant of breath, I managed to reply, "Oh, this is nothing, sir. Mere scribblings, of no interest to anyone. However, if you find any other book here of interest, feel free to examine it." I used one hand to indicate the common texts lining the study shelves, the other hand still clasping the notebook fiercely to me.

A shadow passed across Mr. Culpepper's face. For an instant, I thought I detected black wrath. How consummately bizarre! As if a mouseling such as he had spleen enough to assume a look so threatening! And yet I dare swear I felt a momentary pang of terror in his presence and thought I caught a flare of green in his muddy eyes. Fancy that! Me, terrified by a walking cabbage!

It was, in truth, a passing whimsy, for upon the very next moment, the gentleman dissolved into tears. Holding his plump hands before his face, he sobbed unashamedly. Such honesty and openness of emotion could not help but move me. Setting Mama's notebook down upon a high shelf well away from us both, I then turned to the distraught Mr. Culpepper and inquired as to what the matter might be.

"Doom!" he cried, in accents resonating with echoes of the charnel house. "Oh, I am condemned!"

"Mr. Culpepper, you have the advantage of me," I said, much alarmed. "Shall I fetch you a physician?"

"He could do me no good." The wretch shook his head. Again I had the fleeting impression of another, more conventionally handsome face beneath his unimpressive features. The attic light was never of the best. "The power which enslaves and torments me," he went on, "lies beyond the narrow ken of a physician's care. I shall perish for it, and the supreme irony is that I must meet my fate beneath the very roof which shelters my one hope of salvation."

"Oh sir!" I exclaimed. "I know not what you intend!"

At this juncture, tears of supplication standing in his eyes, Mr. Culpepper made bold to take my hand in both his own and—

But here comes the post! I must seal this missive and dispatch it to you with the assurance that you shall hear more anon from

> Your Devoted Friend,
> Delilah

*   *   *

June 1804

Dear Caroline,

(Albeit I use the term more for Form's sake than out of any delusion that you hold my friendship worthy enough for either of us to refer to the other as "dear.")

How could you? The outpourings of a heart in agony are pooled before you in my previous missive, and all you can think of to send me in reply is an utterly *grovelling* request for the receipt needful for distilling the tansy love philtre to which I gave but passing mention!

I am almost minded to refuse you all further knowledge of what passed between Mr. Culpepper and myself since last I wrote you. As for the philtre . . . I shall think about it. Perhaps were you to evince a modicum of polite interest in my fate, I might be swayed to look favorably upon your request. For the philtre does indeed function as Mamma's notes suggest, of this I have proof positive.

If I choose *not* to send you a vial thereof, console yourself, dear, *dear* Caroline, with the thought that there are plenty of other fish in the sea, as well as in Huntingdonshire. But my decision in the matter remains to be seen, does it not?

Having now attracted some sliver of your attention, I shall tell you what transpired between Mr. Culpepper and myself that rainy afternoon in the attic chamber. I had, I believe, left the gentleman in possession of my hand, and in great distress of mind. He spoke of a great peril threatening him, yet at the same time of salvation's sweet hope to be found under the very roof presently sheltering us.

To be sure, I asked him what he meant by this hope of salvation, expecting to hear him speak of Papa's brother, my Uncle Paul, who holds a cure of souls in Lower Sandwallop and who occasionally takes tea with the family. Shock of the most vivid sort showed itself plainly on my face when instead Mr. Culpepper took the hand already in his keeping, pressed it to his bosom, and most fervently exclaimed:

"You!"

I was at a loss, though not so far gone as to neglect extricating my hand from his clasp. "Forgive me, Miss Delilah," he continued. "I forget myself."

"You do indeed," I averred. "Touch me again and I shall take steps."

With a despairing moan, he turned from me. "Alack!" he cried, overcome. "Have I then alienated my one possibility of help?" He raised his eyes to mine and—O Caroline! How dare you venture to compare the pedestrian gaze of your Huntingdonshire swain to ocular orbs like Mr. Culpepper's, abrim with poetic longing and misery?

"I will tell you a tale," he said hoarsely. "If you will but hear it out, I shall ask no more of you."

What could I do, in simple human charity, save consent? And so it was that Mr. Culpepper related to me a history at once dazzling, baffling, revelatory, and horripilating, concerning as it did myself.

"Your dear mamma bore the maiden name of Crafter, did she not?" Mr. Culpepper asked in tones reserved for those who already suspect the answer to their inquiries. Upon my admission, he continued: "You are therefor connected by blood to a clan whose reputation in certain circles is—Ah, how to put this so that I may not too gravely shock your sensibilities?"

"So long as my own reputation remains untarnished, sir," I riposted, "the peccadilloes of my ancestors do not touch the welfare of my soul."

"Oh, but they do, they do!" he groaned, his plump cheeks drawn into a grimace of sorrow. "For that sept of the Crafter clan which yet flourishes in America is stained most hideously black by their continued, unrelieved, and unrepentant practice of"—here he dropped his voice and glanced about the chamber, as if seeing spies among Mamma's retorts and alembics—"*witchcraft!*"

Caroline, Caroline, could you but have heard the note of cold dread which informed his pronunciation of that word! Why, it so caused my flesh to crawl upon my bones that for various instants I remained unaware of the fact that Mr. Culpepper had once more lost that hesitance of speech which I had previously noted.

I forced my spirits up and drew myself erect. "Sir, you presume!" I declared in martial accents. "Witchcraft, is it? In this day and age?" I made free to laugh his tale to scorn. My laugh was, of course, as light, silvery, and musical as you may recall it, if you recall me at all.

Mr. Culpepper hung his head. "I expected this," he said mournfully. "It all dovetails so neatly with *his* plan. True, who would believe me, speaking as I do of dark forces whose existence is all but forgotten in this age of Reason's clear light?

There is no mind so closed as that which claims to be open to Reason. Yet when I heard from your stepmamma that you cherished a fondness for the Romantic poets who do see fit to give the nod to things Unseen, I had hopes you would at least afford my story fair hearing. Too, when you evinced interest in expanding your own private sphere of knowledge through the unaided study of the Classics—"

"Enough, sir, I pray." I stilled his words, blushing hotly from the shame they had evoked. "You do well to chastise me. I apologize for the haste of my reaction. It is only that an evil reputation touching the American branch of the family might somehow, in the hands of wicked tongues, come to cast an unfavorable light upon my poor, dear mamma's departed spirit. Continue, if you will. I will hear out your proof in this."

Bitter, bitter gall, his laugh! "Hear it!" he exclaimed. "Nay, see it, rather. Behold!" He made a gesture whose expansive nature was intended to take in his entire rotund person. "Learn and pity, dear Miss Delilah, what the dark sorcery of a Crafter's magic has done to one"—here he detached from around his neck a locket which he opened and handed to me—"whose rightful appearance you may here plainly see."

I own I gasped, so grievous was the assault upon my nerves. For upon opening the locket I saw the very face I had previously seen swimming across the fleshy features of Mr. Culpepper as the two of us stood in the rain. There were those same golden locks, those verdant eyes, that face spare yet dominating, the somewhat mean lines of the thin lips forgiven by the unquenchable nobility of the chin.

"This . . . is you?" I am certain I stammered. He nodded. "But—but how—?" I need not have asked. The answer was plain: Witchcraft.

"Need I, to a mind as penetrating as your own, dear Miss Delilah, point out the shabby linguistic jest which Mr. Pericles Factor presently plays out against this entire household? *Factor* is a name which derives from the Latin for one who makes, and *Crafter* . . ."

"—means the same. O horrible!" I cried. "Then he is of my blood?"

"A cousin," Mr. Culpepper averred. "Distant enough in degree to permit your marriage to be free of the banns of consanguinity, even were the truth of his kinship revealed."

"My marriage?" I was understandably aghast at the word. "To him? Does the villain dare to presume—?"

"He dares much," said Mr. Culpepper, "if in so daring he finds himself at length in charge and possession of . . . *the token.*"

He spoke these ultimate two words with such implied import that I must grasp their significance without fully comprehending their meaning. Upon applying to him for further explication, I received the following reply:

"It is a fact well known that those lost souls who devote themselves to the practice of witchcraft must of necessity sell their souls to Satan. In exchange, the Archfiend grants them powers transcending those of common mortals. They may delve into the priviest thoughts of others, mind to mind, without detection. They may—your pardon, Miss Delilah, I *must* speak frankly—influence the emotions of those who have stirred their basest desires. They may effect the transportation of distant objects. And last but not least, they may summon and control a person or object by the utilization of a symbol or token representing that person."

"Or object," I prompted, if only to keep the full implication of his disclosures from my mind. "But how—?"

"—does this concern you?" Mr. Culpepper finished my sentence so perfectly in accord with my own thoughts that one might almost ascribe to him the very powers of dark magic of which he had so lately spoken. "For the reason I have already stated: *the token!*"

I dared not flinch; I must know! "What token?"

"It is rumored throughout the ranks of your eternally condemned American connections," he said, "that while the British branch of the Crafter family has wisely chosen to eschew the questionable advantages sorcery confers, they are still masters of certain . . . heirlooms whose symbolic power is immeasurable. These are passed from generation to purblind generation. They are not many, nor is the power of each equal to that of its brother. Some are no more than gewgaws—a forked branch of hazelwood, the statuette of a satyr, a chaplet of laurel, carefully preserved, a cup carved from olivewood—yet there is one among them whose value transcends all others, a thing whose symbolic power offers the possessor thereof mastery over the paramount force of this rich world."

His speech overawed me. "Mr. Culpepper, do you—can you mean . . . the Divine?"

He shuddered as if with cold and put up a warding hand. "No, no, by no means. By no means need we concern ourselves with . . . that of which you speak. I mean Death, Miss Delilah."

I felt the cowardly blood retreat from my extremities. I stood chilled to the fingertips. "It is not given for mortals to control Death, sir," I said.

His eyes burned strangely. "Not for ordinary mortals, perhaps. But your practitioner of witchcraft is well beyond the tiresome constraints incumbent upon commoner folk." He managed a wry smile as he added, "Can you conceive of the temporal power to be vouchsafed the man who is known as Death's master? Can your simple woman's mind begin to ideate the wealth such a man might amass? From the mightiest potentate upon his throne to the lowliest wretch in his filthy hovel, who would *not* seek out such a man and press into his hands all his earthly goods if they might purchase from him but a day's additional respite from the attentions of the Grim Reaper?"

"You speak a sorry truth there, sir," I replied, myself more grim than the Reaper of whom he spoke. "This, then, is Mr. Factor's purpose? To procure from me the token of which you speak, the object by which Death himself may be ruled?"

"Even so. Being sure of his captive prey, the cunning sorcerer Factor confided in me utterly his goal and the means by which he intends to achieve it, though Innocence herself be trampled into the dust should she stand between it and him." Mr. Culpepper's fluency was perhaps to be assigned to the absence of Mr. Factor, yet I vow I found it yet rather disconcerting.

"Then you know what this token is?" I asked.

"It is the model of a human skeleton in miniature, carved from wood by the hand of Wizard Amer himself, forefather and founder of the Crafter line and first to plunge his soul into the murk of the Devil's service," he told me. "The token passed from Wizard Amer's hands when one of his she-cubs stole it, the better to advance her own career in the black arts, else the old rogue might be living yet. She in turn lost it to a sibling who only understood its use imperfectly, and he was murdered for it by the lover of yet another of his sisters, at her behest."

"O evil!" I exclaimed, as well I might, for Mr. Culpepper was outlining for my revolted ears a family history Mamma had never mentioned—with what good cause!—and which I trust you will never reveal to another living soul, my trusted Caroline.

"Evil indeed," Mr. Culpepper agreed. "Shall I desist?"

"Go on," I directed, steeling myself. "Knowledge is better than ignorance." Somehow, in uttering those words, I thought I felt my dear mamma's approbation warming me.

"Well, I shall make short shrift. The whole sanguinary mess ended with the skeleton transported to England by one Thomas Crafter, who knew nothing of its supernatural value. Only the tales of its virtues remained in the New World, there to be unluckily discovered by the mystic pryings of Mr. Pericles Factor—or Crafter, to give him his true name. He set his mind on recovering the token and exploiting its powers to the fullest. Through family documents, he was able to trace it to England, and it was during his continued investigations in London that I was misfortunate enough to cross his path."

"He is, then, no true acquaintance of yours, Mr. Culpepper?" I ventured.

" 'Mr. Culpepper'!" A sharp, caustic laugh again escaped his lips. "That name! It is no more mine than Factor is his! We met, he and I, at the races. My adored sister Athena—who knows when next I shall see her sweet face in this world, alas!—remarked upon the dashing young gentleman whom none of the Prince's party seemed to know."

"The Prince's party!" I gasped, taken aback by all that such casual mention of His Royal Highness the Prince Regent implied. "You cannot mean—"

He raised a masterful hand to still my words. "All in good time, my dear Miss Delilah. All shall be revealed. We were, as I was saying, at the races. To satisfy a beloved sister's whim, I found a pretense to introduce myself to him. His charm was hypnotic, devastating, even—dare I say it?—fatal. On the strength of my introduction, he soon became an intimate of our set. No doubt the villain perceived our wealth, breeding, and social preeminence as little more than tools for him to use at his convenience at furthering his noxious scheme. There was, need I mention, neither trace nor hint of his American origin when first we commenced relations, else I should never have allowed him such favor." He looked solemn.

"Of course not," I concurred, and unable to restrain the outrage of my bosom at this violation of a gracious man's confidence, I added, "O vilest duplicity, thy name is Pericles Crafter!"

He seemed to regard me tenderly for an instant, and when a zephyrous sigh blew from his pendulous lips I imagined it emanating from his mouth as it truly appeared, thin and unensorcelled. The miniature portrait he had shown me displayed a face whose masculine beauty was almost worthy of a true Prince Charming. O Caroline, our childhoods are not so far removed from us that you cannot recall the nursery tales of enchanted princes, their natural perfections forcibly disguised by witchcraft. Yet there I stood, in Mamma's old attic chamber, living such a tale of wonder!

"You do not know how near the mark you hit when you speak of duplicity, Miss Delilah." He spoke as if the world's weight bowed him down. "The better to prepare his unwitting tools, the sorcerer next used his falsely winning ways to lure my innocent sister Athena into his clutches."

"Say not so!" I begged.

"I must." He was obdurate. "By blandishments and promises he won her heart. By lies he convinced her that I was against the match. By base cunning he persuaded the child to elope with him to Gretna Green where they were joined in holy matrimony. *Holy!* With one such as *he*?" He was upon the point of loosing an oath when my restraining presence calmed him.

"I received his demands in the same post as brought Athena's rapturous announcement of her marriage," he went on. "Now assured of his prey, the demon incarnate dropped all pretense. He spoke plainly as to his blood and opprobrious sorceries. He had conveyed my sister to an isolated country retreat, he told me, and there placed her under a spell of sleep. Athena would not wake again unless he allowed it, and if he chose he might remove that portion of the spell which permitted her to survive without nourishment. This was the threat he held over me. For my part, as I loved my sister, I must meet with him in London, at a time and place of his specification, there to consent to whatever dastardly orders he might put to me. I checked the direction of Athena's letter to me and found that it was addressed in *his* hand. Thus did my broken heart prove that the fiend must have laid the sleeping spell upon my darling as soon as she had finished writing that last missive of bridal joy."

"The knave!" I cried.

"Aye, but what is more perilous than a knave who holds all the cards?" he observed. "He had me. I attended him at the time and place specified. It was a low resort in one of London's least savory quarters, where to buy a man's silence costs a ha'penny more than to buy his life. There, in the back room of a den of thieves and ruffians, Pericles Crafter invited me to share a cup of wine with him. It was not poisoned—of this he assured me by drinking from the same bottle. Ah, but venoms may do worse than kill! I drank, then demanded he state the price of Athena's freedom. He laughed and most curiously replied, 'The potion has prepared you, fool! Soon you will sue for your own freedom right enough, and forget your idiot sister's predicament.' Then, in place of honest speech he began to utter syllables of arcane and awful significance. I grew weak. My sight dimmed. The room swam. Pains of an untellable cruelty racked my body."

"Please, sir, no more! I cannot bear it!" I begged him. You know me, Caroline—or you used to claim you knew me as a sister—and you know with what ease my tender soul bruises for the plight of others.

"Courage, Miss Delilah," the dear, gallant man said. "I have borne as much upon the field of battle. I must speak, lest worse befall. I shall abridge: I lost consciousness. When I awoke, he was stooping above me, a sneer twisting his mouth. He handed me a shard of broken looking-glass, that I might see the metamorphosis his witchery had wrought." Here he touched his face.

"A man's true worth is not measured by mere appearance," I reminded him.

"For you, perhaps," he said. "But how many women share your sterling moral excellences?" As I could say nothing to this, he continued. "Crafter then told me of his plan. He had changed my looks with a foul purpose: I was to impersonate one Horatio Culpepper, of the Darbyshire Culpeppers. His diligent researches as to the whereabouts of . . . the token . . . had yielded fruit. He knew all he needed to know of your family, including the facts of your mother's death and your father's remarriage. He knew that your stepmother had a distant connection, a Mr. Horatio Culpepper, on whom she doted but whom she did not see or hear from with any great frequency. He would gain *entree* to their home and trust discreetly, in the company of your stepmother's supposed connection: myself."

"But surely he takes a chance there," I suggested. "What if the real Mr. Horatio Culpepper should choose this very moment to contact Stepmamma? The wizard would be discovered!"

He drew a deep breath and somberly replied, "Precious few posts run between this world and the next, Miss Delilah. Your American cousin was most thoroughgoing in establishing the safeguards for his plot."

For the first time in my life I felt a pang for my poor stepmamma. To lose one she held dear, solely because his person provided a convenient key by which the black sorcerer Crafter might invade our home! "He shall pay for this," I vowed. I offered my hand. "I call upon your honor as an English gentleman, sir. Reveal to me your true identity, and I will do whatever I may to help you and thwart this blackguard."

He did not take the hand I offered. "Nay, Miss Delilah," he said. "I will not speak my true name to any living soul until I have redeemed it. Ours is a great and ancient family whose fame remains in shadow until I have expunged this smirch upon us."

"Then you will need nothing of me," I said, turning from him in sorrow.

"Can you believe *that*?" In his rage, the spell of disguisement slipped a trifle and I glimpsed the man as he was, magnificent, heroic! "Miss Delilah, our acquaintance has been brief, yet even so I have come to feel that your spirit is somehow— somehow higher, finer, purer than those of ordinary women. Let me entreat but a moiety of the compassion which must of necessity reside within your dear heart for my ill-starred sister's fate. Lady Athena Kirk-Chatenaire might have accepted the suit of an earl, a marquis, even a duke of the blood royal! Instead her young life and hopes were thrown away, squandered for the sake of the illusory attractions of your American cousin. Now he will attempt the same roguery with you. Mastery of your person brings mastery of your property, and that property needs must include the token he desires. I beg you, for the sake of my lost sister, for the sake of your dear, departed mother, for the sake of all English womanhood, *do not succumb!*"

"*Never!*" I swore with more fervency than ever stirred my self's core. In my zeal I was yet able to note that the distracted man had let fall the very information which he sought to hide: his name. Who has not heard of the Dukes of Kirk-Chatenaire? How else explain the intimacy with His Royal Highness the Prince Regent so cavalierly mentioned earlier?

A blush upon his cheeks disclosed that he, too, had realized his error. "Well, Miss Delilah, it seems I must trust your discretion now, being unable to trust my own," he said. "Is my name . . . my honor . . . safe with you?"

"Entirely," I vowed. "Utterly."

"Brave girl!" he exclaimed, and took the hand so lately declined. Pressing it tenderly, his eyes soft with sentiment, he said, "That is well, for it is the hope of my heart that someday—some happy, happy day when all this is behind us—you may condescend to accept the name which you have so courageously agreed to defend as . . . your own."

Enclosed please find a vial of Mamma's tansy philtre, darling Caroline. Trust that you shall hear more anon from

> Your Friend,
> Delilah

*   *.   *

July 1804

My Sweetest, Most Sympathetic Friend Caroline,

Your reply was all that a lonely spirit under siege might wish.

I rejoice to learn that Mamma's tansy potion yielded such satisfactory results and extend my heartiest felicitations upon the occasion of your engagement to Lord Cranbrooke-Purslaine-Dewberry of the Huntingdonshire Cranbrooke-Purslaine-Dewberrys. Pray convey to his lordship my thanks for granting me the liberty to call him "Dewy."

I regret I shall not be able to do so. Soon I shall be dead.

Be not amazed, dear Caroline, at such devastating news. I am certain that by this time you have gathered that my situation is no longer one of social normalcy. The manner by which you have received this missive ought be clue enough, for it shall not reach you via the common post. Such mundane avenues of communication are closed to me now. Still, you *shall* receive it. Although I am imprisoned, he cannot, he shall not, deprive my assaulted soul of this one means of relieving itself.

When I have done writing, I shall apply those teachings of my dear departed mamma's (as preserved in her meticulous Greek) which are supposed to effect the transportation of distant objects through the exchange of equivalent masses. The raw materials for such an undertaking lie within easy reach in this, my cell. He has already ransacked the attic study—indeed, it was his first target, the swine—without encountering the prize he seeks. All else he regards as trash, unworthy of his attention. Therefor I shall be free to send this one last piteous missive to you, the companion of my youth, the friend of my bosom.

Should the object of equivalent mass which I must needs transport hither to permit my letter to reach you at Bath prove to be one of your highborn fiancé's *billets-doux,* I promise on my honor not to read it.

O Caroline, and what matter if I should read it? What harm would it do? The knowledge I might glean therefrom would perforce go down into the grave with me. He has been searching the house, top to bottom, for hours. He has not yet found the accursed *token* which he so passionately desires. Passionately! Yes, there is passion in the man, but not of the tender sort reserved for Love's gentle service. It is for Power alone his heart beats faster—the Power of command over Death itself— and for that Power's sake he is willing to wager the price of his immortal soul!

What is my life to him? A mite, a speck, a fly to be obliterated at a blow! I am no longer his tool, his toy, his foolish puppet. I have served my purpose, to my shame. He cares naught for human life, else why do I now share this attic chamber with a corpse?

Steel yourself, Caroline! The chill which crept over our limbs as we read of such ghastly interludes as this in Mrs. Radcliffe's volumes was but a tame and homely *frisson* compared to the sensation of cold dread which invades me now. I write so that I need not spare a thought to the poor dead man in the corner. Break, heart! We shall not see his like on earth again. He perished in my defense, defying the monster to the last. Ah, nobility! For it is solely in the vale of direst peril that we learn the true meaning of that empty word, and it is only too late that we discover where our untutored hearts most sincerely and worthily ought bestow their freight of Love.

Chivalry, thy name is Pericles Crafter!

Caroline, if I live and Providence grants that we meet again soon, I will thank you to kick me once, firmly, where it may do me some good. I am a goose. Only a goose would mistake unconsciousness for death. Only a greater goose would so lose all proper sense of comportment that she fling herself joyously upon the gentleman mentioned when the signs of life return to him. Only the greatest goose in all the world would so far forget herself that she leave her personal correspondence unguarded so that the gentleman may read it and discover those delicate revelations of affection never intended for his eyes.

Ah, welladay, there is no mending some things. And so we are to be married. If we live.

My mind's eye forms a picture of your expression, and it is not a flattering one. Do not gape so, sweet erstwhile companion, at these words. I was duped, misled, made a pawn by the man I trusted, whose tale of woe, witchcraft, and whimsical sisters I too readily believed. He is no more the Duke of Kirk-Chatenaire than he is Horatio Culpepper! He is not witchcraft's victim, but its master! The face and form he claimed were fixed upon him by my darling Pericles' sorceries were in truth self-inflicted, a clumsy disguise procured by his substandard enchantments whose slippage I did on occasion espy. Had I but known!

But how could I know? Oh, the plausible scoundrel! I had no sooner dispatched my last message to you, my precious friend, than he was at my side, urging me to initiate the scheme we had compounded between us for the purpose of overcoming the supposed "Wizard Crafter." I was to lure poor, unwitting Pericles into the front parlor, on the pretense of showing him some family relics.

"I leave it to you to select the objects themselves," the so-called Duke mewed in my ear. "But I caution you to make certain that they are truly things which once belonged to your ancestor Thomas. These Crafters have a nose for the authentic."

"I cannot include the token he seeks," I replied. "The little wooden skeleton. For one thing, I have never seen it beneath this roof, and for another, it would be unwise to lay such an item before our enemy unless we have a plan for his immediate overthrow."

"Unwise, most unwise to be sure," the glib wretch assured me. "This is but bait, my adored Delilah, the lure to divert his attention while you slip *this* into his tea." He urged a small gray chamois bag into my palm. On loosing the yellow drawstring I found it to contain a measure of acrid brown powder.

"But if you poison him, how shall you ever free your sister?" I queried.

"It is no poison, but a drug whose virtues subvert the mind and subdue the will of whosoever ingests it. I have acquired it only at great personal risk, but I would dare more for dear Athena's sake . . . and your own. The evil Wizard Crafter is too sly to give me the chance to apply this . . . *remedy*—ha, ha!—myself, but he has no cause to suspect you and every reason to desire sight of old Thomas Crafter's keepsakes. Once he has downed the brew and its effects take hold, I may in safety command him to perform the requisite rites to release Athena and restore me. Only then shall I give the blackguard his just reward, a length of good, clean Sheffield steel through the marrow of his rotten heart!"

Sweet friend, as I glance up from these words and see my dearest Pericles riffling through book after book for some means to our salvation, I shudder to recall how it was less than an hour ago I thrilled to hear the vile pseudo-Duke swear to slay him. Heedless girl that I was!

I took the pouch and gave my word that the drug would find its way into the tea, the tea into Pericles. To protect it, I took the precaution of wrapping the pouch itself in the bizarre black handkerchief which that peculiar and most mysterious gentleman had given me upon the horrid day of Mamma's death. (I *have* written to you of him, have I not? As he never called upon us again thereafter, I wonder what might have become of him.) Thus guaranteed against spillage, the pouch was concealed in my bosom.

As the "Duke" had predicted, my unsuspecting darling responded to my invitation with alacrity. When he entered the parlor, he was bewildered to find me there alone, *sans* chaperone. A ready lie, fed me by the "Duke," informed him that Stepmamma and Papa had been called from home unexpectedly. The souvenirs of Great-grandpapa Thomas lay temptingly arrayed upon the table, hard by the tea things. I told him I was willing to postpone our interview, should he feel ill at ease without a duenna, but that for my part I saw no harm in entrusting my honor to his own. His dark violet eyes were alight—with hunger for the wretched *token's* power, I surmised. Ah, how wrong I was!

"I confess, ma'am," he said, seating himself beside me on the divan, "I find these circumstances more than wonderful. Your honor's safe with me. Heaven witness, there ain't a single hair of your head I'd see come to harm."

"Tea, sir?" I asked brightly, interposing a brimming cup. My heart fluttered. Pericles is the finest of gentlemen, the handsomest example of Nature's handiwork. What woman in her right mind would not find herself thrilled to hear such words of devotion laid at her feet? Alas, that worm of a *soi-disant* Duke had envenomed my ear against accepting Pericles' tribute at face value. My heart perceived the truth, my mind insisted it must all perforce be falsehood. Oh, naughty mind!

I attempted to attract his attention to the family relics presently bestrewing the tea table. "Will it please you to examine these, Mr. Factor?" I offered, still using the name by which he was commonly known beneath our roof. "You may handle any you like while I prepare your dish of tea to your taste. Sugar, I believe? And a spot of milk?" It was to be my chance to introduce the drug.

Oh, happiest chance not taken! His eyes still upon me, he picked up the mementos of Great-grandpapa Thomas one by one in quick succession, with all the polite disinterest of one compelled to view a friend's butterfly collection. He was done with them too soon to permit me to bring forth the chamois bag, unwrap it from the enrobing black handkerchief, and tip the brown powder into his cup. All too soon—as then I thought—his tender eyes were fixed upon me again.

"Very interesting," he said, giving me to know it was not.

"Oh, sir!" I protested. "Surely you have not examined these objects thoroughly at all. Why, look. Here among them is a box which might contain . . . some relic of more than passing fascination for you. I have heard that my great-grandpapa Thomas enjoyed wood carving." *There*, I thought, with some smugness. *That should draw his notice from me.*

I was mistaken. "I don't care a fig for your great-grandpap, Miss Delilah," he said somewhat heatedly. "Beggin' your pardon, but we're plainspoke folks back home. All this truck's nothin' to me. What I come here to say—to say to you—to say—"

Whatever he had come to say, he did not say it. Rather a most disconcerting change came over him. His skin paled. A light dew garlanded his noble brow. He held a hand to his heart and swayed as if taken with the vapors. And through all this access of giddiness, I saw him grit his teeth, clench his eyes tightly shut, and I heard him mutter, "The devil! Oh, the ring-tailed devil! His power's still on me, bridling my tongue, but I *will* speak! My heart'll just about bust itself clean open if I don't fight off that potion for your sake and have my say."

I believed him to be speaking of his demonic master and was much troubled. What if he should summon up Beelzebub himself to aid him in all sorts of mischief? To distract him from this suspected spellcasting, I hurriedly seized the very box which I have mentioned and opened it. "Oh, look!" I cried desperately, holding the contents up before his eyes. "What a common-looking stone. Whyever would Great-grandpapa Thomas take such pains to house it in so fine a casket? The box is lined with best Spanish velvet, yet this looks for all the world like an ordinary garden pebble. Did you ever see—?"

"Lord above! A bezoar!" he gasped, and snatched the pebble from my hand. As I stared, dumbfounded at an accused wizard's easy invocation of the Divine, he pressed the stone to his brow, then to his heart. His lips moved over a series of unfamiliar syllables and a faint, rosy luminescence emanated from his person. Then, with a sigh, he slumped back on the divan. "Free," he breathed. "Free at last."

"Free," echoed a cold voice from the doorway. "Free to perish like the vermin you are, Crafter." I beheld the man I still thought of as the Duke of Kirk-Chatenaire, only now he had seemingly reverted to the fair image of the miniature independent of anyone's sorcery . . . save his own!

Pericles rose from his place, the light of battle in his eyes. "Curse you, Renfrew Coister! Aye, and curse me for ever lettin' one of your blood near enough to turn me into the Devil's puppet. If I'd'a listened to my mam instead of thinkin' all her warnin's of old family enemies was so much woman-talk,

you'd never of got near enough to me in Boston to dose me
with your demon-dust."

"I fail to comprehend your complaint, Crafter," the former
"Duke" sneered. "You have benefited amply from our associa-
tion. For one, I have saved your precious *mam* the cost of your
passage to England, taking all our combined travel expenses
wholly upon myself. For another, I have obtained you *entree*
to the home of those very Crafter relations whom she most
desired you to seek out, for whatever foolish purpose."

"She sent me to search out the very thing you're after, you
hound," Pericles shot back. "She got took with a vision of how
some witchy varmint was out to lay hold of old Amer's carving
what Cousin Thomas took off with him to England. That's why
she sent me to fetch it back to where it'll be kept safe from the
likes of you!"

"Your mamma is as meddling an old fool as Amer ever was,
I perceive," the low Coister replied too smoothly.

"You keep your miser'ble tongue off my mam's good name,
Coister!" Pericles shouted, and hurled himself upon the foe.
Woe, with but a gesture of that loathsome man's hand one of
Papa's prized Staffordshire dogs flew from its place on the
parlor mantel to smash against the back of my darling's head.
Pericles collapsed—dead, so I fancied—and the value of the
remaining ceramic dog was entirely spoilt.

"You have slain him!" I exclaimed.

"A needful action," the poltroon drawled, blowing imaginary
dust from his fingernails. "I did not reckon with old Thomas
owning a bezoar. Such stones are found exclusively within the
brains of certain select toads and have the power to instantly
negate the effects of all drugs and poisons. He is quite out of my
power, now. Fortunately, he has served his turn. A clever blind
from which to stalk my quarry." He eyed me meaningly.

I leapt to my feet and dashed for the bell-pull to summon
the servants. The wicked man was there before me, either
through his own nimbleness or by some supernatural agency.
He seized me roughly by the shoulders, brute that he is! "You
waste your time," he said. "The household is dispersed. A spell
of suggestion has sent them all away for an indefinite time, the
better to permit me a full search of the premises."

He cast a scornful eye at the objects which I had laid out upon
the table. "I had hoped," he said, "that you might do still more of

my work for me, sweet Delilah. When I told you to fetch some of old Thomas' gimcracks to 'bait' the alleged 'Wizard Crafter,' I thought Luck might let you bring among them the very token of power I seek. Alas, Dame Fortune proves a chancy jade, as ever. The old geezer must have placed it beneath several layers of warding spells, but no matter—" Here the mountebank reached with one hand into the bosom of his jacket and thrust a forked hazel branch into my unwilling grasp. "We shall find it."

I recognized the dowsing rod and knew its purpose from my delvings into Mamma's notebook. Did the boldfaced recreant actually believe that I would lend my abilities to his cause? I let it drop to the floor and trampled it underfoot. The rod remained unharmed, but at least I felt somewhat better for the defiant gesture. "*We*, sirrah?" I demanded, standing tall. "By *we* do you dare to intimate *you* and *I*?"

Again his hands fell upon me. Oh, how the barbarous fiend laughed! "But naturally, my lovely," he gloated. "For I own that I came to this house seeking one prize, but I mean to depart with two."

"Never!" I flung the word in his face and wished it were a dish of scalding tea. "You, Renfrew Coister—if that is your real name—are a liar, a murderer, and a thief. I know not what pit of the fiery Abyss spawned you, but ere I would link my fortunes to your own, I should sooner hurl myself thither. Be sure of it!"

His eyes grew wide. "That is no way to speak of New Haven," he said. "Very well. You have chosen. Yet while you term me murderer with such high contempt, know that you came within a hairsbreadth of sharing that honorable title with me. What do you think was the *true* function of that powder I gave you to dose young Crafter's tea withal?"

His eyes told me that he spoke honestly, for once, and a monumental trembling fastened upon my limbs at the thought of how near I had come to being the agent of an innocent man's death. Granted, I thought him dead already, but still . . . My tender spirit could not bear it. I tumbled into a swoon.

I awoke in Mamma's study, and the rest you know. I assume that the fiend Coister, by whatever means, conveyed our insensible bodies here so that he might not be embarrassed should any unexpected callers happen to glance in at the parlor windows during his search. Too, the study makes a good prison.

As I write, dear Pericles cons my mamma's notebook, seeking some deliverance for us. It is our sole hope, he says. Like myself, he is of Crafter blood, and as such possesses that Talent which (so he has told me) has long caused our family to be mistaken for those fallen souls like Renfrew Coister who have obtained their powers through diabolic agencies. We Crafters scorn such, relying rather upon the sovereign and holy forces of Education, Observation, and Scientific Method to cause Staffordshire dogs and other *objets d'art* to fly across rooms.

The aftereffects of the subjugating potion by which my Pericles was enthralled have unfortunately so affected his memory that he is at a loss to summon up the incantation proper to the destruction of the fulsome Coister. I regret with all my heart that I came so late to my studies, else by this my own Talent (so my darling calls it, as Mamma did—had I but known!) might prove a match for Coister's vile machinations.

Woe, the time I have wasted in girlhood's frivolities! The portrait of Great-grandfather Thomas glowers at me from its frame, condemning me, in my mind, for my many shortcomings of character. And yet Mamma said that he was kind to her, in his acerbic way. The thought of Mamma makes me weep, and all I have to dry my tears is this *outré* black kerchief which late wrapped the pouch of Coister's evil poison. The temptation to use those fatal grains upon myself is strong. Better death by one's own hand than dishonor at the hands of Renfrew Coister! For of one thing I am certain now, dear Caroline: He is no gentleman.

Farewell, farewell. God knows when we shall meet again in fields Elysian! Yet ere I die, I should cherish some last word of parting from you, my bosom friend. Therefor please find enclosed with this last missive a measure of blue powder folded into a small parchment envelope. Sprinkle half of it liberally over any letter your compassion might see fit to send me, the while reciting the words which you shall find writ upon the parchment itself. I know not whether this will work for you, having no Crafter blood, but it might be worth a try. *Nil desperandum.*

The remainder of the powder, if mixed with two parts sheep fat and one part olive oil, will do wonders for your complexion.

You might therefor perchance care to utilize it the night preceding your nuptials and think of one who once was
    Your Doomed, Unfortunate, and Miserable Friend,
        Delilah

*   *   *

September 1804

My Most Cherished and Beloved Caroline,
    Of course I shall tell you how it happened! I have been *trying* to tell you for months! Owing you so much, and the ties of Family being what they are, can I do less than offer you full explanation for the astonishing events which were a collateral effect of your late resourcefulness, sagacity, and initiative? Perhaps this letter will meet a kinder Fate than all its predecessors.
    In my present circumstances, it is hard to believe that not so long ago I sat bereft, sobbing helplessly into the only kerchief at hand. Its funereal hue did little to lift my spirits. I had just sent you the letter and asked Pericles whether he had found any aid for us yet. Reluctantly he admitted failure.
    "I don't know where your mamma hid her fightin' spells, but all I've found in these books is ord'nary cantrips for easing pain a mite and curing the common cold; nothing special," he said. "There's a little spell of animation here might do us some help, but—"
    "Animation!" I cried, elated. "Do you mean the words are capable of imparting motility to objects otherwise devoid of autonomous motion?"
    "Welllllll, I guess," Pericles replied, scratching his head in that adorably bewildered way he has about him.
    "Then might we not use it upon these very books and cause the whole contents of this library to assault the despicable Coister when he returns to claim my person?" I suggested eagerly.
    My joy was doomed. "We could try," Pericles said. "But Renfrew Coister's slyer'n a frontier fox. He'll have a plain shielding spell up around him when he comes back, you mark my words. The books'll just bounce off."
    "And is that useless spell the best you've found?" I asked.

"Darlin', that spell's *all* I found," he replied. "Page forty-three of that blue-bound book over there." He nodded towards the table where my Greek text lay. Now I knew the full measure of our peril, for I had read that very cantrip while teaching myself the ins and outs of the Attic tongue and accepted it as little more than a linguist's whimsy. Who would use a true spell to illustrate a point in Greek grammar? In truth, the whole of it was scarcely more than five words, all told. The black handkerchief rose to my eyes once more.

My tears disturbed Pericles mightily. He held out a much-used wooden mortar for my inspection. A quantity of chalky green spheres rolled about within. "Don't take on so, 'Lilah. Look'ee here, I took the liberty of mixin' up the stuff as should be sprinkled on the thing that wants animatin'. No reason we couldn't try it anyhow, go down swinging, give old Coister a run for his—"

"Oh, Pericles, how could you imagine that such nonsense could aid us?" I wailed, striking the mortar from his hands. As the tiny spheres sailed across the study, I went on to demand how any man in his right mind could ever mistake a simple practice exercise in Greek like—here I confess to reciting it entire—for magic of true potency!

"And I suppose *you* are the arbiter general for what will pass muster as magic in these sorry days, eh, m'gel?" said a voice whose harsh and thunderous tones made Mamma's small chamber quake to the rafters.

"Well, if that don't beat all hollow," Pericles murmured, coming to lay protective hands upon my shoulders.

I gasped and crumpled the black handkerchief into a soggy ball. The sight I saw, dear Caroline, would have sent a lesser woman into an access of the vapors. For there, fresh from the portrait now an empty frame upon the wall, stood my great-grandpapa, Thomas Crafter.

He was splendid, if dated, in the finery of a previous age. His jowls were much redder, more wobbly, and far more overwhelming in person than in paint. He rolled one of the unused pellets from Pericles' animation spell between thumb and forefinger as he strode towards us. Three paces off, he took a deep, snuffly breath and bellowed:

"Blight and gall, is that the stench of a bloody American I smell? In *my* house?"

"Sir, please!" I exclaimed. "You are speaking of my betrothed."

"What?" The apparition drew near, nostrils flaring, as if he had the power to divine everything about me by scent alone. "One of my direct line to wed a—a—a double-damned, tea-dumping, tax-evading *traitor to the Crown?*"

To his credit, Pericles stepped between us and readily admitted to his nationality. "I heard tell of you, sir," he addressed Great-grandpapa boldly. "I know as how you don't take too kindly to us Yankees. But hate us or not, my mam always did say as how she heard you was a man of business first. I've got a proposition to lay afore you that I think you'll find mighty attractive."

Great-grandpapa screwed up his florid face most needlessly at Pericles' accent—an idiosyncratic locution which I am sure *you* will find charming, darling Caroline. Yet despite his obvious distaste for the American rendition of our common tongue, he showed a spark of interest in the words themselves. "A proposition?" he echoed. A sarcastic laugh made his pendulous lips bob like corks asea. "Do you not think that in my present state I might be a shade . . . *beyond* the temptations of commercial dealings?"

"No, sir," Pericles maintained. "You was born a New England man, like it or not, and it's said we raise 'em so's not even the grave can keep our merchants from a good deal."

This time Great-grandpapa's laugh was not so scornful. "Very well, pup," he said. "And what *is* this deal you would offer me?"

"A plain swap," Pericles said. "Your help for my life and the saving of hers." He made an heroic gesture indicating my modest self. "If you hate us Americans that powerful bad, here's your chance to have one right where you want 'im, and do your worst."

"Is that so?" Great-grandpapa seemed amused. "Well, well. Live long enough and you shall see everything, they say. Die long enough and you shall see more. A noble American, begad! One willing to lay down his life for Lady Fair. And for this, I can have your worthless hide?"

"Aye, sir, and free of tariff, too," Pericles riposted.

Now the laughter which shook Great-grandpapa's jowls was from the heart. "Strike me dead—deader—here's sport! Tell me, lad, when I collect my fee for services rendered, do you expect me to devour you, drink your blood, or merely flay you alive?"

Pericles remained steadfast. "Whatever takes your ghostly fancy, sir."

"Just so, just so." Great-grandpapa wiped away the phantom traces of merriment's tears. "Well, what takes my fancy, boy, is that you say what's brought you to a pass where you're so willing to give your life into these rough hands. Sharp, now!"

"Permit me," I interposed, and with dear Pericles' consent went on to explain, at some necessary length and with as much elegance as my state of trepidation might allow, the circumstances of our present situation. I ended by saying, "Pray succor us, dear Great-grandpapa. If not for the sake of that dread price which Pericles so willingly offers you, nor for the fact that his Crafter blood transcends his abhorred nationality, then for the memory of my dear mamma, your grandchild."

Great-grandpapa gave me a most peculiar look, then turned to Pericles and inquired, "You mean to marry her, lad? Take her back to America with you after you're wed?" And when Pericles assented, added—I know not why—"All that high gale and low dramatics . . . that's vengeance enough on the whole nation of 'em." Before I might ask his meaning, he went on to remark, "Coister, eh? It seems I recall the family—miserable excuses for magicians, all. Couldn't turn bread into toast unless they sold their souls to Satan first. And now this jumped-up scion of theirs wants to command Death himself? Haw!"

"Death," I repeated somberly, dabbing the last few tears from my eyes with the black kerchief. "And my person."

"*He* wants you, too?" I know not why Great-grandpapa was so puzzled by this intelligence. "Hasn't the poor bedlamite ever heard you *talk* for any length of—? No matter. He is also an American. It must be something in the water. Never mind. Come here, child. Let me see that black rag of yours. There is a scent to it I find strangely familiar, and if it is as I suspect . . ." It was a decidedly odd sensation when his hands brushed mine, that he might inspect the black kerchief, but no odder than the veritable storm of guffaws which racked his body once he had completed his examination of that item.

"Great-grandpapa, I fail to see the humor," I said severely.

"You would," he replied, when he was able. "America deserves you. Nay, don't pull that beldame's face with me, m'gel. You're a Crafter, right enough, and there's more than a touch of the Talent to you, unless my nose for such things betrays me. God helps them who help themselves, as your turncoat Ben Franklin would put it. Hark to me, you pair of boobies, and I'll give you the means you need to save your hides without paying me an inch of 'em."

He beckoned us close and whispered certain secrets into our ears before fading from our ken, nevermore to return, if I have anything to say in the matter.

So it was that when a horrid cry of "EUREKA!" reverberated through the house, followed by heavy footsteps galloping up the stairs, I was not quite so moved to distraction as one might have expected formerly. Nor was I at all undone when the study door burst open and Renfrew Coister stood triumphant before us, brandishing a small, exquisitely jointed wooden skeleton in his hand.

For you see, dear Caroline, I had used the black handkerchief and Great-grandpapa's counsel to procure us a little company.

"Put that down, Coister," said the gentleman in black. "I don't like men of your stripe taking liberties with my person."

The astounded Coister goggled at our visitor after the fashion of a herringmonger's best merchandise. His eyes darted from the wooden skeleton to the gentleman in black, perceiving in the fleshless fingers and eyeless sockets of each a distinct resemblance. "It cannot be!" he cried, shaking the articulated simulacrum until the limbs rattled. (Our caller, to his credit, gritted his teeth and by sheer force of Will did his best to remain unmoved by this harsh treatment.)

"Stop that, if you please," said Death (for it was He). "You can't hope to control me with *that* poppet now."

"Why not?" Coister demanded, at his least gracious. "I found it myself, in the bottom of her mother's old bridal chest. She had it disguised as copy of Jonathan Edwards' sermons, but a little prodding soon dislodged that threadbare glamour. I used the proper procedures, said all the right spells, and now it is mine! Control the symbol and you control the thing symbolized!"

"Not," said Death, "if someone gets to the thing symbolized first." He made a shallow bow in my direction, his bony fingers extended towards the black handkerchief. This I had, as per Great-grandpapa's instructions, spread out upon Mamma's table and dusted lightly with a mixture of dried herbs Pericles had gathered from the array of glass containers lining the attic shelves. "Precedence is precedence, Coister, old man. I believe that the lady has first dibs," the Grim Reaper remarked.

"What in Hell's own name are 'dibs'?" Renfrew Coister swore mightily.

O Caroline, it was as if the monumental nature of his blasphemy tore the world asunder! Pericles leapt forward, exhorting him to mind his tongue in the presence of a lady. Coister snarled even worse oaths and drew from the air itself a dagger wherewith to work mischief upon my unarmed cousin. Yet ere Pericles could notice the sharp welcome awaiting him at Coister's hand, the very firmament flashed, there was the overpowering scent of tansy, and in mid-leap Pericles Crafter vanished to be replaced by—

But you already know the manner of Lord Cranbrooke-Purslaine-Dewberry's irruption into Mamma's study, being as you were the agent thereof. *Dear* Caroline! How ingenious of you to use my spell of transportation to exchange the equivalent masses of Pericles and Dewy! Especially since Dewy had a sword.

Ah, could you but have seen the man's presence of mind! How many other youths of his delicate upbringing would have the acumen to perceive, immediately upon arrival *in medias* quite perilous *res*, that the wisest course of action was to draw his blade against Coister's own steel and, with a minimum of fuss, cause the reptile's head to part company with his shoulders?

Of course it did make rather a dreadful mess. The whole spectacle was too much for my already hectic nerves. I believe I heard Death remark, "Well, I'll just be clearing this away for you, shall I?" before I sank into blissful unconsciousness.

The rest you must know: How Papa and Stepmamma, freed from Coister's spells, returned to find me upon the parlor divan insensible, unchaperoned, and alone with Dewy. How, in simple charity, I made judicious application of Mamma's bezoar to free that noble gentleman's rational processes from all previous artificially induced attractions. How he and I both realized that, much as our unformed and juvenile affections had been so foolishly granted elsewhere, more mature considerations of Duty, Honor, and Mutual Respect conspired to but one possible conclusion:

Caroline, I married him.

Given what I have told you, I assume you will henceforth desist from sending me letters which can at best be called ill-thought and at worst, libellous. You can not deny that I have attempted to explain all ere this; no more can you deny that you have destroyed my previous missives unread, for your childish behavior whenever the post arrives has been noticed by the neighbors and placed you foursquare upon the barbed tongue of Gossip.

I am therefor sending you this letter in the hands of my trusted cousin, Pericles Crafter. Your breeding, if not any inborn sense of restraint, should prevent you from staging another tantrum while he is present to await a reply. I rely upon your usually sweet disposition to receive him kindly and cheer him up somewhat. Heaven alone knows why he has turned so sullen! I *gave* him the fusty old skeleton to take home to his "mam" the very day that Dewy and I announced our betrothal. Whatever more could the silly boy want?

I am sure you two will find some common cause in which to pass an idle hour of polite conversation. Why, think of it, Caroline! You might even have some distant kinship to the Crafter line, seeing as how it was your own Talent which allowed you to exchange Pericles for my dear, darling Dewy! Perhaps Cousin Pericles might be able to aid you in the development of this magical gift. May you learn, as I have, that education is its own reward.

It is my fondest wish that together you and he might persuade each other to look back upon the events of which I have written in a more rational, less romantically overwrought manner. Romance is all very well for the poets, but live in *America? Moi?*

Faithfully I do remain

   Your Sincere Friend,
   Lady Delilah Cranbrooke-Purslaine-Dewberry
   "The Alders"
   Huntingdonshire

England
Anno Domini 1807—1815

Perhaps there is something about having the Talent that attracts situations where it is needed. Today we would call that coincidence. In an earlier age: fate or the Hand of God. Whatever the reason, it makes life for most Crafters quite exciting, and can have other benefits as well.

WHOSE GHOST THERE?

by Christopher Stasheff

Anthea was ten years old when she met the ghost.

He was really a very nice ghost, everything considered—but Anthea wasn't in the mood to consider very much. She had just fled into the library to have a good cry, for Nanny had told her, rather sharply, that Mama had no time to listen to Anthea's whining just then. Poor Anthea positively dissolved, but Nanny scolded her sharply. "Away with you, aggravating child! When I've such a headache! You mustn't make such a noise!" So Anthea had run out and down the long, creaking stairs to the first room that had a door to it, which was of course the library, crying as though her heart would burst. She threw herself in among the cushions on the window seat, though they reeked of damp, and wept and wept and wept. With all her heart, she wished that her real Nanny hadn't died, and left her to the mercy of this . . . this stranger, this rude country girl who knew nothing of the proper behavior of a nanny, and cared nothing for Anthea's feelings. She wept on and on as the gloaming faded into a gloomy dusk, not caring that there wasn't a single candle lighted.

"Such a fuss," rumbled a hollow voice. "Why, it's enough to wake the dead."

Anthea gasped and sat bolt upright, instantly furious that anyone should intrude on her grief, blinking her tears away, or trying to—then gasping again as she saw the glimmering old suit of armor where surely there had been none before. And it lacked a helmet! Nothing there but its bare shoulders.

"Who are you?" she cried, looking about. "Why have you brought this pile of tin here?"

"This pile of tin, little mademoiselle, is myself," said the hollow voice—and so help her, the suit of armor stepped away from the wall and clanked over to the tall wing chair, where it sat!

Well, actually, it didn't clank, really. In fact, it didn't make a sound. It only *seemed* that it should have.

"Well, that's better," the hollow voice said. "I've little use for a watering pot. Tears increase the damp so, and my armor's apt enough to rust as it is."

"Why, how rude!" Anthea cried, anger drowning fear. "And how cruel of you, sir, to play such a trick upon a poor girl in her misery! Take yourself out of that suit of armor on the instant!"

"That I fear I cannot do, little mademoiselle," said the armor. "I died in it, so I'm stuck in it, if you follow my meaning— at least, until I find my head."

"Your head?" Anthea could only stare. Well, actually, no, she could have screamed, too—but at the moment, she was far too confused for that. "Why have you lost your head? Over what?"

"Over a battle, actually—though I could say, over a young lady."

"I knew it!" Anthea clapped her hands. "Whenever a proper gentleman has lost his head, there's romance in it! Poor fellow, did she not requite you?" Then she came to her senses, and indignation rose. "Why, this is quite unkind! Who are you, sir, and how dare you play such a prank upon a grieving maiden?" She was rather proud of that "grieving maiden"— she had thought it up herself, without any help from Mrs. Radcliffe or her books. "Come out of that suit of armor, and be done with this deception!"

"I fear it is no prank," said the hollow voice, "and as to who I am, why, I am Sir Roderick le Gos, Knight Bachelor, sworn to the service of the Duke of Kent."

"Le Gos?" Anthea frowned; the name tugged at her memory. Hadn't Father mentioned . . .

"Yes, little mademoiselle, le Gos is the old form of your own name, Gosling. It has transformed itself down through the centuries, but you and I are Gosses still."

"Centuries?" For the first time, a thrill of fear touched Anthea's heart. She quelled it sternly—after all, the chap seemed nice enough. "You can't mean . . . you aren't . . ."

"The family ghost? Yes, I am, actually. Not all that many can see me, though—your mama can't at all, of course, but she's not a Gos by blood. Even you will probably find that you can't see me in ten years or so. But for the moment, we can chat quite companionably—if you don't find my aspect too horrifying."

"Not a bit, for I can't find your aspect at all." Anthea frowned. "Where is it?"

"I carelessly misplaced it some centuries ago, a hundred miles or so to the north and west. It was during a battle against some border raiders, you see—Scots who had the audacity to object to being ruled by King Edward, don't you know, and thought to make his subjects suffer in his stead. It wasn't generally known, but a band of them had managed to catfoot it down from the North Country, bravely resisting temptation all along the way, so they could set up a broil entirely too close to London. They raided and retreated into the forest, where they seem to have made common cause with a band of outlaws, and came surging back out at the oddest moments to wreak havoc and plunder."

"And you had to go to chastise them?" Anthea asked, her eyes round.

"Not 'had to,' I suppose—but Lady Dulcie wouldn't think of having me offer for her, if I hadn't some bit of land and rank to my name. I suppose it's my own fault, in a way—I ignored a feud of long standing, between her family and mine. But the lady was beautiful, and our estates did border one another, and ancestral grievances seemed far less important to me than the lustre of her eyes. Still, there must have been in her some trace of the old malice that bred the ancestral quarrel, for she challenged me to prove my love by joining the expedition against these raiders. I went in the train of my lord the Duke. The Scots fell on us at dawn, and we fought briskly, I assure you."

"Who won?" Anthea asked, her eyes widening again.

"I can't say, actually—I was killed in the thick of the fighting. A scoundrel tripped my horse with the butt of his pike. I fell quite hard, but their blows were only heavy enough to dent and mar my armor. I lugged out my sword and forced my way up to my feet, but just then a great rawboned chap in a kilt swung a huge claymore at me, and the blasted sword rang on my helmet as though on a bell. The straps burst, and off it came. I cut back at him, of course, but he only stepped back till my blade had passed, then leaped in and swung again—and, well, there went my head. I don't really remember much of the rest of the battle, you'll understand—only a dazed sort of feeling that I wasn't all there, quite. There was a confused business of winding through the countryside on a cart, and of some doleful chanting in Latin. Then, finally, my mind cleared, and I found myself looking down at my own tombstone—out there, in the churchyard." Sir Roderick gestured toward the window.

"Why, how horrible!" Anthea exclaimed.

"No, not really—except for those few horrible seconds of blinding pain, but that was over soon enough. And I haven't been troubled with a sore throat since."

"I should think not," Anthea said.

"It is deucedly boring," Sir Roderick confessed, "and one can't really see too well, without a head."

"Can't you get it back?" Anthea asked.

"I suppose I can, though I haven't had much luck thus far. You see, they brought my body back for burial in the family plot, but my head was lost amidst the carnage on the field of battle. I'm still searching for it, of course, but I can't leave the house unless I'm haunting a member of the family—bound by ties of blood and land, d' you see, and none of my kinfolk have ever gone far enough north for me to come near the scene of that battle."

Moved, Anthea cried, "I promise to go there, as soon as I'm old enough! Only you'll have to tell me where it is."

"Would you really? Why, how good of you!" Sir Roderick didn't mention that she probably wouldn't have enough money to go to London, let alone to the battlefield, unless she married—

in which case, she wasn't likely to have the freedom. "Don't go without an escort, though—these Scots are great rough hairy brutes, you know."

"Oh, I understand they've improved recently—quite civilized, Papa says." The reminder of her parents clouded her brow.

Sir Roderick noticed. "Bit of a rum show, eh? To have to leave London and come to this rambling old manor."

"Yes, it's really quite unpleasant! . . . Oh, forgive me! I hadn't meant any disrespect for your family home."

"Yours, too, my dear, though you've only just found it— and it's really quite all right. Windhaven is quite thoroughly run-down, I assure you—not what it used to be at all. Even at its best, though, I confess it did become a bit tedious after the first hundred years. I've taken the opportunity to travel to London with the family, you see, not to mention Bath and . . ."

"London?" Anthea stared. "Was it really you, then, who made those odd noises in the night?"

"Quite so, and I've known you since you were an infant— charming, perfectly charming. I could have stayed with Trudy— your Aunt Gertrude, don't you know—but I thought I'd better come along to the old manor, and see that you were well enough cared for."

"Oh, but I'm not at all! Nanny died, and they hired this horrible, ignorant stranger in her stead, and the housekeeper and the rest of the staff are so tiresome, I could swear they hate children, and . . ." Her griefs came to mind again, and Anthea's eyes swam in tears.

"Now, now, it's not quite so bad as it might seem," Sir Roderick murmured, reaching out an armored hand—but all Anthea felt was a chill on her cheek. "Life's always worth living, don't you know, if only because it might go better in times to come. There will be a troupe of young men dancing attendance on you some day, though you may feel no one pays attention to you now."

"They don't, they truly don't!" Anthea cried. "Mama cares nothing for my feelings, and hardly ever sees me—indeed, at times I think she wishes I weren't there!"

"Painful, bitterly painful," the knight agreed. "Still, you mustn't be too hard on your mother, little mademoiselle— she's had a dreadful disappointment, you know."

"Well, yes," Anthea admitted, "but she doesn't seem to have much time for anyone or anything except melancholy, at the moment."

"Quite so," Sir Roderick agreed, "though I thought she made it quite clear she cares inordinately about her social circle."

"Oh yes, she does carry on so about the loss of her wonderful friends and gay parties!" They had been lost with the Goslings' London house.

"She has cause to rail against the bitter fortune that has consigned her to the country life," Sir Roderick pointed out.

"She would, if her own extravagances hadn't been so great a part of that misfortune!" Anthea returned. She had come rather early to that age at which a girl can find any number of things wrong with her mother, especially one who had been so distant as her own. "And really, she shouldn't call this wonderful house a 'decaying old manse,' or go on about its being so far from the lights and salons of London!"

It was in Kent, actually.

"Decaying old manse!" huffed Sir Roderick, offended. "Does she really? Well, well, it has been let go of recent years. Your father hasn't truly cared very much about it."

"Papa has taken it very badly," Anthea stated. Indeed, Papa seemed to blame himself for Mama's loss. Not that he needed to—she was blaming him quite enough for them both already.

"But it was he who paid all that money, and promised all those sums that he didn't have," Sir Roderick pointed out.

"Never mind that it was Mama who ran up all the bills with her modiste, and insisted on so many servants, and on redecorating the town house, and holding their share of parties and soirees!"

"Don't mind it at all," Sir Roderick returned, "for your father called in the tailor every month in his own right."

"Yes, because Mama kept after him to keep his wardrobe up to the latest fashion, of course, and carried on so about being ashamed to be seen with him, if he didn't."

"There's some truth in that," Sir Roderick admitted, "but certainly no one had to urge your father to run up such enormous gambling debts, least of all your mother."

"That *is* true," Anthea conceded.

"True? The truth of it is that neither of them cared a fig for keeping an eye on their expenses, or to trouble themselves with concern that their expenditures might outstrip their income," Sir Roderick said. "Not that I'm blaming them, mind you—I never much thought to look at the money myself. More concerned with honor and chivalry, don't you know—but it's for a man to provide for his wife and babes, eh wot?"

"The land does that," Anthea muttered, but somewhat uncertainly.

"True enough, but you must take care of the land before it will take care of you—and not take out of it more than it has to give."

Which was exactly what Papa had tried to do, of course—and the long and the short of it had been that they had had to sell the town house, and where could they live after that?

Only in the rambling old manor in which Grandpapa had grown up. And Papa hadn't wished to be there for more than the occasional visit, and hadn't tended to anything that fell into disrepair—so, now that they needed it, the big old house was dank and ramshackle.

"But the land has a great deal to give," the ghost assured her. "Not just in corn and cabbage and tenants' rents, but in the beauty of field and hill and woodlot."

"I haven't seen it," Anthea said shortly.

"But you must!" the ghost said. "Not tonight, of course, for it's raining, but on a bright and sunny morning, or in the glow of a summer's evening. When you step into budding woods and find it thronged with birdsong, when you spy a fox peeking out from a covert, when you come upon a meadow filled with wildflowers, you will find the country is not so bad a place to be."

"It sounds lovely," Anthea said, caught up in his enthusiasm.

"That it is—but not on a gloomy day of rain and wind. Though that too has its charms, if you're snug and dry, before a warm fire."

Anthea made a face and gestured at the cold hearth. "Would I dare to light a fire there?"

"Of course, for the flue still draws well, and is reasonably clean for want of use—and the birds' nests have fallen for the season, so there's little chance of a chimney fire. If you'd set a log on, I'll show you."

Anthea was somewhat puzzled, but she did as Sir Roderick asked, slipping off the window seat and crossing to place a log between the andirons. The bark crumbled in her hands. "I wonder how long this has been here."

"Well, if it's a bit gone to rot, it will light all the sooner." The ghost clanked up beside her and knelt, holding its hands out over the logs.

Anthea followed its movements with her eyes. "How is it that you clank now, when you didn't before? I thought ghosts had no substance."

"We don't, but I wouldn't wish to startle you by coming up in total silence, then speaking at your shoulder." A silver glow appeared around Sir Roderick's gauntlets and spread out to envelop the log. It turned golden; then flames began to dance. Sir Roderick withdrew his hands, and the glow died—but the flicker of a burning log remained.

"Oh!" Anthea clapped her hands. "How marvelous! Are you truly magical?"

"Truly, though limited—I'd no teacher, you see, so it was rather hard to make use of the talent. Took me sixty years to learn that little trick, though rattling chains and slamming doors came somewhat more easily."

Anthea leaned toward him, but felt only a chill and shivered. "The fire's glow does make the room more pleasant." Then she shook her head in irritation. "But there's nothing to *do*!"

"Oh, there are games to pass the time." Sir Roderick stood and paced over to a table nearby. "There's backgammon here, you see, and chess."

Anthea made a face. "Chess is boring. Besides, I don't know how to play it."

"Really? I assure you, you'll find it exciting enough once you've learned."

"I've no desire to."

"Oh, come now! Just to indulge a new friend, eh? It's been years since I've had a game—decades, in fact."

With surprise, Anthea realized that she really had made a friend, though a very unlikely one. Hard on that came fright that she might lose him and be completely alone again—except for Mama and Papa, who scarcely noticed her, and that poisonous Nanny and the chilly staff. She rose with a theatrical sigh and came over to the table. "Oh, well, just to please you, then."

"Truly? I'm ever so grateful!" Sir Roderick pointed at the table, and a drawer slid open. A chess piece floated out of it to settle on the checkerboard inlaid in the wood.

Anthea stared, amazed, and feeling just the slightest *frisson* of fear.

"Dreadfully sorry," Sir Roderick apologized, "but I can't really grasp them, you know. Can't handle anything much over a pound, either. Well, then, this piece is called a pawn, and there are eight of them to a side . . . ."

"How lovely!" Anthea picked up the miniature carving, delighted at the warm darkness of the rosewood. "Is it a medieval soldier, then?"

"Yes, and quite authentic, too, which is why it's just the teeniest bit battered. It can only move forward one pace at a time, unless it's fighting another pawn, in which case it moves diagonally ahead." Sir Roderick pointed again, and another warrior floated out of the drawer, armored like the ghost himself, though with a visored helm. It sat astride a rearing horse. "This one is a knight, and he's the hardest of all, because his horse can jump over anything in front of him—but it always lands to the side, you see."

The miniature knight leaped off the board, sailed two spaces forward, then swerved to the side and settled again. "Like a capital L," Sir Roderick explained. "And this is a bishop . . ."

Anthea listened, enthralled. It made so much more sense when he explained it! Though it helped that the pieces looked like what they really were, not just little knobs and rods. She settled down to make a pleasant evening of it, after all.

They played every day after that, with the ghost carefully coaching Anthea in tactics and gambits. Finally she realized that he was deliberately letting her win two games out of three, and demanded he start playing to win. He claimed that he did, but she was still suspicious of how often she came up victorious.

For Sir Roderick became her great friend, of course. In winter, he strolled out with her in the very earliest morning, as visible by day as by night (though only to her), and showed her the beauties of newly fallen snow and the lacework it made of the branches in the woodlot. She would have thought it a dreary waste otherwise, but with him she was able to see beauties that she never would have discovered otherwise. And she had need of it, for Mama, in despair at having missed a London Christmas, pined away and succumbed to pneumonia, dying between New Year's and Twelfth Night. When Anthea saw her eyes close for the last time, and Nanny managed to pry her away from the lifeless clay, she dashed out of the room and ran pell-mell down the stairs and into the library, where she threw herself down among the cushions on the window seat and wept and wept. She must have cried herself to sleep, for of a sudden, she woke with a start and found herself in darkness. For a moment, the fear was so sharp as almost to make her cry out; then she was able to make out the familiar shapes of tables and chairs, and the racks of dusty old volumes on the walls, by a faint glow that somehow permeated the room. Then that glow brightened and coalesced, drawing in on itself till it assumed the familiar form of her armored and headless friend. "I had to watch over you, you see," Sir Roderick said, almost apologetically. "I couldn't have you waking alone in the dark."

"Oh, Sir Roderick! Oh, thank you!" Anthea leaped up and dashed to her friend, throwing her arms about him—and right through him, and the chill bit into her. She drew back, and the tears started afresh. "Or, Sir Roderick, it's terrible! Mama has quite pined away—and has died!"

"Yes, Anthea," the ghost said quietly, "I know."

"You know? But how . . ." Then Anthea's eyes widened, and she clapped a hand over her mouth—but her thoughts fairly shouted, *Of course! You knew the moment she came forth from her body—for she's a ghost now, too, isn't she?*

"She is," Sir Roderick confirmed.

Anthea was so agitated that she didn't even notice that the ghost had read her thoughts.

"But she hasn't lingered, I'm afraid," Sir Roderick said. "She was a good woman underneath it all, and departed almost immediately for Heaven. She hadn't a fallen head to hold her here, you see."

"No, she had . . . Oh, I mustn't say it!"

"No, you must," Sir Roderick said gently. "'A child who needed her,' is that what you were going to say? Yes, she had, little lady, and she misses you quite sorely—I know, for she's telling me that now, even as we speak."

"Oh, is she truly?" Anthea cried.

"Yes, though she won't be able to do it for long, and not very often—and only another ghost can hear her. When she realized she was about to die, she repented of her silliness in mourning her London life, for then she discovered how precious life had been, even though it wasn't exactly to her taste." The ghost sighed, and Anthea somehow knew he would have been shaking his head, if he'd had one. "Of course, it was too late then, for she'd let the sickness take far too firm a hold on her. She never knew how much you meant to her, Anthea, until suddenly she found you beyond her reach. Now she aches for you, child, and will surely do all she can to comfort and reassure you from where she is."

"Oh, Sir Roderick!" Anthea threw herself into his arms, not minding the chill, snuggling down against the upholstery of the big old wing chair which was all she could feel, and she wept and wept again, in the insubstantial embrace of a ghost.

Papa almost turned into a spectre himself, after that. He became wan and melancholy, and seemed to take very little notice of the life about him. Alarmed, Anthea took every chance she could to evade Nanny—not hard, for the woman ignored her as much as possible—and crept in to be with Papa, and pay what attentions she could, for fear that he, too, might leave her for the buffering of death—and she must have succeeded to some extent, for, though he didn't seem to take much interest in life, he didn't die, either.

It was a strain on her, and she probably couldn't have borne it if it hadn't been for the attentions of Sir Roderick. She had a great deal of lost and lonely time, for Nanny seemed to feel that if she wasn't causing trouble, there was no need to bother with her—she'd far rather drink Father's port with the cook—and Papa wouldn't take much cosseting before he would send her away, so that he might be alone to wallow in self-pity. Hurt, Anthea would wander off to the library and try to nap. There she whiled away the time till evening with napping and reading, for there were a great many books in the library. It was fortunate she did, for Papa either wasn't willing to spend money on a governess, or never thought of it—and in the evenings, Sir Roderick would guide her studies, suggesting books to her, and discussing them after she'd read them. He insisted on a half-hour of mathematics every night, and a deal of science and history and geography, too—but he made it all so interesting that it was almost fun. It never occurred to Anthea to wonder how he knew so much that hadn't been discovered until after he had died, or even that he knew so much of books, when most medieval knights had never learned to read.

But there was leisure aplenty, too, and her grief slackened and sank beneath a rising tide of delight in the brave new world about her. In spring, Sir Roderick showed her the new foals and calves, and pointed out hidden nests with half-a-dozen gaping beaks for mother birds to feed. He showed her a precious little meadow filled with wildflowers, which she would never have found by herself. It was almost as beautiful by moonlight as by day—and she knew, for she came out there herself the next morning, and found it even more enchanting with the day flowers opening their faces to the sun. In summer, he taught her to lie lazily on a hillside making fanciful images of the cloud-shapes above her, to rejoice in the fury of the lightning and the thunder (provided she was safe indoors), and to watch for the Wee Folk to dance beneath the moon. (She never saw them, of course, but he did point out the rings where they'd been dancing.) Then, in autumn, he showed her the glory of the golden wood and the rustling leaves, the cleverness and prudence of the squirrels as they hoarded nuts, the peaceful vista of fields after reaping, and finally, the tucking-down as the little creatures composed themselves for the long winter's sleep, and the geese passed overhead with distant honking in their pointed formation, going south to fabled lands of wonder for the winter.

And always, there was chess—in the evenings, in the boring afternoons of rainy days, and by the fire in the winter. She became so adept at the game that she could handily beat him— thought she was never sure he hadn't let her, and forced him to win a few out of spite. She did wonder how he could see the pieces without a head—but then, she wondered how he could see her, too.

There was less time for that as she grew older, though, for Papa didn't tend to the estate, but let it go as it would, so the land yielded less and less as the years went by, for want of proper management, and the tenants had less money to pay. He wouldn't lower the rents, of course, so those who could left for better conditions, or for fancied jobs in London—and those who stayed were always fearfully behind in their rents.

Then Papa remarried that horrible woman, and Anthea's world came crashing down, what was left of it.

She couldn't understand what Papa saw in her, aside from money—though there did seem to be plenty of that. He called in a tailor and was soon resplendent in new clothes—and off to London with his new wife. The woman made it clear from the first (after the wedding) that she wanted nothing to do with her stepdaughter—so Anthea stayed behind at Windhaven, heartsick and lonely. Sir Roderick consoled her and managed to boost her spirits to the point at which she began to take an active interest in the estate. Within a few months she wished she hadn't, for Papa paid it no more attention than before, merely sending one of his wife's men to oversee the farm—and Anthea became certain the steward was skimming most of what little profit remained. Sir Roderick confirmed this, though he could bring her no proof but his own witness, which wouldn't have been much use in court, so she had to let it pass, and do without a new dress, or new curtains, or repairs to the roof. The servants left as the income ran out, and neither Papa nor his wife showed the slightest interest in putting money into Windhaven, so more and more, she took care of the house by herself, cooking and straightening up as much as she could, though she knew better than to try to clean more than a few rooms by herself. It would have been intolerably lonely without Sir Roderick.

Then Papa had some sort of horrible argument with That Woman, perhaps occasioned by the size of his gambling debts and her extravagances—but the long and the short of it was that he came back to Windhaven, chastised and beaten, and lapsed instantly into melancholy.

Anthea wasn't disposed toward any but the most chilly conduct toward him, but by and by began to pity him, for he was so very doleful. Her old fear of having both parents pine away reasserted itself, and she took to showing him some slight kindness, attempting to chat with him over tea—a very new ceremony, but one which served nicely. He reacted little, or not at all, at first, but she persevered, and gradually he emerged from his dejection and began to respond. Little by little, with Sir Roderick's advice, she managed to coax him into showing some sort of interest in life again, and Papa repaid her attentions with growing fondness and eventually came out of his grief enough to value her company. They played long games of chess in the evenings, and he taught her to play whist, piquet and several other card games, though never very well, and began to enjoy her conversation as she grew older and more knowledgeable. She was amazed at the depth of her own reaction to his attention—she had thought she would never even be able to forgive his neglect, but actually found an almost pathetically eager surge of delight. She did her best to control it, but some of her warmth doubtless showed.

Anthea managed to come by the occasional newspaper, and brought it home to read to him, asking him to explain the bewildering variety of events—for example, who was this Napoleon, and why was everyone so concerned about him? Questions of this sort drew answers of surprising energy from her father, and slowly, little by little, he began to take an interest in the world around him again.

It was too late, though, for the damp and chill of the old house had settled into his bones, and he died when Anthea was only seventeen. Once again, Sir Roderick consoled her through her grief, and brought her out to life and light again—only to have her confronted with a heap of bills that she could not possibly pay. Papa's wife, it seemed, had beaten him to the grave, but not by much, and had left her own stack of debts, which were added to his—so Anthea was sole heiress to a dearth of assets, and a mountain of debts.

In desperation, she turned to Sir Roderick, her only source of support, and he took a midnight flit about the neighborhood to discover an honest and capable solicitor. In the hands of that good man, Anthea discovered that, as a minor, she could not agree to anything legally binding, and therefore could not be held liable, as long as there was a relative to whom such decisions could be referred. It was then that she remembered Aunt Trudy.

Aunt Trudy was Papa's sister, somewhat estranged by irritation with Mama, whom, she felt, should have taken far better care of Papa than she had. When Papa had moved to the country and lapsed into melancholy, he had broken contact with her completely—he had not even learned of her husband's demise, or her sons' and daughters' marriages. Now, though, apprised of circumstances by the solicitor, Aunt Trudy, really Lady Broch, descended on Windhaven to weep buckets of tears at her brother's grave, every one of them sincere, then to press Anthea to her matronly bosom, which was amazingly soft and warm—and something inside Anthea that had been knotted tight, loosened, and she found herself weeping like a watering pot in a real, flesh-and-blood embrace for the first time since she was ten, while Aunt Trudy made consoling noises and soothed her, then put her to bed.

Then Aunt Trudy and the solicitor, between them, tackled the pile of bills and the horror of Papa's books, or lack of them, and called the steward to account. The long and the short of it was that he was let go and sued for monies owing. In his stead a reliable under-steward was appointed from Aunt Trudy's estates, inherited from her husband, Lord Brock. Suddenly, the old manse was under repair, the fields were put in order, and Aunt Trudy was sweeping Anthea away with her to London, just in time for the Season.

London was a mad, exciting whirl as it appeared from the window of Aunt Trudy's carriage. Brief as their acquaintance was, Anthea felt no hesitation at letting her aunt see just how delighted she was with the metropolis. "Oh, Auntie! The Tower itself! Oh, it seems an age since I saw it!"

"An age it has been," her aunt returned. "You were only a child when you left, and you are a young woman now."

'A young woman'—no one had called her that before. The term was sobering—but not for long. Everything looked so much smaller than she remembered it.

"But of course," Aunt Trudy said, "you were somewhat smaller then, yourself."

The enthusiasm and gaiety of the return buoyed Anthea through her introduction to the staff, and particularly Hester, her very own lady's maid—newly promoted for the occasion, and under the constant and unrelenting scrutiny of Aunt Trudy's Abigail.

"Don't fret," Anthea assured her, glad to have someone as nervous as she herself. "If you do make any mistakes, I shan't tell."

Neophyte or not, Hester knew the proprieties, and Anthea had a hot bath to wash off the dust of travel, and a decent dress, not too far from her own size, appropriate for dinner. She felt awkward and gauche under the severe eyes of the butler, the footman, and the maid—but Aunt Trudy put her at ease in minutes, by making quite obvious her delight in having someone to share her meals with again. Anthea hoped she was sincere. It was terrible to think, but she hoped it wasn't mere politeness.

Then, finally, she was in her nightdress and alone in her darkened room, her chocolate cup empty beside her bed, the room shadowed by the flickering light of her candle—and the strangeness began to make itself felt. Surprising as it was, Anthea realized she was longing for Windhaven. "Oh, Sir Roderick," she whispered, "if only I could speak with you now!"

"Why, then, do, Miss Anthea," said the familiar old hollow voice.

Anthea started, nearly leaping out of her skin. "What . . . ? Sir Roderick!"

The suit of armor gleamed in the shadows by her wardrobe. "Why, poor child! I've frightened you. Forgive me—I thought that surely you would remember that I could travel to haunt the family wherever they went."

"Of . . . of course." Anthea sat up a little straighter in bed. "Yes, how foolish of me! I should have remembered! Oh, Sir Roderick, it is so very good to see you!"

"And you, dear child. Surely you did not think I would lose your company if I could prevent it."

"Oh, you are so good! But . . . Sir Roderick, I am no longer a child."

"Of course not, my dear." The suit of armor came over to sit on her bed. "That is why I addressed you so. When you were a child, I called you 'little mademoiselle'—so now, when you are grown, I feel free to call you 'my child.' After all, we are related."

"And I was so grateful for the courtesy then," Anthea laughed. "Shall I be grateful to be called 'child' soon?"

"Yes, and that day is not far off, I believe. Still, I'll call you 'Miss Anthea' till then. May I advise, though, that you only *think* the words when you address me, rather than speaking aloud? I assure you, I'll hear you just as easily, and the servants might wonder at hearing you speak with a man in your own chamber."

"Oh yes, of course!" Anthea immediately shifted her conversation to thought only. *I think I can sleep well now, knowing that you are near.*

"Why, thank you, Miss Anthea. Are you sleepy, then?"

Well . . . not very.

"Yes, I know—discovering my presence was a bit of a shock. Might I suggest a game of chess, then?"

The very thing! Anthea scrambled out of bed, careful to keep her nightdress down, and ran to take out the chess set she had brought with her. She scrambled back into bed and opened the board, laying out the pieces.

The candle burned down before she had him checkmated, but the glow from his armor was quite enough.

There followed a positive whirlwind of shopping, and Anthea came home in quite a giddy mood for the first three days. Aunt Trudy seemed to be enjoying herself just as much as Anthea was; she confided, over dinner, that the shops and modistes had all become new to her again, just by watching Anthea's delight in them.

The next day, Aunt Trudy embarked on a round of visits, calling on friends with Anthea and seeing her properly introduced. She met a dozen girls of her own age or nearly, and if some of them were calculating in their assessment and attempted to patronize her, the others more than made up for it with their quick and ready warmth. Half a dozen of them came to Aunt Trudy's to help celebrate Anthea's birthday on the twentieth of April, just before the beginning of the Season— and the next day, the invitations began arriving. It seemed that Aunt Trudy's friends included several of the patronesses of Almack's, and Anthea had passed their inspection. She was about to be launched.

Her first ball was to be at Lady Fortrain's. She spent hours with Hester, dressing and powdering and primping, and was too nervous to eat more than a few mouthfuls at dinner. Aunt Trudy was quite impossible, urging dish after dish upon her with a roguish twinkle in her eye. However, she more than made up for it by whisking her away wrapped in an ermine-trimmed cloak, into the carriage and off to the ball. Anthea felt quite like Cinderella, and had half a mind to accuse Aunt Trudy of being a fairy godmother. If she didn't, it was half because she feared her aunt might confess to the truth of it. However, she did remember herself enough to say, "Oh, Aunt, how can I ever repay you for this!"

"You may reimburse me when your lands have begun to yield a profit again. For the present, you may gladden my heart with your own joy."

Anthea looked stricken. "But, Aunt—to repay Papa's debts, and undo the damage of neglect, will take eons!"

"Only decades, my dear, and I look forward to a weekend at your house, when it has been suitably restored."

"Oh, of course, whenever you wish! But, Aunt . . ."

"It is only a loan," Aunt Trudy said firmly, "and you are not to trouble your head about it. Affairs of this sort are the privilege of . . . maturity. Yours are flirting and laughing and filling a house with music. I pray you, do it well."

Anthea gave up and flung her arms about her aunt, knowing her generosity for the charity it was, and loving her all the more for not admitting it. "But I will never, ever, be able to repay your kindness!"

"Then you will have to repay it to some other young thing who needs it." Aunt Trudy whisked out a handkerchief and dabbed at Anthea's cheeks. "There now, child." And she gave her a quick peck on the cheek.

Lady Fortrain's mansion was lit up like Guy Fawkes' Night. The stream of carriages passing in front of the door was in almost constant motion, each pausing for a few minutes to discharge its passengers, then moving away to find a place to wait. Coming into that line was another matter, of course—drivers cracked whips and cursed at one another as they jockeyed for position. But inside the carriage, Aunt Trudy sat serenely and calmly, while Anthea fluttered back and forth from window to aunt, exclaiming, "Oh, how lovely! So many lights! So many beautiful dresses!"

"You don't remark or seem to remark upon the people, Anthea," she was corrected.

"Oh, how can I, Aunt? They're too small to see!"

"Don't fret yourself, you'll soon be close enough to view their faces quite well, I assure you."

She was indeed, close enough to face the redoubtable wall of respectability represented by Lord and Lady Fortrain, who greeted her formally and Aunt Trudy warmly. It was strange how their formidable aspects dropped when they began to chat with Trudy.

Freed from the constraint of her aunt's presence, Anthea joined a gaggle of her new friends, to giggle and glance at the gentlemen.

"Oh, do look at young Lord Melchoir, Anthea! They say he has twenty thousand a year, and squanders it all in *utter* dissipation!"

Anthea stared. "One would never think it, to look at him. He looks quite the picture of health and virtue!"

Ermingarde gave a peal of laughter. "Virtue! The only virtue he may have is whatever he steals! Yet they say that Lord Delbert, who makes every attempt to appear the absolute rake, is actually quite honorable in private!"

"Oh?" Anthea smiled. "And how would they know of his private affairs?"

"My dear, affairs can never be truly private! Except, perhaps, for those of Mr. Crafter, there."

"Oh, but he is not truly a gentleman!" Jane objected. "Truly, he may be quite wealthy—but not a cent of it was he born with—it is all come from trade!"

"Nevertheless," Sophie said, "he comes of good family. His cousin is a baronet, after all."

"But such a *distant* cousin, my dear! And this Crafter is actually from the Colonies! America, of all places! Really, one cannot but think he would be more at home in moccasins and a hat made of some small animal than in cutaway and breeches!"

Anthea eyed the young man in question, seeing blond hair with a surprisingly dark skin, standing by himself, quite self-contained, but with an air of interest that seemed somehow forced.

"American? Is he a spy, then? They favor Napoleon?"

"No, by some irony, he served in Her Majesty's Navy, they say—but one never knows, does one? After all, it has been only years since we began the war with the French! If you can call the current situation a war," Ermingarde said as an afterthought.

There was something vaguely sinister about the young man, Anthea thought. "Is he the only eligible bachelor who is not leading a secret life of dissipation?"

Her friends giggled, and the conversation turned to speculation as to who would dance with whom. It was short-lived, however, as one by one, the young men came over to bow and praise, and ask for the compliment of a dance. Before long, Anthea's friends were whirling away to the music, each with several dances already bespoken. Anthea watched and smiled, and tried not to feel too envious.

"Miss Gosling."

Anthea looked up, startled. "Lady Fortrain!"

The imposing dowager forced a slight smile. "May I present Mr. Roman Crafter, late of the exotic lands of the East."

The young man bowed, and Anthea suppressed a slight shiver. So close, she found that he fairly exuded an air of worldliness which she found more repulsive than attractive.

"Your aunt has told me of your interest in geography," Lady Fortrain went on, "so I thought you might wish to learn of Mr. Crafter's experiences in India."

"India! Oh yes, Lady Fortrain, thank you! Really, Mr. Crafter, how did you come to India?"

The grave young man gazed directly into her eyes with such a deep and probing look that Anthea had to suppress a shiver. "It was in the course of private curiosity, Miss Gosling, though it came to be on the King's business."

Lady Fortrain smiled benevolently and moved on. Anthea rather wished she hadn't; there was something decidedly unsettling about Mr. Crafter. Perhaps the steady gaze of those large, surprisingly light gray eyes, so fitting beneath the mane of ash-blond hair—or perhaps it was his excessive leanness, or the bronze hue of his skin. All in all, he gave the impression of someone left out in the sun too long, which he may well have been. Most probably, though, it was the aura of almost fanatical intensity that seemed to surround him like a cloak.

But he was immaculately dressed, his neckcloth pristine and precisely folded, and she certainly had his undivided attention. "I confess to puzzlement, Mr. Crafter. How could private curiosity turn to royal affairs?"

"By the press of events, Miss Gosling. But really, may we dance while I tell you of it? I should very much like to."

"Why, thank you." Anthea took Crafter's arm and stepped out onto the floor, repressing a shudder at his touch. As they began to move through the paces of the dance, his eyes never left hers, and to ward off his intensity, she pressed. "Do go on, Mr. Crafter. What were these events that took you to India?"

"That was a matter of trade, Miss Gosling, as much as of curiosity."

She was surprised at his boldness in so openly admitting to being in trade. He seemed almost brazen, in fact. "Trade, Mr. Crafter? Has your family no land, then?"

"Why, yes, a considerable amount, and they are ever acquiring more, I understand—though it's rather inaccessible to me, being in America."

Brazen indeed! Would he proceed to tell her to which spymaster he reported? And why did he make no mention of his English relations?

"I was chosen to serve in His Majesty's Navy," Crafter explained, "and given very little choice in the matter."

"You mean you were—impressed?" She was shocked—and somewhat thrilled.

"My father was, actually—we were passengers aboard a ship bound for Jamaica. The captain of the man-of-war that overhauled us thought Father would do splendidly as an able-bodied seaman, never mind that he was en route to represent the Government of the United States in a Crown colony—and thought I would do as a powder monkey, being only ten at the time."

"A common seaman?" Anthea gasped.

"Not willingly, I assure you. I was privileged to take part in the battle of Trafalgar, though I can't claim to have seen anything but the powder supplies and tunnels, and the wounded. Through a rather unique set of circumstances, I was fortunate enough to be able to contact some relations of mine . . . ."

"Not a baronet, by chance."

"Ah, you have an ear for the gossip! Yes, I've a cousin of that rank, though it was the squire in Ireland who bought a commission for me. That protected me from the worst of the life of a foremast hand, and gave me a pittance to save in the bargain. I sold out when I attained my majority, repaid my cousin, and invested in the British East India Company."

Anthea found it interesting to note that there was an Irish cousin that gossip did not speak of—but then, one frequently didn't speak of the Irish. "How did this lead you to India, though?"

"I desired to be sure my money was being put to good use."

"To be sure of it! Really, sir, if one cannot trust the East India Company to increase one's money, whom can one trust?"

"No one, I begin to think—for the mismanagement and nest-feathering I witnessed were quite disheartening. I determined to take a hand in affairs, and managed to impose some discipline—but in the process, I became an informal envoy to a rajah's court."

"A rajah!" Anthea breathed, all agog.

"A small one," Crafter temporized, "though his palace was large enough, and had the requisite peacocks to announce visitors—and if I can't speak of piles of jewels to either hand, I can at least assert that his wives did seem to be entrusted with a substantial portion of his capital."

Anthea laughed, almost in spite of herself, and Crafter responded with a smile of amusement. "The Rajah, it seemed, wished to forestall the incursions of the Company by treating directly with the governor-general, who is at least nominally in the service of Crown as well as commerce—so there I was, a subject of His Majesty and an emissary to him, one and the same."

Anthea laughed again, and would have liked to ask him more, but the music ended, and Crafter stepped back, releasing her hand with a bow. "Thank you for the dance, Miss Gosling. May I look forward to repeating the pleasure?"

"I . . . I think perhaps the third gavotte." Anthea examined her programme carefully, which was rather difficult, as it was completely blank. However, she inscribed Mr. Crafter's name, then curtseyed and said, "Thank you for your fascinating conversation, Mr. Crafter. I shall look forward to more accounts of your exotic adventures."

Crafter smiled and bowed again, then left her—and her friends flocked around immediately.

"Really, the Man of Mystery himself, Anthea! Did he tell you of murderous deeds and mysterious doings?"

"Is he as ominous as they say, Anthea?"

"You laughed quite well, Anthea. Was he truly amusing?"

Then everyone fell silent at the approach of three gentlemen, and someone drew breath rather sharply, for at their head came Lord Delbert, his eyes sparkling as brightly as the diamond in his neckcloth, crowned with a mane of raven hair, his bright blue eyes seeking out Anthea as he bowed. "Miss Gosling! May I have the pleasure?"

Her friends stared as Delbert led her out onto the floor, and Anthea thought he must surely hear the pounding of her heart.

"Where have you been hiding, Miss Gosling?" Lord Delbert asked. "You have never graced London before."

Anthea gave a little laugh. "Not since I was ten, your lordship. We have been living in Kent in the interim."

"How naughty of your parents, to hide away so dazzling a beauty!"

Anthea's face flushed with pleasure, though she told herself it was only empty flattery. Still, she knew that she was pretty enough, and that the light of the massed candles showed the auburn glints in her hair to their best advantage. "La, sir! You must not speak so!"

"No, I must, for beauty deserves tribute. Do you remember much of the town, Miss Gosling?"

"Only Saint Paul's and Saint James's, Mr. Delbert."

"Then you must allow me to show you more of it! There are such brave sights, Miss Gosling. We must begin with the Park . . ."

By the time the dance ended, he had claimed three more, and had cajoled her promise to allow him to call on the morrow and take her driving in his phaeton.

On the way home, Anthea chattered and exclaimed without pause. Aunt Trudy listened with a fond smile, prompting her with a question whenever she seemed to be slackening. She was only just beginning to run down as they came home. When they had come in, though, and the footmen had divested them of their cloaks and the maid had brought them Cambric tea, Anthea finally realized that Aunt Trudy had been much more quiet than was her wont. "Did some aspect of my evening trouble you, Aunt? My dances with Mr. Crafter, perhaps?"

"Crafter? Pooh!" Aunt Trudy waved him away. "A pleasant enough gentleman, certainly, though contaminated with the aroma of trade. There is some justification for him in the rumor that he enjoys it as other men enjoy their horses or cards, but it is nonetheless déclassé. Still, he is impeccable in his conduct, to the point of dullness."

"Then is it . . ." Anthea swallowed. "Lord Delbert?"

"Delbert has the face and form of an angel, and the tongue of a devil," Aunt Trudy said, frowning. "There is nothing to be said against him, of course—he comes of excellent family, and has never been observed to be improper. Still . . ."

Anthea's heart plummeted at the "still."

"There are rumors," Aunt Trudy went on. "Nothing definite, you understand, all very vague, but there is some question as to why he is still a bachelor in his thirties."

"No doubt the arrow of love has never found his heart!"

"Or has found it all too often," Aunt Trudy said grimly. "I wouldn't dream of denying you his company, Anthea—but I would urge caution."

Aunt Trudy had good reason to recommend wariness.

Nonetheless, Lord Delbert called the next day, and his conversation and bold gaze quite thrilled Anthea till her blood seemed to bubble in her veins. His visit was almost concluded, and he was just soliciting again her promise to drive in the Park with him that afternoon, when the butler brought in Mr. Crafter's card. Aunt Trudy looked up and nodded, and the butler bowed and departed. Lord Delbert, however, seemed not to have noticed, so he was still chatting with Anthea quite amiably when Crafter appeared in the doorway. Lord Delbert looked up, and rose to his feet as Crafter presented himself with a smooth and somehow sinister grace that flowed into a bow. "Lady Brock, how good of you! Miss Anthea, a pleasure! And yourself, Delbert."

"Bit out of your territory, ain't you, Crafter?" Delbert said with a devilish grin. "Too far from the counting-house by half."

"A distance which I would recommend to you, milord," Crafter said, returning the smile.

Delbert flushed angrily, to Anthea's surprise, and turned to bow to her. "Until this afternoon, Lady Anthea."

"Until then, my lord," she murmured, and he rather ostentatiously kissed her hand, then turned away.

Puzzled, she turned back, to see Mr. Crafter following Lord Delbert's exit with amusement in those gray eyes.

"Please be seated, Mr. Crafter," Aunt Trudy urged. Anthea drifted into a chair.

"Thank you, Lady Brock," Mr. Crafter sat. "I fear I have clouded a bright afternoon."

"Not at all," Aunt Trudy said briskly. "I am sure Lord Delbert is far more entertaining in the phaeton than in the drawing room. Tea, Anthea?"

"Yes, thank you, Aunt." Then Anthea fell silent, at a loss for a topic.

Mr. Crafter slid smoothly into the momentary silence. "Are you enjoying the Season, Miss Anthea?"

"Oh, yes! It is so gay, even festive! Really, I am so glad to be back in London!" The statement gave her the idea for a possible topic. "And yourself, Mr. Crafter? Did you find your return to London pleasant, or would you have preferred to remain in India?"

"I assure you, I blessed the cool breeze of England," Mr. Crafter said, smiling. "India has its attractions and fascinations, but it is, when all is said and done, alien, and I found I'd no wish for it to be otherwise."

"Did you tire of it, then?"

"For the moment," Mr. Crafter said judiciously, "though I would not be loath to return at a later date. It is not one large country, you see, but a host of small ones. I saw only a tenth of it, perhaps not even that."

"But their customs! Surely they don't differ from one kingdom to the next?"

His eyes brightened; she realized, with a start, that he hadn't expected her to know that many of the independent states in India were sovereign kingdoms. "There are small differences between neighboring countries, but there are great ones between the North and South . . ."

And they were off into a discussion that was, in its own way, just as fascinating as Lord Delbert's visit, though much less exciting. Anthea found, to her surprise, that Mr. Crafter listened to her opinions with respect, and never contradicted them—he only narrated such of his own experiences that confirmed or denied what she had read. Aunt Trudy finally had to call a halt to the conversation, though she confessed that she herself was loath to. Nonetheless, the ladies did need a few hours to prepare for the afternoon, so Mr. Crafter was dismissed. He did not, upon his going, kiss Anthea's hand, or even try to— but he looked long and deeply into her eyes, and said that he hoped they would have occasion to chat again. Then he bowed to Aunt Trudy, and departed.

"A man with a somewhat checkered past," Aunt Trudy sighed, "but a fascinating one! Though I fancy most your age would find his accounts boring, Anthea."

Anthea was rather surprised to find that she hadn't.

The drive in the Park was a scintillating pleasure, the more so since several women they passed looked rather nettled to see her in Delbert's phaeton—but after the third such glance, Anthea did begin to wonder as to the nature of their envy. Was it only that they wished to be where she was—or that they already had been? Of course, a gentleman might drive with any number of young ladies, in fifteen Seasons—but had there been more to it than a drive? And there were the half-dozen who took one look at Delbert and turned their faces away, driving resolutely past him with stony gazes. That seemed to amuse Delbert, but he made no mention of it, only kept up with his stream of lively and amusing gossip, setting Anthea alternately to laughter and exclamations of disbelief.

But when they came home, he assisted her down from the carriage with both hands and did not let go, but stood looking down into her eyes, his own with such a glow as to set her heart a-flutter, then pressed his lips to her hand in such a way that she knew he aspired to higher things.

So it went for several weeks, Lord Delbert's visits exciting and stimulating to the emotions, Mr. Crafter's stimulating to the mind—and if Lord Delbert's attentions aroused feelings that not only exalted Anthea but also somewhat frightened her, Mr. Crafter's were oddly soothing and reassuring.

Her life was not a perfect whirlwind of suitors and gatherings, though—there was responsibility, too, as she found out when she noticed how pale and wan her maid, Hester, appeared to be one morning. "Are you ill, Hester?" she inquired.

"No, not at all, miss. Just too late arising this morning, it would seem."

"Didn't you sleep well?"

"Oh, well enough, I suppose, miss." But Hester was growing more and more agitated, and now that Anthea looked, her eyes were red-rimmed and swollen—not terribly much; rather as though she had bathed them in cold water to reduce the swelling, but still noticeably. She caught her maid's hand and softened her tone. "What is the matter, Hester? Truly, you may tell me without fear."

Hester hesitated, irresolute.

"I swear I shan't betray you," Anthea pressed. "But if there is trouble, do tell me of it! Two may see a way through where one would not."

Then the floodgates sprang open, and Anthea was alarmed to find herself the crying-pillow for her own maid. She consoled and comforted as best she could, and when the wave of tears had slackened, the story came out between sobs. It was a footman of another household who was the cause of the problem, it seemed. Hester had met him when the two households had joined for holiday festivities, and had fallen in love straightaway. He professed that he felt as she did, and pursued the matter with all the eloquence and soulful looks at his command. Swayed by passion as well as love, she had yielded to his pleading, then had been horrified to discover that she was with child. Her lover had been even more horrified, protesting that he could not wed her till he had gained the rank of butler, which was still several years away. When she had pointed out that the child would not wait so long and that she would lose her place because of it, he had retorted that he had no desire to lose *his* place, and had told her to "take care of the thing."

"Oh, but you mustn't!" Anthea had cried, aghast even though she wasn't quite certain of the meaning.

"I would never think of it, miss," Hester replied, eyes dry but swollen thoroughly now. "I shall bear the babe if it is my last living act—but, oh!—how am I to manage? Your aunt would throw me out into the street if she knew! What am I to do?"

Anthea hesitated between fear and propriety for a moment, then clasped Hester's hand firmly and said, "You must have faith in your mistress."

"Oh, I do, miss! What do you bid me do?"

"Not just myself, Hester—Aunt Trudy."

"Oh, no, miss!" Hester pulled her hand free, shrinking away. "She'd fly into a rage if I told her! She cast me out on the instant!"

"She would do no such thing," Anthea said firmly. "You know her, Hester—she is a kind and understanding person, who would never condemn another woman for being swayed by love. Come, we must tell her." And taking Hester by the hand, she swept her off, protesting, to Aunt Trudy, her confidence in her aunt so great as to surmount any doubt.

That confidence was not misplaced, though Aunt Trudy was saddened by the news, then lectured Hester on her folly. Hester, to her credit, only acknowledged the truth of her employer's words and asked Aunt Trudy's pardon, which was given instantly. "But what are we to do with you, girl? We can't have you staying here to suffer the ridicule of your fellow servants, and have your shame known to the world."

Hester's eyes filled again. "I would never think of shaming you, milady."

"Nor would you ever do so." Aunt Trudy embraced the poor maid. "You are of my household, Hester, and it is not my custom to desert my people in their hour of need. But where shall we send you when your condition can no longer be hidden?"

"Aunt Trudy?" Anthea said diffidently.

"Yes, child?" Aunt Trudy looked up. "She is your maid, after all, and you must accept some measure of the responsibility for her well-being. What can you recommend?"

"Send her home. To my home, I mean—to Windhaven."

"The very thing!" Aunt Trudy clapped her hands. "None know you there, Hester, and heaven knows there's need of you. The housekeeper is compassionate and gentle, I've seen to that—though she's stern about duty, mind! Your secret would be safe there, and we can legitimately send you to see to your mistress's affairs for several months—really, there wasn't a single room in the house fit for a young lady, and you've wit enough to see to the transforming of a suite, Hester. The babe will be safe there—"

"Oh, yes! It was a wonderful place to grown up!—Your pardon, Aunt," Anthea said, lowering her eyes.

"Given gladly," Aunt Trudy replied. "There are tenant families who would be glad enough to have one more if there were a little money to help feed it, and if you're minded to have the child adopted. However, there are also wetnurses available to tend it, if you don't wish to give it up but have it reared in the manor. For you know, Hester, that we'll expect you back in London within the year."

"I would want nothing more, milady! Oh, thank you, milady!"
And the tears flowed again, but this time it was Aunt Trudy
who took the maid into her arms and risked water-spotting
her gown.

Life proceeded at its normal, and rather dizzying, pace;
Hester remained in attendance on Anthea, for it would be a
few months more before her condition was so pronounced as
to require her removal. Anthea found that there was a bond of
sympathy established between herself and her maid now, and
she felt free to confide in Hester, especially in regard to her
feelings about her two foremost suitors. She did not explain,
though, that she rather hoped neither of them would encounter
Sir Roderick, for she didn't believe Hester would be reassured
to learn of the family ghost of Windhaven Manor just now.
Besides, Sir Roderick had assured her that only family, or those
extremely gifted with that Talent the Celts termed "fey," could
see him. There seemed little danger of that, though, for Sir
Roderick had been oddly absent since the Season's beginning.
To be fair, Anthea would have had to admit that she hadn't
had time to chat with him, and he apparently didn't want her
to slacken her breakneck course.

Lord Delbert's attentions became more and more ardent; he
began to steal a kiss in the garden, and in the drawing room,
when Aunt Trudy was absent—kisses that became longer, his
tongue dancing lightly over her lips in a pattern that sent thrills
coursing through Anthea's whole body. She knew she should
have slapped him, told him to desist—but was afraid that he
might.

Mr. Crafter, on the other hand, was unhappily the soul of
propriety—Anthea could have wished for the opportunity to
compare his kisses with Lord Delbert's. He did, however, spend
more and more time looking soulfully into her eyes, and once,
when she protested that a man of such broad experience and
depth of learning should find an unlettered chit like herself
to be boring, he assured her, "Nothing could be farther off
the mark, Miss Gosling. You are astonishingly well-read for
so young a lady, and have a lively and inquiring mind that
entrances me." Then his gaze sharpened in that disconcerting
intensity of his. "But more—there is some quality about you
that attracts me mightily, as the steel to the lodestone. You

have some element of empathy that far exceeds that of most people, and I suspect you have an inordinate sensitivity which you are at pains to hide." Anthea felt alarmed, and her face must have shown it, for he broke the tension with a puckish smile. "Besides, you're the best opponent at chess I've had in many a year. Will you play?"

She would, but she found herself wishing that it had been another game to which he had invited her. She wasn't quite sure what it was, but she wished it.

It was Lord Delbert who named it, one night when Aunt Trudy was detained with the housekeeper. He pressed Anthea to him, kissed her far more passionately than ever before, then whispered, "I can no longer live without you—I must have all your favors at once, and for all my life! Run away with me tonight, to Gretna Green!"

And Anthea, to her shame, said yes.

Delbert swore her to silence, claiming that if Aunt Trudy knew of it she would prevent them for more months than he could stand—that he would positively wither away from unrequited love. Anthea doubted that, but she was as impatient as he for the wonders his presence promised, though she wasn't certain what those wonders were; so she refrained from telling her aunt, though she felt dreadfully guilty in doing so.

But she had to tell Hester, of course. After all, she couldn't have packed by herself.

Aunt Trudy had to attend the soiree, even though Anthea had a headache—it was, after all, a social obligation. As soon as she heard the carriage depart, Anthea was out of bed and changing into her travelling clothes. She felt horrible at deceiving Aunt Trudy, who had been so good and kind to her, but Love was master of all, and surely her aunt would understand when she came back wedded to one of the most eligible bachelors of the *ton*.

She and Hester dragged the portmanteaus down the back stairs. There, in the mews, was a carriage, with Lord Delbert, all smiles, right beside it. Anthea hesitated at the sight of the enclosed vehicle, knowing she would have no chaperone—but Lord Delbert swept her up in his arms, kissing her deeply, and the blood began to pound in her veins, and she knew that the love for him that ached in her breast was all that truly mattered.

Then they were in the coach, and Anthea caught a bare glimpse of Hester waving as they were whirled away. Then Delbert's lips closed over hers again, and she could think of nothing else.

It was the most romantic evening of her life—champagne and passion in a closed coach, kiss after kiss, growing more giddy and more silly as the miles passed. At some point in all the jesting and jollity, she mentioned how he would love Windhaven, as soon as it was restored. He seemed to still beside her then. "Restored? Is it so awfully run-down, then?"

"Oh, yes, and buried under a mountain of debt! But Aunt Trudy tells me that it will yield income again, in ten or twenty years."

"But surely you will inherit from her when she dies."

"Perhaps something, though I wouldn't wish to claim it, she has been so wonderful to me already. But she has two sons and two daughters, so of course the bulk of her estate must go to them." She suddenly realized what she was saying, and gave a self-deprecating laugh. "How silly of me, to discuss such mundane matters!"

"I am fascinated with every word that drops from your lips." Lord Delbert turned away; a cork popped, and liquid poured. It was a moment longer before he turned about again to offer her another glass. There was more champagne and more passion then, his kisses becoming ever more ardent—then a sudden unaccountable weariness came over Anthea.

"It is the strain and the excitement," Lord Delbert soothed. "Sleep, my love. I would have you fresh and vivacious when we arrive at the first inn." Then waves of sleepiness engulfed her, and Anthea drifted off into dreams of bliss.

Anthea, waken! came Sir Roderick's voice in her mind.

The dreams had become more and more carnal; she dreamed of lips pressed to her naked flesh, light fingers caressing her until she ached with longing. But Sir Roderick's voice was commanding, and she wakened, though her head throbbed and the whole world seemed shrouded in fog. She wondered that the wine had been so strong—then realized that those light fingers were caressing her in more than dreams, in the very life, far more intimately than they should, and Lord Delbert was gazing down at her with a smile of rapt delight—and not at her face. His breath was coming in ragged gasps, and his face was flushed. She cried out in shock, and he looked up at her with a devilish grin. "Wakened so soon, my pretty? Well, that will only add spice to the adventure."

"But, my lord . . . Gretna Green . . . can you not wait . . . ?" Though part of Anthea wished he wouldn't.

Delbert threw back his head and laughed, and there was a note of cruelty in that laughter. "Foolish girl, there will be no Gretna Green! What need have I, a lord, of a ceremony?"

Anthea stared, electrified. "But . . . love . . ."

"Say 'money,' rather. I'm ocean-deep in debt, silly wench, and needed a rich marriage to bail me out. The rumors said that you had estates—they mentioned nothing of debts! Still, if I cannot have relief of one kind from you, I'll have another."

"My lord!" she protested, flinching away—but his arm prevented her, circling behind her. "My aunt!" she cried. "Your reputation in the ton . . ."

"And would you be foolish enough to speak of it? I assure you, none of your predecessors have! Though even if you did, what matter? I'm finished in London, anyway, if I can't have a sea of silver right quickly. I shall have to leave to wander the Continent, so what matter Society now? Be sensible, wench, and lean back and enjoy it, for you'll not have such another night again!"

She didn't doubt that, though not as he'd meant it. She remembered the young women with stony faces, and realized, with horror, that she was about to join their ranks.

"Don't tell me that you had no notion of this," he said with a sneer, "for I could tell by your kiss that you had mind for one thing only."

"I never had! Shame on you, sir, to think so of me!" Then Anthea realized that the motion of the coach had stopped, that it was still. "Where . . ."

"On a country track far to the north of London, my dear, and the coachman has taken the horses far away. There will be none to disturb our lovemaking."

"My lord, if you love me, you will wait!"

"Love?" Delbert's lip curled in a cruel sneer. "What is love but the yearning of body for body? Don't tell me that you haven't felt it, my lass, for I've known the heat of your body and the pounding of your heart—here, even here." The cupped hand tightened.

"I know what kind of girl you are, Anthea, even if you do not—and your being here, alone in a closed coach with me, gives proof of it!"

"No!" she cried, trying to writhe away from him, but the arm that was curled about her tightened, holding her securely, as he laughed.

A delaying tactic, my dear. A wager, Sir Roderick's voice said in her mind. *A game of chess.*

Anthea's heart leaped to know she was not alone, though she blushed with shame at the thought of Lord Roderick's witnessing her disgrace, and knew there was little he could do. But it was even as he said—the longer she could postpone the inevitable, the less inevitable it might become. "A wager, my lord! A game of chess! If you win, I shall not resist you— indeed, I shall surrender myself to the passions you claim to detect!"

"A wager?" Delbert drew back with a gleam in his eye. "That might add spice to the encounter. Chess, d'ye say? Foolish child, do you think you could best me?"

"It might heighten the pleasure, as you say," Anthea said, her voice trembling.

Delbert heard; his grin widened. "And my forfeit, if—ha, ha!—I should lose?"

"Then you will let me go, my lord, unharmed and intact, and will say nothing of this night's doings to anyone."

Delbert frowned, but the gleam remained in his eye. "High stakes, but why not? I've played for higher. Where are your chess pieces?"

They were in her portmanteau, and she had them out in a trice, managing to rebutton her bodice as she did. She laid out the pieces, then began the longest game of her life—not merely because of the suspense or the stakes, but because, as Sir Roderick's voice pointed out to her:

He will never let you go unmolested, even should you win. Your only hope is to prolong the game—the longer, the greater the possibility of rescue.

She saw the truth of it in the anger that flashed in Delbert's eye when she took a pawn. Thereafter, she was careful to lose steadily, never taking a piece of his unless she had lost two of her own, but prolonging each capture as much as possible. Meantime, she tried to ignore the caresses of his voice as he described the pleasures she would experience when this opening game was over, and tried to fight against her body's longing to surrender. Yet when she grew too distracted, Sir Roderick's voice was ever there, counselling, *pawn to queen's knight six . . . king's bishop to queen's rook five . . . Beware of pawn take at queen's bishop four . . .*

Three hours passed, and Lord Delbert began to frown. In fear, Anthea sacrificed two pawns and a knight, though she had to call his attention to the latter. "This game tires me," he growled ominously, and Anthea's heart thudded, for she knew she dared not lose. She began to win, and Delbert to grow darker and darker of mood. Then, when he had only a rook and a knight left to his king, while she had two rooks and won her queen back, he snarled and threw over the board. "Witch! You could not have brought that to pass! Come here, and I will show you the glories of the path to your master!" And he surged toward her, hands outstretched.

Anthea screamed and threw herself at the coach door, knowing it was futile, that she could never wrench the latch open in time—but Sir Roderick had been at work, and the panel gave way. Delbert's rush carried them both tumbling out of the carriage. Anthea fell clear and bruised her head, but Sir Roderick's voice beat through her brain, and she found her body lifting from the ground. *Run, child! As far and as fast as you can!*

She had a brief glimpse of Lord Delbert, half in and half out of the coach, cursing and thrashing. Then she found her feet and was off, tripping and stumbling over the uneven ground of a springtime field. There were woods to her right, and the road, but she knew she dared not run on it, for he would surely be faster than she. Ahead rose low hills, and she dashed for their cover. If she could only last till dawn! Surely he would give over the chase when there was fear of discovery!

But she heard the pounding of his feet behind her, his snarling rage, then his sudden howl of fright. Glancing back, she saw the glowing suit of armor with sword uplifted, and heard Delbert yelling in horror. Roderick had made himself visible to Delbert. She saw no more, for she turned away and ran for her life. He might give over, daunted by the spectre, but she doubted it; his passion and anger were such that he might very well overcome his fear, and seek her out still, defying the ghost.

Her breath was coming in ragged gasps, and she was more hobbling than running, when she finally came among the low hills. She stopped, swaying, seeking a hiding place, tempted to merely sink down against the nearest slope—but she heard Lord Delbert's howls of anger, then his maniacal laugh of triumph. "Spirit of battle or spirit from bottle, what matter? You cannot harm me in either case!"

Then she heard the pounding of hoofbeats and a cry in the night—Delbert's voice, in rage. She risked a look back and saw a horse and rider swooping out of the darkness, blocking her pursuer, the man leaning down to cuff Delbert aside.

"Crafter!" Delbert shouted furiously. "What in hell do you think you're doing!"

"Punishing a rogue and a scoundrel," Roman Crafter snapped. Anthea was amazed at the cold hardness of his voice. "Get back to your coach and wait for your horses, Delbert, or you may not live to regret it!"

"Remember your station, you oaf!" Delbert roared. "Do you dare touch a man of the blood?"

"Station? You forget, Delbert—I'm American. We don't believe in such things. Show me your quality with your deeds, not your birth."

"That I will, in a trice!" Delbert bellowed. "Just get down off that damned horse, Crafter, and I'll show you your place!"

Roman gave a low laugh that raised chills along Anthea's spine—and leaped down from the horse.

With a roar of triumph, Delbert pulled a pistol from his belt and levelled it at Crafter's head.

Then Anthea could not believe her eyes, for suddenly the pistol began to glow, a glow that brightened into a streak of white light that surged down Delbert's arm toward his heart. He screamed and threw the pistol away, but the white light still clung to his arm, and a voice from nowhere rang out: *Shall I kill him, young Roman?*

Run, girl! Sir Roderick's voice rang through her head. *He has bought you time, but may yet pay with his blood! Flee!*

Anthea did, turning and running, suddenly as frightened of Roman Crafter and whatever spirit accompanied him, as she was of Lord Delbert.

She knew that one or the other of them would be after her, no matter who won. In a panic, she looked about and saw a patch of deeper darkness against one of the hillsides. She hobbled to it with ragged, sobbing breaths, reached out—and felt the hillside give way into a low cave. Weeping with relief, she dropped to hands and knees and crawled in. There was still a chance Delbert might find her, but it was less than before.

Something glowed in the dark, something that stretched upward into a tall and glittering form.

Anthea cried out, and shrank back against the wall of the cave.

He stood in silhouette against an eldritch glow that seemed to come from the walls of the cavern itself, a tall, unnaturally thin man with silvered hair.

Anthea crouched rigid, staring up at him.

He lifted an arm in a bell-sleeve with a gold-embroidered cuff, beckoning.

Anthea wasn't ready to rise. "What do you want?" she whispered.

The figure stood still a moment longer, then came to kneel beside her. He was unbelievably handsome, with large, slightly slanting eyes, a high forehead and long, straight nose, high cheekbones above gauntness, and a full, sensuous mouth. The lips curved in a courtly smile. "We have need of you." His voice was rich and melodious, and his eyes drew her, compelling.

A thrill coursed through her; it was just like every folk tale she'd ever heard or read, and she didn't doubt for a moment what he was. She rose slowly, as unable to resist as to think, while the Faerie lord's gaze was on her.

He was taller than Anthea by a head or more. He gazed down into her eyes, smiling, and she felt herself being drawn into the huge, dark pools of his pupils. . . .

Then he turned away, moving silently into the depths of the cave, depths that she had not realized were there, and it came to her that this was not a hill, but a barrow, a hollow hill that her people had long thought to be neolithic burial sites, but older people had known for the dwelling places of the Faerie Folk. She followed the elfin lord, her heart hammering in her breast.

The door was set into the sides of the tunnel, and seemed as old as the rock around it, made of dark, rich oak, waxed to a gloss that seemed to let one look deeply into the grain. The Faerie lord turned the lock with a huge key and stepped aside to bow her in. Anthea followed, heart hammering in her breast; how could anyone come through that door, if the Faerie locked it behind him? Once she was through, she could never depart without his leave—but curiosity impelled her forward as much as his compulsion, and she could not even think of turning back.

Lock it he did, then stepped on past her, murmuring, "Come." She followed, marvelling at the richness of the panelled walls through which she moved. An archway opened to her left, affording a brief glimpse of a *drawing room* elegantly appointed in an antique style, but the Faerie lord strode past it without a glance, and Anthea had to follow.

They came to the end of the hall, and another rich old door, partly open. The Faerie pushed on through it, and Anthea, following, stepped into a chamber so wide that the huge canopied bed in its center seemed small. The walls were hung with tapestries; between them, walnut panelling glowed. The floor was covered with an Oriental carpet, and the bed-hangings were satin and velvet.

The Faerie lord knelt beside the bed, taking the hand of a lady who seemed so exquisitely fragile that she seemed to float between the sheets. Her hair was long, and so light a blond that it seemed almost silver. Her face was delicate, fine-boned and high-cheeked, and her eyes were huge, her lips red and full. But those high cheeks were hollow, and her skin was very pale. One look at her made Anthea feel heavy and *lumpen*—but also made her feel healthy.

Magnificently healthy, when she saw the emaciated infant lying on its mother's breast, eyes still closed, little mouth working at its fist. Its crying was so thin as to sound like the mewing of a tiny kitten. Anthea stepped forward, a wordless cry drawn from her, reaching out toward the baby—but she halted a few feet away, not daring to touch something so fragile.

The Faerie lady looked up at her, and once again Anthea felt herself drawn into huge, dark eyes. "I am height Lolorin," the lady murmured in a low, husky voice, weak with strain, "and this is my lord, Qualin. Wilt thou nurse our child?"

Anthea looked up, eyes wide—and realized that the man, though he still knelt, was strung as tightly as a violin, seeming ready to leap, just barely held in check by Lolorin's hand on his, his eyes burning as he gazed at his child. "I . . . I cannot,"

Anthea protested feebly. "I . . . I am not a mother, and have no milk to give."

"That, we can amend," the Faerie lord said, his voice deep and cavernous, and Anthea felt a thrill of alarm mixed with a dreadful yearning. "A small spell, and thy breasts will swell with milk."

"But . . . but I am a virgin . . ."

"Thy breasts will take no heed," Lolorin assured her, "and the milk will be good."

But Anthea was in a quandary. The sight of the infant pulled at her, so deeply that pity and her longing to help it became an almost physical pain—but . . . "I am young, and have tasted so little of life! I have suitors, I have barely begun to live . . . ."

The Faerie lord stirred. " 'Tis true. Name thy nurse's fee, and thou shalt have it."

"Oh, don't speak of fees!" Anthea cried. "If the baby grows strong, that will be enough!"

Qualin's eyes glowed, but Lolorin said, as though the words were dragged out of her, "She doth speak without thought. Consider well, mortal, for if thou dost consent, thou wilt be bound to us for a year and a day—'twill be that long at least ere my babe can subsist on fare other than thine. And human milk is vital, for the aura of thy own kind hath enervated the folk of Faerie. We have weakened with age, and the decline of mortal folks' belief in us. So tenuous hath our existence become that Faerie mothers' milk hath grown too thin to sustain an infant long."

"We would not ask this of thee," said Qualin, "save that our child must have a human to nurse, and thou art the only woman who hath chanced to come within our purview; I lack the vitality to go abroad to sue. Yet thou hast come near our hollow hill, alone and at night—and thou art one of those born with the power of magic about thee."

"I?" Anthea gasped.

"Indeed. Hast thou never felt it?"

"No, never!" But then Anthea remembered her contact with Sir Roderick, and his mention that she could only see him because of an inborn Talent, which might fade as she matured. Apparently it had not—or she had not grown up as much as she had thought.

" 'Tis that quality of magic," Qualin said, "that touch of the fey, no matter how minor, that doth enable thee to see and speak with us of the Faery world."

" 'Twill be long ere another so gifted haps to come within the aura of our powers," Lolorin murmured. "It will, I doubt not, be too late for my babe. Wilt thou not give aid? For if thou dost not, surely he may die!"

"Oh, do not lay such a charge upon my soul!" Anthea buried her face in her hands, torn. "I would not see your baby die—truly, I wish to save him—but I wish to save my own life, too! I wish to dance, and to speak with other girls. I wish to be have young men fall in love with me, and woo me, and court me; I wish to dance at balls and drive in the Park!"

" 'Tis only a year," Qualin protested. "Your life will still be there when thou dost return."

"Nay," said a deep voice from the doorway. "It will be vastly changed."

Anthea spun about, and Qualin surged to his feet with an oath.

There, in glowing silver armor, stood a knight with a drawn sword in his right hand—and, tucked in the elbow of his left, a head!

But it was a living head, if a ghostly head can be said to live—and its lips moved as it spoke. "The lady is in my care, and I will not permit her to be harmed." The head wore no helmet, and the rugged face was young and handsome, though it too glowed silver beneath a wavy mass of hair.

"Sir Roderick!" Anthea cried. "You have found your head!"

"Yes, Anthea—and I must thank you for bringing me to the battlefield on which I lost it." Sir Roderick held his sword out before him, where it floated, point fixed on Qualin. Then he took the head in both hands and set it on his shoulders, giving a half turn as though to lock it in place. Qualin took the opportunity to lunge, but the sword parried easily and riposted, sending Qualin back on guard. "How didst thou come here!" he spat.

"I followed my kinswoman," the ghost answered. "Blood calls to blood, and I had but to answer that call. Your locks mean naught to me, for I am a ghost." He smiled grimly, his eyes never leaving Qualin's. "And know, Anthea, that you will pass far more than a single year here—for though it may seem only twelve months to you, in the world outside, seven years will pass. Your friends will be matrons and young mothers; the gentlemen so smitten with you will be husbands burdened with the management of their estates. Your aunt will be seven years older, if she does not pine away for grief at your disappearance."

"Aunt Trudy! Oh, I could never do that!" Anthea turned to Qualin. "Is this true?"

"It is," he said reluctantly, eyes still on the ghost. "And who art thou, stranger, who comes thus to imperil mine heir?"

"Her ancestral ghost, who has known and cherished her since childhood. I do not wish your child any harm, but I will not see my own deprived of youth and the few carefree years of romance God grants to her. Avaunt, eldritch lord, and stand aside! This lady is not for you!"

"I shall not let her be torn from me!" Qualin ground out, and lunged forward.

"No," Anthea screamed—but swords not of steel met with a fearful clash . . .

And held. They stuck together as though they were magnets of opposite poles, and an eerie silver light played over both blades, melding them together. Qualin spat an oath and wrenched at his, but it would not budge. "What magic have you wrought, fell spectre?"

"No enchantment of mine." Sir Roderick, too, was wrenching at his blade. "Some other force comes. O glow upon our swords! You are a spirit of your own form!"

"Even so." The voice was a thrumming in the air, a deep vibration within their skulls. "I am a spirit foreign to the land, but strong enough withal, especially on such a night as this. Give over, Faerie lord! Give over, ghost! For I shall hold thee bound till thou dost cry 'Hold, enough!' "

"Never shall I bow so!" Qualin raged. "What hellspawn hath brought thee here?"

"A spawn of mortal folk, and not of Hell at all," said a resonant voice behind Anthea. She spun about with a gasp, and saw a gentleman in breeches and Hessian boots, though his coat and neckcloth were gone and his shirt torn wide open, showing a manly, muscular chest. "Roman!" she cried, then blushed. "I mean, Mr. Crafter!"

"The same, Miss Gosling." But Roman's gaze was fixed on Qualin and the ghost. "I don't believe I've had the pleasure."

"Wouldst thou speak as though in a drawing room, thou fool?" the Faerie lord snapped.

"Why not?" Roman said, with airy disregard of the circumstances. "We may as well be civilized, after all, since we cannot do one another harm. Anthea, would you do the honors?"

Anthea noticed the use of her Christian name alone, but knew it was no time to charge him with a breach of etiquette. "Mr. Roman Crafter, may you be pleased to make the acquaintance of Qualin, a lord of Faerie, and his lady, Lolorin, with their child. The knight is my old friend, Sir Roderick le Gos, late of Windhaven Manor."

"Quite late, I should judge, from the cut of your armor." Roman looked Sir Roderick up and down. "Still, it is becoming; you must give me the name of your tailor. I thank you for your kind intercession on behalf of Miss Anthea, Sir Roderick."

"It is my pleasure," the knight responded, "for I am privileged to think of her as my ward, though not in the eyes of the law—and you shall have to answer to me, Mr. Crafter, if you wish to know her better."

"Why, Sir Roderick!" Anthea protested, blushing furiously.

"I gather he is the senior male of your house," Roman inferred.

"If you are being so civil as to make introductions," Qualin ground out, "might we know the name and style of this creature who has bound our swords?"

"My apologies," Roman murmured. "He is a creature of the sea, and I made his acquaintance during a storm in the tropics. We got on famously, and he has chosen to accompany me for a brief space. In fact, it is through him that my cousin purchased my rise from powder monkey to midshipman, and thereby to ensign and, eventually, captain."

"Yet he advanced by his own ability," the spirit hummed. "Call me, as he does, merely 'Erasmus.'"

"Saint Elmo's Fire!" Anthea cried.

"Excellent, Miss Gosling," Roman said, with surprised pleasure. "Not too many landlubbers know the term, or that 'Elmo' is the shortened form of 'Erasmus.' Yes, he has that name among the superstitious, though to tell you the truth, he has as little to do with saints as with demons—though I promise you, he can give living mortals quite a shock. Yet he seems to have taken a fancy to my inquisitive turn of mind."

"And to your boldness and talent in dealing with spirits," Erasmus hummed. "What say you, Roman? Shall I free these two banty roosters?"

"Banty roosters!" Sir Roderick choked.

"You will have to forgive my friend," Roman apologized. "He has taken up many idioms that he learned from me in my youth—oh, very well, my early youth. But the question he asks is valid. Will you both sheathe your swords and try to deal in reason, if he releases you?"

"Well, I will attempt it," Sir Roderick huffed.

"And I." But Qualin's eyes glittered dangerously. "Yet I warn thee, I will not permit the lady to be taken from us, if she doth choose to stay."

Roman glared at him for a space, then said, "Fair enough. She is, after all, her own person. It is your decision, Anthea, and we will all abide by it. Agreed, gentlemen?"

Ghost and Faerie grumbled assent, and the glow drifted away from their swords to hover, a sphere of light, by Roman.

Anthea paled, and almost cried out in protest. Was she to be left without support in this? Though she did have to admit that she did not want to be compelled to a course of action she would not like, it would nonetheless be wonderful if someone else could only tell her what it was she wanted—and could be right.

"Please acquaint me with the nature of the contretemps," Roman said. "Apparently the issue is the freedom of Miss Anthea Gosling. But why should there be any contention against it?"

"First tell me," Qualin growled, "who you are, and how you came into my hill."

"I am Roman Crafter, late of His Majesty's Navy, and later of the United States of America."

"What is that?"

"A country in the West, beyond the Isles and the ocean."

"It cannot be." Qualin's eyes burned. "Mortal eyes cannot see the Western Haven."

"Quite right; the only ones we see are quite mortal, I assure you, and though they have their own population of elementals and spirits, none of them are of your race. As for myself, I had the bad fortune to be impressed into the British Navy, and the good fortune to meet Miss Anthea Gosling. When Erasmus told me that she had been spirited away by an a utter cad, I rode as quickly as I could to overtake them. I lost their track on the road, but Erasmus cast about and found them for me, and I arrived in time to spare her the worst of his attentions. Yet when I'd done with him, she had fled, and I was quite concerned for her further safety. Erasmus was good enough to seek you out again and unravel the spell that barred the entrance to this hill. I felt your presence and followed."

Anthea stared. "But—the door . . . the lock . . ."

Roman frowned. "What door?"

"That huge old door in the hillside! He used a six-inch key to open it!"

Roman shook his head, gaze still on Qualin. "Only a bush, and a cave mouth."

Anthea's breath hissed in. "A glamour! It was an illusion that Qualin cast." She looked up at the tall Faerie lord. "Did you think I would be more willing to help if I thought you lived in a rich house?"

"Aye, certes. If 'tis not so, thou art quite unlike all others of thy kind." Qualin's gaze stayed on Roman.

"Then," Anthea breathed, "everything else I see is also a glamour. Take it away, please! You cannot expect me to dwell in the midst of a lie!"

"Thy kind ever have," the Faerie lord snapped; but Lolorin murmured, "My lord, I prithee—let her see what is real."

Qualin stood stock-still for a moment; then he shrugged, tossing his head. In the blink of an eye, the tapestries and carpet were gone, as were the rich wooden panels behind them. Damp rock walls showed in their place, webbed with niter where they merged into the cave's roof. The four-poster bed was gone; Lolorin lay on a heap of old straw atop a rocky shelf, and her coverlet was several old furs sewn together, with patches of hair missing. Her gown was only linen, stained with age, and Qualin's glorious raiment had faded to the dun colors of an old, threadbare tunic and hose.

"This is the truth thy kind so praise," Lolorin said. "Why, I cannot tell—I had liefer live with glamour."

"So would most of us." Anthea felt her heart sink.

Even Roman looked somber, but he said, "You cannot expect a gentlewoman to live under such conditions!"

"Glamour will warm and comfort her," Lorlorin protested.

"The lady is safe." Qualin's tone was brittle.

"Be sure we shall not maltreat her; we have too great a need of her."

"Need?" Roman turned to Anthea with a frown. "Would you acquaint us with the nature of that exigency, Miss Anthea? Surely you did not come into this hill of your own free will."

"But I did, Mr. Crafter," Anthea explained, "at least, into the cave that is the mouth of this tunnel. I sought to hide from Lord Delbert . . . ." She shuddered at the thought of him.

"Do not fear," Roman said quickly. "He is fled to the Continent, and will trouble you no further." His eyes hardened. "I made quite sure of that."

Anthea nearly asked what Roman could have done that would have made him so certain, but her courage failed her.

"I take it," Roman went on, "that Lord Qualin then appeared, to entice you further in."

"Why, yes," Anthea admitted, "though I can scarcely blame him, since he did it to protect his own child."

"Child?" Roman glanced sharply about the room. "Ah, yes! The lady Lolorin, and the babe you mentioned. I take it they have need of a mortal nurse."

Anthea blushed. "So they have explained it to me—and I am the only human woman they have come upon. If he does not have human milk, the baby will die."

"So I have heard." Roman frowned at Qualin. "But I confess to confusion. Has your race, ever so powerful, now grown so decadent as to need the services of a mortal nurse?"

"Nay!" Qualin exploded. " 'Tis thy race that hath done it, thy kind that have filled the land with Cold Iron; thine air doth reek with the fumes of the blood of the earth! The insidious aura of unchecked Cold Iron doth pervade the aether, and doth sap the strength from our limbs! Even here, in the fastness of the Welsh mountains, doth that vibrating reach—even here, far from all cities, doth it deplete us!"

" 'Tis true." Lolorin's eyes seemed even more huge. " 'Tis therefore that my frame cannot bring forth milk rich enough for my child."

"Unchecked Cold Iron?" Roman frowned. "What is this you speak of? Men have used Cold Iron in every way they can, for millenia!"

"Not so," Qualin replied, "for your smithies have grown huge, and pour out vast quantities of the stuff—and more and more of it is alloyed and purified into such as was once reserved for swords!"

"Of course!" Roman lifted his head, understanding coming into his eyes. "Steel has a broader and stronger aura than mere iron—and there is more and more of both abroad, as horses are shod and wagons multiplied! Tell me, is it the Midlands that are especially noisome to you?"

"Aye. Where once was our haven, there are stinking piles of brick that are filled with bits of Cold Iron! Their aura pervades the Midlands; they blight the land!"

"Mills," Anthea whispered.

"And their ramshackle towns," Roman agreed. "Small wonder the Faerie Folk are vanishing."

Anthea frowned. "But the tales of your kidnapping mortal wet nurses go back hundreds of years!"

Lolorin nodded. "Cold Iron began it—and as thy kind spread its use, so didst thou use it to hew down our trees, which did shelter our kind, and without which we cannot endure. Thus we retreated from thee and thy metal, for 'tis poisonous to us. We weakened, yet we persisted—till now."

Qualin nodded stiffly. "Our folk began to flee, when they found that scarcely a house could be found in all Britain that was not filled with nails of Cold Iron. Aye, they did fly to the Western Isles, where I trust they remain to this day."

Roman frowned. "The Western Isles that I cannot see?"

"Thou wouldst not, nor any of thy kind—nay, nor will any of thine instruments of alchemy reveal them to thee. Of all the sons of Mother Earth, only those of the Blood may find them, or the roads that lead there."

Anthea looked up at Roman. "What instruments of alchemy are these?"

But Roman only answered, "I never did like being excluded . . . ."

"There is no aid for it," said Qualin. "Thy kind have not the eyes to see these Isles. Yet our folk did, and most fled; yet some did cling to our earth, and what remained of our forests, for 'twas the land and the trees that did give us birth, look thou, and we despaired of living without them. Aye, some few of us do bide in determination."

"How is it that the aura of Cold Iron weakens you?" Roman said softly.

" 'Tis counter to the coursing of our strength," Qualin maintained. " 'Tis too measured, too harsh. It doth disrupt all our magics, without which we cannot live."

Roman nodded. "No wonder you fled as far from the cities as possible."

"Not enough," Anthea whispered, staring at Qualin. "It is leaching the life from you. How can you bear to stay?"

"We are intractable," Lolorin said, her voice low. "For look you,'twas our land ere any of thy kind did come here, this Britain, this England—and how could it be either, an there were no Faerie folk here?"

Qualin nodded. "Therefor we bide."

"It must be immensely lonely," Anthea breathed.

"I' truth," Lolorin whispered, "there are few enough of our kind that bide in all England—in all Europe, mayhap in all the world."

"But how can you endure?" Anthea asked. "Even after this child has grown . . ." She looked down at the baby, which looked up at her, wide-eyed. She smiled tenderly. "Oh, Roman! I cannot leave so sweet a child to perish!" She looked up at Lolorin, her eyes swimming with tears. "How unfair of you, to show me the baby, when you knew it would tug at my heart as strongly as any man could!"

Lolorin only smiled, but with sadness and longing.

"Her point is well taken," Roman said, his voice low. "She must be free to go where she will, without coercion—and when she chooses."

Qualin's mouth tensed with impatience. "Thou shalt have her so, when the babe no longer hath need of her."

"How long will that be—a year? Two? She is a free woman, you know."

"She shall not be our slave," Lolorin said. " 'Tis as thou sayest—she shall be handsomely paid, and we shall dismiss her in a year and a day as promised."

"In your time, perhaps. But how long will that be in our time? Seven years? Fourteen?"

Qualin didn't move, but something in his eyes showed that Roman had hit home. "We shall ensure that it be no longer in thy time than in ours."

Roman shook his head. "It is not enough. You cannot ask her to forfeit her youth."

"Thou dost presume." Qualin seemed to draw inward, compacting, like a tiger readying itself to spring. "Thou dost not chaffer with the Old Ones."

"If the lady's freedom is at stake . . ."

"Nay!" Lolorin cried. "Wilt thou two, in the pride of thy manhood, give the lass greater cause to weep than she already hath?"

"I do not wish it." Anthea's voice caught in a sob.

"Which?" rapped Qualin. "That the man be hurt? Or the babe starve?"

"I do not wish it! Neither! I cannot stand for Mr. Crafter to be hurt, or the babe! But if only I can save the infant, I will!"

Roman turned to her, appalled. "But you are too young to cast away seven years of your life, Miss Gosling, no matter how much good you may do with them!"

"Speak honestly, mortal!" Qualin snapped. "It is not her youth that thou dost care for, but herself! Thou dost wish to have her for thine own! Do not dissemble!"

Roman turned to stare at him, nonplused, and Anthea felt the blood drain from her face. Was there truth in what the Lord Qualin said? But surely there must be—the Faerie Folk could see to the heart of any mortal.

But Roman had recovered his poise, and turned to her with a bow. "I surmise you find the choice unbearable, Miss Gosling."

"You . . . surmise correctly, Mr. Crafter."

"'Miss Gosling'! 'Mr. Crafter'! Can they not be done with such pretenses?" Qualin burst out. "'Tis plain to all who see him that he is in love with thee, and plain to anyone who can hear the heart, that thou art in love with him! Canst thou not at least call one another by personal names?"

Anthea blushed and lowered her eyes, her heart pounding. She heard Roman's voice, slow and wondering. "Miss Gosling . . . Anthea . . . No, I've no right to ask!"

"Yet I will answer, though not at this moment," she replied. "I shall call you 'Roman,' though, if I may."

"I would be honored. And may I call you 'Miss Anthea'?"

"You may not, sir," she retorted. "'Anthea' will do." She was gratified to hear him let out an awed breath.

"Well, *there* is some vestige of honesty, at least," Qualin said, and Lolorin added, her voice low, "We cannot ask thee to stay with us now, Anthea, if thou art in love."

"Unless . . ." Qualin looked up, eyes burning. "Thy lover would stay with thee?"

"Instantly," Roman said quickly.

Sir Roderick coughed into an iron fist.

"That is, if the proprieties could be observed," Roman amended.

"Indeed." Qualin's lip curled. "And where are we to find thee a minister, or a chaperone?"

Sir Roderick looked up, as though at a sound, then said, "That may not be so vast a chore as you think. If you will excuse me a moment?" He disappeared.

"What . . . what could he have heard?" Anthea stammered.

"There is another matter I have neglected to mention," Roman began, but footsteps—of more than one person—echoed in the passageway.

Qualin whirled, backing up to shield Lolorin with his body, and she tensed behind him. She didn't move, but her eyes seemed to grow even larger. Shaking his head, Qualin lifted a hand slowly, wrist turning in a complicated pattern as the fingers seemed to stroke the air. He began to chant in words that Anthea and Roman did not know, and the cave walls disappeared, replaced by the rich wooden panels and the tapestries. The floor was carpeted again, and Lolorin lay once more, richly garbed, in the four-poster bed.

Then Sir Roderick stepped out of the tunnel—and beside him were Aunt Trudy and Hester.

"Aunt Trudy!" Anthea cried, and lowered her gaze. "Oh, forgive me!"

"In an instant, child." Aunt Trudy bustled over to her and caught her hand, chafing it, then touching a palm to her forehead. "Lord Delbert is another matter—but you I'll forgive in an instant, the more so because I feel certain you've learned the reasons underlying some of the strictures surrounding a young lady. There, child, are you well? Such a deal of damp! And really, who are these people who live in so unseemly a location?"

"I might ask the same of thyself," Qualin snapped. "Have a care how thou dost address a lord and lady of Faerie!"

"A lord of Faerie?" Aunt Trudy turned, staring. "My heavens, it's true! Well, I am the Lady Gertrude Brock, wife to the late baronet—and I trust it will not be necessary to call upon his aid! Yourself, sir?"

"I am the Lord Qualin, and my wife is the lady Lolorin. Our son is only a fortnight aged, and hath a need of mortal aid. Wilt thou grant him such?"

"Sir!" Aunt Trudy cried, drawing herself up.

"I feared not," Qualin said, thin-lipped. "But if not thee or thy niece, then who?"

"I . . . I am not wellborn, Lord Qualin," Hester said hesitantly, "but I am human."

"Hester!" Aunt Trudy cried. "You speak out of turn!"

"Yet such speech is perhaps welcome." Qualin's eyes glowed, and Lolorin pushed herself a little further upright, hope in her eyes. "Wouldst thou nurse my babe then, mortal lass?"

"Oh, the poor wee thing!" Hester cried, and ran to the Faerie's bedside. She caught up the baby and rocked it, crooning. "Oh, how could I turn away, with one who would need me so! Yet I fear there's little good I could do it for some months yet, for my milk has not yet come."

"You are with child?" Lolorin's eyes swelled.

"Yes, milady, though the father will not acknowledge my babe." Hester bowed her head ruefully.

"That doth matter naught," Lolorin said, "and a small spell will suffice to bring thy milk before its time. Yet know, mortal woman, that if thou dost stay to nurse my babe a year, seven will pass in thy realm outside this hill."

Hester stilled, and Aunt Trudy said, "I really cannot allow a servant in my employ to be so badly used."

"We will not use her ill, but well," Qualin said with surprising force. "She shall be honored, and shall live in luxury—and when her service is done, she shall have Faerie gold aplenty." He turned to Hester. "Name thy fee!"

"Oh . . . why . . ." Hester looked up, startled, but Aunt Trudy nodded slightly, and she said, "Why . . . a hundred pounds, I should think."

"A thousand," Aunt Trudy said. "Ten."

Qualin glared at her, then shrugged. "One thousand or ten, what the matter? She shall have it, and Faerie magic shall grant her a safe and easy birthing."

"But what of my child, after?" Hester wondered.

"What of yourself?" said Aunt Trudy. "Your son we can foster easily enough—but how shall you live when your service here is over?"

"Why . . . I had not thought . . ."

"I shall take you back into my household gladly, if I am still alive," Aunt Trudy assured her, "and I intend to be—but one never knows . . ."

"I shall surely be able to provide for her, Aunt," Anthea offered, "and I shall be pleased to have her services."

"Oh, will you, miss?" Hester cried. "Oh, thank you!"

"Though there will be small need for it, if you've ten thousand in your own right," Aunt Trudy finished. "Such a dowry should attract a worthy husband—but we should speak of love, Hester. How will you feel to lose seven years with young men?"

Hester shrugged. "I've little enough interest in them of the moment, milady—and it may be they will be better when I return."

Roman turned a grunt into a cough, and Sir Roderick said, "I doubt that exceedingly, young woman."

"Well, then, mayhap my Robin will have position enough to want a wife and babes," Hester said, then shrugged. "Though I'm not so certain I would want him anymore. 'Twould be hard to find any other husband, though, when I've already a babe."

"If thy mistress cannot find a home for thy child, he shall have one here," Lolorin said firmly. " 'Twould not be the first time a mortal lad hath been raised in the Faerie realm."

Hester turned to stare at Lolorin, her eyes growing huge. "Oh, milady! If you only could . . ."

"We can, and shall."

"And there, I think, is Hester's trouble solved, at least for the present," Aunt Trudy said, "though you must call on us, Hester, as soon as you have come back to the daylight world."

"Oh, yes, ma'am! And I'll be forever grateful!" Hester dropped a curtsey.

"And so, I think, you have no further need of myself, Lord Qualin, or of my niece," Aunt Trudy said.

"No, none at all." Qualin was standing by the bed, one hand on his son's head, one hand on Lolorin's shoulder. "Go in peace, mortal folk—and I thank thee for thine aid in this."

"It was our pleasure, I'm sure. Anthea?"

"Oh, thank you, Hester!" Anthea rose and followed her aunt out of the tunnel, very much aware of Roman's presence behind her. Not that she needed to worry about making conversation, though—Aunt Trudy was doing splendidly at that, and not leaving much opportunity for anyone else. "Well, really, Sir Roderick! I didn't even begin to recognize you! Your head, at last! After all these years! Oh, it is so very good to see you again! But how has this come to pass?"

With a shock, Anthea realized that she had not been the only lonely child to be reared at Windhaven.

"Really quite remarkable, Trudy," Sir Roderick replied. "By excellent chance, that cad Delbert laid a route straight past the battlefield where I lost my head, so many centuries ago. Really quite a bit of luck, that. And as to your seeing me again—well, I fancy your contact with Anthea may have had something to do with it. But it's mostly the result of these Faerie Folk, d'you see—they fairly exude magic, they're surrounded by it, and I've no doubt it amplified your own gifts and woke them again, in a fashion . . . ."

Anthea realized, with a start, that they had come out into the light of false dawn—and that Aunt Trudy and Sir Roderick were moving off to the side, not at all obviously, but moving quite a deal faster than they seemed to, and there was quite a bit of space opening between the two of them on the one hand, and herself and Roman on the other. The ball of light had emerged behind the American, and was waning in the half-light, disappearing with the deep-chimed admonishment, "Call me at need, Roman."

"I thank you for all your assistance, Erasmus," Roman said, then turned back to the lady. "Well, Miss Anthea, it would seem our long night is nearly done."

She took a breath, nerved herself up to it, and said, "Just 'Anthea,' if you please, Roman. I believe I did give you that permission."

"Anthea," he murmured, and his voice caressed her name as though it were a fabulous jewel.

Then, somehow, fantastically, insanely, he had taken hold of her hands and was gazing deeply into her eyes and was saying, "Anthea, the Faerie lord is right—I am a fool to dissemble any longer! I have loved you since I met you, and every succeeding acquaintance, every word from your tempting lips, has made me love you the more! Desire for you burns so deeply in me that it will drive me mad, if you do not assuage it by a promise to wed me! Marry me, I beg of you, and I swear I shall do all that I may to ensure your happiness!"

"But . . . but Mr. Crafter . . . Roman . . ." Anthea caught her breath, and what was left of her senses. "How . . . how can you still wish to be with me, when you have . . . had to confront the fact that I am . . . haunted?"

"Haunted? Oh, now, sweet lady!" Roman stepped closer, as though to reassure her. "It is merely that you have the sensitivity, the gift, to see what others cannot!"

"But do you not see that I must be fey? That I must be one of those born to—" She forced herself to say it. "—to a weird? And that I come from a family so accursed? And that my children, in all probability, shall be so, too?"

"Children! Oh, Anthea!" Roman pressed closer still. "If they were my children as well as yours, you may be sure they would have the Talent—for do you not see that I am one even as yourself? Nay, I assure you that in my family the Talent does not only run—it is a virtual torrent! For six generations, my family have cultivated their gifts, learning the science of magic! The trait has bred true, and has grown and grown." He took her by the shoulders and held her off at arm's length. "How can you think that I would be put off by meeting with Sir Roderick, when you yourself have seen my own supernatural friend? And he not inherited, but discovered and befriended by me myself!"

"Then . . . you do not know what it is to have a family ghost!"

"A ghost? No, but there is a will-o-the-wisp that has been our friend for a very long time, and it is rumored that we are long-lived because an ancestor made a friend of Death himself. Nay, there has scarcely been a single Crafter who has not had his own spirit-friend, and they march in a legion to the aid of the present generation when they are needed! Oh, Anthea! That *I* could be put off by only *one* ghost? Nay, nay, sweet lady, especially not when the damsel who is 'haunted' is a lady of such beauty, intellect, and charm!"

She gazed up into his eyes, blinking. "I . . . I don't know what to say . . . ."

"Then say 'yes,' " he pleaded, "and kiss me."

She did. Both.

A few yards away, Sir Roderick appraised Roman's technique with a practiced eye. "Not terribly experienced, I'd guess, but I wager he'll learn."

"I'd wager he will delight in it," Aunt Trudy said tartly, "and so will she, though I suspect I'll be hard put to make them wait for a wedding."

"Trudy!" Sir Roderick gasped.

"Oh, stuff and nonsense! Did you think William and I had lived as plaster saints all those years? A chaperone must know her duties from the inside, Sir Roderick—and don't tell me you don't know that, for I seem to remember you making a few timely interruptions when I was fresh from the schoolroom!"

"I did," Roderick sighed, "and from the look of these two, I'll have another generation to attend."

At Sea
Anno Domini 1812

One of the best known limitations on magic is that of water. Like Cold Iron, flowing water is inimical to most magics, at least those based upon the powers of land and sky. Vampires are said to be unable to cross flowing water and many spells can be escaped by simply crossing some sea or river. Water, it seems, has it own magic which is powerful and quite alien to men. To those who tap this watery magic, it can mean great power, but a power that often brings with it the burden of an even greater evil. Stand on the beach of any ocean and you can feel the fascination and the strange power emanating from the waves. So all seamen become superstitious, and those who fight among the waves soon learn to respect and fear the power that dwells beneath the waves.

IRONSIDES AND COTTONSEED OIL

by Ru Emerson

The road that ran from Baltimore through Annapolis was wide and well-tended—fortunately for the young man who walked down its center at an hour when most honest young men were long since asleep. David George Crafter Holywell moved slowly, as much because of near-complete darkness as for the load he carried. There was no light save the few stars that could be seen above the circle of tall trees, scarcely enough to set the road apart from the deep, wet ditches that flanked it. Earlier, when he'd been fresh and walking quickly, he'd stepped offside and nearly tumbled into the brackish, green-slimed standing water he could smell whenever the light breeze died.

"Well," he murmured to himself, "by now there'll be no chance of anyone to come after and persuade me home." The sound of his voice, faint as it was, seemed to echo through the woods all around him—alarmingly, he thought. He swallowed, set his lips together in a firm line, and trudged on, left hand picking carefully at the strap of his heavy canvas bag in an attempt to relieve the pressure against an aching collarbone and now-tender muscle where the weight of the bag was beginning to become a problem. The shift helped for one long moment; after that his arm began to go to sleep and he had to shift it back again.

I should not have brought so much with me, he thought tiredly. *What more does a seaman need than himself and his wits—and a hand to set to the papers?* But then, after this last argument with his mother and father, his only clear thoughts had been *Annapolis*, and *Go, now*!

The road ahead was suddenly much clearer, and moments later he strode into the open. With a sigh, he knelt and shed the sack that held his one decent change of clothing; his winter cloak and the new, heavy stockings his mother had knit him; the tools he'd made for himself the previous summer, when he'd helped build the house for his sister and new brother-in-law. Atop all were the precious sketchpad and crayons, the soft lead sticks that had caused so many arguments with his father the past two years.

Davy flexed his shoulders cautiously, winced and reached back to massage them and his neck. His head ached. "Ah," he said softly, and turned a little to look back the way he'd come, "but I've done nearly half the distance already tonight! By morning, when they find my message, I'll be already at the docks along the bay, and with any fortune at all have signed my seaman's papers. Even *my* father can't gainsay the Navy Department!"

God knew David Alan Holywell had gainsaid everything else his youngest son wanted for his future. *How many times have I heard him say it—bellow it, rather—this past year?* "I'm a plain carpenter, no nonsense about *me*! I'll not have a gimcrack for a son, fussing about with pretty scribblings; that's no living for a true man!" He'd been equally adamant in his arguments with Davy's mother. "And there'll be none of this other nonsense, plants and candles and odd smells all the day and night! Let your sisters spread this uncleanly family craft to their young, I'll none of it." When Amanda had suggested the study of medicine for Davy, her husband had simply laughed at her. "And how shall I find the money for him to learn such a profession? He'll stay at home, learn a decent, honorable trade, marry a proper girl when the time comes, and care for us in our dotage."

Davy wiped sweat from his forehead, closed his eyes briefly and shook his head. He could feel his chest tightening, his breath coming short and painful, the headache growing worse. "Leave it be, that's all behind you now," he told himself flatly. The tightness remained; finally, he sighed and began repeating his mother's soothing litany which she'd had from her father and he from his mother right back to his many times great grandfather Amer. Possibly beyond that; no one really spoke about those beyond many-times Great-grandsire Amer. Odd, though, how simply working his way back through his mother's family relaxed him a little. Perhaps because Amanda, his mother, had recited it to him so often when he was very small, he'd thought it simply another of her songs to send a little boy to sleep. Amanda, daughter of the explorer Jedediah Crafter Moss, who was twin brother of Jebenzum, both sons of Amelia Ruth Crafter Levy, daughter of Lucinda Amelia Crafter Greene— and so on.

Davy gave his neck one final rub, fumbled out his water bag and drank before climbing reluctantly to his feet and pulling his canvas sack up with him. It felt heavier than ever. He glanced over his shoulder before setting out down the road once more. Toward Annapolis and the Navy shipyards, toward two years aboard an American frigate and a chance to fight the British as his great-uncle Jeb had done.

The woods were closing in and the road began to climb toward a low ridge. His steps slowed; he squared his shoulders then, lowered his head so he wouldn't have to watch the grade, and forced himself to as strong a pace as he could manage. Just a few more yards, he assured himself at each step; just up to the top, where he would be able to see lights along Chesapeake Bay, and he'd take a proper rest. Eyes fixed just before his toes, he was unaware of the shift in the air near the top—a shift that became a spiral of faint, greenish light. He saw it only as the light spread and touched the road. He stopped short, the sack hitting the ground with a thump as he set both fists on his hips and glared at the whirling mass. There were two sad, reproachful eyes in the very center of it.

"Sprite," Davy warned, "that had better not be you!"

"Happen that is a very poorly put speech." A lisping, oddly accented voice came from the swirl of pale green. "Were you not taught how to speak proper gentleman's English? But— what if it is not me?"

"Are you playing with me?" The young man bared his teeth. "Begone, at once! Leave me in peace!" No answer. The eyes were more visible now and, if possible, even sadder. Davy cleared his throat and set his legs astraddle—as much to keep his knees from shaking as anything. For some reason, he had always found it difficult to argue with the little, near-invisible being that was his mother's friend—or ally—more than he did with either parent. Possibly because of those reproachful eyes—more likely because this was the only one of the three that never won an argument by sheer volume. "If Mother sent you—and if you think," he went on sharply, once he was certain he could trust his voice, "if you *dare* think I'll turn and follow you home like a tamed pup, you're very much mistaken!"

"Happen I know better than to try and persuade *you*." The voice was high and piping, like a reed flute; it never failed to amaze Davy just how much sarcasm such a voice could express. "There is a lead shot somewhere out there which bears your name. Or a salt wave." Silence. When it became clear Davy intended to outwait it, the sprite fetched a little sigh and went on. "Your mother—"

"Don't bring my mother into this," Davy warned.

"—is upset," it went on, as though he hadn't spoken. "But she has been upset ever since your brother John argued with your father and left home. It is not possible for *any* of you to agree and leave the poor woman in peace, so she can concentrate upon her work?"

"I have done as much, can't you see?" The young man grumbled. "I am gone now. With only herself and Father about, and he off at work so much of the time, perhaps she'll find that concentration." It was the sprite's turn to hold a stubborn silence and the boy's to sigh then. "All right, that *was* rude and inexcusable. But why can't they understand? I can't take pleasure in building if it's under my father's eye; he carps so, no one could do a proper job. Mother's notion is no better; she'd have me dabble in the family craft and I have no talent for that."

"That is not so," the sprite objected.

"I haven't," Davy said grimly. "I will not have. I do not want it. And then, to keep me safe from those who'd hang me as a warlock, she'd have me cover craft with medicine! Sprite, does no one ever *listen*? I do not want to be a doctor! The very thought of mending broken bones or great bleeding cuts makes me ill, and Mother only laughs and says I'll become used to it once I begin!"

"Happen you might. But I see the matter distresses you—"

"It angers me very much—"

"—and so you'd go to sea instead, to fight the British, where men die in droves," the sprite said accusingly. "For a lad who does not care to see blood, happen you seek it in plenty."

"That isn't necessarily true, you know; after all, my uncle didn't die, and *he* sailed clear into the Mediterranean, after the Barbary pirates. He came back wealthy enough to buy a good patch of land west of the Cumberland Mountains, and if he now chooses to dabble in family magic and send a reek of herbs and spells up his chimney, why, he has no neighbors for two days' ride in any direction to complain of it, has he?" Davy squared his shoulders and drew a deep breath. "Your reasoning is flawed, as always. It's not all dying, or why would anyone choose to go to sea?"

There was a little silence; the whirl of light became agitated, then stilled again. *Got you, once again,* Davy thought, suddenly cheerful. Whatever other talents the sprite might have, its grasp of logic was pitiful, and when it couldn't respond to his arguments, it invariably gave up at once.

"Ask this of *me*, who cannot even approach the great water," the creature replied. "And would not, even if I could," it added loftily.

Pretending indifference, Davy thought. *I've won.*

"There's the matter of pride, too," Davy went on, and somehow kept the triumph he felt from his voice. His mother's companion was notoriously touchy about losing arguments and it had plenty of ways to make its displeasure felt, literally. This was scarcely the time to find himself covered in an itchy rash. "Those new men in the Congress, those Young War Hawks as they call themselves, they have a good grasp of what is important, you know. Why should we let these arrogant Britishers run the sea as they please, taking our ships, our men, our cargo—telling us what we may and may not sell and buy and in what ports? We fought a war against them and won it in 1783. Was that all for nothing?"

"Happen I know nothing of these politics," came a rather prim response. "You will not be persuaded, then?" Davy shook his head so hard, fine brown hair swung free of the confining black ribbon and tickled his nose; he sneezed. "Knowing that once you board a ship your mother will have no bond with you? That I shall not? Water, you know," the sprite reminded him as Davy frowned and shook his head in confusion. "Happen that water, especially so much salt water, nullifies power."

"There isn't such a bond between me and Mother," Davy said evenly. "You must think I am my brother John. Don't tell me there could be such a bond, either; perhaps I am more Father's son than John is, but there's no Crafter Talent in *me*."

"That is not so, but we will leave it for now."

"We had better." Davy ran a hand across his hair, snugging loose ends back into the ribbon as best he could. "Give over, sprite. You're accomplishing nothing save to make me unhappy; you won't change my mind. Do you think I haven't thought it out? I can't live at home anymore. I feel like a mouse between two cats. I can't please either parent, so I'll please neither."

"And please yourself instead?"

"Perhaps. Is that so wrong? I won't know for certain if the sea pleases me so much as I believe it will until I've tried it, shall I? But it's more than that, didn't you listen?"

"Patriotic duty," the sprite replied sourly. "Happen I heard what you said, and a pretty little speech you made of it, too. Never mind. If I cannot persuade you, will you at least heed a little sense? Your brother John lives not far this side of your destination. Why not talk with him a little, sleep at his hearth, arrive to sign your paper awake and alert?"

Davy opened his mouth to say no, then closed it again. He picked up his bag, shrugging his shoulders forward in an effort to stretch outraged muscle. He felt a momentary qualm as he set one foot before the other—*if this is a trap of Mother's!*—but he rejected the fear as foolish, almost at once. His mother wouldn't have found that note yet, surely;

this wasn't a trick or a trap on the part of the argumentative little being to ensnare him somehow and keep him from his destination. The sprite wasn't—dishonest—like that. Nor was Amanda; if she'd discovered her son missing and wanted to bespeak him, the sprite would have said as much. Or his mother would somehow have found a means to communicate with her power-poor son.

And besides, stopping to talk to John, now he thought of it, was a very good notion. John had gone through enough arguments of his own with their father to understand how Davy felt; he'd never try to turn his youngest brother from his present course. And John lived near enough to the shipyards and docks; he might know which of the frigates was in port, or, if there was more than one, which was the best. One couldn't hope to find a berth with the great Captain Decatur, of course. But a ship, any of the frigates which might take him into the open sea, and perhaps set him upon a course against those arrogant English . . . .

There was only one small problem: While he'd heard indirectly from John the past winter—a short note to Davy had been enclosed in a letter to their sister Lucy, congratulations on her marriage—he knew only that John had a small acreage and a furniture shop outside Annapolis. *Somewhere* outside Annapolis. Davy scowled at the sprite. "I don't suppose *you* would know how to find my brother's front door on a night such as this?" he asked belligerently.

The strap of the heavy bag slid from his arm and rose into the air, began moving uphill in the midst of a faint, greenish light. "Happen," came the rather smug response from the center of that light, "that I do."

It shouldn't have surprised Davy when he, the spin of green light and his bag—floating at an unnerving knee-height off the road—came to the end of a narrow side lane some time later to discover John sitting on the stoop, the light of a dying fire visible through the open door. *John might well have felt my presence, if this—this well-nigh-invisible porter— did not simply inform him when he persuaded me to come this way,* Davy thought peevishly. *I could almost envy them that. Think how wonderful to bespeak anyone else with the Talent, anywhere.* Think—to know at once what his uncle Jeb was doing, how his sister Jemmy was settling into her new life in Boston. Of course, it would also mean that, like with Jemmy, there'd be no escape from his mother's rather high-pitched and near-constant reproaches . . . . *Doesn't matter; I cannot manage it anyway. They can, and all I can feel is a certain envy and a good deal as though my mind has been invaded against my will.*

He had to swallow anger, then; he didn't want to growl at John, after all, and it wasn't really the sprite's fault he was tired, footsore, cross—and suddenly not certain he'd done the right thing, now his goal was so near. Be blessed if he'd let either of his companions know *that*, though. He dropped onto the stoop with a heartfelt sigh and clasped John's arms, hard.

"You've grown considerably," John said, and drew him close for a hard embrace before leaning back to eye him critically in the fading red light. "Enough to scramble into a frigate's sheets, I suppose, but not so tall as to tangle up in them." Davy opened his mouth and shut it again without saying anything; his elder brother laughed quietly. "Come, now. You can't be surprised I know why you grace my doorway at such an ungodly hour. But, come in, it's grown cool this past hour or so and there's a bucket of hot ale and a loaf on the hearth." He scooped up the bag the sprite had dropped just inside the room and let Davy precede him. "Here, take the settle close to the fire, doff your outer things and your shoes. So, Mother won't have a doctor in the family after all?"

Davy laughed sourly for reply, took the thick, warmed mug and gratefully inhaled steam. "As likely Father will have a partner in either of us to hand him nails."

"A pity," John said quietly. "All the same, I learned a good deal from both of them, things I can use now I've been a year or so away from the constant arguings. This house and all its furnishings are my work, and I make enough from the sale of my tables and the like that next year I'll be able to wed my young woman and build her a better and larger house." He sipped at his own ale, set it aside. "You might have gone to join our uncle out West, you know; the sea isn't precisely a safe profession just now."

"But, that's the entire point, isn't it?" Davy rested his mug on his knee and leaned forward. "To teach the English and the French a lesson, that we won't be pushed about. And the sea wasn't safe when Uncle Jeb went against the Barbary pirates, was it? Or don't you remember the things he told us of that war?"

John smiled, shook his head and reached for the mug, which he set in his younger brother's hands once again. "I'll not argue politics with so avid a supporter of the Young War Hawks. I know better. Your mind's clearly made up, and you're old enough to have a right to your own choice."

Davy heaved a quiet sigh and drained his cup. "Thank you, John. I knew you'd be sensible."

"I'm not so certain that's what I'm being; still, it's your decision. I'll go down to the docks with you tomorrow if you like, and see if I can be of any use. They say the *Constitution* is in port just now. No doubt her berths are full but—well, perhaps not. And I do know her captain."

Davy's fingers tightened on the mug and he bent over his empty cup to hide the sudden grin. The *Constitution*! Stephen Decatur no longer sailed her, but she'd been his flagship when the great Captain defeated the Barbary pirates in their own harbor! He brought his head up, blinking; John had been speaking and he'd missed a good deal of what his elder brother had said.

"Never mind." John laughed briefly and waved a hand. "I can see your thoughts are all for a frigate and sails and cannon. I would not trade with you for the world and all in it. But I do worry that you will have no contact with any of us—myself, the sprite, Mother." As Davy scowled and shifted, John waved his hand again. "No, don't say it. I know you will have it the family Talent never found a seat in you."

"More fool he," came a faint, whispery voice from somewhere along the shadowy mantel. Davy transferred the scowl to the least greenish light there; it faded. "Happen he's wrong," the voice added in the tone of one getting in the last word.

"I am not," Davy snarled. He managed a rueful grin and shrugged then as John caught his eye and winked. "John, I'm sorry; I'm tired from so long a day and night, and truly, didn't I try to learn from Mother? *You* know I did. And what did I accomplish, save to break her favorite alembic, and to spill something that made a hellish smoke and roused Father's displeasure to a fever pitch?"

"That you cannot work with Mother means nothing," John said. "Didn't I say? I broke enough things, trying to deal with her, and it was purely impossible. Fortunately, I was sensible enough to bring a copy of the book with me, and I did have the additional sense to try certain things for myself once I left home. You cannot think how much simpler it all was." He tossed the still dark mantel a grin. "I did have help, of course."

"Happen you had Talent as well."

"Thank you, my sweet."

"Yes, but what is it good for?" Davy demanded irritably. "It seems to accomplish nothing save to band witch hunters into vicious packs, or to create dreadful smells and suspicious neighbors, or to anger people like Father, who want none of it."

John sighed. "I know. I felt that way once. I still wonder why he wed Mother; doubtless he thought she would give it all over once he had her safely in his house and bed."

"I wonder one hasn't murdered the other," Davy grumbled into his empty mug. John took it from him, refilled it and handed it back.

"A mystery not discoverable by science," he agreed. "I often wonder why the sprite remains with Mother—"

A low growl came from the mantel. "Happen *I* have no choice," it said.

Davy considered this, sipped gingerly at the hot, spicy ale. "Oh," he said finally. And, after another long, thoughtful pause, "I'm sorry."

"Happen I take enough pleasure with others in Family. Amanda can be borne."

"Don't get involved in a discussion with the sprite," John suggested. "Or you'll be the rest of the night trying to sort it all out, and you'll come out feeling confused, to say the least. And sleepless."

"And I do need to be alert." Davy drained his mug, set it aside and impulsively held out his hands. "John. Thank you—"

"Don't say it," John broke in. "Give me a real proof of your gratitude, why don't you?" He got to his feet and beckoned as he moved into shadow. Davy followed cautiously, shuffling his feet in case of furniture hiding in the gloom. John was a darker shadow against a small window; then the window was blocked and a moment later he struck a light. He beckoned again; Davy came up to lean against a woodworker's bench, with tools neatly placed on the far end and two half-turned chair legs placed across them. The rest of the surface was neat and barren, not so much as a speck of sawdust or a wooden peg anywhere in sight. All along the back of the bench were closed cabinets, many of them locked. John tugged one cabinet door open, bringing out several glass containers and a burner. The cabinet next to it held bottles and boxes of chemicals, neatly marked, with John's heavy, leather-bound copy of the family notes set into a niche above them, which he pulled out and began to page through. Davy repressed a sigh, rolled his eyes ceilingward, and clasped his hands behind his back, watching in silence as his elder brother apparently found the page he wanted. He studied it for several moments, then lit the small burner and began mixing certain powders and poured them into a long glass tube. When he added liquid to this, it began bubbling even before he moved it above the flame. Davy eyed it warily and took a step back. John saw that and cast him a quick glance and a smile.

"It's safe enough—or will be. Can you spare me a drop of your blood for it, though? There's a clean pin stuck in the inside of the cabinet door—there, pushed into the wood. Just one drop—careful!" he added as the younger man jabbed the end of his smallest finger and pressed, forcing a thick red blob to the surface.

"What is it?" Davy asked nervously. The bubbling liquid was now hissing and spitting, and the smell, though faint, was unpleasant. "I hope you don't intend that I drink that!"

John laughed. "Don't worry. No, it's a charm of sorts, a protective thing. Something to do with the notion of your blood being protected from harm; at least, Uncle Jeb has used this one before. He had one aboard ship when they went against Tripoli, or so he says, and he claims it turned a sword or two pointed his way."

"What, did he rub it on?" Davy's nose wrinkled. "I can readily see it would turn away the ladies."

John laughed again and shook his head. "You must have paid less attention to Mother than I did. When was there ever such a spell in this book? Silly, it goes into a little brass bottle with a spoonful of whale oil atop the liquid, and you *wear* it, either about your throat or in a pocket. A stoppered bottle, before you

ask. The bottle gets a coating of whale oil. You'll have to rub
it in well, repeat it now and again. The drop of blood is in a
watery liquid, the brass and oil surround it. And oil and water
don't mix, so your blood is doubly protected—and, therefore,
so are you," John finished cheerfully.

Davy's forehead puckered and he shook his head. "I'm sorry.
That's not making any sense at all, John."

"Wait." John closed the book and returned it to its niche
before he reached for a small brass bottle, a larger bottle filled
with liquid, a copper funnel and a soft rag. He closed and locked
the cabinet on the book, then transferred the spell-stuff into
the little brass container, added a little liquid from the large
bottle before stoppering the brass one. He set it aside, poured
liquid from the large bottle onto the cloth and handed cloth
and brass bottle to his younger brother. "Here. Rub that in
well. You won't want it all over your clothing." Davy's nose
wrinkled involuntarily; the oil was particularly fishy-smelling,
not a particularly well-rendered batch of blubber. "Come now,"
John went on. "Don't you remember one of the first things
Mother taught us? The symbol is the referent." And as Davy
shook his head he added, "You must remember, surely. You
create a symbol—the liquid with your blood in it, representing
you—then you do something to it—protect it in a hard shell,
like this brass bottle—and so long as the symbol is safe, so is
the referent. Simple, yes?"

"Bah," Davy said. "But it won't work at sea—will it?"

"Uncle Jeb said *his* did. Though nothing else of the family
knowledge did, try as much as he might."

"Well." Davy continued rubbing. The small bottle shone
nicely now. He could wish it didn't smell quite so awful, but
perhaps John had a purpose to using what had to be badly
rendered whale oil. "At least this is small enough no one will
notice it. As to the rest, how would Uncle Jeb have managed
something like this"—a sweep of Davy's hand took in John's
laboratory—"aboard a ship, where a man has the space of his
hammock and not much else to call his own? Of course he had
no recourse to the family Talent!"

"There are ways; you haven't read enough of the book,
have you?"

"As little as possible, John. As you well know. All the same,
I don't remember any way for one of us to set up a laboratory

in the midst of outsiders. And if it is there, it is knowledge I will *not* need, John. Any more than I will need our mutual small friend. Besides, it's already warned me often enough the past hours that it can't come to my rescue once I'm at sea, or even talk to me."

"Do not look so pleased," came a small, peevish voice from somewhere above the bench. John took the bottle, examined it briefly, then bent down to rinse his funnel and the glass tube in a bucket under the bench. He dried them on an unoiled corner of Davy's cloth before returning everything to its proper place. When the wooden doors were closed once more, he turned and handed Davy the bottle and a long leather thong to tie around his neck.

"Here. Return my favor at the docks tomorrow by swearing you will keep this on you at all times."

"I—well." Davy turned it over thoughtfully. "Well, all right, I swear."

"There are odd things on and under the sea," John went on. "Remember some of Uncle Jeb's stranger tales. Not so much the fighting at Tripoli, but some of what he swore he saw not so far off our own coast."

Davy stuffed the bottle inside his shirt—he could always stuff it in his bag later, he decided—and grinned. "He'd had a sight too much grog, John. Must have. Sea serpents and mermaids?"

"You deny they might exist, knowing the companions *our* family has?"

"When no one else saw them?" Davy retorted. "Too much grog."

"Well—remember what he said. It's a curious world, after all. Come, though; we'd better be abed if you intend to go abroad early tomorrow." Davy merely nodded. But once he'd settled into an old spare comforter before the fire, John paused on his way to his own bed. "Do keep an open mind, will you? And I know all about the limited space aboard a ship; I've been asea once, you know—if only to Boston. I also know you've the Talent if you choose to use it, little brother. There may come a time you want to bespeak family, or our small friend here, or even possibly desperately need to. Don't ask why; I don't know why. I just see there might be a possibility. A ghost of a hint of a mere chance. I don't know how any of us could help, either; before you ask *that*. Just—think about it. Honestly, Davy, I don't think that's too much to ask, is it?"

Davy gazed up at him for a very long moment. It was an odd request, coming as it did from a man who never exercised an open mind in either his alchemy *or* his furniture-making, however well he performed in both fields. Finally, he nodded. "If you feel so strongly about it."

"As strongly as you feel about this mad venture," John said, but he said it so solemnly, Davy couldn't bring himself to argue his brother's choice of words.

John had him up and on the way as the sun was just beginning to cast early golden light over woods and fields. There was dew on the bushes lining the lane; a thin coating of it kept down the dust on the main road. Davy's ears were buzzing and he had to stuff his hands into his pockets so John would not see how they trembled. His heart was pattering rapidly against his waistcoat as they came onto a broad cobbled avenue and walked down it for some distance. There were gulls everywhere, white against blue sky, raucous voices cutting through the noises of wooden cart-wheels against stone; two women arguing with a street peddler; the distant calls of merchants and customers down a narrow side-street where he could see the high-piled tables of an open-air harvest market. And then the tangy, unmistakable odor of the wharf: a compounding of fish, gulls, pitch and kerosene, salt water, something that had gone well past ripe, exotic odors he couldn't begin to identify.

John led him down a shaded, narrow alley and once more into brilliant sunlight; Davy blinked rapidly, slowing as his eyes adjusted. Sun reflected off the water to his left; to his right were stone and wooden buildings, barefoot and barelegged men everywhere—men in blue-and-white-striped shirts and pale, short breeches carrying bags and parcels from buildings, across wooden planking that rattled and echoed underfoot. They all had one destination. Davy stopped short, eyes wide, mouth agape. Just before him, rocking gently, stood what must surely be a frigate: a long, graceful ship, larger than any he'd seen before. Three great masts rose to an astonishing height. John nudged him and he pulled his mouth closed with an effort. If anyone of those men had seen him, staring like a bumpkin! Apparently they were one and all too busy, though. He schooled his face to what he hoped was casual interest as they walked on, but he could feel the blood warming his face as he stepped past the bow and was able to read the lettering there: *Constitution*. In something of a daze he followed his elder brother through the door of one of the buildings.

Midday. Davy's admiration for his brother had gone up considerably when Captain Hull greeted him by name—John's chairs and table graced the captain's cabin, it seemed. *He* had felt exceedingly inadequate when, pleasantries done with, the Captain turned to study him. Davy sat up straight, hoping he didn't look half the fool he felt. The Captain finally shrugged. "In such times, I ordinarily would prefer not to accept a green boy aboard my ship—the British want her badly, you know; it's not sense for her to carry any but highly skilled and experienced sailors. But he's got a look about the eyes, and I lost a man two days past, broke a leg as he came ashore. Not such a problem, save that I'm already short three others this past month. Think you want to join the Navy, eh, boy?"

Davy nodded, swallowed. "Yes, sir." He flushed as the older man laughed, but it didn't sound like a malicious laugh.

"Aye, well. I like enthusiasm. It might carry as much as experience, unless the man in question is a gunner. We'll keep you from the guns though, shall we?"

"I—yes, sir. I've—I know carpentry, I've apprenticed under my father, I have my own tools—some of them . . . ." Davy's voice faded to nothing, and he bit his lip to keep from stammering on. To himself he sounded like a prattling babe. Captain Hull merely nodded.

"Carpenter, is it? Well, I've a full carpenter, but a ship can always use another man with a knowledge of hammer and nails." Somehow, it was all done: A clerk was brought in from a back room, papers produced. Davy and Captain Hull both signed, with John a witness to his brother's character and willingness to join the American Navy for a period of two years, during a time of declared war against the British, for a pay of $13 a month. Another hour, and he was issued two changes of rough, slightly too-large clothes and blankets. Most of his bag was left in John's hands, but he'd another, smaller canvas bag for his tools, and the Captain had been pleased to see his sketching materials. "Perhaps we'll come one over the British,"

the Captain had said cheerfully, "and you'll record it all for me."
He was gone then, leaving Davy and John alone together. Later,
Davy could remember nothing of his last conversation with his
brother. There had been a half-dozen men his own age and a
Marine Lieutenant Bush to bring him aboard ship, to show him
his hammock and where to stow his few personal things.

There had been an odd-tasting, extremely hard biscuit to
chew on while several of the younger men showed him around
the ship, from the storage and the powder magazines to the
galley and the messes, all around the decks. At the Lieutenant's
suggestion, they didn't try to take him into the rigging, even
though the ship was still at port.

By early evening, though, she no longer was: Her hull
thoroughly scraped and cleansed of barnacles, her thirty-seven
new sails unfurled, new guns in place and a full load of
powder below decks, the *Constitution* sailed slowly out into
Chesapeake Bay.

Davy was given simple chores—helping to tighten lines;
clearing spare ropes from the deck; checking that the boats
were all properly fastened into their locks, that the colors had
been folded neatly, where they could be quickly retrieved and
flown if the Captain so ordered. In the meantime, after the
British fashion, the frigate would show no colors at all in
hopes of luring an unsuspecting enemy ship into range of its
24-pounders.

He worked with a will, and by the time he went to his
hammock felt comfortable with the sailors in his mess—eight
young men altogether, who would eat the same meals and share
watches. He found the constantly rolling deck a minor annoyance only; fortunately, it didn't seem to bother his stomach.
But there was a distinctly queer sensation under his ribs as
he lay back and closed his eyes. Odd. Had John been right
after all? Somehow, for the first time in his life, he felt alone.
He dismissed that impatiently. He never had been connected,
Crafter-fashion, to his mother, his uncle Jeb, his sisters. Not
even to John, closest of all his kin. Certainly not to that
maddening sprite. That reminded him; he drew the brass bottle
from the inside pocket where it had been hidden under his shirt,
slid it into a little leather pouch in his canvas tool bag. *Yes,
John, I did promise*, he thought drowsily. *But I didn't say for
how long—and I don't see how you'll ever know, anyway.*

• • •

Two days. They were in the open Atlantic now, though Davy could easily make out the coast to port. Lieutenant Bush had more or less turned him over to his mess and several other common seamen, with orders for them to show him what they did and when, and to teach him proper shipboard behavior. The Lieutenant himself was busy working with the gunnery crew, and with repositioning the kegs of powder down in the after powder magazine.

Davy spent most of his first day with Andrew Vincent, a poor city boy his own age from Philadelphia, and with Henry Clay, not much older and nearly dark as a Moor, who'd grown up as Davy had on a farm.

Between them, he learned how to tie down lines the right way, where to go if the ship came under attack and the big guns were brought into play. ("You don't want to be underfoot, Davy; it's chaos with men loading and cleaning, powder boys everywhere, and the firing enough to make you deaf. Besides, they'll have your ears if you *do* get in the way, same as if you so much as *whisper* once a ship's been sighted. Dead silence from sighting until first shot, it's a rule from the days against Tripoli.") He learned how to fold his hammock and stow it in a minimum of time; spent hours before the ship left Chesapeake Bay in scrubbing the main deck where feet had trailed mud back and forth between the after companionway, the main hatchway, and the gangway, leaving dirt, dust, mud and trickles of substances that leaked from the bags going below. He polished cannon; he learned to knock even two-day-old ship's biscuit against a hard surface before biting into it—and somehow managed not to yelp in surprise and disgust at the weevils that scurried away.

Once they were on open sea, he actually had the opportunity to break out his tool bag, to make repairs on an oarlock in one of the boats hanging alongside. That felt good; he was doing what he knew, serving as a carpenter aboard ship. Immediately after, though, he was sent to mid-deck with oil and rags to polish the huge, spool-like oaken capstan used to weigh anchor.

It wasn't what he had expected, Davy thought as he rubbed and polished dark wood and brass. Being Navy during a declared war, one would expect more to do with fighting, boarding a captured ship. He'd been issued a dirk, of course; everyone had some sort of blade in case they boarded a ship or were, God

forbid, boarded themselves. But most of his time thus far—
almost everyone's time, he realized in looking around the main
deck—was spent in cleaning and polishing, repairing ropes and
sails. Uncle Jeb had talked about cutlasses, guns, falling masts,
fires—nothing about scrubbing planks and steps. Well, but why
describe such dull moments to an eager young nephew?

There were a few good things about so much boring, grueling
physical labor, however: It kept his mind from wandering onto
subjects such as the unpleasant sensation of very deep water
beneath the ship; of something *in* that deep water which might
not wish men aboard ships well; of the growing unease at being
truly cut off from his own kind and an accompanying anger
that assured him he was making up such a sense of disquiet.
Because there *was* no contact between himself and others of
Crafter stock—and those who served the Crafters. Was not and
never had been! Unlike his mother and his brother John, who
had both had the Talent strong almost from birth.

They'd have been lost aboard a ship. Both of them, Davy
realized, were set in Crafter ways—or what they saw as its
ways. With them—like most of the rest of his kin—it was
everything from that blessed book, no single variation permitted; everything just as many-times Great-grandfather Amer had
worked it out.

"It's Wednesday," Andrew announced as he came running
up, bare feet slapping against hardwood planks. "That means
a drill, to see how fast the gunnery crew can set up, and how
quickly the rest of us get into position. Stay right close to me
for now, unless Lieutenant Morris—that's him, there, d'you
remember?—unless he sends you elsewhere. Pay no heed to
what the other boys try to tell you; it's your first Wednesday
and they'll try mischief. And remember, once Lieutenant Morris
gives the first order, *keep yourself quiet*."

No one tried mischief. The Lieutenant passed him several
times where he stood with half-a-dozen other common sailors
near the mizzenmast, buckets of water at their heels and four
of the more experienced ready to climb into the sheets at
need. Davy watched in awe as the gunports were opened and
the massive weapons rolled forward, as boys raced back and
forth across the deck with powder buckets—empty buckets,
since there was no danger, and no barrels set out for gunnery
practice. The drill went on for well over an hour as the ship

continued its smooth, even course northward along the coast. Aside from the slap of feet against decking, the faint screech of a wheel that needed oiling, the scrape of metal as one of the crews opened the port on the cannon, a total, skin-prickling silence held.

As soon as the drill ended, Davy and his group were put to work trimming sail—Davy safely on the deck right at the base of the mast to catch lines and hand them to one of the others to tie off. "Of course, we'll be rocking madly once we actually engage the British," Andrew said. "Keep that in mind; since it's your first voyage you'll want to find something to hold onto." He grinned. "Be glad you're not one of the sheet monkeys, up there in the rigging when the ship's rolling." Davy looked up, and quickly back down again. He could feel the blood leaving his face. All the same, if a man knew his way about up there—well, there'd be time and a way, another voyage, wouldn't there?

The hope faded. Just now, with the drill scarcely over, recalling the grim and unnerving silence in which men and boys had worked to ready the ship for battle—well, all at once, he didn't feel quite so hopeful about the length of his future. *I chose this? Of my own free will? Mother's right, and so was Father. I must be mad!*

The night was warm, the sea almost calm; worn out, he slept hard, barely woke when the boatswain's mate came clattering through at change of watch after four hours, and went right back to sleep again.

Late afternoon. He was in the bow, helping Andrew oil the wheels on the 18-pounder kept there, when a cry came down from high above. One of the men on the foremast had sighted four ships landward; moments later came another cry, from the mizzenmast—another ship off the starboard. Davy came partway upright to stare toward what he'd been told was the New Jersey shore; Andrew touched his shoulder and pointed farther south. "No colors. They could be the *President*, you know, Commodore Rogers' ship and the rest of his squadron. Scuttlebutt has it we're looking to find him." He turned to look back along the deck and up at the rigging. "Sure enough, see? They're slacking, standing off to wait for the seaward vessel to come in."

"Oh." Davy considered this. He swallowed. "What if it's theirs instead?"

"What, all five of them?" Andrew laughed, clapped him on the back and bent again to his assigned task. "Consider what a prize it would make!"

Prize. Davy swallowed again. Perhaps, once he had a moment, he'd go in search of that little brass bottle John had concocted for him. After all . . .

The sun went down, and the *Constitution* moved very slowly forward; the unknown ship was well in from the horizon, not yet near enough to make out markings. Davy, on evening watch with his mess, watched anxiously as the sky slowly grew dark and a few stars came out. At one point the Captain and Lieutenant Morris went by, deep in discussion; the fact that they sounded worried didn't do anything to ease the pain in his stomach.

Full dark. Half-a-dozen men bearing lanterns scrambled into the foremast rigging, spreading out in the pattern that would mark *Constitution* to another American frigate captain. No response. The sea all around them remained dark. The boatswain pounded down the deck, returned moments later with half-clad sailors. For all her size, Davy discovered the ship was highly maneuverable; she came about in short order indeed and began sailing south, moving slowly in light wind. Behind her, no sign of light, no sound of movement. They might have been totally alone.

Davy crossed to the rail as his watch ended and spent several long, fruitless moments peering into the night. For the moment, the usual sensation of an underwater presence was gone; buried under crushing dread, no doubt, unless it was the influence of the little charm bottle he now wore. His palms were damp, and he jumped when a hand touched his arm.

"Gently, my friend." It was Andrew. "I've no doubt it's the *President*, you know. There's any number of reasons they might not have responded to the signal." They both considered this in silence. "Though," Andrew went on thoughtfully, "it's known the British use witchcraft of some sort to locate American ships." Davy saw the motion of his mess-mate's head as the other turned to look at him, and wondered briefly if he'd been somehow found out. He laughed.

"Witchcraft! Not really!"

"Well—something like it, they say. Witches can't work on water, of course."

"What, did the Devil give them special abilities, then?" Davy asked dryly. "Since it's for God and King, of course." Andrew chuckled.

"Well—actually, a friend of mine was taken by them, conscripted because they said he looked and sounded Brit, even though he had proof he was born in New York City. Imagine! *He* says there was a man aboard the *Little Belt*, kept largely to himself in a special chamber full of bottles and evil-smelling smokes. *He* wasn't allowed inside, of course; no one was save this man and his servant. But he saw once, when the door was ajar, bottles and boxes and an enormous book propped against the bulkhead."

"A book," Davy echoed blankly. He shook himself quickly. "I've heard of such things," he went on, hoping he sounded only mildly interested—and not at all knowledgeable. "Men who create magic with written spells and so on. Alchemists, aren't they?"

"Truly? But why would anyone want to turn lead into gold aboard a ship?" Andrew asked.

"I've heard they do other things, besides that."

"Oh." Andrew considered this, finally shrugged. "There's another thing, though—one that's common knowledge among us, although a landsman might laugh at it." He eyed his companion sidelong once again. "This ship. She's lost some of her protection, coming into Chesapeake Bay." He settled his elbows on the rail and stared at the froth of water trailing alongside the ship. "She—you see, after she was commissioned, the men who built her rubbed the copper sheathing and the planking with oil. Probably coming new to the sea you'll think it a fool's gesture, or you'll think it smacks of witchery. All the same, when Commander Decatur took her into the Tripolitan War he knew, and so did all her men, that it would be well-nigh impossible to take her or sink her. Now—well, Captain Hull meant well. And the hull *was* thick with growth, barnacles, oysters—he said it was hung about like a grape arbor. So he took her into fresh water to kill off what growth he could, then had her scraped. She's fast now; before that she sailed like a tub. But when they scraped her—"

"They took away the oil?" Davy asked quietly as Andrew hesitated.

"Just so. You'll laugh—"

"Not necessarily. There are odd things in the world, after all. If she was scraped though, why couldn't she have been re-oiled?"

Andrew laughed briefly. "Two reasons: The oiling wouldn't have worked well underwater, and the Captain had no interest in trying to haul her out of water. More importantly, he has a mind above such—well, the kindest thing he's called it is a fool's notion."

"I see."

"I thought you should know, since you've signed aboard for two years. And in case the older men say odd things. Some of them think they can sense something unfriendly below the hull, now it's unprotected. Some think the British will be able to find and take us now."

"And you? What do you think?"

Andrew shook his head. "I think she's a good ship, with a good captain and a good crew; they'll have to fight hard to win out against the *Constitution*. I cannot feel anything odd about her, or the sea. The Captain claims it to be poppycock and won't hear any of it." He sighed. "I don't *think* I can feel anything odd. Although, sometimes, in a watch—but a man can imagine anything in the late hours of a watch, can't he? I forget, you haven't taken one yet. Well, you'll see." He smiled in Davy's direction, the flash of teeth visible in the very faint lights on deck. "The rest of our mess is below; we'd better go, too. Tomorrow looks to be a very long day." Davy thought much later that he couldn't have understated matters more if he had tried.

Tired as he was, sleep evaded him for some time, and when the change of watch came around, he was still awake—still considering Andrew's words. Alchemists—there *were* other alchemists in the world. Oil on the hull of the ship/no oil. Things beneath the water. Alchemists? British alchemists? A number of his relations had returned to England after the war ended; was it possible another Crafter was out there?

Dawn. The change of watch was still nearly an hour away when the boatswain's mate came bellowing and clattering through the welter of hammocks on the berthing deck, waking everyone, tumbling men to the planks. He had to raise his voice above the angry rumble but he managed it, and silenced them all with his first words: "Five British ships; we're surrounded! Up and out!" He didn't need to say anything else; the men raced onto the deck.

The *Constitution* looked small indeed with the British full ship of the line before her. Retreat to shore or to the north was cut off by four smaller ships. Davy came to an abrupt halt near the mizzenmast, and in the utter stillness on deck, he could hear Lieutenant Bush naming them. "*Africa*; carries sixty-four guns. That's *Shannon* to her rear, *Guerrière* off our port, both thirty-eight-gun frigates. *Aeolus* and *Belvedira*, thirty-two guns apiece." He sounded frighteningly calm, Davy thought. By the faces of several of the younger men around him, he wasn't the only one who thought as much. But Captain Hull was as outwardly unemotional.

"A good catch, if we could take them. Perhaps, however, an extra application of sail, and a strategic turn to the south?" Men were already swarming aloft. But as the ship began to move, the wind gave one final puff and fell away entirely. Sails went limp against the masts, and high above, someone began cursing.

"Enough!" someone else shouted, and silence fell. It was quiet enough, all of a sudden; they could hear the English angrily fighting their own sails.

Captain Hull came down the deck, officers right at his heels. "Launch boats. Pick the best we have to row them. Get rope, run it out from the bowsprit to each boat." And as someone began to protest, "Don't look at me so, man! What choice have we? She moves better than any British tub; we'll tow her out of this trap. Head south." He stopped between mizzen and main masts, and looked around at his waiting, silent men. "The rest of you, pay heed. We'll win free of this, if there's any way good men and a good ship can." He passed on; one of the officers gestured to those nearest him. "You, you and you, get all the buckets you can; you and you, begin forming the lines to pass the buckets across the deck and into the rigging. The sheets have to stay wet; they'll hold whatever air comes, wet. You, you and you—" He pointed out three of the older sailors. "Below with you, at once. Get whatever help you need to bring up rope, all the spare length we have. Go!" Men scattered, and Davy found himself in the midst of a brigade passing buckets of sea water toward the mizzen.

Later he found it hard to focus on any one thing. It seemed to take forever, but somehow, slowly, the *Constitution* eased her way between the British ships, out of the trap, towed by her own rowboats; as she came into open water, gunners ran to open four of the gunports. Thus far, fortunately, the British were holding fire—perhaps to avoid hitting their own ships. Surely that wouldn't last.

The sun rose; they inched southward, the shoreline scarcely seeming to move at all. Wet sails hung limp and dripping in the morning heat. And now, Davy could look back and see the nearest of the British ships moving, towed by her own boats, oars dipping in and out of a brilliant blue sea. The heat increased; sweat dripped from Davy's hair into his eyes, from the end of his nose and his chin; the brass bottle was stuck unpleasantly against his breastbone. He could almost make out individual men on the nearest pursuing ship; could see cannon through the open ports.

When the hair lifted from his forehead, he didn't immediately take it in; others, more experienced, cheered briefly as the breeze bellied the *Constitution*'s wet sails and she moved out of range. He had wit enough to stay where he was, near mid-deck, out of the way as men with more experience ran to catch up the men and boats as she passed them; he helped coil and stack wet ropes, and prayed they would not be needed again.

Half an hour later, the breeze died, and not long after, Davy saw a splash portside. "Oh, Lord, that's *shot*," he whispered. The man passing him buckets laughed grimly.

"Of course it's shot! They've rotten aim, though, the Brits, be grateful."

Other men pelted past them, dragging an enormous length of newly spliced ropes while three others struggled after with a sharp-bladed anchor. "Ah, God." Someone nearby sighed heavily, one of the older men, Davy thought. Someone knew what was afoot and didn't care for it much.

No one did, when it was explained to them; so desperate a chance as to seem a madman's or a fool's. The kedge anchor was being rowed as far ahead as possible, half a mile of rope tied to its end. Once the anchor was dropped, men would have to haul on the rope, towing the ship forward a step at a time.

It went on all day; Davy was vaguely aware of men splicing more rope, another anchor being attached to that, another line formed to alternate the anchors. Now and again there would be a brief respite—just enough breeze to allow them to bring in the boats and rest those manning the ropes, manning the oars, climbing into the rigging with buckets of sea water. He heard the nervous murmuring around him as the order was given to dump most of the ship's drinking water. Late in the afternoon, he came a little more aware as the heat eased and a light wind held for four hours. There was food—something—he never remembered what.

There were, always visible, five sets of sails. Never very far behind, despite everything they had done.

Somehow, somewhere, he lost the brass bottle; over the side, perhaps, one of the times he'd been on the dipping end of the bucket brigade. It didn't really matter; he was too exhausted to care. Save that now he was aware not only of malice beneath them, but of something—some*one*—on one of those ships behind them. Someone who was somehow capable of working magic aboard a ship, over open water! A part of his mind wondered at that; it never occurred to him, tired as he was, to wonder that Davy Holywell was able to sense the other at all.

Another day, another night; a third day. There was a difference now, though; the *Constitution* was slowly making headway, and they could see dark clouds building above the line of trees that marked the shore. Davy, who had been at the base of the mizzenmast most of the day, passing up buckets of water, was pulled back and given a short rest as skilled men swarmed into the sheets. Andrew was at his shoulder. "It's only a squall, but look! The Captain's reefing the heavy canvas, as though he expects a howler. Watch, the British don't know these waters as well; they'll copy his move, and once the storm hits, we'll shift."

They did; dark cloud, wind and blowing rain hid the ships one from another and orders were bellowed out. The boats were caught up on the run as the ship gathered speed and canvas was reworked. An almost chill wind blew sweat-soaked shirts against men's breasts, and the *Constitution* broke away. An hour or so later, as the sky began to clear, they could see the British, now well out of reach.

A cheer went up, a round of grog passed around the deck, and three-fourths of the men, including Davy's mess, sent down for their first real sleep in three days.

By morning, they could still see the British, but barely. An hour later, another cheer went up as someone high in the mainmast called down the welcome news: All five ships turning away.

"We did it!" Men hugged each other and there was pandemonium on the main deck. The euphoric mood lasted all the way to Boston Harbor.

Davy felt it, too. But his joy was tempered by worry—that sense of someone on the other side, working magic against them. He wasn't doubting his own feelings by now, though he didn't know what he could do about them. All the same, he had a nagging feeling that someone was going to have to do something to counter the British. A good ship, good men—it might not be enough, if someone was compounding spells against them. But who could he tell? Who could—or more correctly, would—do something about it? His brother John—but he could almost see John shake his head, assure him that there was nothing in the book for a situation like this, and no one could use Crafter magic aboard a ship, hadn't he paid attention?

Boston—they were going to Boston to replace the drinking water that had been pumped out to lighten the ship. He had family in Boston, of course. Perhaps someone there could do something for him.

"*Someone* will have to," Davy murmured into the gun shackle he was repairing. "Because I certainly cannot."

He learned with the rest of his mess that the stay in Boston Harbor was to be an extremely short one. "Captain doesn't want to chance being caught by orders telling him to stay there, I'd wager," one of the older men said. The others laughed. "But I wonder how he'll fund provisions and water," someone else murmured. "Wasn't I in Boston, not so long ago, either? There's no money in the Navy's purse there."

"Captain won't be slowed by such a triviality," the older man replied. "Wager he knows a dozen men who can fund fresh water and a few more barrels of meat, anyway. Be grateful, all of you, we've only been a few days out; we might otherwise have wound up stranded in Boston Harbor for certain."

All I would need, Davy thought grimly. In spite of the past few days, the British still looked better to him than a return to his family. All the same . . . He caught Andrew's attention and bent close to speak with him privately. "What chance he's right, we'll only have a little time in port?"

Andrew considered this. "Good, I'd say. Especially if we must borrow for food and drink, the Captain will be careful not to trespass on his friend's bounty. And they're all too right about orders; Washington's still run by old men and they don't want to risk their investment in wood and copper and canvas."

"More importantly," Henry Clay added from the other side of the little round table, "the British must know where we're going; five ships might be enough to blockade the harbor. Didn't we leave Annapolis as quickly as we did in order to avoid that, after all?"

"I'd heard as much," Andrew admitted. He turned back to Davy. "Whether they will let us have any time ashore, beyond letting us set foot on the docks to load food and water, I don't know."

"It was what I wanted to know," Davy said. "I've kin there. One or two I wouldn't mind seeing, but several I'd feel better if—" He shrugged, smiled briefly. "You know."

"Quite well," Henry replied. "Though it's unlikely any of *my* kin would be as far north as Boston. But if we put in anywhere my father might come—" He sighed gustily. "Never mind." He chewed, swallowed and suddenly looked much happier. "You know, if we sail into Boston, I'll wager we do it proper. You know, all brasses shining, flags in place, everything in full polish." Davy groaned; his mess-mates laughed. "I know, it sounds like work, and after the past three days, too! Don't let them tell you otherwise, Davy, that was *not* an ordinary bit of work. This, though. When we sail into Boston Harbor, you'll see it was worth it."

It *was* hard work; but as Henry had said, when they found themselves surrounded by small boats and cheering folk, with more cheering folk on the docks awaiting them, it truly was all worth it.

Andrew had been right also; the men weren't allowed full leave. But the Captain did permit six-hour excursions by those not actively working to shift powder or load supplies. Davy, uncertain of what welcome he could expect from his Boston uncle, sent a message instead of simply going to visit, and very much to his surprise, found an open carriage waiting upon the dock when he was freed from duty.

James Crafter Greene looked older than Davy's father, but it was difficult to tell; David Holywell's dark hair was half gray, Uncle James's heavily powdered. He was a rather distant but polite man, something Davy appreciated after the hysteria of his own household. He listened as they rode across town, made no comment until Davy had finished his tale—a tale he'd tried to hone into neatness the past two nights. To his own ears, he sounded too young, excitable—and his heart slowly sank as they rode on in silence. Uncle James—who called himself Jeb—rested his chin on the handle of his cane, staring straight ahead.

He roused himself just as his nephew was about to begin stammering out an apology for having bothered him. "Mmmm . . . Well, yes. Haven't ever been to sea myself, simply watching boats in the harbor makes me ill. I have heard things, though—men I know, a couple of fellows who serve me now, spent a year or so in involuntary service to the British. Impressed, you know. One has aided me in my research now and again. What you say about something underwater, something ill-humored. Possible, very much so. Captain should've re-oiled the hull, eh?"

"Well, sir, I can see his point," Davy allowed cautiously. One never *did* know what might get back to the person being discussed. "He hadn't the time, the British have been trying to set blockade—"

"Aye, mmm. The British. That's another thing entirely, isn't it? Too bad you don't know more about this fellow aboard the *Little Belt*, eh? Think it's one of ours?"

"I thought you might know better than I, sir, who among family that went back to England might—if there's anyone male and of the right age."

James rubbed his jaw against the cane. "Don't know. Doubt it, though. There are rules about what we do, all in the book— didn't your mother show you? Should've given you a chance to make your own copy, if she hadn't the time. Hear your father keeps her busy." James cast his nephew a rather malicious grin, and Davy found himself liking the man.

"Well—she did. I'm not—I haven't—"

"I heard you weren't confident about your Talent. It'll come, boy, it'll come. About your ship. What do you want of me?

You know anything we do won't be effective once the ship's asea. That's why I doubt your wizard is a Crafter; none of us could work anything in a ship's cabin, you know."

"I know." Davy managed that much; he had to turn away as though to gaze at the city around him so his uncle wouldn't see his irritation. Narrow-minded—He sighed quietly. It wouldn't work. It wouldn't be any use whatsoever. His only other hope had just slid right from under his feet. "Sir. What I'd like, if you can provide it—"

Uncle James returned to the docks two evenings later, this time in a closed carriage. Davy found a shipmate to trade excursion time with, and came down the gangway just as it drove up. His uncle's driver pulled the carriage off next to a quiet wall, closed the door snugly on the two men and wandered off to gaze at the ship and speak with one of the officers. Inside, James tugged curtains hard across the windows, then tied long, blue ribbons that ran from each corner, across the sides, across front and back. Only then did he relax. "They're treated; no one will hear or see anything. Brought everything you asked for."

"Thank you, sir. I—"

"Don't know what you'll accomplish—"

"Happen," came a small, prim voice from a dark corner, "he might accomplish good things." And, as Davy sat open-mouthed, staring into the corner, it added, "Think the distance between Annapolis and Boston so great I do not cross it?"

"I should have known better." Davy sighed, glanced at his uncle. "Did you send for it, or did it come of its own, knowing I was here to annoy?"

"Annoy!" A small, vexed sound like a smothered sneeze followed the single word.

James looked from one to another, mildly perplexed. Davy shook his head. "Never mind, sir. This is not a thing I'd have chosen to do; it may take all the time we have for me to do it right. Right," he added as he saw and sensed the other two stir, "as I see it, at least."

"I won't argue that with you," James said mildly. "After all, Great-great grandsire Amer had to start somewhere, too, didn't he?"

"Begin," the sprite added softly. "Happen you need assistance—happen I am here to give it."

It should not have been as complex as he made it; Davy was certain of that. Protection for the *Constitution*, that came first. With, if he had worked it out properly, communication of some kind—at least a sense of connection—between himself and the sprite. Though if the former precluded the latter, he scarcely cared, so long as his ship had its former guard between itself and the depths.

And so, a very small model of a frigate, one Uncle James had bought from a craftsman that very afternoon. It had been in a bottle that, according to Uncle James, lay in shards in his own workroom. The box Uncle James set in his lap contained several different kinds of oil and a number of other liquids. Davy sorted through them, finally separated out witch hazel, a lotion that smelled strongly of rosemary, and a bottle of cottonseed oil. His uncle peered at it, shook his head. "Sea spell, any kind of water spell, you want the whale oil, boy."

Davy shook his head in turn. "No, sir. At least—not at first. Not if I'm to try and preserve communication with our small friend there."

"Small. Huh."

"For that, I want a land-base oil. I—here. Can you hold this out for me? By the ends of the masts, please." He pulled a broad painter's brush from his shirt, mixed oils, poured the result into a small tin cup and began painting the mixture all along the ship. His uncle watched, turning the little model when one side was completed, turning it back so Davy could make certain he'd covered all the hull, including the massive rudder and each of the two small boats hanging from the sides. Davy shook his head. "We've three boats—ah well, it's the best one can do; we'll simply have to hope." He set aside brush and tin, examined the model closely and finally took it and set it atop the box. "Nearly dry. Uncle, you brought the other—?"

James held up a small brown bottle, the bottom of which was covered in paper and heavily waxed. "Far-sight spell. Won't work out there; of course you know that."

"It's all right." *It will if I have anything to say or do about it*, Davy promised himself grimly, but he wisely kept that to himself. He was becoming increasingly tired of the stick-in-mud attitudes of his family—at least, those of whom he knew. "The box of tobacco, you did that for me?" It was a long and narrow hand-carved smoking box, such as a fond uncle might give his nephew; inside was a clay pipe, a bag of tobacco—and underneath, a false bottom, and within the small space that provided, a finger-sized bamboo tube that held liquid. Similar to the liquid John had brewed to fit in a brass bottle, altered by Davy to—he hoped—fit new circumstances.

"You see? It's all ready but the binding matter. I brought a pin." Davy watched in silence as the older man pricked the end of Davy's thumb and let two drops fall into the liquid, then James jabbed his own smallest finger and pressed it to spill two drops of blood into the tube. Davy didn't feel any different; he didn't know if he should, and James clearly thought poorly of his alterations to a written spell. Davy ignored that and went on. "And the powder—?"

"Here. Doesn't take much."

"It must not." Davy stared at the ball James handed him. It was small enough to fit inside his shirt unnoticed; strung as it was on a fine plaited blue thong, it might have been a keepsake. James showed him the catch that opened it, showed him how to slide the covers from the halves once it was opened, to give him access to the powder. Stuff that could supposedly stop a full-powered, Devil-sanctioned witch in his or her tracks, could nullify all but the most carefully crafted spells. *Magic do-everything dust*, Davy thought irreverently. There was a drawback to it, of course; the user had to be near enough the enemy, or the source of the spell, to actually touch it. Well, one never knew, did one?

Hadn't his brother John asked him to keep an open mind, after all? *John, I wonder if you ever thought I would take you this way?* Davy thought. He nearly dropped the little ball when the answer came immediately: *No, Davy, but you always were one to chart your own course, weren't you?*

He folded up the ball and draped the cord around his neck before turning to glare into the corner where the least hint of pale green light gave away the inhabitant of that cushion. "Did you do that?" he asked severely.

A sigh out of proportion with its maker's size answered him. "Happen," the sprite said at last, "I did no such thing. Happen you asked your brother a question; as a polite man, he answered."

Davy closed his eyes. "Tell me that didn't just happen," he begged. "Tell me my mother won't be harping at me next."

"Happen Amanda might not know. She's sealed her work-room to keep your father's shouting from breaking her concentration. You amaze me," it added acerbically. "First time in all your years, you bespeak someone and *this* is all your reaction?"

"Oh, come," James said quietly. He'd been following the conversation with difficulty, but the sprite's last words seemed to make sense of it for him. "Don't you know how to block Amanda—or anyone else you'd rather keep out of your mind?"

Davy shrugged. "Until just now, it wasn't important. Is there time left, that you can show me, sir?"

"Isn't likely she'll be able to bespeak you, anyway; it's something you have to want."

"Like asking your brother John a question," the sprite added helpfully.

"Well—yes. Here," James added and leaned forward to take hold of his nephew's forearms.

He couldn't follow what his uncle was trying to show him; James seemed to think his lack of understanding would probably protect him from his mother better than anything else, at this point. "Come back later," the older man said finally, "when you've a longer leave. See what we can't show you." He laughed quietly as he took the box of powders and liquids, with the little treated ship still balanced atop it. "I'll keep this safe meantime. Who knows, by the time you return, you may be teaching me. If all this works—"

If I live to see it work, Davy thought. Suddenly, he felt extremely foolish. *I wasted an entire six hours off. I could have gone into town with the others, seen a little of Boston. Well, at least of the pubs along the wharf.* He managed to keep that from his uncle James, and somehow the two of them managed to convince the sprite it would look terribly odd for him to walk across the dock with a spiral of pale green light above his shoulder. "And I cannot trust you to stay unseen," Davy added sternly. The corner went very dark and still.

A replacement bottle for himself—he considered that as he went up the gangplank and he heard his uncle's carriage drive away. He could have made one similar to the one John created for him. He rejected the thought after a moment. No one else aboard ship had such a thing. And if there were evil things about—in the water, aboard an enemy ship—he wanted to *know*.

Four days later, the *Constitution* sailed back into the Atlantic; there were wagers cast all across the decks and into the rigging as to just how many hours they'd beaten orders to remain in port, and, in actuality, it later emerged that sealed Navy orders arrived a mere eleven hours after they cleared the harbor.

It was different, this time: Davy was accepted as part of the crew, friends with the other members of his mess. He *belonged*, he realized, perhaps for the first time in his life. It was a good feeling. He felt comfortable enough now to bring out his sketching materials during his off hours; he drew his mess-mates, various parts of the ship; his captain draped over the rail, earnestly discussing something with the boatswain; Marines drilling; one of the powder boys sitting with his back to the rails, laboriously copying his letters on a flat piece of wood.

Different, too: The *Constitution* was far enough at sea this voyage that he could scarcely see land, even from high in the mainmast. But he wasn't cut off as he had been last time. It wasn't as though he could bespeak anyone, even if he'd wanted to. He knew they were there, though, and once, hovering on the edge of sleep, he was nearly certain he sensed the sprite.

Away from land once again, he knew he wanted nothing to do with the family Talents—it was expedience that forced it on him in Boston, that was all. Whether he'd accomplished anything besides temporarily soothing his own worries remained to be seen. In the meantime, he had well over two weeks asea, learning knots, how to climb the mizzen in a stiff breeze and take in sail while seated on a swaying cross-member, ankles crossed so a sudden plunge into a trough wouldn't send him flying—heady stuff, frightening at first, but exhilarating, too.

Constitution came across a few small prizes during that period: two open boats the British had taken from the Americans, a shipload of fruit from the Caribbean; several impressed American sailors being rowed from Halifax to a point north. By the time they headed southeast once again, Davy felt as though he'd been aboard for the better part of a year.

Mid-afternoon; he and his mess had just finished reworking the lashing on the bowsprit—hard work in a high wind—and were about ready to head below when a voice came down through the sails: "Ship on the horizon, to the north!" And, not long after, "British ship!" Along with the rest of the men, Davy ran toward the rail and peered into the distance. All around him, men gabbled excitedly: "Which, d'you think?" "Flying her colors? Big one, then, spoiling for a fight." "Found the ones to give her a fight, hasn't she?" The boatswain shouted them down finally, and in the ensuing silence came a cry from above: "Look at the sails, look at her topsail! What it says! It's *Guerrière!*"

It had to be fate: *Guerrière* had been one of the five ships that nearly trapped them off new Jersey; *Guerrière*, whose captain had written a challenge across his topsail, "THIS IS NOT THE LITTLE BELT," after that 22-gun sloop of war was mistaken for *Guerrière* and severely crippled.

Guerrière, which carried someone who was using, if not Crafter magic, then something very similar. Davy felt a familiar sensation; whoever that someone was, he was aware of the young alchemist-by-blood-and-not-choice on the American frigate. "Davy, come on." Andrew had hold of his elbow and was tugging at his arm. "Buckets, remember?"

"Buckets," Davy echoed dutifully. His mess had the job this watch of scattering sand and ash all across the main deck in case of battle. To keep footing safe, whatever else spilled on the deck. *Blood,* he thought as he ran for the main companionway with the others. *Perhaps my blood.* He buried the thought then. Not a good way to be thinking just now. Besides, if that other could somehow hear his thought . . . .

Ash and sand were scattered; guns moved into position and ports slid open; powder was loaded and boys stood ready with full buckets. Dead silence. The British ship, near enough now so that every man aboard the American frigate could read the arrogant message on the sails, was not yet near enough to engage.

Davy's legs were beginning to ache from standing so long in one place. The ships were jockeying for position, and now the British were beginning to fire. Shot tore through the mainsails, ropes slithered down to the deck. Four of Davy's mates swarmed aloft to fix them once again.

Davy caught hold of ropes, passing them to those who would reattach them along the rails; he was working automatically, thinking furiously as he went back and forth between main mast and rails. There wasn't any way he could get to the *Guerrière*. He couldn't be certain the man he thought of as his own adversary was being useful to the British at this moment, but he didn't want to chance that happening. If there were only some way of getting that powder from where he stood to where the other was!

The sky, already gray, grew darker. Surely they could not be more than fifty yards apart now! Through the ringing in his ears, Davy heard a ragged-sounding Lieutenant Morris beg the Captain to let them fire; heard the Captain's calm denial. Nearer; nearer; Davy was certain he could have thrown a knife from where he stood and buried it in the other ship's mast. Suddenly the Captain bellowed out an order, *Constitution* turned broadside, and every gun on the near side spoke as one.

The *Guerrière* seemed to explode into splinters; another round and yet another, her mainmast fell. Andrew, balanced above the deck on the rack that held boarding pikes against the mainmast, gleefully shouted out, "We've made a brig of her!" and someone shouted back, "One more shot to the foremast, and we'll make a sloop of her!"

More firing, and *Guerrière* nearly staggered into *Constitution*; Davy thought he saw the Marine Lieutenant who'd first taken him about the ship leap to the railing and fall back; saw a sword-waving officer on the other ship fall wounded or dead. And then, somehow, the *Constitution* was free, sailing into open water—dragging the other ship's mast with her.

Andrew shook his arm, hard. "Pay attention; we have repairs to make before we can go back and take them. Didn't you hear orders?" Davy blinked, nodded. He hadn't heard anything but the roar of cannon for what seemed a lifetime. Suddenly, it was still again, the only sounds the creak of rigging and the clatter and bang of gunners reloading; the slap of rope against the sanded decks, bare feet against sandy hardwood as someone ran back from the bow. Someone nearby groaned; men were carrying a wounded Marine below, and someone else covered Lieutenant Bush with a spare piece of canvas.

Davy caught rope, handed fresh-cut ends on; the little ball around his throat seemed warm. *Happen you might get a bit of wood from that ship and dust it. Symbol is referent, remember?* He jumped as the tart little voice filled his mind. *Sprite?* he thought nervously. No response. "I'm going mad," he whispered. But it made sense, didn't it? John's little lecture on symbols and referents—well, why not? There were pieces everywhere, long, deadly looking splinters of mast, bits of gold and white-painted stuff that must have come from the figurehead. And not far from his foot, what looked like a chunk of railing. He bent down and caught it up, turned away as though fighting a sneeze, and quickly pried the little ball apart, caught powder between thumb and forefinger and dusted it over the chunk of wood. He coughed, hoping that would cover what he'd just done, shut the ball and dropped both it and the wood down his shirt. No one seemed to have noticed, fortunately. Nothing felt different, either. *Must have dreamed the nasty little being,* he thought. *Happen you didn't,* came the sharp reply. *Happen this is no place for such as myself,* it added, and all sense of it was abruptly gone.

Rigging and sails once more in proper working order, the very few wounded sent below, his crew at the ready, the Captain had *Constitution* turned and brought back against what was left of *Guerrière*. The arrogant British topsail was soon gone, along with all her masts; her Captain dying, over a hundred of her sailors dead. Men worked frantically to bring over the wounded, and then the rest of *Guerrière's* crew, when it became clear she could not be saved.

Davy managed to get himself stationed at the rail, where he could watch the British as they came across. Thus far, he'd seen a handful of impressed Americans, the badly wounded Captain, a heart-rending number of bodies, hurt and bleeding men everywhere. No one who might constitute a sorcerer. He was beginning to wonder if he truly had imagined the entire thing—if he'd imagined anything which wasn't this ship, this time and place.

A tap on the arm aroused him; Captain Hull stood by the rail. "You, boy; you're my artist, aren't you? David Holywell, you see, I remember. Think that name would look good on a series of canvases to commemorate this battle, don't you? But—well, we can speak of that later." He gestured and his voice became grave. "We're going to have to burn her; Captain Dacres says before we do, he'd like the Bible from his cabin. Think you can fetch that for him?"

"Sir." Davy bobbed his head and scrambled onto the rail before the Captain could change his mind. *As if he knew what I wanted, one chance at that ship.* The Captain's cabin was aft, of course. It took him several moments to find it, and then to find the Bible; the chamber was all velvet and fancy furnishings. He caught it up, staggered as the ship rolled.

I'll take one quick look, just one, he thought. *This deck only.* He swallowed hard, then started toward the companionway, peering into open doorways as he went. Two beyond the Captain's, he found what he was searching for: a small, well-lit chamber, low-ceilinged. It reminded him of the corner where John kept his tools and chests. A table ran the length of the bulkhead, closed cabinets from edge to edge. Several bottles lay on the floor, and from a shattered tube came a coil of ruddy smoke. He nearly missed the man who lay half in shadow beneath the table. He knelt, gazed into a stranger's set and unseeing eyes. It could have been family; he couldn't tell. It no longer mattered. If there was a book, it was locked inside one of those cabinets, and would go to the bottom of the sea with the rest of the ship. With the dead British alchemist.

"With me, if I don't hurry," Davy whispered. He stepped back out of the room and ran for the companionway.

Much later, he and his mess-mates stood against the rail and watched as flame shot toward a cloudy night sky. All over the ship other men watched in silence as the *Guerrière* burned and finally sank beneath the waves.

Davy touched the little ball through his shirt, then quietly freed the bit of dust-treated wood and let it fall into the sea. *Happen you might regret that.* The tart little mind-voice again.

Doubt it, Davy replied tersely. Somehow he wasn't surprised the sprite was back with him.

John's mind-speak, however, took him by surprise. *At least you stopped them this time.*

Did I? I doubt that, John.

I don't. You blocked someone using power the way we do. He might have—John hesitated.

Might have what? I don't know that he did anything that might have harmed us. I don't know that I did anything worthwhile, either. Silence.

Happen you have us to speak with, the sprite reminded him. *Because of him, others like him. Something worthwhile, isn't it?*

Pleasant in its own way, I suppose, Davy responded. Behind them, the last flames faded and sky and sea merged into one utter blackness.

And under pressure, John put in finally. *Just think, once you're free of that ship and home again . . .*

Davy nearly laughed aloud. *Home? Oh, John, I'm sorry. But—don't wait for that, don't count upon it. This—this here, this ship, these men—for the first time I can remember, I'm happy. I'm at home here.*

After all this? Two mind-voices demanded incredulously.

After all this.

But, brother, I do beg you, think if you did so much under such circumstances, consider what a fine master of the family craft you could become!

Dear brother John. Whatever I've done, I still fail to see any real point to it all. Besides, if I find I ever do want something else to do, Davy added happily, *I won't lack. You're not the only Crafter to take a commission from Captain Isaac Hull, you know. I think it will take at least four full-sized paintings to do justice to today's battle, don't you?*

Boston
Anno Domini 1821

Most of the Crafter family spread across America. One group chose to stay in the growing, vibrant port city of Boston, where, it should be noted, life was not any less perilous than along the frontier. Perhaps among all the Crafters this group was the most adept at remaining inconspicuous and concealing their power. Sometimes this isn't easy, particularly when a great evil threatens.

MISS CRAFTER'S SCHOOL FOR GIRLS
by Jody Lynn Nye

". . . Providing Instruction in Deportment, French, Embroidery, Latin, Astronomy, Algebra, and Cooking," read the discreet brass plate next to the door of the large house on the edge of Boston. "Miss Amanda Crafter, Headmistress." A school cousin Davy's prize money had helped to open.

Within the study in the front of the red-brick and white-granite building, the same Miss Amanda was going over the advertised agenda with the parents of a prospective pupil. A straight-backed woman of thirty-five with severely coiffed black hair, Miss Amanda exuded confidence and the deportment she promised to imbue in her students.

"I assure you, Mrs. Gentry, your daughter will receive instruction here which will ensure her warm reception among the very best people. We intend to fit out our girls to grace any room, and to excel in any walk of life in which they may find themselves."

"I do not doubt the quality of the education, Miss Crafter," Mrs. Gentry said, delicately. "I only doubt whether you'll succeed in getting any of it into Madeleine. She's . . . resistant to outward influence."

"She's a willful hoyden," the Reverend Mr. Gentry grumbled. "She's driven away six tutors and governesses in as many years. I've got a business to run, imports and exports, you know, beside my duties to the Church. I cannot continue to be called away to reason with people she has offended."

"Ours is not a large institution," Miss Crafter pointed out. "Therefore we are able to give close attention to the needs of each girl. At present we have seventeen pupils. Your daughter would raise that number to a most pleasing total of eighteen. I and two other teachers serve as their schoolmistresses, their chaperones, and occasionally their confidantes. I would be happy to make available to you their references."

"Well . . ." Mrs. Gentry considered, "that is a rather better ratio than Mr. Grimes's school . . . ."

"My dear," Mr. Gentry said, "the man's a Roman Catholic. I told you I wouldn't consider him."

"But my dear," his wife countered, "his is the best school in Boston."

A gentle 'hh-hhm' distracted them from their argument and back to the present. Mrs. Gentry realized with horror that she had made a breach of manners in making such a comparison aloud. "Oh, I am so sorry, Miss Crafter. I didn't mean to imply that your institution was in any way wanting."

Miss Crafter smiled. "I find it entirely natural, Mrs. Gentry, that you would want the best of everything for your only daughter. Would you care to have a tour of the school before making a decision?"

"No, thank you so much, madam," Mr. Gentry said, rising. "It isn't necessary. What appurtenances you have will be of no interest to us. We shan't be attending. I believe Madeleine will be happy here, don't you, my dear?" He assisted his wife from her chair.

"I agree. Miss Crafter, thank you. When may we send Madeleine's things?"

"Tomorrow or thereafter," Miss Amanda said, after a moment's consideration. "I make it a policy to have the girls room by twos. We will have to prepare her room and choose a roommate for her."

"She has always had a room of her own," Mrs. Gentry began, affronted.

"Pray, Mrs. Gentry," Miss Amanda said, interrupting her smoothly, "consider the pleasures and responsibilities of co-existence with a girl of her own age and class to be one of the first lessons she will learn."

Madeleine Gentry arrived two days after her luggage. A tall girl with a thick mass of honey-colored hair and the promise of an attractive figure, Madeleine was accustomed to ruling a situation. Her dainty features had fooled more than one governess into believing she was sweet and tractable. Madeleine prided herself on being daring, willful and unmanageable. Arriving in the room first, she had taken the only comfortable chair, a deep green velvet armchair, and drawn it close to the small fire. She regarded the slim, dark schoolmistress who came to meet her in the parlor with open disdain.

"Well, Miss Gentry, I hope you had a pleasant drive," Miss Amanda said, sitting down in the straight-back chair next to hers. To Madeleine's annoyance, the schoolmistress seemed not at all upset that Madeleine had disposed herself in the green armchair. In fact, it would appear that the stiff, unpadded ladderback was her usual seat. Though her delicate bones might rue it, Madeleine vowed to take that one the next time she was summoned into the headmistress's presence.

"I suppose you'll be asking me about the weather next," Madeleine said, assuming a bored posture.

"Not if you don't choose to discuss it," Miss Amanda replied. "I thought we might have a few moments to get acquainted before I showed you to your room and introduced you to your roommate."

"Yes, Mother told me about that," Madeleine said. "I won't have it. You may give me a room of my own."

"Miss Gentry," Miss Amanda replied evenly, "that is impossible. All our pupils share rooms. They may switch between themselves occasionally as special friendships crop up and the friends wish to stay together; I encourage that. But as you are a member of an even number, there are companions enough for all. Rose Keating Adams has agreed to be yours. You should be pleased. Rose is a charming girl, and of very good family."

A black servant girl brought in tea and arranged the tray on a table at Miss Amanda's right hand. "Thank you, Emily," Miss Amanda said, smiling at her. The girl bobbed a curtsey, and left.

"I hope we will at least have servants? I will require the services of a maid to help me dress in the mornings."

"Early in the day," Miss Amanda replied, "the house staff is engaged in preparing the morning meal and lighting fires throughout the house. If you should prefer to be dressed rather than fed and warmed, I am sure we can come to some arrangement. But I believe that if you approach your roommate in the spirit of cooperation, the two of you can do up one another's laces."

The schoolmistress had an answer for everything. Madeleine was cross, but decided to continue her air of boredom. "Very well, I would like to see my room."

Miss Crafter smiled. The girl was not used to having her confrontational demands answered. "Follow me. Later, we will introduce you to your classmates."

That afternoon, Madeleine joined the school for luncheon. Her seventeen classmates were seated at three wooden tables spread with plain white cloths. Each was presided over by one of the mistresses. At the table with the eldest girls there was an empty chair next to the tall one occupied by the mistress. As Miss Crafter led her toward her place, Madeleine walked with her head high, trying to conceal her nervousness. The girls stared at her, and whispered behind their hands, but she caught the gist of one murmur.

"She's so pretty. Look at her hair." Madeleine felt better after that.

"Girls, may I present Madeleine Gentry? She is our new pupil. I hope you will make her welcome."

While they dined on their simple fare, the pupils pressed Madeleine with eager questions. Her prospective roommate, Rose Adams, was among the most curious. Rose had shiny black hair with purple and red highlights in it like a blackbird's wing. She was not pretty, with her pinched-looking little nose and hooded eyes. Madeleine felt no competition from a face such as that. She knew then that she would have no trouble becoming influential among these innocents. The only thing which troubled her was the tedious prospect of schoolwork.

She had always been an indifferent student, never having found a reason to apply herself to her books. It showed, embarrassingly, during the very first class in algebra the next afternoon.

The youngest student, Priscilla Townsend, kept looking around at the other students while she was calculating her assigned equation. Madeleine noticed that the others seemed eager to encourage her, and smiled and nodded when the child met their eyes. In a flurry of mouse-colored braids and red cheeks, Priscilla rose to her feet and announced her solution.

"If x is two, then the answer is six," she said. Miss Abigail smiled at her, and the other girls murmured their approbation. Priscilla was evidently the school pet. Madeleine was disgusted. The little girl, relieved at her triumph, flopped into her chair with a sigh.

"I feared I would never get that," she said, very low. She felt Madeleine's eyes upon her and tilted her head to meet her eyes.

Madeleine sat back languorously. "Only a silly pipsqueak like you would think that it was important to get it."

Miss Abigail, Miss Amanda Crafter's younger sister, who was teaching the class, overheard that, and called upon her. "Madeleine, perhaps you would care to do the next sum?" She wiped the slate clean with the damp cloth hanging by a string from the easel, and scratched in a new line of numbers.

The girl perused the baffling equation on the slate, and made a vague attempt to reason it out. The style of the mathematical phrase looked familiar, but not enough to give her a clue as to how it worked. She decided to guess. "The answer is eight."

Miss Abigail hid a smile. "You did not need to work it out on your own slate?" she asked.

"No, of course not," Madeleine said.

"Then it might surprise you to know that the correct answer is seventy, mightn't it?"

"I don't care," Madeleine replied, in the same airy, disinterested tone. "I see no use for these equations in my future life. I will have servants to do that kind of calculation."

"And what if you find your servants are cheating you?" asked Miss Abigail. "You won't know how to tell."

"They would not dare. My husband will take care of those details," Madeleine said, with a proud toss of her head. There was a titter behind her, and Madeleine turned red. She vowed to track down the girl who laughed and make her sorry.

Reckoning for her own transgression was not long in coming. Miss Amanda Crafter was waiting for her outside the door of the classroom when the session broke up for tea. She took Madeleine's arm in a friendly way, but Madeleine realized that the grip was sufficiently strong that she couldn't break away if she chose.

"I have an assignment for you, Madeleine," Miss Crafter said. Her voice sounded pleasant, but it did not match the disappointed expression on her face. She drew the girl into the sitting room and closed the door. "I won't keep you from tea with the others. You will have some free time between French instruction and the time you should dress for dinner. I would like you to write an essay on the elements of friendship."

Madeleine stared at her. Had she overheard her remarks to the class brat? It was impossible. The doors of the schoolroom fit tightly, and they had been closed the whole time. "An essay?" she repeated weakly.

"Yes, I think two pages would be sufficient." It was evident that she did know all about it. Madeleine swallowed. Miss Crafter continued. "If you can't apply any of your own experience to your thesis, I suggest you examine your surroundings for material. You may learn something."

"It's as if she has eyes in every cupboard and corner," Madeleine grumbled, later on, when she and Rose were dressing for the evening meal. She had scrubbed the ink off her fine, white hands, and had noticed a spot on her cuff. There wasn't time to see to it now.

"Sometimes it seems that way," Rose admitted. "She hates a sneak, so none of us can guess how, with no one to tell her, she knows everything that goes on. One of the others suggested it must be black witchcraft. I pointed out that Miss Amanda wears a cross, which would burn her if she practiced evil. Perhaps there are speaking tubes in the walls?"

Rose was as unflappable in her own way as Miss Crafter, moving through her days with sunny tolerance. All of Madeleine's attempts to make the Adams girl angry and move out of their shared room failed. She had even stolen the girl's best and most prized embroidered shawl to wear to church on Sunday. Rose had noticed, but still would not react.

"You look very well in cream," she had commented, arranging the folds higher on Madeleine's neck for the best effect. Annoyed, Madeleine had contrived to dip the fringes of it into the morning coffee. Even that had raised no criticism from her roommate, who simply removed the stained fringes and added new ones.

"I made it, I can mend it," Rose laughed, when Madeleine asked her about the change. After that, she left the other girl's things alone. There were more likely victims in the school.

The girls were expected to be in bed at nine. When the clock struck, the lights were extinguished by one of the servants, who went from room to room giving one last warning to frenzied letter writers and young needlewomen with their arms full of mending to put their tools down for the night.

"No!" Madeleine shrieked, as Emily descended on her lamp and turned it out. She was in the act of writing another letter of complaint to her father about her treatment at the school. She felt for the inkwell with her free hand to keep it from being knocked off the table, and rounded on the servant, who held a candle to see by.

"Relight that!" she demanded.

"Apologies, miss, but it's time."

"I'll decide when it's time. I'm not finished."

Emily shook her head. "Rules, miss. Good night." She turned away, throwing her shadow huge and wavy on the wall.

"Am I supposed to undress in the dark?" Madeleine shouted.

Rose, already in bed, threw back the covers and sat up. "Come on, Madeleine. I'll be maid to you. There's a full moon to see by."

"No. I wasn't finished with my letter. I will see Miss Crafter," Madeleine said, storming toward the door.

"You won't find her," Rose called after her.

"Why not?" Madeleine asked.

"At night, she's never around. We hear her tiptoe away, and

then we hear mysterious voices in the night," Rose said, her voice vibrant with excitement. "We think she's part of a secret society . . . or something *else*."

Madeleine's mouth opened into the letter O. This smacked of wild tales told to her by her elder cousins, who had traveled to India and other strange places of the world. "Well, I will get to the bottom of this," Madeleine said, sounding a little less sure. "But I won't go to bed at nine like a child. At home, I'd just be getting ready for parties at this hour."

"Oh, don't! What if there *is* something going on?"

Rose's words intrigued Madeleine. Mysterious voices in the night, tiptoeing away secretly . . . Was she about to stumble into the midst of a coven with Miss Crafter as its chief witch? She'd heard that such people danced around fires naked— imagine! Madeleine tried to conceive of a fire blazing in the center of Miss Amanda's neat sitting room, and people in their altogethers sitting around it sipping tea. The picture made her giggle nervously.

She crept down the steps, listening. The staircase seemed long and very narrow in the dark, almost as though the walls couldn't wait to close in on her. A lone gas flame burned low in its sconce on the landing. Madeleine stood in its light for a moment as if gathering its energy to go on.

Towards the ground floor, she heard voices. They appeared to be chanting rhythmically together, though she couldn't make out their words. Madeleine followed the sound all the way down. It led her to the door of Miss Crafter's sitting room.

Daringly, Madeleine grasped the door handle. It felt reassuringly ordinary. The smooth bite of its cold, smooth surface gave her the jolt she needed to turn it and push the door open.

There were a lot of people in the room, but disappointingly they were all fully clad, and the flicker of flame came from gaslights and a small fire in the grate, not a bonfire. Gradually, Madeleine realized that all except for Miss Crafter, who was standing beside the fire pointing at a slate, they were black. Surprised at the interruption, they turned to look at her, their eyes rounded, showing the whites around the irises. She saw that every pair of them held a book between them. The voice she had heard was the cook's assistant, Leah, reading aloud a poem by Lord Byron. Miss Crafter turned to confront Madeleine's accusing glare.

"You're teaching slaves to read?" the girl demanded, outraged.

"Ladies, that is all for tonight," Miss Crafter said, turning back to the group. Immediately, the servants rose and began to move the chairs away from the fire. Miss Crafter rounded on Madeleine. "I see that it is past nine o'clock. What are you doing still awake?"

"What are *you* doing?" Madeleine retorted. "Teaching black slaves to read. Ha! I would almost rather that you *were* practicing sorcery."

Miss Crafter's lips pressed together and tightened into a white line. "For your information, they are all free women. They work for their education, prizing it above fancy clothes and a life of ease. *Every one* of those girls knows more Latin than you do. They apply themselves. They ask questions when they do not know something. They are *interested*, which makes them students any teacher would prize. They pay in the only coin they have, their work, while you do not even show appreciation for the instruction you receive. Goodness knows why you feel education is worthless to you."

For a moment, Madeleine wondered if the teacher had it in mind to sentence her to corporal punishment. She was justified: Madeleine had broken the rules rather flagrantly. The pointer she held would leave painful strokes on the palm or back of one's hand. The same idea must have occurred at the same time to Miss Crafter, but she rejected it. She put the stick firmly away from her. It was the first time Madeleine had seen Miss Crafter become excited, and she wondered if she had found a vulnerable crack in the imperturbable headmistress's exterior. Could this be used for blackmail? No, even better, Madeleine decided. Even better than blackmail: liberty.

"Well?" Rose's voice hissed at her across the darkness. Madeleine was at last in bed, marched up the stairs and assisted to undress by Miss Crafter herself. "What did you find?"

In a hushed whisper, Madeleine began to narrate her adventure, detailing the chanting noise, and creeping up to clasp the door handle.

"Ooh! You're a brave one." Rose gasped. "I would have died of fear!"

"And I turned the handle, and pushed open the door . . ."

"Yes?"

"And there was Miss Crafter . . ."

"Yes?" breathlessly.

"Teaching the servants to read poetry!" Madeleine concluded, her voice rising. Hastily, she clapped her hand over her mouth.

Rose giggled in the dark. "Really?"

"Cross my heart. Can you imagine?"

"What's wrong with that?" Rose wanted to know.

"What a waste of time!"

"No, it's not." Rose quickly changed the subject. "None of us others would have dared go down to see where the voices were coming from. I think you might be quite mad. That's what we'll call you. Mad Madeleine!"

Madeleine protested, but privately, she was pleased. When the others heard the tale, they picked up on the nickname, praising her courage. She didn't mind at all. It meant they thought her daring beyond any of their ken.

She meant to be more daring yet. Miss Crafter's all-seeing eye appeared to be shuttered while she was teaching her night class. Mrs. Madison, the wife of the new President, was to be honored at a party held by Madeleine's aunt two days hence. Madeleine had an invitation card.

That night, when the lights were down, and her roommate was safely asleep, Madeleine rose from her bed. She had purposely left her cupboard door ajar, so it made no noise when she opened it and took out her party dress. She stole out into the hall with the dress bundled in her arms to keep the crisp silk skirts from rustling. In the cupboard under the stairwell, she dressed swiftly, and wrapped herself in a dark cape. When she tiptoed past the parlor door with her shoes in her hand, she heard the respectful voice of Emily reciting a Latin poem. Madeleine recognized it as the same one she herself had botched badly only that afternoon. She felt the urge to burst in on the lesson and cause a disturbance, but it would curtail the fun she was planning to have elsewhere.

Her great-aunt's house was only a few streets away. The card, which Madeleine kept in her hand the entire walk, had been kept hidden from all eyes underneath her lace box. She didn't want Miss Crafter to know about it, since she would surely tell Madeleine's father, who disapproved of his aunt's parties, considering them to be filled with louts and coquettes. It was unlikely that he would be there, even for the honor of meeting Mrs. Madison, so Madeleine felt she would be safe from discovery.

The party went on until four o'clock in the morning. Madeleine had two glasses of champagne, which made her limbs feel rather loose as she staggered back to the school. Congratulating herself on her stealth, she made her way back to her room without awakening the house, and fell heavily asleep.

She was awakened late the next morning by Rose, who shook her urgently. "Madeleine, you must get up. Can you hear me?"

"Go away," Madeleine muttered.

"If she does not open her eyes by the time I count five"—Miss Crafter's precise voice came from across the room—"Emily is going to pour the pan of cold water she is holding onto the pillow. If Miss Gentry's head is still on it at that time, there is nothing I can do to keep her from getting wet. One, two, three . . ."

"I'm awake!" Madeleine exclaimed, sitting up. The sudden flood of sunlight into wine-shot eyes sent a spear of pain piercing through her brain. Rose caught her arm as she swayed. Emily set the pan of water down on the floor and helped the girl out of bed.

"You slept through breakfast," Miss Crafter informed her. "Are you ill?"

"No, not at all," Madeleine assured the headmistress, willfully ignoring the pain in her head. "I . . . woke in the night. It was some time before I fell asleep again." That much was true, Madeleine told herself smugly.

"If you have recovered, then please get up," Miss Crafter commanded. "Classes will begin in twenty minutes. I shall expect to see you there. You have prepared your analysis of your stanzas of Homer, have you not?"

Thankfully, Madeleine remembered that she had. Rose had helped her with some of the Latin vocabulary the afternoon before.

The rest of the day was a blur. Madeleine found herself dozing in class, dropping off, it seemed, only seconds before Miss Abigail or Miss Letitia called upon her with a question.

Still, no one guessed the truth, and Madeleine felt she was free to carry on her evening carousing.

Invitation cards came now and again by messenger, and were conveyed sealed to Madeleine's room. She opened them and kept them hoarded under the collars in her lace box. She confided their existence in no one, not even Rose, who, in spite of Madeleine's earlier cruelty and constant inconsideration, was fast becoming a close friend. No one seemed ever to suspect that she was living a secret life.

"Soon, I will tell the others, and they will marvel at how I carried on so boldly, right under Miss Crafter's nose!" Madeleine told herself, hugging the notion to her like a treasure. She dressed in the dark cupboard again that evening, and tiptoed out of the house, never noticing the tiny line of blue light through which she passed as she trod over the threshold.

Before she was more than a hundred yards up the street, a figure rushed out of the rear door of the school, and hurried after her.

At the end of one day, when the classes had been especially hard and the mistresses more than usually strict, Madeleine felt she needed an evening's diversion to put herself at ease. She thumbed through her growing collection of invitation cards to see if there was anything going on that evening. Alas, there was nothing.

A new diversion was called for. Madeleine considered the possibilities. It was an indecent hour to call upon any of her friends. She couldn't go home. Her father would cane her for running away from school, and haul home her things under a cloud of disgrace. But wait—her father's warehouse on the wharf was not far away. She could easily get there on foot. The rear of the school pointed toward the waterfront. All of the servants were in the parlor, doing equations or some similar nonsense on their slates, so the way would be clear. She put on her clothing and sneaked down the back stairs, then made her way through the dimly lit streets to her father's warehouse on the waterfront, near the mouth of the Charles River.

As soon as the door closed behind her, Madeleine felt a rush of exhilaration. Such a daring trip was frightening and exciting at once. Rumors told of terrible dangers to virtuous young girls if they strayed onto the waterfront. Even Miss Amanda Crafter, when she went to meet the trading ship commanded by her affianced, Captain Gregson, always went with an escort, most often one of the footmen, and always during the day. It would be something to go down and come back again without being caught.

It was a little tricky finding her way, since she had never approached it from Miss Crafter's before. The streets were ill-marked, and no one was in the long rows of shops to help her. Every window was shuttered, which she found more intimidating than if they had been open and full of strangers.

At last she emerged onto the waterfront. It seemed most sinister. The very gaslights were less bright overlooking the Charles River. The wharf near her father's warehouse was deserted except for a few men smoking in the dark, leaning against a bollard; a stray dog, and the horrible squeal and scurry of rats. Madeleine had a strong constitution, but she felt she couldn't tolerate seeing a rat. By the echo of their scratchy feet on the boardwalk, they were surely each the size of a small dog.

Gentry & Co. was one of the largest buildings on the inner curve of the river. There was room for three ships to moor before it. At present, none that sailed for her father were in port, but by the heaps of crates and boxes marked with the names of foreign parts sprawled on the dock, it hadn't been long since they were there.

Madeleine knew that her father had a habit of leaving a door key hidden. The location was known only to his warehouse master and himself, but Madeleine had wheedled it out of him long ago, and she knew if it was still here, it would be in the same place. Reverend Gentry didn't trust the memories of others to be as facile as his own in recalling changes.

The heavy bar of metal was where it had always been concealed, hung on a nail inside the rain-butt at the rear of the building. Rolling up her sleeve, Madeleine felt around in the barrel. The water was very cold, chilling her fingers so much they went numb just as she clutched the key. Gasping, she fished it out, and stood massaging life back into her fingers.

Two watchmen wandered past the building, chatting. She hoped they weren't stopping at Gentry & Co. She held her breath until they turned in to the next warehouse and unlocked the door. Swiftly, Madeleine took the dripping key around to the front and let herself in.

The darkness within the warehouse was velvety and fragrant. Madeleine lifted her nose and inhaled the strong smells of spices, tar, sea water, tobacco, and glue, all familiar and pleasant as perfumes to her. They were scents she had known from childhood. This warehouse had been a second home and a playground to her. Reverend Gentry liked to bring his little girl with him, to "teach her the business, after all, she's my only child," as he always said.

She had made it here all the way from Miss Crafter's without being detected. Now she wanted a token to prove that she had been here. If she ever told one of her schoolmates the story, she needed proof. There was no need to go off into any of the storerooms to find goods. Even the offices, situated in the center of the building, were filled with crates of merchandise just arrived or awaiting shipment.

Madeleine opened the door of her father's room. The best things would be in here. There were several boxes crowding the heavy wooden desk. A tightly made, straw-filled box held books of some kind. Madeleine scratched away some of the straw and pulled one of them out. A Bible. Ha. That would hardly promote the image of a daring adventuress she wished to project. The same went for the old wooden cross on the wall.

The next crate held brass candlesticks. A pretty simpleton she'd look carrying around a candlestick waiting for someone to ask her about it. There must be something small and portable, yet rare and fascinating. Madeleine knew her father kept the oddities and expensive items locked in a strongbox in his desk.

As a child, she had discovered how to make the locked drawers open without a key. No man could do it: the opening in the base of the desk near the back was only the size of a child's hand. It was barely big enough to pass Madeleine's more grown-up one, but the lock snicked open. She rose from the dusty floor and hurried around to pull open the drawer. With a crow of success, she unearthed her quarry. Beneath her father's leather-covered ledger was the strongbox.

The box was not heavy, and it rattled when Madeleine shook it. Amid the other noises, she heard a clinking sound within. Perhaps there was jewelry! That would suit her purposes perfectly.

The lock was a good one, which she could not open without a key. She knew her father had one, and very likely the warehouse master did, too. Her father was not a forgetful man, so his would be on his ring of keys, but the warehouse master did occasionally misplace things. She went across to his office, a smaller chamber on the sea side of the building, and searched there, feeling along the top of the wooden paneling and along the underside of chairs.

The key turned up in a very clever place. She opened the big clock which stood next to the cloak rack and peered into the depths of its cabinet. On a hook rested a square-mouthed key. Madeleine took it off the hook to test its size, and discovered it fit the winding nuts on the clock's face. When she bent to replace it, she discovered there was another key behind it, a tiny one, hardly more than a slip of pressed metal. She carried it back to her father's room in triumph.

She took the box from the desk and laid it under the window so the faintly wavering light of the street lamps would illumine what was within. The key fit into the lock and turned, yielding smoothly without so much as a click. Her hands trembling with excitement, she lifted the lid.

Most of the small items were curiosities carved of wood or ivory from the Spice Islands or as far away as Africa. Two of them were hideous miniature idols. She didn't like the crude, blocky style of the carvings, and the staring eyes and protruding tongues made her quail at touching them. Impulsively, she seized the mass of necklace strands beneath them, and succeeded in turning the idols over, so they were no longer looking at her.

The necklaces were more to her taste. She sorted through them happily. The colorfully painted beads of one appealed to her, as did the smooth amber plaques of another. The trouble was that none of these were what she could wear undetected until she chose to reveal her excursion. They were all too exotic in appearance.

At the bottom of the box was the very thing she had been hoping for. A small, leather bag yielded forth a necklace of gold. The burnished beads were no larger than the ends of her fingers, but felt surprisingly heavy. Her father had brought home a little figurine of gold one day when she was a child, and let her play with it. It had been made in the shape of a woman wearing only a belted shift and carrying a long bow.

"See that, poppet?" he said. "Real gold is as heavy as lead, and it has a smooth texture like chamois. There's nothing else like it in the world. Nothing." He held the figurine up fondly to the light, admiring the carving. "Such graven images have caused even strong, morally sane men to give up the ways of God."

In the center of the necklace lay a short pendant. Madeleine couldn't make out the shape, but thought that it looked rather like a half-formed face.

The beads felt between her fingers the way the little goddess had. They were real, pure gold. This piece must surely be worth a small fortune. It would be a perfect token. She could explain to her father later on why she had borrowed it.

Somewhere in the distance, the Old North Church's bells rang the hour, and the other, younger church clocks joined in the chorus. Madeleine realized that she had been gone a long time. She tucked the necklace in its bag into her pocket, and slipped out of the building, locking the door and replacing the key in the water barrel.

She slipped back into the school and undressed in the cupboard, slipping her nightdress on. She bundled her clothes untidily into her clothes cupboard and rocked the door gently into place until it looked as if it was closed.

The next morning she wore the gold necklace openly to class. It aroused so much attention among the other girls that Miss Crafter asked her to put it away.

"Such expensive baubles are out of place during school hours," she said. "If you care to wear it when you dress for dinner, you may."

"Yes, Miss Crafter," Madeleine said, outwardly obedient. Inside, she was most satisfied by the reactions to her token.

It was exclaimed over by the others at teatime.

"It's just like your hair," ten-year-old Priscilla said, admiringly.

"Where did you get it?" Rose asked teasingly. "A lover?"

Madeleine smiled coyly. She enjoyed being the center of attention. She wanted to tell all about her secret trip, but a little voice told her not to. Instead she said, "I got it from my father. He has a trading company, you know, a most prosperous business. He obtains curiosities from all over the world."

"Where's this one from?" one of the other girls begged.

"I can't recall," Madeleine said airily. "I have so many things from so many places. This may be from China, or the Indies; I don't know. My father hasn't told me."

The Reverend Mr. Gentry was very agitated when he and her mother came to take Madeleine out for a drive at the weekend, and took her home for a special tea. She hid the necklace under the clothes in her cupboard, hoping to bring up the matter to him while they were out, but she couldn't find a good moment to mention it. The mood never quite seemed suitable. The weather was chancy, which she knew always put him in a temper.

"Your father is much upset," her mother said, during a moment alone when Mr. Gentry went upstairs to have a smoke in his den. "Someone broke into the warehouse and stole a very valuable piece from his office. He has asked everyone, but no one can remember the last time it was seen. A gold necklace. There's some history behind it. The man who found it went mad and jumped overboard into the sea. He was drowned. Your father considers the necklace unlucky."

Guiltily, Madeleine elected to say nothing. She would simply have to put the necklace back, very quietly, and hope she was as clever and as fortunate about not being caught as she was the first time.

When Mr. Gentry returned his daughter to the school, he requested a private word in the parlor with the headmistress.

"You're doing wonders, Miss Crafter. Madeleine's learning something! The girl actually recognized a few quotes of poetry I threw her way while we were out. I'm impressed. But judging from some of the stories she's told us, it sounds like she's scarifying some of the other students. Miss Crafter, you'll have to scare the devil out of her to make her stop. The love I have for my only chick doesn't blind me to her domineering streak. Far from it. By the way, how have her secret sojourns been going?" He laid a finger beside his nose in a conspiratorial fashion.

"Quite uneventfully, Mr. Gentry," Miss Crafter replied. "Since I wrote to you, she has not come back under the weather from any party. The hostesses all responded most kindly to my notes begging them to look after her at their affairs, and chaperoned her as if she were a daughter of their own. My servant John has seen to it that no harm befell her on any of her transits to or from a house. Her secret life appears to be making her a trifle less abrasive. Her self-satisfaction has kept her from striking out against the more humble members of our household, and I believe she is finding friends among the rest of the students. In any case, her secret journeys have meant that she has learned to clean her own boots, if only to keep one of us from inquiring how she got mud on them in the middle of the night."

"Well, well," Gentry said, laughing. "I see no reason why she shouldn't go on attending her parties, if it's doing as much good as all that."

The affair of the necklace preyed on her mind so much during the following week that Madeleine couldn't find the heart to kick up a fuss during classes. Miss Abigail regarded her new pupil warmly, hoping that Madeleine had finally settled down to being a part of the school. She said as much to her sister as they sat before the fire one evening with the mending.

"I don't think so, Abby," Miss Amanda opined. She pulled a needleful of thread through the rip in the hem of a linen sheet. "I believe she may have something on her conscience."

The effect of wearing the necklace had been so successful the first day that Madeleine began to wear it all the time. She knew that the mistresses disapproved of her wearing it during lessons, but she felt a twinge whenever she tried to leave it off. A little voice within her chided her as she touched the clasp, telling her not to leave it behind in her room.

The servants might steal it, the voice whispered.

"Certainly they wouldn't," Madeleine argued, weighing the chain in her hand before slipping it into its bag. "They'd have their characters blotted for all time. They'd never get another job as house servants in Boston. They might as well go and cut sugar cane in Jamaica." Madeleine quashed the little whine firmly.

Then one of the other students, the voice insisted. *They're all envious of your treasure.*

"Even if they are, they couldn't conceal it," Madeleine said, taking the chain out of its leather bag and replacing it about her neck. She admired the effect in the glass. The shining, yellow circlet was very fetching on her. "It's mine now." She had entirely forgotten about returning it to her father.

Yes, mine, the inner voice said. *All mine.*

Thereafter, Madeleine kept the necklace on her at all times or by her when she was bathing. Gradually, she became unwilling to have the others play with it or pass it around as she had before. With the fledgling skill of needlework she had acquired under Miss Letitia's careful tutelage, she made a small bag of cloth for it, and wore it under her skirts at all times when she wasn't permitted to wear it on her neck. The bag reposed at night under her pillow. Clutched in her hand, it gave her a certain kind of comfort, but the little voice continued to preach distrust.

Over the course of the next few days, odd things began to happen around her, though never to her. One morning on the way to breakfast, one of the other girls, Deborah, made a sly comment about Madeleine's ineptitude in math class as she started down toward the dining room. Madeleine was just about to retort, when Deborah slipped and fell down the stairs.

She shrieked, unable to stop, until she tumbled in a heap on the landing. Exclaiming, the other girls raced down to her.

"Something nudged me from behind! Mad Maddy must have pushed me," Deborah said. She tried to move her ankle, and her face screwed up in pain.

Miss Amanda appeared at the bottom of the stairs and rushed up to the group.

"What happened here?" she demanded.

"Madeleine pushed me down the stairs," Deborah began, and caught Miss Crafter's glance. "Well, *something* hit me in the back, and I fell."

"Under what circumstances would she have done such a thing?" Miss Amanda asked.

Deborah grew shamefaced. "Well, I'd just made a little jape at her expense, but to resort to violence—!"

"I never," Madeleine protested. "I swear by the Bible and the Constitution of the United States that I was nowhere near her when she fell."

"Don't swear, Madeleine," Miss Crafter cautioned her. "Can anyone substantiate that?"

"I can, Miss Crafter," Rose said. "Maddy was near me, more than an arm's length from her. Deborah simply fell." Her hand described the arc of Deborah's inelegant descent.

"She's going to need cold compresses," Miss Amanda decided, after examining the ankle. "It will be all right in a few days. It isn't broken. There, that will be a lesson to you, girl, not to make sport of others. It may be that your own conscience tripped you up."

"Yes, Miss Crafter." John, the manservant, appeared, and Deborah was helped, with difficulty, back to bed.

Deborah was confined to her room for three days until Miss Crafter pronounced her fit again. Miss Abigail visited her in the afternoon to give her a reading assignment and to hear her recitation of a French fable.

It was only the first of the accidents that seemed to occur around Madeleine. Miss Letitia skidded and slipped on a perfectly dry floor in the schoolroom when she made a derogatory comment about Madeleine's progress in algebra.

"I think Mad Madeleine's found a guardian angel," Daisy, one of the younger girls, suggested.

Part of friendship is play, and the others were beginning to be frightened of the run of bad luck that befell people who did or said anything ill to Madeleine, even in fun. They began to leave her alone. Having lately become accustomed to having friends, Madeleine felt lonely and bereft.

Never mind, the little inner voice said. *You have me.*

Miss Amanda had not failed to notice the strange run of circumstances that dogged Madeleine Gentry.

"She was up to some kind of ill behaviour," Amanda told her sister. "I thought something like this might happen the night she interrupted the servants' reading class. Madeleine is just the kind of girl who will see how far she can go, and press out against her limits every time until she is stopped. That first morning that we found her drunk, I spoke to Mrs. Harper, who confirmed that the girl had been at her party the evening before. I wrote to her father, informing him of her behavior. I had discovered long ago that she had a small hoard of invitation cards for various parties. She has been accustomed to an active social life. Barring her getting ill on punch or champagne and sleeping through the next day, I thought that if these little outings took the edge off her energy, she might become a useful member of our society.

"He informed me that if I could see to it that she would come to no harm, he was agreeable that she should be allowed to continue attending the parties, and if I chose, there was no reason to inform her I knew she was going." Miss Amanda smiled. "Reverend Gentry understands that his daughter enjoys thinking she's gotten away with something she knows is wrong. Stolen fruit is sweeter than that to which we are entitled. Up until now, I thought our ruse might be working.

"I missed her only once, when she went abroad one midnight without a set destination. It wasn't until a few days later that I realized she had gone out without my knowing it. Something happened to her that evening, and I believe that her alteration in behavior is a result of it."

"I wonder what it could have been?" Miss Abigail said.

"I don't know," Miss Amanda replied, tapping her fingers with her pen. "And I am terribly afraid we are going to find out. Something about the current run of circumstances reminds me of a story told me by Captain Gregson, in which an outside influence took hold of an innocent life, and subtly altered the aura around it."

"You can scarcely use the words 'innocent life' to refer to Madeleine Gentry," Miss Abigail said, laughing. "Wandering fearlessly abroad by herself at night like a gypsy."

"That's exactly why I do say she is an innocent," Miss Amanda said. "She hasn't the sense to know that she might be placing herself in danger."

The advanced cooking class consisted of the six eldest girls under the tutelage of Miss Letitia. She was pleased with their progress, having guided them over the course of weeks through the mysteries of the kitchen from the simple preparation of vegetables to the killing and dressing of a fowl for the oven. The latest week's adventure was the making of bread.

Even Madeleine was able to eke savage pleasure out of folding, pummeling, and throwing down the heavy mass of dough. She was floury to the hairline before Miss Letitia checked on her portion and pronounced it ready to set aside for rising.

"But it's getting soft now," Madeleine complained, brushing stray hairs off her hot face. "Should I not continue?"

Letitia smiled. "It is precisely why you should not continue. When it reaches this texture, soft and elastic like the flesh of your cheek"—she touched the girl's face gently—"then it is perfect. Any more, and the bread will refuse to rise correctly. It will be tough and fibrous."

Disappointed, Madeleine surrendered her bowl of dough. Hers, along with the other girls', was put away onto pantry shelves and left to ferment.

"That will take a while before we need to see it again," Miss Letitia said, with an air of mystery. "Therefore we will undertake another project in the duration. Rose," she directed, "will you find the sack of brown sugar, and you, Elizabeth, the white. Daisy, please measure out a cup of butter—no more. Madeleine, since you are the strongest, please take that bag of nuts and the hammer and bowl, and begin to break them out of the shells. The meats need not remain intact. Deborah, as Madeleine passes them to you, please chop the nuts into pieces about this big." She held up her finger and thumb about a centimeter apart.

Rose, her eyes dancing, asked, "Are we making sweets?"

"We are," Miss Letitia confirmed. "You have worked hard and well, you have earned a treat. We have pecans, we have peanuts, we will make nut brittle."

The girls clapped their hands for joy, and began to assemble the ingredients.

Candy! Madeleine loved sweets. Willingly, she set to work on the nuts. The peanuts she set aside to open with her fingers, but the pecans took skill and care with the hammer. If she struck them too hard, they smashed into greasy powder. If she struck them too lightly, they slipped out under the hammer's face and spun across the wooden tabletop. The right tap cracked the shell neatly around the center, and she could pull forth a whole nutmeat.

"My parents are coming at the weekend," Deborah said, as she deftly chopped the nuts into fragments and whisked them into a bowl. "Mother wrote that if I have improved in French she will buy me a new bonnet."

"How nice!" Daisy exclaimed.

"Madam Levallier on Market Street makes lovely spring hats," Madeleine put in. "I remember my mother—"

"Where will you go?" Daisy interrupted.

"I'm not sure yet. Of course, my grandmother thought I should make it myself, but Mother said I should have a *fashionable* hat for this season."

"I've heard that the fashion in France is an arrangement of pheasant—" Madeleine began.

"Perhaps if you do well in Astronomy," Daisy interrupted again, making a mischievous face at Deborah, "she will buy you a dress to go with it!"

The other girls laughed. Madeleine felt put out that she was being ignored, but her task demanded her whole attention. There were a lot of nuts in the sack, and each needed to be treated as carefully as the first. If she lifted her head to join the conversation, she was likely to miss the nut she was breaking, and bring the hammer down on her fingers.

The girls whose only jobs were to measure ingredients soon joined Miss Letitia at the stove with the huge iron frying pan. It took Deborah only a moment at a time to chop up all the meats Madeleine produced, so she could come and go between her place at the table and the merry group watching the sugar melt over the fire, leaving Madeleine alone.

Madeleine felt her cheeks grow pink, and the bubbling of anger rising inside her, as she watched the others chatting happily, leaving her out. Savagely, she brought the hammer down on a nut, and missed. She struck her own finger solidly, and shrieked. There was a tremendous crash inside the pantry, and the girls spun around. She glared at them, holding her throbbing hand.

Miss Letitia looked from Madeleine to the pantry door. She ran over, threw it open. Every pan of bread was upside down on the floor, with the exception of Madeleine's.

"Madeleine, you've spoiled a week's worth of bread," Miss Letitia chided her.

"I didn't do it," Madeleine protested, surprised. "I hit my hand, that's all."

"That was a spiteful thing to do," Miss Letitia insisted. "And to compound your action by lying! For shame!"

Madeleine started to speak, and decided nothing she could say would change the angry teacher's mind. Still clutching her wounded finger, she fled the room. She dashed to the front hall, yanked open the door and stumbled out of the house. As she passed the parlor, a heavy bronze figure on the parlor mantelpiece rose up into the air, and crashed down, breaking the marble mantel in two before dropping into the fire and scattering embers and ashes.

"Don't let the sugar burn, girls!" Miss Letitia called, as she ran after Madeleine.

Miss Amanda heard the crash, and arrived in the hall with Miss Abigail only a step behind her. "What is amiss here?" she asked, viewing the mess through the open door of the parlor. "Great heavens! What is all this? What is going on?"

Miss Letitia explained. "And then she must have broken your mantel. What a wretched brat! Mad Maddy, indeed!"

Miss Amanda went into the parlor. She scooped the embers away from the statue, and brought a cloth duster to try and lift the bronze out of the fire. "It's impossible. She couldn't have done this. I can't raise this alone. Captain Gregson brought this to me, and placed it on the mantel himself. I couldn't move it. When the girls dust they have to go around it unless they have John's help." It took all three women to move the statue onto the tiles surrounding the hearth.

"Madeleine is strong, but to do this she would have to be a freak," Miss Abigail commented.

"People have tremendous strength when they are in a fit of rage," Miss Letitia suggested.

Miss Amanda shook her head. "No, something else has happened. I sense it. There is something amiss here greater than just a girl's hurt feelings. Letitia, will you keep order here? Abigail, come with me." Miss Amanda removed her shawl and put on her coat and hat. "Have Emily summon a coach for us," she said. "There's no time to harness ours."

The two sisters hurried to the Gentry house. Mrs. Gentry was surprised to see them, but invited them out into the garden.

"We need to speak privately," Amanda said.

"What do you mean, Madeleine is missing?" demanded Reverend Gentry, after Miss Amanda explained.

"She ran out of the house," Miss Amanda repeated patiently. "She appears to have had an altercation with some of the other girls, but I fear there is more to it than that. I believe she left the house on the sly one night that I do not know about, and something very odd happened to her then."

"What?" Mrs. Gentry demanded, and Miss Amanda realized that she knew nothing of her agreement with Mr. Gentry. "I thought that yours was a respectable school. How could you have allowed such goings-on?"

"Now, now, my dear, I knew all about it," Mr. Gentry said, clearing his throat abashedly.

"She has never been without protection," Miss Amanda said. "Nor without chaperonage. You must take my word for that."

"She's done no more than we'd do if she was going from our home," Reverend Gentry said, trying to placate his wife. "But what other problem is it you allude to?"

"I can only pin down her change in behavior as far back as the day she began wearing a gold necklace. She has been telling the girls that it came from you. I wonder if you would tell me what you know about that necklace, Mr. Gentry?"

"The necklace!" he exclaimed. "Big gold beads and a little face-like thing in the center?"

Miss Amanda inclined her head.

Mr. Gentry struck the arm of his chair. "It was stolen a couple of months ago from my offices. I never dreamed that my own daughter . . ." He threw up his hands. "I suppose I ought to have guessed. Nothing else was taken, though there were items of far greater value in the warehouse. Madeleine's always been a magpie, loves shiny baubles. I had it locked up in a drawer, but she knew where to find the keys."

"Why was it locked up?" Miss Amanda pressed him. "It is not strictly because it is valuable, is it? Otherwise would you not have had it at home?"

"No, frankly speaking," Mr. Gentry said. "It's supposedly responsible for the deaths of two men. One killed by the other, who threw himself over the side of the ship that brought the necklace home to me from the Spice Islands."

"As I feared," Miss Amanda said, her forehead drawing down gravely. "My fiancé has told me many mysterious tales of the islands. He's mentioned artifacts that can drive men mad."

Mr. Gentry snorted. "Personally, I don't believe a word of it. The darkies on my crew said it had bad *joujou*, but you know how they are. Once I heard that, I knew the story wouldn't stop at the wharf. I couldn't sell it in Boston. No one would touch it, and as a man of God, I don't think I could stomach making money off such a profane thing. I was going to have it smelted down."

"Where would she have gone, Mr. Gentry? Mrs. Gentry?" Miss Amanda pressed them. "If she felt she was in trouble, where or to whom would she run?"

Mrs. Gentry looked hurt. "I always felt that if she was unhappy, she would come to me," she said. "Or my husband's aunt, though she knows that we don't approve."

"The warehouse," Gentry said, without hesitation. "From a small child, Madeleine always liked to hide in my office or in the storerooms. My men know her. Do you think she's there?" he asked, as Miss Crafter stood up. Miss Abigail followed suit.

"I'm sure of it," the headmistress said. "Will you accompany us? I fear we may need help with . . . her."

Madeleine cowered in the corner of her father's office, listening to the inner voice enumerating horror after horror that ought to befall the cruel women who had teased and abandoned her. *Fire and woe shall be their part! They should revere you, hold you up as a superior being.*

"I don't understand," Madeleine wailed. "Why should they do those things?"

It's what you've always wished, isn't it, having them admire and worship you? It should come true.

"No, I don't want it."

But you do. You crave their admiration. You've always wanted it.

"But not that way, not through terror. I want them to follow and admire me because . . ."

Because they like you? None of them like you. What reason have you ever given them? You scorn their offers of friendship, make fun of them, steal their belongings, bully and berate them.

"Oh, God, if that was ever true, I am sorry for it now!"

Whatever was within her caused a huge shudder to pass through her body, and she shrieked in fear as the inner voice commanded: *Don't speak that name again, or I will rend you apart, like the hurricanes tear up the huts of the islanders.*

Madeleine subsided, sinking over her clasped hands in utter despair. She wished she had learned more prayers than the last lines after which she could say "Amen" and escape from the dreariness of church on Sundays. Her father had never managed to instill in her any of the fiery faith he felt, the exaltation he knew from God's love. She felt that she was far away from her Creator's help. All she could remember was the poetry she had learned at Miss Crafter's school. She had thought the words so beautiful, but there was no protection in them, no comfort.

She wished Miss Crafter was there with her. The headmistress seemed cool under any circumstances, but would she even care if her most obstreperous pupil was in deadly danger, especially from an unseen foe? No one would believe her if she told what the voice had been saying to her. A sob broke from her lips. Madeleine knew that she was alone with this demon, and she didn't even know what had made it choose her to plague.

The voice within began to speak again, laughing at the despair of its prisoner-host. Madeleine tried to shut it out, burrowing into her dusty corner like a lost waif.

"Madeleine?" her father's voice called from the front of the warehouse. She could see him and a clutch of other figures silhouetted against the afternoon sky. "Are you here, my dear?"

"F-f—" she began, but the voice within seemed to have control of her vocal chords, and choked off her reply.

"There you are, Madeleine," Gentry said, spotting her in the corner. "Come out of there, my dear. We're not angry. We want only to talk to you."

Madeleine rose gladly, but to her horror, her throat was emitting a snarling sound, like the growls of a beast.

"What is wrong with my daughter?" Mrs. Gentry cried. "Miss Crafter, I am holding you responsible. You have no control over these girls. She is worse than ever she was at home. I'm withdrawing her from your school."

"Now is not the time to discuss it, Mrs. Gentry. Get down!" Miss Amanda grabbed the angry woman's arm and dragged her behind a packing crate.

Without seeming effort, Madeleine picked up the desk chair. She held it effortlessly over her head, baring her teeth in a hideous laugh, then sent it hurtling across the office to crash into the wall behind them.

"My daughter!" Mrs. Gentry protested, trying to free herself from Miss Crafter's iron grasp.

"That's impossible," Gentry goggled. "Plainly impossible."

"Conservation of energy," Miss Crafter said decisively. Miss Abigail, crouching behind her, nodded. "We must tire it out. All it has to draw on is Madeleine's strength. I do not believe," she said, almost irrelevantly, "that she ate any lunch."

"What in the name of Hell's court has that got to do with it?" Gentry said, rounding on the schoolmistresses.

"Robert!" Mrs. Gentry shrieked.

Translucent and twice the height of a man, a gigantic image of a head appeared between them and Madeleine. The girl recognized it as the image on the pendant, and she could tell by the shock on her father's face that he recognized it, too. Her hands flew to her neck, and she fumbled with the necklace, but could not get it to come off. Her father advanced on the face bravely, with one hand held up before him in a warding gesture. The face laughed, its booming voice coming from Madeleine's throat.

"Avaunt, ye demon of Satan," the minister cried.

Miss Amanda stopped him. "Mr. Gentry, that won't work until we can get that necklace away from her."

"My daughter!" Mrs. Gentry cried again.

At a look from her sister, Miss Abigail led Mrs. Gentry out of the way, crooning little pleasantries to her in the soft voice she used when one of the girls was ill, and made her sit down.

"What do you mean?" Gentry demanded. "She's a young girl. We will walk over and take that accursed necklace away from her."

A crate flew across the room and crashed in front of them, scattering books and straw and splintered wood. Miss Crafter jumped, but didn't cry out. Madeleine, panting, her face contorted beyond recognition, glared at them. Reverend Gentry took his handkerchief out of his pocket and dabbed his sweating face.

"It will not be that easy," Miss Crafter said.

"What has happened to my daughter? She must be possessed."

What are you doing to them? Madeleine cried, though no sound escaped her lips. It appeared only that she was snarling wordlessly as her hands lifted a heavy vase from beside her father's desk and flung it. *Those are my parents!*

You have no family now. You are timeless. I control where you will go and what you will do.

Let me go!

You took me unto you willingly. I cannot decline service so offered. I grow in power with every moment I am with you.

I reject you! I am a free woman.

No longer. The voice sounded bored. *Kill them, and then we will go.*

No! Madeleine screamed. But her body would no longer obey her commands.

Her hands went out in a shoving gesture, and Miss Abigail went backwards over a low box. Madeleine knew then by the feel of invisible flesh against her palms how Deborah had been caused to fall down the stairs. This creature, this demon inside her, could touch without touching. It aimed the same attack at Miss Amanda, who whisked her forearm before her upper body and head as if she were swatting flies, and Madeleine stumbled forward, having missed her target.

She has knowledge, the demon growled. *This will be more difficult.*

Madeleine's arms reached high into the air, and tore at nothingness. Suddenly, the ceiling over the heads of her parents and teachers shattered and fell, showering them with wood and plaster. Her mother screamed and began to pray out loud. That angered the demon.

She said the Name! She must be killed! I don't want to hear the Name!

Stop it, Madeleine begged. *Leave her be.* With an effort of will, she forced her arms part of the way down, but they sprang back easily against her strength.

I can cause their flesh to rot on their bones, the voice sneered. *It's a lingering, painful end. If you love them, would you not want them to die quickly?*

Yes—I mean, no! I don't want them to die at all!

Too late!

Madeleine could only watch as her hand reached out and grasped a fistful of air. The windows on the quay side of the building shattered, and all the glass flew toward her father and Miss Crafter.

With an astonishing display of strength, the headmistress yanked Mr. Gentry behind her and made the warding gesture again. The shards stopped an inch from her face and fell harmlessly to the floor.

"You—what are you?" Mr. Gentry stammered, pulling away from Miss Crafter.

"Only a seeker after truth, Mr. Gentry," Miss Crafter assured him. "Do not fear me. There is little I can do that you could not, with a little instruction. I am not evil, I promise you. But *that* is." Her finger stabbed in Madeleine's direction. "Do not abandon your daughter now. She needs you."

Gentry swallowed. "What must we do?"

"We must exhaust the demon's potential," Miss Crafter explained carefully. "So long as it centers on Madeleine, it will have only her energy to use. Once that is gone, we would have a moment of respite to drive it away before it can batten on to another human host."

The voice soon became bored with the schoolmistress's lecture. With nothing more close at hand to throw, Madeleine's captor began to draw to it phantasms of the deep. Madeleine felt her mind whirling with terror as the images of sailors dressed in rags, with greenish-white faces and sunken eyes, tramped past her and her astonished parents and teachers. They were followed by the skeletons of sunken ships that sailed into the warehouse, passing through the walls. She screamed, soundlessly, feeling herself sinking into madness.

The visions of the sea's dead took their toll on the defenders as well.

Mrs. Gentry was beyond hysterics now, clasping her handkerchief between her hands and staring wide-eyed. Mr. Gentry picked up a prayer book from the litter on the floor and turned to Psalms. He began to read aloud, his voice gaining energy with every line.

" . . . Yea, though I walk through the valley of the shadow of death, I will fear no evil, for Thou art with me . . ."

"Go on," Miss Crafter encouraged him, her eyes never leaving Madeleine's face. "It doesn't like that."

" . . . And I shall dwell in the house of the Lord forever!"

"Keep reading," Miss Crafter commanded.

Gentry flipped back a few pages, and declaimed. "Fervently do I love Thee, O Lord, my strength. The Lord is my rock, my fortress, and my deliverer . . ."

Madeleine pointed all the fingers of one hand directly at him. As he stared in disbelief, a fireball erupted from her hand and slammed directly into the book he held. It was immediately consumed in roaring red flames, and he dropped it to the floor.

"Madeleine! That was the word of God!" Mr. Gentry exclaimed in outrage. He stooped for another prayer book from the scattered heap on the floor, and continued to read.

The figure facing them sagged every time the Holy Name was mentioned. Madeleine's hand was scorched at the finger-tips, and her limbs moved slowly, painfully, as it sought to launch another attack upon them. Miss Crafter called to Miss Abigail.

"We are nearing the end. Lend me your strength, sister! I believe that this is it."

Miss Abigail stumbled over the debris on the floor until she gained a place beside her sister. Building and holding a wall of compressed mental strength before them, they moved toward Madeleine from both sides, angling to trap her into the corner.

The girl struggled and squirmed in torment, but her eyes pleaded for them to do something. Her hand was badly burned, and the hand she clutched it with was swollen and sore from her earlier accident. Slowly, inexorably, Miss Crafter pushed her prisoner to the wall, then stepped before her sister's protective barrier and dropped her own.

Immediately, Madeleine's hands went up, fingers curved to scratch at her face. Miss Crafter grabbed the girl's wrists in one hand, pulled her forward, and flicked open the catch of her necklace. She felt a tremendous jolt, but there was no real power left in it. The chain sagged and slid off. She released Madeleine and caught the gold, retreating swiftly. Miss Abigail bravely stood her ground.

"Mr. Gentry, now we require your expertise."

The minister advanced on the cowering figure of his daughter, a cross held high and the prayer book open in his hands. "Avaunt, ye evil spawn of Satan. Begone from this place and the body you so foully possess against the will of the pure soul within. Begone! In the name of the Lord God, begone!"

He pressed the cross to Madeleine's forehead, and to each of her hands. There was a flurry of struggling; then the twisted expression left Madeleine's face. The girl slumped against the wall and sagged nervelessly to the floor.

"Has it been destroyed?" Mr. Gentry whispered, his voice hoarse, as they knelt at Madeleine's side. She looked as if she was at peace.

"I don't know. I suspect it has only been driven away," Miss Crafter said. "It is difficult to destroy one utterly. The law of conservation of energy would support that theory. My affianced, Captain Gregson, has said that evil presences like this one travel bodilessly from place to place until they find a host to help them do their foul work."

Mr. Gentry regarded her with admiration. "You're quite a woman, Miss Crafter. Your fiancé is a fortunate man. I am certain that there are more things you might be able to teach my daughter."

"Such as first aid," Miss Amanda said briskly, propping up the girl's head on her bundled coat. "I would say that was the most important subject at the moment. The first thing to do is to get her to a couch, and find salves and cool compresses to put on her burns."

"Miss Crafter, I want Madeleine's things sent home today." Mrs. Gentry had rallied, and bore down on the schoolmistress with an imperious air. "When such things can happen to a child under your care, it becomes plain that you are not a fit person to entrust them to. We are withdrawing her from your school."

"Oh, nonsense, Winifred. We are not," Mr. Gentry said, standing up and brushing his hands together. "Madeleine got into this scrape by herself. If it wasn't for Miss Crafter, she might not be out of it yet."

"But I don't understand!" Mrs. Gentry wailed, breaking down. "The—the skeletons, and the ships . . . . W-w-witchcraft! They're evil sorceresses. It must be reported."

"Not unless you want your own daughter tried," Gentry replied. "How else would you explain the crates she threw? My favorite chair, crushed to firewood? You watched Miss Crafter and Miss Abigail. They weren't brewing up some hell's drink over a cauldron. I saw them walk toward Madeleine, and take this damned necklace away from her. Nothing else. And that puts me to mind," he said. He dropped the gold necklace to the floor, and put his heel on the face in the middle of the chain. With a grunt, he ground the pendant into the floor. The bottom of it snapped loose and skittered across the boards. "I'll have it melted down today, if I have to buy the damned jeweler's crucible to do it."

Madeleine was conveyed to her parents' home and put to bed. Miss Amanda sent Miss Abigail back to the school to assure the pupils that their schoolmate had been found, and except for slight injuries to her hands, was all right.

When Madeleine awoke, she was surrounded by a wealth of small presents and cards. "What is all this?" she asked. Her voice was hoarse and rough, but it was her own.

"They were sent over by your schoolmates," Mrs. Gentry said, bringing the little bundles to her one by one. Encumbered by the bandages on her hands, Madeleine slowly unwrapped the packages.

Rose had sent the embroidered shawl, with a card bidding her to keep it always. Madeleine smiled at that, and at the other little gifts. One small box touched her especially. It was full of irregular shiny brown squares studded with golden nuggets.

Madeleine smiled weakly. "It's the candy we were making. I didn't get to see it poured out and worked."

"You shall," Mrs. Gentry said, wetting the cloth and replacing it on her daughter's right hand. "I'll make a special request that they repeat that cooking lesson before you leave the school for good."

Madeleine frowned thoughtfully. "Mother, why did she come after me? Miss Crafter, I mean. Because you and Father would have been angry if she let me run away?"

Mrs. Gentry pursed her lips, and patted the bandage into place. "I think she cares what becomes of you. Goodness knows you've made it difficult. But I think she's equal to you and whatever you've done."

"I think she's better than that," Madeleine said. "When I was watching from inside, it felt that it was happening to someone else. She was wonderful. She always remained calm, as though she'd done it before. I wonder if she has."

"I've never heard of such a thing," Mrs. Gentry began, and stopped. "But I can't think of a woman I know who would admit that it happened to her. I have no intentions of speaking about that day to anyone else, and I think it wise that you do not, either. There's something uncanny about those women. If you don't want to go back, you shouldn't."

"But I do," Madeleine protested. "There's so much more I want to learn. There are certainly subjects in which she is expert that are not on the syllabus." She half closed her eyes, peering speculatively at the ceiling through her eyelashes. Already, she was beginning to calculate the advantage her newfound knowledge could gain her.

Mrs. Gentry was outraged. "Madeleine, you were nearly killed. Any feeling person would leave well enough alone. You are incorrigible."

Madeleine opened innocent blue eyes at her. "Mother, you wouldn't want me to change, would you? I thought you sent me to Miss Crafter for an education. I'd say I've only learned part of the lessons she has to offer."

Missouri
Anno Domini 1834

Many things attracted those who settled the American frontier. For some it was the opportunity to acquire land, or amass a fortune. For others, it was a way of escaping debts, or even fleeing the law. In many cases they succeeded in building a new life. Nat Singer was the direct descendant of Amer Crafter and inherited many of the family's most powerful gifts. He fled West when, for all his skill, he could not avert the one tragedy he feared most. And, perhaps, to get away from his unnatural abilities, which now seemed to him more a curse than a gift. Talents that only reminded him of what he had lost. Trouble was, travelling a thousand miles to the edge of civilization doesn't give you any more distance from that which is a part of yourself.

THE DREAM COUNTRY

by Robert Sheckley

In early June, 1834, a stranger walked into the southern Missouri town of Oak Bluffs leading a big chestnut horse. The chestnut was limping badly, favoring his left forefoot. The stranger was a tall man in his early thirties. He had a short black beard, and wore a floppy black felt hat with a wide brim, such as you see further west of here. Although he was dressed in frontier style, in buckskin and moccasins, his skin was curiously pale and unweathered. His hands showed no sign of hard use; they were more like the hands of a clerk than an outdoorsman. Just within the town, a boy of ten or so stared as though he'd never seen a man on foot before.

"Hey, mister! How come you're walking?"

"Horse came up lame."

"So you'll be wanting another horse?"

"Looks that way." He looked at the kid and liked what he saw: a tow-haired boy with a freckled country face. The man's severe features broke into a smile. "I suppose you got one to sell?"

"No, sir, I ain't got no horse to sell. But I know where you can git one."

The frontiersman found a nickel in his pocket, flipped it to the kid.

"All right, son, tell me about it."

The kid grinned. "Masterson's livery stable, just right next door to where you're standing."

The man had seen the livery stable sign for himself. The kid was a wiseguy. But he had a soft spot in his heart for wiseguy kids, having been one himself, way back when he'd lived in Boston. Where he was going he didn't expect to see any more kids like that very soon.

"Thanks a lot," he said.

The stranger took a few steps, entered the livery stable and made his request to the leather-aproned man shoeing an old dray horse.

"Sorry, mister," the proprietor said. "I'll be glad to take in your horse. But I ain't got no fit replacement."

"Can you tell me where I can find one?"

The liveryman shrugged. "You could try some of the ranches around here, I suppose. Not that it would do you any good."

"Why's that?"

"I know most of the stock within fifty miles of here, and there's nothing for sale you'd be interested in. Still, there could be some new horseflesh I haven't seen."

"I'll check anyway. But not on this lady." He patted the mare's neck.

The liveryman thought for a moment. "I'll put up your horse as long as you like. And I've got a mule I could rent you. Flo's not very quick-like but she's good enough to get you around."

When the stranger came out of the livery stable leading a mule, the boy was waiting.

"No horse?" the boy asked innocently.

"Nope. He didn't have one that was suitable. I suppose you didn't know that."

The boy looked embarrassed. "I'm sorry, mister. I guess I did know. But I wanted that nickel."

"Nothing wrong with that. But you can earn it now. Do you think you can find me a place I can sleep for a night or two while I wait for a horse to turn up?"

"Sure, mister! My ma lets rooms and she's the best cook in Oak Bluffs!"

The boy started out at a trot. The man followed more slowly, leading the mule.

As the pair approached the white farmhouse, much like other farmhouses in those parts, the boy took off at a run. He raced up the wood plank stairs to his house, across the wide porch, through the dark wood door with a half-moon window, and was gone.

In a few minutes he reappeared on the porch, hand in hand with a tall woman. A dress of linsey-woolsey draped her ample figure. A white scarf knotted her smooth red hair at the nape of the neck. She smiled. Her face was lovely, albeit careworn.

She quickly assessed the stranger, liking what she saw. "Billy says you're looking for a place."

"Yes, ma'am," the man answered. He awkwardly removed his hat, shifting from one foot to the other. "My name is Nat Singer. I can't pay much. Got to save my money for a horse. But I've got two strong hands and a liking for work. I'd be happy to take up the chores and whatever else for my lodging."

Well, the money would have been nice, but Emma could use someone to milk the cows, clean out their stalls, and help deliver the butter and cheese into the town proper.

She nodded. "Looks like you've found yourself a room."

Emma looked Nat Singer over and she mostly liked what she saw. He was a good-looking man, just a couple of years older than her. There was a certain refinement about him, almost a softness which was refreshing after too much exposure to the rawhided, salty, and profane men of the West. There was something else about Nat Singer, something not so nice lurking behind his soft black beard and earnest brown eyes. But no one's perfect. Emma decided Nat looked fine to do the chores around the place, which had been piling up ever since Lemuel Skelly's death. He'd been the last hired hand, and the Shoshone had picked him off one time when he'd been riding over toward Devil's Lake looking for stray steers. Now the Shoshone were mostly gone from the land. People said the Kiowa had displaced them, and the Kiowa had a bad name, especially after the mess they'd caused in Kansas. But they weren't mostly seen around here and so no one paid them much mind.

And so Nat Singer began work on Emma Hawkins' farm. Emma raised dairy cows, and provided about a quarter of Oak Bluffs' milk. She also churned some of it into butter. Her vegetable garden grew tomatoes and zucchini and string beans. She raised some of the best strawberries in the state. She had a good-sized pigpen and did her own slaughtering, assisted by one of the drunkards from town. She kept her own counsel.

Nathaniel Singer was the second oldest son of Martin and Fay Singer. Martin was a descendant of Amer Crafter, who had brought his supernormal talents to the Colonies from England in the early years of the seventeenth century. The Crafters were a family of some distinction: people with exceptional talents in witchcraft.

All the Crafters did not follow the family tradition of magic. Some turned their back on the trade. Others, like Nat, had an ambiguous and uneasy relationship with the occult arts.

A wild youth, highly intelligent but headstrong, and with a strong inherited talent for witchcraft, Nat had grown up in Salem and witnessed the Puritan excesses of its citizens. Experimentation in witchcraft had brought him great successes at first. And then came the incident when his magic couldn't help, when he'd lost his wife, Agatha. Nat decided that New England, with its crabbed spirit and intolerant ways, was not for him. He dreamed of going West, toward room and freedom from dogma.

His feelings about magic were violent and ambivalent. He hated it but was drawn to it. This led him into a series of lucid dreams. His dreaming brought him frequent visions of that mysterious unknown Western country to which he was going. There were great expanses of dun-colored land under an enormous sky that seemed larger, more pellucid, than those that overarched New England. In his visions he saw great prairies and deserts, and cliffs of many colors. He could see the great bend of a river. The place was hot and dry. There was cactus and juniper. The sun was brilliant, merciless, all-seeing, unforgiving. There were Indians in this land and they were different from the Iroquois and Hurons he had known. They did not shave their heads like the northern tribes. Their dark hair was shoulder-length, and they bound it back with colorful headbands. They were horsemen who had been fighting the Spanish for over a century.

Those savage horsemen were still far away. Nat thought about them, and so the quiet days passed, and Oak Bluffs seemed a peaceable place. But it was soon after this that he began to pick up the scent of something wrong. At first he didn't want to acknowledge it. If his sense was right, there could be trouble, spiritual trouble of the sort he was trying to move away from. He'd left the difficult problems of innocence and evil behind him. He was going to a new place, a place that did not know the demons and dangers of the Old World. Agatha and he had dabbled once too often in that. Now he had to move fast. He didn't want to stay in this place. Something smelled bad here. There was an almost palpable sense of evil in this place. Bad things were going to happen here. But he wouldn't be here when they happened. That was certain.

Nat was supposed to make himself useful. It was evident that he didn't know beans about farm life. It was plain that he was a city man. But he was willing to turn his hand to whatever came up, and he was quick to learn. The first task was rail-splitting, and then fence-mending. Some of the cows had been escaping from the southern pasture. This fence had to be built up at once. The rail-splitting was tough work for a man who wasn't born and bred to it, but Nat quickly picked it up. He was inexperienced, but clever with his hands. Things had a way of coming together nicely under his long, blunt fingers. Billy, who followed him around and watched him, marvelled at how quickly the city man was able to accustom himself to farm life.

Nat found the work pleasant and not too onerous. He had long wanted a practical introduction to what he had encountered before, only theoretically, in books studied at Harvard.

Although most forms of farm work seemed pleasant to him, one chore was somewhat irksome. The widow had decided just weeks before he'd come that a new cesspool had to be dug below and to the right of the existing one. The old one was filled to overflowing, and had been further flooded by recent rains. The new one, marked out in somewhat firmer soil, would be a long-term job, taking one man most of the summer.

After a few hours of backbreaking work, wrenching out the granite lumps that this land seemed to be composed of, Nat mopped his brow and sat back to consider if there might not be a better way to go about this.

It was a fine afternoon. The sun was already halfway down the sky. Billy wasn't with him today. The widow had been sending the boy to the new school started by an itinerant preacher. Nat surveyed the land, then took out his billfold. He sat down on a little bluff, made himself comfortable, and began searching through it. At last he found what he was looking for. It was a scrap of parchment he'd gotten from the Boston Common Copying Room. On it was a list of names, none of them likely to be familiar to most people.

He read it. *Endymore*. That was the one he wanted.

He paused and looked around. He was alone. He didn't like what he was about to do. He reminded himself that he'd sworn not to go back to the old ways. He was going to a new country, and was giving up the old ways. But the pit was very difficult to dig. And there was no one around. So . . .

It took but a moment to trace the pentagram in the dirt. Several twigs, cleverly bent and joined, served as the focus figures. He was harder pressed to find the pinch of manna dust. It wasn't the sort of thing one carried around every day. At last, searching around the floor of the meadow, he found a mole's lair, and within it, some fine powdering dust left by the female from her recent heat. He sprinkled this around the pentagram, and then began the chant. His words rose, thin and without timbre, in the bright June air. He felt the familiar sensation of queasiness in the pit of his stomach. The chant proceeded from his mouth, haltingly at first, for it had been a long time since he'd last invoked an earth spirit, but then with more celerity as the familiar pattern reasserted itself. After a little while he noticed a whirring in the air, like a tiny dust storm. It seemed to spin just out of his peripheral vision, tantalizingly close, yet refusing to be looked at. He didn't try to focus on it. He knew from considerable experience how some spirits resist firm definition.

"Well, and who are you?" a voice said, somewhat crossly.

"My name is Nat Singer," Nat said. "I stand under the protection of the seal."

"Glad to hear it. Otherwise I would have blasted you. Why do you rouse me from my sleep? I was just having the most remarkable dream. In it I had been elected king of the Hindu pantheon of gods, and I was just deciding—"

"Excuse me," Nat said. "I'd like to hear the story some other time. Right now I need to ask a favor."

"Of course. Why else would you have called me up? All right, what is it?"

"You are a demon of the earth," Nat said. "I would like you to move some earth for me."

"One of those mountains, I suppose?" the spirit said.

"Nothing so grand. Right here on the ground I have marked it out. It is an area about fifteen feet on a side by twenty feet deep."

"You would disturb me for a task as minuscule as that?" the spirit said.

"I'm afraid so. Although it's a minor matter for you, for me it would involve considerable effort."

"I suppose it would," the spirit said. "What will you give me if I do this?"

"I am not bound to give you anything," Nat said. "You are one of the spirits bound by King Solomon himself, bound to do the work which an initiated person such as myself requires of you, as long as it pertains to your realm of magic, the earth."

"True enough," the spirit said. "But it is not a bad idea to do me a little favor anyhow. Who knows how long the Seal of Solomon will bind me in place? And, the seal once broken, who knows how terribly I might wreak vengeance on those who made light of me?"

"What is it you want?"

"Just make a little prayer to me, sometime just before you're going to bed."

"A prayer to you? But you have no real power. You can't grant wishes in the general sense. What would be the point of directing a prayer to you?"

"It would make me feel good, that's what good it would do," the spirit said. "But if it's too much to ask . . ."

"No, not at all. I'll get around to it. But for now, the dirt, if you please."

"Oh, very well. Stand back."

Singer stood well back from the outlined area. For a few moments nothing happened. Then he saw what looked like a sword of glass appear in the air. It plunged down into the ground, and brilliance coruscated from the blade. Deeper and deeper it slid, glowing silver-hot and throwing off fiery red sparks, penetrating the hardened earth like an ice pick sliding into butter. Tendrils of smoke arose from where the fire burned in the earth, and there was a crackling, groaning sound as rocks were cleaved asunder by the blade's glassy brilliance. Soon a glowing line surrounded the outlined portion of earth. Then, as Singer watched, the earth began to rise in a solid block, coming up out of the ground as though propelled on a huge hydraulic screw. Higher and higher it rose, a solid chunk of earth bound together with tree vines and filled with pebbles and larger stones. Earthworms and tiny insects fell from the mass of earth as it rose, higher, higher. Then it came entirely free of the surrounding earth and was poised for a moment, suspended ten feet above the ground.

"Where you want it, boss?" the earth demon asked. "What if I drop it over there?" He indicated a direction several miles away with a wisp of smoke.

"Not there!" Nat said. "That's where they just put up the new warehouse. They'd have my hide if I buried it under a mound of dirt."

"Well, where am I to put it?" the demon demanded. "You can't expect me to go on holding it here forever. Although I'm certainly capable of it."

"Take it up to space," Nat told him.

"What part of space? Space is a pretty big place, you know."

"Put it on the moon," Nat said. "On the dark side so it won't show in telescopes."

"Got it, boss," the earth spirit said. "Check with you later." The big cube of dirt trembled for a moment, then shot straight up into the air. In two seconds it had dwindled to a speck, and in one second more it was gone entirely.

It was only then, after the thing was gone and the deed was not to be undone that Nat realized he had left himself a problem.

How was he to explain the manner in which this hole had appeared without invoking the forbidden subject of witchcraft? Surprisingly, no one asked, at first.

Work went on. Then there came a day when Nat and the widow had to go into town for supplies. This simple trip had some unexpected consequences.

Emma Hawkins looked over her list. Feed for the chickens, sugar, cornmeal, and some strong lye soap.

Nat and Billy brought the carriage around to the front of the house for this trip into town. Billy held the reins while Nat helped Emma aboard.

Billy liked to drive, giving it all his attention, while Nat and Emma softly talked about the work of the day ahead. And about the square dance in town that night.

"Seems like everyone's going," Nat said offhandedly. He wanted to ask Emma but didn't know if it would be proper.

"Seems so," Emma answered. She looked away. Was it two, three years ago she and the late Mr. Hawkins attended their last dance? Wasn't a dance they missed, except those when she was heavy with Billy. And then Lem had to go get himself killed by that drunken Shoshone Indian.

"I'd be proud to take you," Nat said, surprising himself with his boldness. He blushed a hard red. Emma looked at him, amused by his embarrassment. "And I'd be proud," she said, "to go with you."

They were both silent the rest of the way to town. Billy tied up the horses while Emma and Nat went into the general store.

The store smelled of flowers, fresh flowers in a tin bucket for sale at a nickel a bunch. Barrels filled with flour, sugar, molasses, and meal neatly lined one wall. Blue glass bottles filled with ointments and tinctures shone in the sun which came through gingham curtains at the front window.

Emma gathered the items on her list while Nat passed the time of day with the proprietor.

"Needing a horse, are you?" the grocer asked. "Heard about a shipment from Kansas coming to town soon. Good horses, I hear."

"How much a head?" Nat asked, feeling the ten-dollar bill he kept in his right pocket.

"Five, ten dollars, I'd guess . . ."

The grocer's voice trailed off as Red Swenson burst in the store's rattly door.

The first thing anyone noticed about Red Swenson was his size—Red was tall and round as a grizzly—and the shock of orange hair that drooped from his forehead in long, loose curls.

Today, Red's blue-denim-colored eyes were streaked with blood from last night's bout with the bottle. Clearly, the bottle had won.

"Seems you cheated me," Red hollered, barely focusing on the grocer. "Bought three sacks of cornmeal from you, and when I got them home I found 'em full of worms."

"I checked all that cornmeal myself," the grocer said.

"Maggots, I tell you," Red shouted, shifting his gaze to take in Nat as well.

The grocer looked around nervously. Wasn't but a week ago that Red had asked for a refund on food he'd bought here. And before that, yes, he'd been here about a week before. Same complaint. The grocer had given him back his money and Red had headed straight for the saloon.

"If you'd bring in the meal I could have a look at it," the grocer offered meekly.

"You doubtin' my word, Sam? You mean you don't believe," Red asked, his voice rising to a shriek, "that Red Swenson, son of Han Swenson, who was a pioneer in these parts, is telling the truth?"

Swenson balled his meaty fists and advanced on the grocer, who backed away toward the cash register. Better lose a little money than get cracked, he figured.

Red would have had his money, all right, if Nat hadn't suddenly stepped between him and Sam. "Now just a minute here," Nat said, putting a strong hand on Red's shoulder. "Seems you ought to bring in the bad meal so Sam here can have a look at it. No worms in this bin here, far as I can see."

Suddenly Red's eyes focused on this stranger. He was built strong, but was a good bit smaller than Red, and lean, like a man who hasn't eaten so well for a while.

"You talking to me?" he asked. "You're the one from back East, aren't you? Came here to Missouri and got yourself a woman master. And you're talking to *me*?"

Nat tried to step away, but Red put his hands on both his shoulders and held him in place. The big man's face came down toward Nat's, his mouth hard and foul with the smell of whiskey. "Seems we should talk about this outside," Red said in mock friendliness. "Seems like you got a lesson to teach me in manners, so let's have it."

Nat felt a furious heat rise to his temples. With a shiver, he felt his dormant powers spread through his body like a net of subtle electricity. He could throw this braggart halfway into the next county . . . .

No, he thought, *not here, not now*. Maybe another time he'd meet up with this big, foul-breathed man again and show him how much brawn was worth when it was matched up against witchcraft. But not now.

Nat glared at Red but backed away. Again Red thrust his huge head toward Nat, but the whiskey went bad in the big man's stomach. He grabbed at his belly and staggered toward the door. Just made it to the other side to retch.

And that should have been the end of it. But there is a perversity that rules these things, because after that, the way Red Swenson told it, Nat put the evil eye on him, making him sick with a peculiar gesture that sure looked like witch-stuff. This, combined with the rumors about the miraculous cesspool, was enough to decide the Reverend Harrelson to pay Nat a visit.

The Reverend Harrelson was blunt and didn't beat around the bush. "Young fellow, there's been some bad talk about you going on."

"I can explain all those things that happened."

"I'm sure you can. But I don't think that I would be quite satisfied. There seems to be some evidence of deviltry."

"Reverend," Nat said, trying to laugh, "you can't be seriously thinking I've got some kind of special powers?"

"I'm quite serious," Harrelson said. "I've had my doubts about you ever since you got here. I suggest you ride out as fast as you can."

"I'm just waiting till I can buy a decent horse."

"Don't wait too long. And don't let me hear any more about this sort of thing. We will not stand for unrighteousness in these parts. I don't have to tell you what we might do."

• • •

In Oak Bluffs and its surrounding region the fine days of late June gave way to an intensely hot summer. The sun rose and poured forth brassy heat from a cloudless sky. The nights were unrelieved by even the faintest stirring of air. On the northern and northeastern horizon storm clouds gathered, but never came to anything. The land baked under the sun, and the early crops gave sign of possible failure unless there was rain.

Rain, that was what was needed! The farmers talked of nothing else. They discussed previous years, and no one could remember a worse summer since the terrible summer of '79, or was it '78?

Josiah Thomas, a local farmer, came over to visit, and he brought along Edgar Hartley, another farmer. They sat in the widow's parlor and drank her tea and looked uncomfortable. Emma could see they had something on their minds, but she couldn't guess what. It was stifling hot in the small, boxlike room. Even though Emma had hung up dampened sheets to give off a little coolness, it was barely perceptible in the still air.

Nat Singer was down in the barnyard when Billy came out and said his mom wanted him to join the visitors. Nat cleaned up and came in. The two farmers talked to him for a while about this and that—where he'd come from, where he was going, what he thought about the new political campaign, his opinions on Indians, where he stood on the slavery issue. Finally they got down to the real purpose of their visit.

"We have reason to believe," Josiah said, "that you might be a rainmaker."

"Whatever gave you that idea?" Nat asked.

"There's been talk about you having special powers ever since you dug out that new cesspool for Miz Hawkins. That was mighty skillful work, Mr. Singer, and uncommonly fast."

"I explained that," Nat said. "It was a shift in the Earth's crust. A very minor landslide. These very minor landslides do occur, you know. They just disturb one area and don't touch another right next to it. Well, that's what did it."

"Dug your cesspool for you," Henry hazarded.

"Yes, it did. And no one can prove different!"

Josiah raised both hands in a gesture of placation. "Have it your own way! It's none of our business! Oh, it's true, there'd be some who'd take it hard on moral grounds if they thought a man was dealing with black magic and witchcraft. But if that man was working for the good of the community— why, then, even the most fanatic, like old Reverend Harrelson, would have to think a second time before trying to make anything of it."

Nat phrased his next statement carefully. "I would like to help the community, of course. But I am not a rainmaker, and you will never get me to admit I am. But I could try . . ."

"That's all we ask," Josiah said. "Just try. But try it soon, acceptable, Mr. Singer?"

Once he had made up his mind, Nat wasted no time. He went out late that afternoon, when the sunset was turning the western sky to a glory of purple and orange, he walked well away from the house, and found a quiet spot within a small stand of cottonberry trees. He quickly made his preparations, drew the pentagram, lighted a candle he had prepared previously, and called up the earth spirit.

"You again?" the spirit asked.

"Sorry to bother you so soon. But I need your help again."

"Am I never to have any peace around here?"

"Stop complaining," Nat said. "I happen to know that you elemental spirits sometimes go for decades without anyone calling on you to do anything."

"Sure, but are we free to turn our attention to something else? Not by a long shot! We have to always be on hand, standing by in case some character like you, with a couple of magic spells stolen from I don't know where, wants us to do something he's too lazy to do himself, or too unskillful."

"I've heard enough," Nat said. "Will you do what I require of you or do I need to lodge a complaint?" He began a series of gestures.

"To hear is to obey," the spirit said, without much enthusiasm. "What is it this time?"

"Rain," Nat said.

"I beg your pardon?"

"I said, *rain*. A nice rainstorm. A goodly quantity of rain."

"Rain!" the spirit said. "I think I understand you now."

"Yes, rain, and please be quick about it."

"Oh, yes sir, you want rain quick? I can get it for you quick." And the spirit vanished.

Nat had a vague sense of dissatisfaction with the conversation. The spirit had seemed too pleased with himself over something. Should he have been more precise about what size rainstorm he wanted, and for how long? Surely one didn't have to do that . . . .

But, as it turned out, that was precisely what he should have done. Because the storm came in minutes later with an impressive crash of thunder and skirmish of lightning, and it was the mother and the father and perhaps even the granddaddy of all storms seen in that area since men could remember. Afterwards there was argument over just where it had begun. Some said it had been brewed in the Great Lakes. Others claimed it blew in from the far Pacific. Wherever it came from, it was more like a tornado than a summer storm. The rain fell in sheets, and those sheets came down in long, slanted lines. It was an amazing display of water, and it drowned out over half of the farms in the neighborhood, beat in many roofs, tore down a lot of fences, and in general played merry hell with the course of life. The farmers got their rain, but they had to replant anyhow because the storm washed the seeds out of the earth. And when it was all done, Nat was something of a hero, but also under suspicion. For even though he denied having anything to do with the rainmaking, his denial carried more of a sense of complicity than any degree of assent would have done.

The summer days wore on. Occasionally there were rumors of Indian war parties on the nearby frontier. A lot of tribes were on the move. It was said that the Comanche, displaced by pioneers entering Texas and beyond, were gathering on the Missouri-Kansas borders. Although the Comanche and Kiowa, fiercest of the plains fighters, made up most of the war parties, there were a lot of others as well: displaced Cheyenne and Sioux, disenfranchised Shoshone and Blackfoot. They had all come under the power of a single man, and this itself was an unprecedented event in the life of the Indians. This shaman was named Two Coyotes, and it was said that he was Kiowa-Apache. By all accounts he was a big man, barrel-chested, and well into middle age. He had a broad broken beak of a nose, a steel slab of a jaw. His eyes were dark, unblinking. It was said he could go into a trance and remain there for long hours, and in this trance he could travel to far places without his body, and could see the results of future actions.

The Government expressed concern over Two Coyotes. But there was nothing to do about him. He hadn't caused any trouble yet. And even if he did, short of an outright attack on a town or settlement, there was no law that said Indians couldn't organize.

These concerns were far from Nat's mind, however. New Indian leaders were always coming up, holding forth for their little hour upon the stage of history, and then vanishing back into the shadows. There hadn't been a strong Indian leader for a long time now. Everyone knew the Indians were too independent, too fragmented, to successfully organize against the white man. In this year of 1834 the tribes didn't pose as much of a menace to a place like Oak Bluffs, Missouri, which had been settled country for more than fifteen years at this point.

Nat was out in the field above the farm, ploughing a field with a team of mules which the widow had rented from the livery stable. It was another fine day. The mules plodded along, pulling the plough. Nat had trouble holding the thing steady. It would take him time to learn how to plough a straight furrow. But he was learning. There was a blackbird singing in the nearby bramblebush that afternoon. Was it trying to tell him something? What portent was it? Because the essence of magic is that suddenly a time comes when everything is a sign and a portent, but you don't realize that until later.

And so the blackbird's song. And then the plough made an odd sound; it struck something solid. Something that was not stone. It was—wood? Nat stopped the team and got down into the furrow and began digging in the soil. The earth was sunbaked again. Nat took off his coat. He had to work hard to break up the clods and force the spade deeper into the soil. Funny, this was well-tilled soil, yet it resisted his spade. At last something seemed to give way, like a barrier crossed, and the digging became easier. As he scooped out a few more spadefuls, his nose wrinkled in disgust. Phew! There was something ancient here, and ugly, and evil.

Nat straightened up, half-deciding to dig elsewhere. Then his expression hardened. There might be something wrong with this place, but he couldn't walk away from it. That was the worst thing to do. The smell fascinated him at the same time as it repulsed him.

He dug deeper, taking out the earth with increasingly careful movements so as not to break anything that might lie beneath. Soon he came to a bone, unmistakably human, its rounded end just peeking through the brown earth. Carefully sweeping around it with his hat, he uncovered more bones. And then something came into sight that took him a moment to recognize. It was a deer's antlers, stained reddish-brown by the mineral-rich soil. A little further down he came upon a human skeleton, interpenetrated by the antlers so that the whole thing looked like a single chimerical beast, a deer-man or a man-deer.

Nat bent low over this thing, and the bad smell came up to strike him. He was frozen for a moment in fascinated horror that was almost pleasurable. Then he tried to straighten up, but was pulled short by something attached to the skeleton in the shallow grave. He realized later that it was his neckerchief, which had caught in the creature's bones. He tried to pull free, but the bones resisted. He tried harder. The neckerchief would not break loose. Instead his pull brought the entire skeleton to an upright sitting posture, the skull grinning into his face, the antlers rearing above the ruined head. Nat became aware in that moment that something was not so much attacking him as playing with him. He wrenched the neckerchief free, and with a blow broke the skeleton apart, bones scattering every which way, the skull rolling to his feet. Moved by some obscure compulsion, he picked up the skull and put it back with the rest of the bones.

"Thanks very much," the skull said.

"You talk!" said Nat.

"Good afternoon to ye, Nathaniel. You play pretty rough when you wrestle, I can tell you that."

"Did I hurt you?"

"No, you did not, Nat. We dead spirits are pretty immune to the trials of the flesh. Though we do permit ourselves the one in order to feel the other."

Nat had now recovered his poise. He sat down on the edge of the shallow grave and said, "You don't talk much like an Indian."

"That's because I'm not." The skull then proceeded to tell

Nat a story. He said his name was Propertius. He had been a centurion in the time of Marcus Aurelius. He had been serving at Cadiz in the 4th Dalmatians. He'd received his orders to proceed to Britain. He'd sailed his ship just beyond the gates of Hercules when suddenly a great storm had come up. He and his men had been blown many miles out to sea. If they were not to die of thirst, they knew that they had no choice but to continue on across the western ocean, to a great and mysterious land that the Romans had recently discovered.

This land they called Atlantis. It was a great continent, and it was populated by red men who wore feathers in their dark hair and were very fierce. Marcus Aurelius kept his knowledge of this land a secret. There was no reason to disturb people about it yet. More exploring was needed before a public announcement. Already Marcus Aurelius had rough maps of the place. It was a huge land, much larger than all of Iberia. And it was there for the taking. Only primitive Indian tribes inhabited the place. If the Germans pressed Rome too hard, there was the new continent to retreat to. But the key to taking it was logistics. Through his mapmakers, Marcus Aurelius was aware of two rivers; the ones now called the St. Lawrence and the Mississippi. The question was, did they connect?

The centurion Propertius wanted to find out about this for the emperor. He and his men started inland from the site of present-day Baltimore.

"I had half-a-dozen sailors," he told Nat, "and a squad of Thracian recruits, the only survivors of our ocean crossing. On the southern Atlantean coast I collected some more men. There was a Roman colony in Charleston in those days, but they were few in number and a miserable bunch. The emperor always said he'd send reinforcements. He was never able to.

"We marched inland through a thousand perils. I would have succumbed over and over to one or more of these dangers if it had not been for my amulet. It was very old, that amulet, Babylonian work, and Marduk, the spirit who resided in it, watched over me. We marched inland, searching for the great southern-flowing river. One by one the Indians took their toll of us, and still we hadn't reached the river. At last we came to this place. And here a great company of Indians fell upon us. We fought like furies, and each man killed his tens and twenties of the red men. But success was not to be ours that day. I asked Marduk, *Why have you forsaken me?* And Marduk said, *It is written in the stars that you should not see another dawn. There is nothing I can do in this regard, for it is so written by Ananke, the Necessity that rules our lives. I have come to prepare you for the end.*

"The next day, just as he foretold, I was killed. My bones have lain here ever since. My spirit cannot be released until they are buried. Stranger, if you bury me, and cast the eagle buried with me into a great river, I will tell you where to find the amulet."

Nat did as the centurion asked him, and laid Propertius to his final rest with an impressive Latin prayer. Then Nat asked, "Where is the amulet?"

"Tomorrow go into the fields and search for it. I will ensure that you find it," a voice answered from the grave.

"Whatcha looking for, Nat?" Billy asked. They stood in the upper pasture behind the farmhouse.

"I'll tell you when I know," Nat said.

They were walking through thick grasses along the bank of a small stream. Sycamore and hemlock grew near the edge. Something stimulated Nat's witch-sense. That something was close, very close, almost within reach. Nat felt along the bank until his fingers encountered a small round hole. Carefully brushing the branches and leaves aside with his free hand, he drew a small object from the earth.

"Wow!" Billy said. "What's that?"

"Indian medicine," Nat said. He put the object into a rawhide pouch he carried on his belt. He secured the top of the pouch with a length of rawhide, and tied it with a large and complicated knot.

"Is it very strong medicine?" Billy asked.

"You could say so," Nat said.

"Is this Indian magic?" Billy asked.

Nat didn't answer. Billy had never seen the man quite so taciturn.

Late that night Nat lay on his bed in the front room. He'd put out the little oil lamp, because a three-quarter moon gave enough light to get around in. He lay on the ticking, hands locked behind his head, watching the shadows weave and turn and dance on the wall and ceiling. An elm tree near the house moved its branches up and down in the light breeze that blew in from the west. The wind carried a lot of smells. There was coyote and black bear in that breeze, and the subtler odors of Emma Hawkins and Billy. A sweet odor of grass and trees wafted in from the prairie. And there was another smell, and it didn't take Nat long to recognize it: Indian. He was smelling the dream-smell of Indian.

He suddenly realized the smell had grown very strong. Something was in the room with him. He could almost see it, there in the darkest tangle of shadows.

Aware of the danger, Nat slowly sat up on the bed. He couldn't remember for a moment what he had done with the amulet. That's what had drawn the thing to his room. He was annoyed at himself. He had only himself to blame. He had grown careless. He had forgotten that although he might be through with magic, magic might not be through with him. Where was it now? He looked around the room, dappled with leaf-patterned moonlight, and then he saw the charm, on the rough little table beside the pewter washstand. He reached for it. Something closed around his wrist.

People laugh at the notion of things that go bump in the night; but it's not so funny when they're bumping into you. Nat's impulse was to tear himself free of that cold, dry, other-worldly grip. But Nat had spent years resisting fatal first impulses like that. It is well known that apparitions are powered by your own fear. Panic is the switch that turns control of your body over to whoever is panicking you. The man who would live through these night matters had better be steadfast, because nothing else will suffice.

Nat forced himself to remain motionless as the hand tightened around his wrist, increasing the strength of its grip gradually but inexorably until it took all of Nat's resolve not to fight back. For a moment he wasn't sure he could succeed. The urge to react was almost overwhelming, an instinct as old as man himself. But he resisted.

Gradually a hazy, luminous collection of green-blue lines began to form in front of him. They sketched out the ectoplasmic figure of a man, nearly transparent except where the lines terminated in the solid dark density of his hand. Nat knew that all of the spirit's energy was concentrated into materializing and maintaining that hand. And already the crisis was passing. The spirit couldn't maintain his grip for long. Already it was loosening.

Then, abruptly, the hand released its grip, but the fingertips remained in contact with Nat's wrist. The disembodied hand, attached to nothingness by luminous lines of energy, crept up his arm, hunching itself up like a big tarantula. It crawled up his shoulder. A cold, ethereal forefinger poked at Nat's cheek and tried to find his eye. But it was an empty threat. Nat could already feel the hand softening, dissolving back into substanceless ectoplasm.

In the morning, Nat called on the earth spirit.

"What is it now?" the earth spirit asked. "What happened last night?"

"I need to know what's going on," Nat said.

"Simple. The shaman Two Coyotes followed you by the dream-scent to the place where you were sleeping. He wants the amulet back. It was his, lost by mistake. He's coming for it."

"Where is he?"

"Nat, this is the last service I'm going to do you. This one is above and beyond the call of duty. If you want this one, you have to promise to let me go at the end of it."

"I swear."

The spirit lifted Nat up and took him out over the land. Swooping low, invisible, Nat could see the rise and fall of the hills and the deep channels in which the rivers flowed. He could see the Indian host gathering. They were mounted, and there were a lot of them. There were Cheyenne and Shoshone, and Arapaho and others, and above all there was Kiowa, a small tribe but very fierce, and leading them was the shaman.

Squat and bold he sat bareback on his painted pony. Nat came down close and peered at him. He could see the man closely, see the very pores of his skin. And then suddenly Two Coyotes became aware of him, despite his invisibility, and swung around, searching . . . .

And then they were back, Nat and the spirit, back at the place where they'd begun.

"He saw me!"

"Well, I did the best I could."

"What happens now? What do I do?"

But the earth spirit was gone.

Nat saw that he'd have to warn the people of what was coming. But how could he do that? What would they say? What would they do to him? How would they think he got this knowledge?

And so this was the matter that perplexed Nat Singer. So much did he think about it that finally the long-awaited moment of buying a horse was almost anticlimactic. The beast was a large black stallion with a hard mouth and a suspicious eye. A dangerous creature, and the story was it had trampled its previous owner to death, catching him in the stall, back in Virginia. Nat didn't know if this was true. He did know that the horse had been ill-used. Old scars from a braided whip still lay about its flanks and withers. Nat walked around the horse, keeping his distance from possible flying hooves. He looked into the horse's eyes, touched its heaving flanks, did a reading and a prognosis there on the spot. This horse had seen some bad times, but it wasn't a bad horse. Some steady work and some decent care and it would be good as new again. So he bought the horse, and drove a hard bargain, getting him for nine dollars. That left him one dollar with which to start his new life.

But he couldn't rejoice in his new life. There arose before him continually now a vision of the catastrophic attack that was coming to the town, sliding through the distant plains like smoke.

Nat sought out the advice of Marduk, the Babylonian spirit who resided in the amulet.

It was easy to raise Marduk. He was an ancient spirit with much experience in discourse with mankind. When Nat called him, that morning, sitting in a little copse of trees above the widow's house, the Babylonian spirit appeared almost immediately, as if he had been sitting at the edge of Limbo waiting to be called up.

"I want to know about Two Coyotes," Nat said. "He tried to kill me. He knows where I am. Why hasn't he renewed his attack?"

"Not much doubt about the reason for that," Marduk said. "He doesn't want to risk a physical attack on you. Not at a time like this, when the Indians are staying quiet and preparing for new mischief. He won't attack you again as a spirit because he didn't have the strength to kill you that way before."

"Do you think maybe he'll leave me alone?"

Marduk chuckled. "You know enough about these matters, Nat, to know that Two Coyotes will never rest until one of you is dead. He's coming for you, Nat. But he's expecting to find you in the Dream Country."

"I don't think I know about that," Nat said. "Where is the Dream Country?"

"It's the region of the mystic world where a man can wander when he does his dreaming. Wizards and shamans can go there at will."

"What makes Two Coyotes think I'll go there? It's a region one goes to voluntarily, isn't it?"

"That it is, Nat."

"Well, you're not going to find me there!"

"That is wise," Marduk said. "You are to be commended for your cautious nature."

The sound of Marduk's ironic voice grated on Nat's nerves. The spirit wasn't being very sympathetic! But it didn't matter. Nat knew he had to get out of there, away from Oak Bluffs, far away, before the Indians came down on the town and began their next war. He had to leave. Now. It was as simple as that.

That morning Nat found Emma in the kitchen as usual. She was doing the week's wash. Her abundant hair was tied back with a bit of bright yarn, and her sleeves were pushed back, revealing rosy forearms. There was a glow of health upon her. Nat had never seen her look so pretty.

"Morning, ma'am."

"Morning, Nat."

Nat willed himself to make some small talk, but none came. He had chided himself for a long time on this problem in his makeup. He had found life in the civilized East almost impossible because of this inability of his to make chitchat even at the dance they had attended. After stumbling around with tame words for a few minutes, he got straight to the point.

"Mrs. Hawkins, I have reason to believe that you and the boy are in grave peril."

She gave him a quizzical look. "Whatever are you talking about, Mr. Singer?"

"I have sure knowledge that there is going to be an Indian attack on this settlement, Mrs. Hawkins. It will signal the beginning of a full-scale Indian war throughout the Middle West, extending God knows how far."

"I see," she said. "And when is this Indian attack supposed to take place?"

"I am fairly sure it will commence within a day or two. Perhaps tomorrow morning. Surely not long after that."

"And how did you come by this knowledge, Mr. Singer? You didn't find it in the bottom of a jug by any chance?"

"I beg pardon? Oh, I see what you mean. No, I have not been drinking!"

"Then where did you come by your knowledge?"

He hesitated. "Ma'am, that is difficult to tell. Could you not just take my word for it?"

"No, I could not. Nor could the rest of the town. Because if there is a danger such as you say, everyone here ought to be told about it. Is that not so?"

"Yes, ma'am, it is."

"And who else have you told?"

"You are the first."

"And to what do I owe this honor?"

"I am afraid no one will believe me, ma'am, and they will force me to admit things that are better not spoken of."

"Things like what, Mr. Singer?"

"But those are the things I prefer not to reveal!"

"Nevertheless, if you want me to take any credence whatsoever in your wild words, you had better tell me something."

"Yes, I suppose I'd better," Nat muttered. "The fact is, Mrs. Hawkins, I have some little knowledge of magical arts, and the impending Indian attack has come to my attention through them."

"You are claiming that you are a warlock?" she asked, her voice flat and unfriendly.

"No, not exactly," Singer muttered. "But I do have certain . . . powers . . . at my disposal. What I say is the truth, Emma, as God is my witness! The Indians are coming! I beg you to believe me."

"What is it you would have me do?" she asked.

"Take the boy and whatever valuables you can pack in the buckboard, and head West. The Indian attack will engulf this town and the regions within a hundred miles east of here."

"And what of you, Mr. Singer?"

"I will accompany you," Nat said.

"I see," Emma Hawkins said. "You and I and the boy are
to escape this menace. But what of the rest of the towns-
people?"

"They would never believe me," Nat said.

"Have you even tried to convince them?"

"I have not! The Reverend Harrelson would have me strung
up within the hour if he heard I was making talk like that. He
has his suspicions of me anyhow."

"And so do I, Mr. Singer, so do I. I do not like this style of
speaking. If there is any danger, which I seriously doubt, you
should go to the town council and lay your suspicions before
them openly and honestly. Then, if they will not heed you,
you will have done what you could. Even if there were such
a danger—could you have believed I would go away with you,
stealing away like a thief in the night from the place where my
husband is buried, abandoning my neighbors to their fate and
thinking only of myself?"

"There's Billy to be considered, ma'am."

"Billy is no more a coward than I am. He will stay here with
me. I see you have your horse, Mr. Singer. I suppose you will
be on your way, then?"

"Yes, ma'am. That is what I suppose."

"Then sooner would be better than later, Mr. Singer. I believe
on work and wages we are quits. It would be convenient if you
were gone by morning. I had thought better of you when you
first came here, Mr. Singer. I had thought . . . Never mind!
Please be on your way as soon as you can!"

Nat went to the little copse of trees in the upper meadow.
It was late afternoon. The golden light was already taking
on a tinge of evening pallor. Blackbirds sung merrily in the
trees. Nat lay down on the grass. Almost immediately a voice
said to him, "Gotten yourself into a proper mess now, haven't
you, Nat?"

"Is that you, Marduk? I didn't call you."

"No. But I took the liberty of appearing anyway."

"Well, you're right," Nat said. "Damn but this is a bad
situation! I don't even know when this Indian attack is to

take place! Not exactly. Soon, but I don't know exactly when. Emma doesn't believe me. The folks in town won't believe me, either."

"Let me set your mind at rest about one thing," Marduk said. "I've done a little investigating on your behalf and I know when the tribes plan to attack."

"When?"

"The attack will begin in the morning, Nat, at first light."

"So soon? How could it be so soon?"

"There's no way it could be any later. Two Coyotes has been having a lot of trouble holding the tribes together. They don't really trust him. Fear him, yes, but not trust. Dissident voices have been raised in council, demanding that he postpone the uprising, make one more attempt at reconciliation. His whole enterprise is foundering, Nat. Without him there to whip them on, there'd be no rebellion. Many tribes have lost their first fury, are inclined now to accept the inevitable."

"Can't someone talk to the tribes?" Nat asked. "Isn't there someone who could point out how disastrous a course the shaman is leading them on?"

"Why yes, there is such a person," Marduk said.

"Who is he?"

"You know him well," Marduk said, "although in another sense you don't know him at all."

"You refer to me?"

"No other.

"The tribes would not listen to me! I do not speak their language!"

"You speak a universal language," Marduk said. "I refer of course to the power of sorcery. If you but defeat Two Coyotes in the Dream Country, the tribes will understand better than any words could tell how hopeless his pretension is. They will go back to their tents. Many lives will be saved."

"You expect me to fight the shaman? I am unskilled at these battles of sorcerers, Marduk. And I am a long time out of practice. How can you expect this of me?"

"Oh, you're quite right, of course," Marduk said. "Who could expect you to stretch out a finger or put yourself in a moment of possible harm for the sake of saving the lives of a few hundred settlers and a few thousand Indians? It is unthinkable to ask that of you. I most humbly apologize."

"That's not fair," Nat said.

"How not?"

Nat was silent for a long moment. Then he said, "I perceive on second thought that what you say is fair enough."

"I thought you'd come to it," Marduk said. "You're not a bad sort, Nat. Just a little spoiled."

"Yes. I see it now."

"Well, I've made my point," Marduk said. "Come on, Nat, let's get out of here, you and I."

"No," Nat said. "We have something to do first."

"Have we indeed? And what is that?"

Nat rose and started down the pasture toward the river bank.

"Where are you going?" Marduk asked.

"To wash in the river."

"You surprise me," Marduk said. "This is a curious time to take a bath."

"Ritual ablution is customary in these cases," Nat said.

"What cases, Nat?"

"You know very well what I'm talking about. It's time that Two Coyotes and I had this thing out."

"Bravely spoken! But aren't you frightened? This Indian is formidable!"

"There's no time for fear," Nat said. "No, nor for courage, either, or hope. This is the time when a man does what he has to do."

"The widow would like you a little better," Marduk said, "if she heard you talking now. To the river, then!"

The Dream Country is reached by way of the Land of Sleep. This Land of Sleep is a place all people know, though they have no control of themselves once they are there. For most men, dreams are simply things that happen to them. For Nat and others trained in the magical art of dream mastery, sleep is a state that can be entered consciously, a place that has a climate and a scenery and even a characteristic lighting and color. These qualities change from time to time, but the main characteristics of the Dream Country remain constant.

And so this time Nat found himself in a dream-forest, with purple trees and red clouds that lay in clumps on the forest floor. He continued, and his intent made all directions easy, and soon he found himself in front of a wall. He stood a moment and looked at it, then sighed and made a motion. As his dream-hand rose, a hole appeared in the wall; a dream-hole in a dream-wall. And Nat entered, and he was in the Dream Country.

This was a place where shapes were malleable and unfixed. Colors ran one into the other, and sounds behaved as if they hadn't quite made their minds up, wavering eerily up and down on the scale. It was not a good place, but Nat moved forward, and strove to pick up the details. One moment the place seemed a forest, the next it had turned into a great desert with mountains in the near distance shaped like stovepipe hats, and colored in brilliant yellows and fuchsias. Nat kept on moving forward, and if he had any doubts, now was not the time to exercise them, because he could see, far ahead, a tiny black dot against the gloriously colored swirling background of lights that marked the shaman's entrance.

Two Coyotes advanced on him and then stood close enough for Nat to make out the shaman's strong features. Two Coyotes spoke, and since he spoke in the universal language of dreams, Nat could understand him.

"So you have come! I thought you would not dare!"

"Obviously you were wrong about that," Nat said. "And there's quite a lot else you're wrong about."

The shaman grinned. "How sad, tiny, and insignificant your words sound! Come to your death, then!" And so the combat was begun.

No tongue in the world is equipped to tell of the combat of dream-warriors in a dream-space. Such contests are the essence of the uncanny. These are deeds that take place on the border of what is reality and what is spirit. Such deeds cannot aptly be recorded in the mundane language we use to speak of pecks of lima beans and bushels of corn. The recording muse felt faint when faced with the challenge of describing the ineffable, but managed to point out that the Indian advanced along the line of his best capabilities, his physical prowess, his lithe and pantherlike passion. Whereas Nat was a representative of another culture entirely. It was his way to examine the onslaughts which the shaman perpetrated. His rationality led him to find an object interesting even when it was trying to kill him. Due to this psychic setup he was almost drowned when the shaman, drawing strength from the depths of his being, commanded a cataract of water to fall in its broken white-waved immensity on Nat's head. The waters rose around him, churning and frothing as wind-spirit energies whipped their surface to a stinging froth. Nat could see for himself that if a dream-warrior died a dream-death in a dream-place, death would come, too, back in the place his body was. So Nat summoned up strength and fought his way out of the flood that washed over him, forming handholds on the rapidly passing river bank, and then creating hands with which to hold on to the handholds. And this strategem sufficed, and for the moment he could lift himself above the raging waters.

But he found that he had merely passed from one peril to another. Because now he was assailed by birds, small and large, some bright of feather and some dull, a raging conflagration of birds, and these attacked him with beak and claw and insensate rage. They came at him in a dizzying whirl of wings, clawing with their taloned feet, and striking with their beaks. Nat countered at once, more rapidly than the time before, because now he was growing more adept and accustomed to the rules of the combat. He dodged the flailing beaks and clutching claws for a moment, then created a shield of shiny black obsidian. With this on his arm, he interposed its adamantine surface between himself and his winged attackers. The foremost of them dashed themselves to bloody pulp against his shield, and the rest drew back for a moment and buzzed together in a hovering black cloud of beating wings. They seemed to come to some decision, because in a moment they had returned to the attack, but this time they had changed shape, and Nat found, coming at him from all sides, snakelike creatures with the many tiny hooked claws of leeches. They came in a torrent, and Nat had to devise a perch for himself so he would not be engulfed by them entirely. He did so, and he was beginning to think again, because clearly something was needed here, some expedience, because the shaman's attacks were mounting in ferocity and Nat had never been at his best in dealing with animal analogues.

The moment of analysis gave him the clue he needed to move to the next step. His own countermove, coming right up! And so he suddenly created a locomotive, alive with fire in its belly and steam bursting out of its joints. Its great rods moved in and out of their cylinder boxes, and the vast mechanism moved forward, laying track as it came, like a gigantic metal monster with a steel skin and copper eyes.

With this one coming at him, the shaman hesitated one fatal moment. The locomotive was new, even in the East. He was from one of the wild tribes that had never seen the white man's ways up close. He had heard of this monstrosity that the white man possessed, but this was the first time he'd seen it. And as terrible as the locomotive was, it was even more terrible when viewed in its dream state, where all its potentialities for harm were in view.

The shaman tried to interpose a mountain. Quickly Nat countered with the dream image of the latest tunnelling equipment from St. Louis. His bit of purest diamond cut through the granite of the shaman's refuge, penetrated into the depths of the mountain, ate through the walls and sought out the shaman himself within. As the drill bit came toward him, Two Coyotes knew fear at last.

Then the locomotive came through the tunnel drilled in the rock and began to stalk the shaman across the quivering metaphoric surface of the Dream Country. Two Coyotes retreated, created a fastness of hills just behind him, a place where he could retreat and hide. But before he could do that, Nat had interposed another dream entity between the shaman and his refuge, and this dream entity was a cotton gin. Its belt-driven shafts went up and down; it rolled forward on bicycle wheels; its headlights shone with the lambent glow of commercial magic; steam oozed from its joints as it came toward him.

Then Two Coyotes saw his peril, and steadied himself for one final blow, his last forlorn hope.

Next morning, the old boatman at the Mississippi station sat up when he heard a halloo from outside. The man who greeted him was tall and thin, dressed as a Western frontiersman. He rode a tall black horse.

"Can I get a passage across the river?" Nat asked.

"That you can, stranger," the boatman said. "But it'll cost you a dollar."

Nat took a silver dollar out of his pouch and flipped it to the boatman. "That's the last of them."

"What you gonna do for money?" the boatman asked.

"Maybe where I'm going I won't need any."

"Place like that sounds like Heaven," the boatman remarked. "You wouldn't happen to be a religious man, would you, mister?"

"Not particularly. Why do you ask?"

"A man would need a lot of faith to be travelling alone in these parts with Two Coyotes and his tribes on the loose."

"Haven't you heard?" Nat asked. "Two Coyotes is dead."

"How did that happen?"

"No one knows. He was found this morning. Seems like he died in his sleep. As soon as the bucks saw he was dead, they started to disperse, giving up the attack and returning to their various people. The news is all over Missouri by now."

"Well, I'll be dinged." The boatman scratched his head. "You travelling alone, mister?"

"Looks like it."

"You can go down to the boat any time. I push off inside of the hour whether anyone else shows up or not."

Nat led the horse down the gentle slope toward the boat tied up to a makeshift dock on the Mississippi. He was alone. He took a sack out of his bag, untied it, and emptied broken bronze that had been an eagle into the water.

"Good luck, centurion," he said.

Then he bowed his head and said, "Earth spirit, thanks for your help. I wish success and happiness for you. This is the prayer I promised you."

Then he took out his pouch and took the amulet from it.

"Marduk?"

"Yes, Nat?"

"I'm going on. To the West."

"Without the widow, Nat?"

"She wouldn't want to go where I'm going. Up into the mountains. To learn."

"From the Indians?"

"Yes, from them. I only wish I hadn't had to kill Two Coyotes. Least I can do is learn something about those people. But listen, I've done with witchcraft and now I am going to cast the amulet into the river and let you go free."

"That's right kind of you, Nat," Marduk said. "But don't bother."

"Aren't you going to leave?"

"You make such an excellent packhorse, Nat, I thought I'd stay around for a while. This amulet is quite comfortable, too. I've lived here for a couple of millenia. Why give it up now?"

"You're staying with me?"

"Put the amulet away and get on the boat. It's time we went to that Western country."

OPPRESSION

by Judith R. Conly

Their bodies, torn by whip and shackle's jaw,
Are sundered from their kin and hearth and name.
Our flesh, once threatened by self-righteous flame,
Is sheltered now by insulating law.

Our minds, whose arcane visions shy from sight,
Shield sanctuaries to contain our spells.
Their thoughts, thick-sown within their earth-dark shells,
Wither anticipating frost-hued blight.

Their souls, craving release from earthly strife,
Invoke eternal bliss with mortal breath.
Our spirits, reconciled with weighty Death,
Can celebrate creation, savor life.

Our fortune, wed to Lady Liberty,
Has freed us from the prison of our past.
Their future, bondage-fouled and mired fast,
Must pave a road to human dignity.

Texas
Anno Domini 1836

By the seventh generation the Crafter Family had spread across most of the Eastern states and territories. Some on their own, others accompanying husbands who shared their families' adventuresome attitudes. One of these was the least likely to have travelled to the rough Mexican territory called Texas — where she found that even in an isolated corner of nowhere her magic could touch the lives of others.

REMEMBER THE ALMOST
by Morgan Llywelyn

Looking out across the flat, dry, dun-coloured prairie baking in the heat, Lena longed for the sight of a tree. Any tree except the feathery, arid mesquite scrub that made the landscape look even drier. Her eyes were hungry for something green and lush.

She remembered summer in New England. Maple shade and emerald grass. Sparkling streams. It seemed like a memory of Heaven, though she knew she was conveniently forgetting five months of winter and snow up to her shoulders and bitter cold.

During those times too she had longed for the sight of something green, but not as acutely as she did now, in this Godforsaken sod hut on the Texas prairie.

She stood in the open doorway and hugged herself consolingly with her thin arms. She did not need to look down at them to know they were desiccated, with all the moisture baked out of them. Same as the rest of her. She did not even look in her grandmother's mirror anymore, the precious rosewood-framed oval she had brought unbroken clear across the country. She did not want to see her rabbity face, her red-rimmed eyes. They seemed as ugly to her as this sunbleached land.

Staring into the glare of the summer day made her eyes water and she stepped back into the shadows of the house. It seemed to Lena like some dreadful punishment, having been born an albino. She could not stand the sun. Yet her family thought she was so special! "Born silver, and with a caul!" Cousin Emily used to exclaim when telling others about young Lena. They had showed her off, at least among themselves. A very special Crafter.

So how did I end up here? Lena wondered bitterly for the hundredth time.

The answer, of course, was outside plowing, trying to dig fertile furrows into infertile earth with the help of one spavined mule and an endless supply of determination. Tell Joseph Peabody he could not do something, and he would set out to do it if it harelipped Hell. That was a favourite saying of his: "I'll do that if it harelips Hell." Against such a will Lena Crafter had been helpless. She married him because he insisted, and let him bring her to the great plains of Texas because he would have it no other way. Joseph had been determined to find a Garden of Eden where others found rattlesnakes and scorpions.

Well, he hasn't found it yet, Lena thought to herself, sighing. He thought having me would make the difference, that I could somehow magic things for him. He listened to the talk, and I listened to those high and mighty dreams of his, and here we are. Both of us.

Us and the mule.

She went to the door again and stared out until her eyes started to water so badly she had to turn away.

Joseph was in a bad mood when he came in for his dinner—a stringy jack rabbit boiled with turnip greens. Lena had never said she was a cook.

"What is this mess?" he asked, looking down at the food on his plate. One of Grandmother Reliance Crafter's best Spode dinner plates lovingly carried from New England. The others on their shelf were gritty with the dirt that blew constantly around and through the cabin.

"Jack rabbit," Lena said, stating the obvious. "It's all there is unless you go hunting."

"Tarnation, woman! Where would I find time to go hunting? If we're going to make a crop I have to get the field plowed."

"They say that's caleche, out there. Hardpan, Joseph. Even if you plow it, how do you expect anything to grow in it?"

"You're my wife, you'll help me."

This was a resumption of an old argument. Lena sat down on the other chair—they had only two—and braced herself.

"I've told you and I've told you, I can't wave my hands over the earth and make things grow."

"You're a Crafter, damn it. All my life I heard stories about your family."

"Not from us, you didn't."

"No, but everyone else knew. Some of your kin were witches and wizards; you can't keep a thing like that secret in a place like New England."

With a patience that had long since worn thin, Lena told him again, "We aren't witches and wizards, at least not the way you mean it. We have a Talent, that's all, and it manifests itself differently in different members of the family."

Joseph took a bite of rabbit, chewed hard, swallowed harder. It was an old buck with meat like leather, for which he would somehow blame Lena, she knew. "Magic is magic," he said stubbornly, glaring at her.

"There are all sorts of magic, and my Talent doesn't qualify as magic anyway," she tried once more to tell him. "The Natural Philosophies, that's what I'm good at."

He shrugged. "Fancy word for another kind of magic."

"No it isn't. Why won't you understand? You aren't stupid, Joseph, you've just closed up your mind."

He took another bite, worked it around in his mouth, then spat it back onto the plate and stood up. "You're the one who's closed your mind. You won't help me even though I know you could. You hate me for bringing you out here and this is your way of getting even!" He stalked from the cabin.

Lena was not sure whether he meant refusing to work magic was her way of getting even—or feeding him tough rabbit.

But she could not help either one. She had told him the truth; her share of the Crafter gift was almost entirely of a scientific bent. And no power on earth would have tenderized that rabbit.

She scraped his plate into the slop bucket to feed later to their one razorback hog in his pen behind the house. He wouldn't be of slaughtering age until autumn, and autumn was a long time away. "If I had the Book, maybe I could hurry the seasons," Lena said to no one in particular. On the prairie it was easy to start talking to yourself.

But she didn't have the Book, or even any of its copies. Her share of the Crafter legacy was tailored to her particular gift; she only had the various discoveries other members of the family had made before her.

No magic at all, she thought wearily. But at least I have something.

She went to the small chest that held her personal things and took out her glasses with a pride she did not even bestow on the mirror or the Spode.

Lena had made the eyeglasses herself. From sand and heat and power, she had fashioned the lenses, pouring her creative will and her need into them until the finished product was exactly what she needed to enable her albino eyes to see as clearly as anyone else's, even in strong sunlight. But when Joseph was around she no longer wore them, because he would begin saying, "If you can do that, why can't you do what I need?"

She wiped the polished lenses on her apron, flinching at the gritty feeling of the cloth against glass. Scratching them undoubtedly. When they became too scratched she would have to make new ones, and it would be hard to do without Joseph catching her at it.

"I've certainly fallen short of my family's expectations," Lena said to the room at large. The dirt-floored, sod-walled, one-room cabin in a wasteland that had become her home. "Born silver with a caul, indeed!"

The seasons passed. They did not hurry, but they passed. Joseph coaxed a grudging, parched crop from the poor soil; they slaughtered the pig; the mule died and they went into debt to buy another. Life was hard and getting harder. Lena dreamed of going home to New England, but she was too proud to admit how wrong she had been, back in the days when she was delighted to have found a man who didn't mind her looks and insisted on marrying her. She wouldn't go creeping back and let the family pity her. In her way, she was as stubborn as Joseph.

In time her eyeglasses became so scratched she could not see well enough to do the sewing and mending. If she did not get new eyeglasses, soon they would be wearing rags. So Lena waited until Joseph had to go into town, and then she took her small Talent and her great need out onto the prairie, to search for sand.

Her greatest gift was the wisdom handed down by Amer Crafter. Every one of his descendants had the phrase drummed into their heads from childhood: A thing is what you think it is. So Lena began by thinking that the coarse beige prairie grit was the finest silica. It had been much easier when she had white Atlantic beach sand available; then she had made fine eyeglasses for many Crafters, a family devoted to reading and studying and therefore subject to eyestrain. When Joseph learned the extent of her gift, he had been scornful. "You can make eyeglasses?" he asked incredulously, staring at her with his perfect, uncorrected eyes. "Is that all?" They were in the wagon coming to Texas by then, however, and it had been too late to take her back.

So now she concentrated with all her might to transmute Texas prairie into eyeglass-quality silica sand, and while she worked, she dreamed. Not of Joseph. But of maple shade and emerald grass, the things her eyes were hungry for.

To her relief, Joseph stayed in town longer than he had meant to, and she was actually doing the final polishing of the lenses when she heard the creak of the wagon outside, and his voice yelling at the mule. Lena quickly hid the new eyeglasses in her wooden chest and went to meet her husband at the door.

To her astonishment, he had someone with him. Sitting on the plank seat of the old Springfield wagon was a giant of a man, sun-bronzed, wearing the remains of what had once been a fine coat with silver buttons. His dark hair was tousled by the omnipresent prairie wind, but without her glasses Lena could not make out his features. She could only tell that he was big. He dwarfed Joseph.

She watched as the big man leaped with surprising agility from the wagon, and went around to the back to untie the sorrel saddle horse that had followed them. The horse was big, too; it had to be, to carry him. There was a rifle scabbard with a rifle in it, tied to his saddle, and a bedroll and canteen, but not much else. Whoever he was, the big man travelled light. Saddlebags were his only luggage.

Lena's astonishment grew as her husband ushered the stranger toward their sod hut. Joseph acted as if the man was royalty, all but bowing to him. Lena had never seen her husband so impressed; at least, not since the first time he had dinner in a Crafter house.

"This is my friend Jim," Joseph said by way of introduction. "We met in the town. He was coming this way on his way further south, and I offered him hospitality for as long as he cared to stay with us. I knew you wouldn't mind."

You knew no such thing, Lena thought irritably, but she smiled at the stranger anyway. Now that he was up close she could see him better. He had a blunt, rugged face, with a powerful jaw and a sensuous mouth—and the most remarkable eyes she had ever seen. He looked out of those eyes as an eagle might, Lena thought.

"You're very welcome to what we have," she said, stepping back to allow him to enter. His shoulders filled the door frame, temporarily blocking the light. "I'm afraid I didn't catch your name . . . ?"

"Bowie, ma'am," was the reply, soft-spoken for such a big man. "James Bowie."

"He's famous," Joseph threw in. "What I mean is, lots of folks in the town know of him. He was in the Government at one time, and . . ."

"I was born in Kentucky and now I've come to Texas," Bowie said gently. "That's all there is to know about me, all that's important."

"You invented that knife," said Joseph.

Bowie's lips turned up very slightly. "Oh yes. That. That's what they'll put on my tombstone, I suppose. No matter what else I do, people remember the knife."

So you have a small Talent too, Lena thought. Glancing at his body without seeming to, she took careful notice of the wide leather belt around his waist, and the sheath that held a massive throwing knife. She wondered if he had made it the way she made eyeglasses. Probably not. He did not have a Crafter look about him.

Still, she liked the man and he made a pleasant change from Joseph's company. He was courteous and considerate, with Kentucky manners that put Joseph's dour Yankee ways to shame in Lena's eyes. She silently hoped Bowie would stay for a long time, but he had other plans.

"I'm on my way south to help fight for Texas," he told them over supper that night—a supper to which he had contributed a tiny bit of real ground coffee from the leather poke in his saddlebag. "There's a big battle brewing, I hear, and I like a good fight, especially when brave men are defending something they believe in. Texas has a right to be free, even if the Mexicans don't think so. The Republic of Texas. I like the sound of that."

"We've been calling it a republic for a while," Joseph said as if he were taking actual part in the struggle for the region's independence.

"A thing is what you think it is," Lena murmured, and Bowie shot her a searching look.

"It is that, ma'am," he agreed. "You keep on calling Texas a republic and I'll help make it one, if I can."

That night, as Lena and Joseph lay in their bed, he whispered to her, "Ain't he a cracker?"

"Bowie? I suppose he is. I've never met anyone like him."

"A genuine hero, he is. Like one of the old Green Mountain Boys. It's a privilege to know him. Why, if I didn't have you to look after, I'd throw a saddle on the mule and ride off with him."

No you wouldn't, Lena thought. That's just a dream, the way I dream about trees and grass. But it was somehow comforting to learn that Joseph did still dream. Once there had been something in him that drew her . . . was it still there? Inside that leathery, dried-out man, was there still a young lad who dreamed bold dreams of taming the frontier and taking her with him?

Bowie was up before dawn, even before Lena, and went out hunting. She heard no gunshot, but he soon returned with a good-sized buck deer. He carried it out behind the sod hut and skinned it, swiftly and expertly, with the famous knife.

"Thought I'd contribute my share to the dinner," he told Lena.

He was only going to stay long enough to rest his horse, a day or two at the most, but while he was with them he made himself more than than useful. While he was out helping Joseph dig a new well Lena had a chance to finish her eyeglasses. She carefully poked the old lenses out of their wire frames, warmed the frames just enough to make them malleable, and fitted the new lenses into them. As she worked she thought about dreams, and magic. And maple shade.

When the glasses were ready she slipped the wire curves over her ears and looked around the cabin. Everything seemed blurred. She went to the door and opened it, looking out. It took a moment for her eyes to refocus and adjust to the light, and then she saw . . .

Maple shade.

Lena almost fainted. She tore the glasses from her eyes and looked again. In front of her was nothing but baked prairie, with heat mirages shimmering like lakes in the far distance.

She put her eyeglasses back on. Maple shade. Emerald grass, sparkling streams. No doubt about it, they were perfectly clear and perfectly real.

She took the eyeglasses off again and rubbed them, very slowly and carefully, with her apron.

A thing is what you think it is.

Had there been some other saying in her childhood, a corollary to that bit of Crafter wisdom that she had forgotten until now? She searched her mind. Then it came to her. She could almost hear her father saying, as he had once learned by rote, "You see what you think you see."

Lena put the eyeglasses back on. Maple shade.

She walked out of the sod hut and stood under the trees. The lush green trees. Their coolness enveloped her. The dappled light soothed her. The colour nourished her hungry soul.

I made these while I was needing, *she thought.*

Was it possible she had a gift for magic after all? For magic suffused with science, or science with magic, a true blending of Crafter skills? How could such a thing be without her knowing?

Born silver, and with a caul. Born with obviously great gifts that had gone undiscovered. Her Talent for making lenses had been a small part of the whole, she saw now. The few tools she had brought with her, the small cache of equipment hidden away in her wooden chest, was only the lesser part of the ability to give vision.

To give vision. She mouthed the words almost reverently.

Jim and Joseph did not return until sundown. Both men were grimy and weary, and as they sat at table they talked of well-digging. Lena took no part in the conversation. She fed them venison—too fresh, but a blessed change from salt pork and jack rabbit—and busied herself beside the fire, thinking her own thoughts. Hugging her discovery to her as a child hugs a treasure.

Joseph went to bed, but Jim Bowie could not sleep. He had told them he planned to leave in the morning, and now he was pacing the cabin restlessly, like a tiger in a cage much too small for him. Lena sat close to the fire, with her glasses perched on her nose once she was sure Joseph was asleep. She was hunched over, mending the rips and tears in Bowie's coat before he rode away. Sewing buttons back on.

He paused to look down at her. "I didn't know you wore spectacles."

"I have weak eyes," she said, not looking up. "I'm . . ."

"I know, it goes with albinism," he replied easily.

"You know about such things?"

"I know a bit of this and that," he said with disarming modesty. "But where do you get spectacles way out here? Or did you bring them with you?"

"I brought some, but they had to be replaced. So I made these."

"You put the old lenses into new frames?"

"Oh no, the frames are fine. I made new lenses."

Bowie took a step back and stared at her. "How in the world. . . . ?"

Consumed with shyness, Lena huddled in upon herself. "My little white rabbit," her father had called her, long ago.

"I have . . . I have this ability . . . well, I mean to say . . . all my family are talented, you see. Very talented. I was the one who wasn't, though they thought I should be. And I was almost blind into the bargain. My father finally took me into Boston and bought me spectacles, and that made things better. I spent a lot of time holding them, touching them. And then one day I just sort of . . . knew. How they were made. I did some experimenting, and I found out what to do. Sort of. The knowledge seemed to come from my fingers, you see?"

He wrinkled his forehead, obviously not seeing at all.

Lena shrugged. This was something you could never explain to anyone who wasn't a Crafter. "It's a talent, that's all. When my family discovered I was trying to make and polish glass, they got me the things I needed and I've been doing it ever since. It's nothing, really; anyone could do it."

"Anyone could make a knife," James Bowie said softly, staring past her now looking into the fire on the hearth.

Lena nodded. "I suppose."

His laughter startled her. "You underestimate yourself, little lady. And you impress me."

Lena began sewing very hard. "You mustn't say that," she murmured. "My husband used to say that once. But . . ."

"But it's been a long time, is that it?"

She nodded, wordless.

Bowie locked his thumbs and stretched his arms at full length in front of him. Lena could hear the joints crack in his mighty arms and shoulders. "At least you still have a husband," he said. "My wife died. I miss her. Very much."

"Is that why you want to go fight somebody?"

"You *do* impress me," he said again. "And I suppose you're right."

"Were you happy together?"

Bowie considered the question. "Almost, I guess you'd say. That's as good as anyone gets."

Lena smiled then, a smile so sweet her plain face was nearly pretty in the firelight. "We were almost happy too, now that I think on it."

"Then you should hold onto that, ma'am. It's something to envy, like your talent."

Lena felt her face flame. "My talent's nothing special." But even as she spoke she remembered seeing the trees and the grass through her new spectacles, and knew she wasn't telling the exact truth.

"I'll be the judge of that," Bowie said. "My eyes aren't as young as they used to be, so how about giving me a look through those eyeglasses of yours?"

She stiffened. "I . . . I don't think so."

"Why not?"

She must choose her words carefully. "You can't tell what you might see, that's all. I said my family expected me to have a talent, but I didn't tell you what sort. Where I come from, there are those who say, well, who say we are witches."

"Witches! This is 1836, little lady, not the Dark Ages!"

"I know, and it is absurd. That doesn't begin to describe the, ah, gifts my family have. But . . . I'm just trying to tell you these aren't the ordinary sort of eyeglasses, and I wouldn't want you to draw the wrong conclusions."

"I make my own judgments," Bowie said briskly. Before she could stop him, he plucked the glasses from her nose.

"Please don't!" Lena cried out as firmly as she could without waking Joseph.

"Tell me why not." The big man folded his arms, with the eyeglasses firmly held in one hand, and looked down at her with a manner so strong, so compelling, she could not resist. It was like Joseph all over again.

"I'm just afraid you might see something that isn't real," Lena said. "Not real as folk think of real, anyway. Those glasses show you what you want to see."

Bowie smiled. "I'd say that would be something pretty special. What do they show you, that you want to see?"

She was embarrassed again. "Trees," she said in a low voice.

Jim Bowie told her, "I've seen trees. Where I come from there's nothing but trees, it seems. What I need to see is the future."

Lena drew in a sharp breath. "My great-grandfather . . . I mean, I've always been told it's not a good idea to try to see the future."

"Maybe for me it is," said Bowie. "My wife's dead, the only life I cared about is behind me. Maybe I'd like to know what's ahead. If I don't like it, I could ride away from it."

Lena shook her head vehemently. "That's not right; you should never try to change the future."

"Maybe," said Bowie. Then he put on her eyeglasses.

Helpless to interfere, she sat staring up at him, wondering what he saw. Perhaps the glasses only showed green trees and grass. But she didn't think so, not from the way his expression changed. Even in the firelight she could see he had gone pale beneath his sunburn.

Without thinking, Lena jumped to her feet and snatched the glasses away. She would never know what instinct prompted her to look through them herself, but for just one moment she saw what he had seen before it faded.

A Spanish mission made of sunbaked adobe, with a bell set above the door. Men on the walls, firing long rifles; men in military uniforms, a few of them, but most of them in buckskins or rough frontier clothing. Some were already dead, lying tumbled half-over the wall with their blood running down to the parched earth below.

What seemed to be thousands of other men, all dressed in red coats, shouting in some foreign language—Mexican?— were charging the mission, obviously intent on killing the last defenders. It was a scene of carnage and horror, yet also of great heroism. Those few brave men on the wall . . . with the flag of Texas, bullet-tattered, still flying . . .

The image faded. Jim Bowie was looking at her.

"What was that?" she asked breathlessly.

"Where I'm going," he said. "A place called the Alamo."

"But you'll . . . you'll die! They were all being killed!"

"*Will* all be killed," he corrected her calmly. He was no longer pale.

"Is that what you need?"

Jim Bowie smiled, the sweetest, saddest, yet most hopeful smile Lena had ever seen. He reached out and touched her cheek with two fingers, then glanced toward the sleeping figure of Joseph on the bed.

"I think I'll leave now," he said. "I'm kind of anxious to get on down there."

"But . . ."

"It'll be all right, little lady. And I thank you. Until now I wasn't sure I was doing the right thing, but you've given me the vision I needed." His smile widened as if he was enjoying the play on words.

"But you mustn't go now!" Lena protested. "What about us? What will I tell Joseph?"

Bowie was already gathering his things, with the silent grace of the giant and the strong. "Tell him you love him, when he wakes up," Jim Bowie advised.

At the door he turned for one look back before he disappeared. "Remember the almost," he said.

Appomattox
Anno Domini 1865

The American Civil War was a great trauma to most Crafters. While they universally despised slavery, it pained them to watch so many brothers and cousins die fighting one another. Even to those who served in the armies of either side, the slaughter sickened them, for they could actually put themselves inside the opposition's mind. A few of Amer's descendants could not accept this and deserted, others still served with distinction. Many of those Crafters who lived on the frontier or deep in the mountains of Tennessee and Kentucky chose not to fight for either side. This is not to say that they didn't play a major role in the conflict or what followed.

A CURSED BOOTY
by Brian M. Thomsen

Drake, Wellman, and Wagner weren't brothers. That was obvious to the weakest of sight in the countryside. Drake was tall, lanky, and lean, and had not yet seen his thirtieth summer; Wellman was short and weathered and nigh unto sixty with a scalp as white as snow; and Wagner was a burly, bearish fellow, more akin to a Viking warship than the Appalachia countryside, of an indefinable age of masculine prime. The blood bond of brethren, however, could not be stronger than the bond of the road that these three shared. They had traveled together for the last four years, looting war's plundered, selling their ill-gotten gain, and avoiding conscription by the armies of the North and South. They lived a dream existence; but of recent, those dreams were replaced by nightmares.

"No! No! Stay away, you red devils! Stay away!" cried Drake, obviously still in a deep sleep, despite his position on nightwatch.

"Wake up, ya durn fool! You'll wake up the whole country-side. Don't you know there's a war going on. We don't need no damn Yankee or Johnny Reb on our backs," said Wellman, shaking the young man back to consciousness.

"It was horrible! I was surrounded by Indians, and they were coming at me from all directions," said Drake, now awake but still quite shaken.

"You were supposed to be on watch," the older man admonished. "Where would we be if some no-good scalawag snook his way in here and helped himself to our loot? We couldn't rightly call in the sheriff, you know."

"The loot! Oh no! Let me check," said the now fully awake younger man, who then scurried to undo the tarp from the buckboard.

"Calm down, young'un," said the older man. "You'll wake Wagner."

"He already has," said the bearlike man, wiping the dust of sleep from his eyes. "What's going on?"

"Drake fell asleep on watch and had a nightmare," said Wellman, realizing that they were all up for the duration.

"Nothing seems to be missing," said Drake, returning to his companions. "Funny thing, though. Remember that writing desk we got from that burnt-out schoolhouse?"

"Yeah," answered the older man, "we sold it to that widder woman yesterday."

"That's what I thought," said the younger man, scratching his head, "but it seems to be back on the buckboard, or at least one that looks just like it, anyhow."

"Ah, you're still dreamin'," said Wagner, not at all pleased to have been roused for no reason.

"Am not. The dream was horrible. I was riding at the head of a company of cavalry when we were cut off by a horde of painted savages, screaming for blood. Everybody was dyin' and it was horrible."

"Cut the bull crap," said Wagner, getting hot under the collar. "Now I know you're lyin'. That was the dream I had last night. I must have told you about it yesterday. What type of fool do you think I am?"

"Now calm down, Wagner," interrupted Wellman. "I'm the one you told about your dream yesterday. Drake had gone into town for supplies, so he couldn't have heard our conversation. You both just had similar dreams, that's all."

"Yeah, well, I didn't wake up everyone with mine, and besides, I didn't fall asleep when I was supposed to be on guard duty," said Wagner, still ready for a fight.

"But what about the table? It's still on the buckboard," insisted Drake. "That widder woman is gonna be awful upset when she can't find somethin' she already paid for."

"No more than that schoolmaster in the other town who we 'helped' sort through the ashes. Why don't we just sell it to someone else? Twice the return on our investment," suggested Wagner.

Wellman smacked his double-size companion across the face. " 'Tain't you learnt nothin'? How many times do I have to tell you? Never sell anything within a stone's throw of where you stole it from."

"But we didn't steal it from the widder," Drake insisted.

"Who do you think the sheriff is gonna believe? A widder with two brats who saw her pay cash money for it, or a trio of scalawags in the slightly used furniture and supply business," contended Wellman. "Besides, it's bad luck to steal or sell the same piece more than once."

"Well, what should we do, then? Move on?" asked Drake.

"No sense in that after we handed out those leaflets sayin' we'd be here all week. Wagner, you chop it up for kindlin', and Drake, you get the coffee brewin'. Nothin' like a breakfast fire to get rid of incriminatin' evidence."

"But how did it get back here?" asked Drake.

"Ah, git back to work before I wail you for sleepin' on watch," said Wagner, putting a close to the talk of the table and nightmares.

Round about noon, their campsite lot was visited by a stranger who was even older than Wellman. Ezekial Crafter wore a threadbare buckskin with a grizzly robe draped over his shoulders to hold back the spring mountain cold. His beard went through various phases of grey before settling on snowy white closest to his face, and on his shoulder rested the largest raven they'd ever seen.

Wellman adopted his best drummer persona and approached the old-timer.

"G'day, guvner. Can myself or my humble associates interest you in anything in particular. I am Wellman, proprietor of this humble roadside establishment, and these are my partners, Mr. Wagner and Mr. Drake."

"G'day, good sir," said the stranger. "My name is Ezekial Crafter. I have a cabin not too far to the west from here, and I am looking for a certain item of furniture for my, how shall I say, work."

"Well, everything we have is up for sale, yours for the askin' at the right price," drummed Wellman. "Now, what exactly are you looking for?"

"I'll know it when I see it," said Ezekial. "Mind if I browse?"

"Not at all, not at all. Just be sure to let us know if there is anything we can help you with," said the old thief, wondering if it might be worth their while to stop by his cabin on their way out of the county.

Ezekial returned a few moments later carrying the small pine table that had been the subject of conversation that morning. "This is the exact item I've been looking for."

Can't rely on those two to do anything right. I guess I'll have to be the one to get rid of it, bad luck be damned, thought the aging thief. "A wise choice. Come let us settle accounts."

That night, Wellman, too, was visited by visions of death. Rather than the mountainous countryside of Appalachia, he found himself in the plains of the west surrounded by a small contingent of Union soldiers. He then noticed that they were being attacked by Indians. From out of nowhere, a feathered savage appeared, ready to run the terrified Wellman through.

Now you of the flowing locks will die, screamed the messenger of death.

Wellman was awakened from his slumber of terror by Drake and Wagner, whose sleep had been disturbed by his screams.

"The Indians were attacking. I could even feel the stab of the red devil's lance. I felt like I was living through my last few moments of life," cried the old thief, still shivering in terror.

"It sounds like the same dream I had two nights ago," said Wagner.

"And mine too," said Drake, who just noticed what was set upright by Wellman's side, and cried, "Look!"

There was the pine table that had been sold twice, and chopped into kindling once, as new as the day they had stolen it.

"Why are we going to him? Shouldn't someone stay behind to guard the camp?" inquired Drake, who was more than a little uneasy about this night journey, the old stranger, and the persistent table.

"We've all had the same dream, and we're all in this together. That old coot seemed to recognize the table, and probably knows more about it than we do. He said his place wasn't too far. In fact, that's probably it over there," said the thief, pointing to a shack that was in the clearing they had just reached.

"Well, he better have a few answers," growled Wagner. "I'm sick and tired of lugging this table around."

"And the curse that goes with it," said a voice from the dark.

"And the curse that, hey, wait a minute! What curse?"

"Step inside fellows," said Ezekial, who was now visible by their torchlight. "I'm afraid that you've all bitten off a bit more than you can chew."

The three thieves took places around Ezekial's fire and listened as he screed the history of the table that was set before him.

"Many years ago, there was a woodworker named Wilkes who made the finest furniture in the country, until an unscrupulous landowner discredited him with stories of black magic and debauchery. Almost overnight the town's perception of him changed from an honest craftsman to an unwanted pariah. His goods were confiscated, and he was sent off to prison, but before he left, he cursed the thief who stole his good name, and cursed the goods that he stole.

"The landowner furnished his mansion with Wilkes's furniture. Wilkes died en route to the prison when the party he was in was attacked by a group of renegades. Not too long after the landowner went crazy, claiming that his nights were filled with dreams of torture that wouldn't stop. He died in a madhouse.

"The curse was passed on to all further plunderers of the Wilkes furniture, invading their dreams with visions of the death of the plunderer."

"So why can't we just get rid of it?" asked Wagner.

"It follows the trail of dishonesty. It can't be bought, sold or destroyed," concluded Ezekial. "Probably until death do you part."

"So what can we do about it?" asked Drake.

"Pray and repent," said the old stranger.

The three thieves left the pine table at Ezekial's, even though he warned them that they would be seeing it again. None of them were looking forward to the many sleepless nights ahead, nor to meeting death at the hands of savages.

When they arrived back at the camp, dawn had long come and gone. They were greeted by a sheriff's posse, and the widder woman who claimed they had stolen back the table they had sold her. The pine table was discovered among the pieces on the buckboard, along with several other items stolen from a neighboring county.

The three thieves were put in chains, and with their illgotten booty, were escorted to the jailhouse at nearby Appomattox Court House.

"Well, at least it will be hard for those Indians to kill us in jail," said Drake, trying to look on the bright side of things from their cramped cell.

"Hey, jailer. What's all the fussing outside?" called Wagner, always afraid of missing out on a party or a brawl.

The jailer leaned back in his chair and smiled. "Looks like you boys are in luck," he said. "The judge will probably be in a good mood. The war's over. Lee's across the way at the McClean house as we speak, signing the surrender papers with Grant."

Wellman had taken up a place at the window, watching a young Union general wrestling with two Confederate generals, rolling around on the ground in front of the McClean house, laughing like schoolboys.

The jailer offered Wagner a cup of coffee. "You boys should be right proud. Looks like that table of yourn is being used by those two generals to sign them papers. You may be going to prison, but you're also part of history in the making."

The Union general had disappeared inside of the house, so Wellman returned to his friends. "If this surrender is true," he said, "we should be out of here in no time, whether by amnesty, or just plain opportunity."

Suddenly, they heard a commotion outside. The young Union general was bounding down the steps of the front porch, then onto his horse, yelling, "Got me a souvenir! Got me a souvenir!" He took off down the road, still yelling and whooping, the cursed pine table balanced on his head.

The jailer returned to his seat and chuckled. "Looks like that boy Custer just stole your piece of history."

The three thieves looked at each other and laughed.

"What did you say his name was?" asked Wellman.

"General George Armstrong Custer," the jailer replied. "He's Major General Sheridan's right-hand man, and a bit of a hothead too. I wouldn't be surprised if that boy didn't stir up a peck of trouble, now that he doesn't have a war to fight. Maybe he'll go to Washington, or maybe the western frontier."

"Maybe he'll go fight Indians," suggested a relieved Wellman.

"Not a bad idea," replied the jailer.